ASLEEP
FROM
DAY

ASLEEP
FROM
DAY

A NOVEL

MARGARITA
MONTIMORE

BLACK WING
BOOKS

ASLEEP FROM DAY by Margarita Montimore Published by
Black Wing Books
www.blackwingbooks.com

© 2018 Margarita Montimore

ISBN: 978-0-9995114-0-4

Cover by Terry Montimore

Visit the author's website at www.montimore.com

First Edition

For Terry, with love and squalor

"Reality" is the only word in the language that should always be used in quotes.

Anonymous

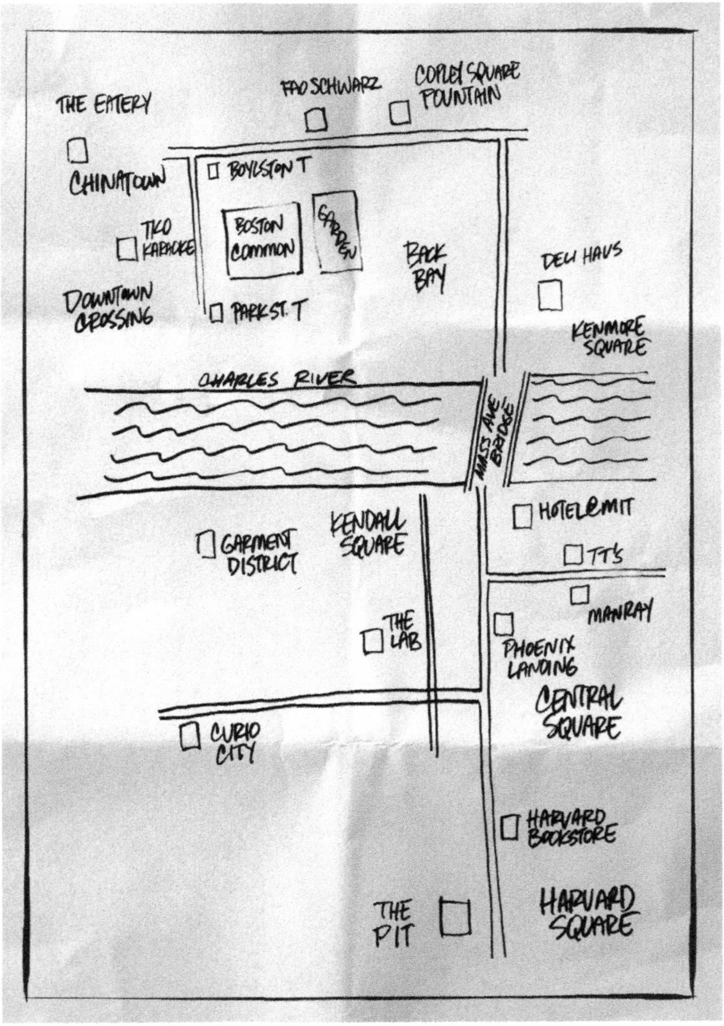
THE EATERY
FAO SCHWARZ
COPLEY SQUARE FOUNTAIN
CHINATOWN
BOYLSTON T
BOSTON COMMON
GARDEN
TKO KARAOKE
BACK BAY
DELI HAUS
DOWNTOWN CROSSING
PARK ST. T
KENMORE SQUARE
CHARLES RIVER
MASS AVE BRIDGE
HOTEL@MIT
KENDALL SQUARE
GARMENT DISTRICT
TT'S
MANRAY
THE LAB
PHOENIX LANDING
CENTRAL SQUARE
CURIO CITY
HARVARD BOOKSTORE
THE PIT
HARVARD SQUARE

CHAPTER ONE

What's the last thing you remember?

A rumble, a static rush, the world on a dimmer switch.

Outside, everything was gray.

But inside, a galaxy of color and light. Fireflies behind my eyes, neon in my bones. A nerve net of bioluminescence.

Radiant with hope. Glorious.

Do you know where you are?

In the heart of a storm. Give me lightning. Give me the flood. I've bled the sky of pigment, devoured its clouds. They remain like honey on my tongue, crystalized with promise. Nothing was ever sweeter.

What happened?

Something incredible.

Something terrible.

No more color. Fade to grey.

I've been robbed of this elation.

Stay with me.

I have the weirdest taste in my mouth. Metallic, like I've been sucking on pennies, and spicy—no, not spicy. Stinging. Blood. What the—? I move my tongue and feel tiny pebbles. They're sharp, cutting my gums and the insides of my cheeks. Not pebbles. Teeth? No. Glass.

I turn to spit out pieces of broken glass, but there's something around my neck and I can't move it. Okay, don't panic. I push the glass out of my mouth with the tip of my tongue and pieces roll down my chin on a trail of saliva and blood. Now let's turn on a light in here.

I open my eyes. Huh.

What is this place? There are shelves of equipment, strange monitors, dials, wires. Some kind of . . . storage room? The image blurs and wobbles. If my head is a handheld camera, whoever's operating it has a serious case of the shakes. I can't get a steady picture and I have no idea what this place is.

Have I been kidnapped?

That thought should trigger some modicum of fear. But it's like I'm trapped in a block of ice and fear is on the other side of it. I can barely muster any curiosity to figure out where I am. The rest of it—how I got here, if I'm safe, hurt, etc.—will have to wait.

So let's see. The room is tiny, and moving, and noisy. There are beeps, the hiss and tinny chatter of a walkie-talkie, the looped bellow of a siren.

Seriously, where am I?

Nowhere good, a black whisper warns, and a fog in my mind parts, clearing a path for fear, the belated guest.

The image finally snaps into focus and it registers: an ambulance.

Why the fuck am I in an ambulance?

I sit up with a—nope, I can only lift my head maybe an inch.

Why aren't you panicking more?

Because it's getting foggy inside my head again and blurry outside of it. I could really use a nap. It's so chilly in here. And bright. Might as well close my eyes and deal with this in the morning. Ah, the dark is much better.

Hang on. Let's get some questions answered first, maybe make sure I'm not missing any limbs. I try to sit up again and a hand on my shoulder prevents me from rising any further. No, it's not just the hand. I'm strapped in.

"Nice to see you coming around, but don't try to sit up. My name is Leo and I'm a paramedic. Do you know today's date?"

I squint but can't make out the face above me.

"September ninth, 1999," I mumble.

"It's actually September tenth," he corrects me. Close enough.

"What happened? Am I hurt?" *Of course you're hurt, genius. I doubt you're tied to a gurney, with a mouthful of glass, just joyriding in an ambulance.*

"It's going to be okay, Astrid, we're almost at the hospital."

How does this guy know my name? Why am I going to the hospital? *Because that's usually the drop-off destination of ambulances. Try to keep up here.* What happened to me?

My head is so damn heavy. Back down it goes, more blood, more spit trickling out of the corners of my mouth. I form words but can't speak them. I manage a garbled whisper, but it's drowned out by sirens, rattling noises, and the tapping of heavy rain on the ambulance roof.

I need to take stock. I'm mostly immobile, but am I paralyzed? I try to wiggle the toes. Okay, those work fine. Fingers? The ones on the left hand move then seize up in pain. Blinded? Obviously not, but my vision is still fuzzy at the edges. Obviously, I can't move my head much, but I shouldn't anyway, in case I have a concussion. *Or worse.* Go away, black whisper, I don't need you scaring the shit out of me right now.

Back to my self-assessment. Do I feel pain anywhere else in my body? Now that I mention it, *hell yes*. Where? Everywhere, especially my left side.

Why can't I remember how this happened? I keep asking the paramedic, but he won't tell me. Why won't he answer me?

Oh yeah, because he can't actually hear me. Because my lips are barely moving and no sound is coming out.

It's an effort to form any more words or keep my eyes open. Is there a cold, heavy blanket over me? Uh-oh, those blurry edges are going dark. It's like someone pushed me into a deep well and I'm falling in slow motion.

"Try to stay awake, Astrid."

Fingers snap in front of my face.

Cut it out, ambulance man. You're messing up my nap. It's so much nicer with my eyes closed. All you do is boss me around with "Don't sit up" this and "Stay awake" that. The darkness is quiet and doesn't make annoying demands.

"Astrid. Astrid!"

His voice is like a megaphone in my ear. *Where is your mute button, ambulance man?*

I think I found it. It's here, further down in the dark.

I hear two voices, growing fainter as they speak.

"She's out again, but vitals are stable."

I'm not out, yet, ambulance man. Give a girl a break, would ya? It's not my fault I have anvils on my eyelids. Besides, the light in here is too bright. And you are too loud. But I can still hear you fine . . . Mostly . . . Kind of . . .

"You'd think people would know not to drive like assholes in this kind of rain."

"What is this, third one today?"

"Fourth. You hear about the wreck by the BQE? Five cars and a motorcycle. Two fatalities."

"This one got lucky."

"So to speak."

"So to speak."

"Want to get breakfast after this?"

"It's lunchtime."

"So? I want breakfast. Couldn't you go for some French toast or pancakes?"

"Maybe eggs. Some strong coffee, bacon . . ."

"Extra bacon."

How about taking my order, ambulance man? I'll have —

Darkness.

CHAPTER TWO

I'm in a bubble bath, submerged to my neck, wearing an eye mask that smells of wet autumn leaves.

A city cacophony surrounds me: car horns, pedestrian chatter, police sirens, church bells.

You need to get going.

I sit up and remove the mask.

Water and suds splash over the side of the antique claw-foot tub I'm in. They should be hitting the tile of a bathroom floor but, instead, they hit cement.

I'm on a sidewalk in the middle of Boston. There's the spire of the Prudential Tower, the façade of the historic public library, a hotel that looks assembled from candy glass and bobby pins.

I instinctively cover my chest with my arms, but there's no need for modesty: I'm already clothed, in a blue sundress.

People file around me in their city uniforms: the students, the workers, the tourists, the layabouts, the privileged. They carry with them their accessories: dogs, children, shopping bags, toolboxes, cameras, backpacks, the cinematic cliché of the grocery bag with carrot greens and baguette peeking out of the top.

Nobody notices me.

I climb out of the tub and another wave of bathwater sloshes against the sidewalk, washing away a cigarette butt into the gutter.

You're welcome, Boston. I just made you a little cleaner.

I brush off mounds of soapsuds like ephemeral shoulder pads and wring out the soaked skirt of my dress that was made for twirling.

I have no shoes on, but the ground is warm beneath my bare feet.

I better go. I might be late.

I start walking.

CHAPTER THREE

Friday, September 10, 1999

You should've missed your bus.

   "That's too bad," he said.

   Who said? Who is he?

   Don't worry about it right now. Open your eyes.

   I squint at the ceiling. Acoustic tiles and fluorescent lights come into focus. This room is bigger than the last one, brighter and quieter. This room isn't moving, but the bed I'm lying in could be floating in water or my body floating an inch above it.

   I turn my head by degrees, first to the right. There's a guy lying on a bed across the room, a space for a third bed between us. He sips something from a straw stuck into a Styrofoam cup, but looks more like someone stuck a giant straw into him and sucked him dry, leaving a husk of a man. He could be thirty or sixty. His skin resembles orange parchment paper. He's dying.

   Am I dying, too?

Maybe I'll find a better view on my left side. There's an IV stand with a few clear pouches hooked up to it, plastic tubes trailing down from them like jellyfish tentacles, which meet up at the crook of my elbow. Whatever's being fed into my veins burns, but I don't mind. The new pain is closer to my skin's surface, distracts from the deeper ache in my body. The burning gives way to a disembodied, vaguely undulating sensation. Who cares if I'm dying? Who cares about anything? I could drift away . . .

Not yet.

Focus.

Okay, so I'm in a hospital room. I don't remember being removed from the ambulance or being brought in here. I don't know which hospital this is or who knows I'm here or how serious my injuries are.

Too bad. Too bad . . .

Question marks ping-pong around my head, buzz in my ears like pesky insects. They demand that I be more worried, that I ask many things. I want to shoo them away.

There's a murmur of voices past the IV stand.

" . . . could've been so much worse . . ."

" . . . can't even . . ."

When I look for the source, a question settles at the tip of my tongue: Am I really awake?

Sitting at the foot of my bed is my father, Robin. So far, so normal. A woman cries into his shoulder. I can't place her because of the wedding veil that eclipses the side of her face. A veil that matches the gown, whose thick satin folds, shaped like ornate cake frosting, overflow into my father's lap.

Who wears a wedding dress to a hospital?

"Do you think she can hear us?" the bride asks. Her voice is dry and husky and would suit a middle-aged chain-smoking truck-stop waitress, but she's sounded this way since grade school, as long as I've known her. It's my best friend, Sally.

"Excuse me, sorry to bother you," a policeman says from the doorway.

No bother, officer. Join the party.

They could be Village People 2.0: Concerned Dad, Policeman, Bride. Is it already Halloween? Jesus, how long have I been out? What should I be? Hospital Patient? No, too obvious. I'd rather go old school and be the construction worker.

"She's awake." Sally shoots up. "Astrid, can you hear us?"

"I want a hard hat." My words are heavy and slurred, like someone hit the Slow Motion button on my face. Must be the drugs. I try to sit up . . . Terrible idea. Not gonna happen. Holy hell, am I in a lot of pain. It's like I woke up the Big Bad Pain Monster and he's having his way with me, walloping me with big sucker punches. I must've really pissed him off, maybe ran over his dog or slept with his wife; moving only makes him angrier, more violent.

Too bad. Too bad . . .

My eyes dart back and forth, looking for a way out because this hurts so much.

You should've missed your bus.

"This party sucks," I mutter before passing out.

"I'd like to buy a vowel. An *O* . . . I'd like to solve the puzzle . . ."

My eyes are gritty when I open them, my mouth sour. Head feels like it's crammed tight with jagged rocks. The room smells of chicken soup and Lysol. The orange man two beds over watches *Wheel of Fortune* on the small TV suspended from the ceiling. His eyes are blank, like the missing letters of the puzzle the contestants try to solve.

"Again? Why am I here again? I'm trying to wake up," I murmur. This dream is like the last one, except now my IV is broken and the painkillers don't work. This dream is worse than the last one.

I don't belong here.

On TV, Vanna White shakes her head.

"I'm sorry, that's not the correct answer," Pat Sajak says.

"Fuck this. Wake me up when it's over." I narrow my eyes at the cold light and wait for sleep to take me to my next dream. Should be any second now . . .

"Astrid, honey, you *are* awake. You've been out for an hour," my father says.

My throat clenches. Since when does he call me *honey*?

If Robin is here, it must be serious.

Someone takes my hand. It's him. Since when is he touchy-feely?

All this tenderness is too much. There's a prickling behind my eyes and — no, no, I can't do this. But I don't have the energy to hold back my tears. Shit. Crying in front of other people is one of my least favorite things in the world.

"Something happened and I can't remember." My whole face feels like it's been stung by bees and I try to move my mouth as little as possible. "Why does it all hurt?"

Robin hesitates. "You . . . Do you need a nurse?"

"I . . . don't . . . know." The pain is mystifying. I've never broken any bones (until now?) or been through childbirth or passed a kidney stone, so I have no frame of reference, but if this was, say, a CIA torture situation, I would've spilled every national secret by now.

A swishing on my other side and Sally says, "There should be a button somewhere."

"No nurse." I don't want more people in here, or more drugs to cloud up my thinking—not yet. First I need to get a what-the-hell-is-going-on baseline here. Though I can't get over Sally's outfit. "You look so pretty," I tell her. The pale champagne of the fabric makes her long blond hair glow. "Angelic."

Her lips quiver. "Thanks."

"But why the hell are you in a wedding dress? Was I in a coma so long I missed your big day?"

"Don't be silly." She forces a laugh. "You weren't in a coma."

The way she says it doesn't match my jokey tone. Was I *almost* in a coma?

"Aren't we supposed to be having your bridal shower tomorrow?" I ask.

The corners of her mouth droop. "It *is* tomorrow."

The question marks come marching in, and on TV the wheel is spinning spinning spinning, and I'm more than a vowel short of solving this puzzle. Everything looks like it's been washed out, gray, like when you first learn to use watercolors and mix them all together. My cheeks are damp with tears and I don't even know what day it is.

No, wait. I do . . . Saturday.

"Why is it tomorrow?" Good lord, what a question. I sound like a five-year-old having an existential crisis.

Sally dabs at my face with a tissue, but then her lips tremble and she starts to cry, too. (For the record: Seeing other people cry? Also pretty high on my list of least favorite things.) Robin, the man who taught me to loathe and restrain tears, stands awkwardly, like he's all of a sudden unsure of what to do with his arms. He does better when he has a script with stage directions; all those years of theater and improv is still not his strong suit.

I'm pretty sure I know the answer, but not 100 percent sure, so I ask, "Am I dead?"

The absurd question cuts through the tension. Sally covers her mouth and snorts, then my father lets loose a snicker, and I start laughing too. This sets off fireworks of pain around my ribs and stomach, but oh well.

"Of course you're not dead," Robin says. His laugh trails off and face goes from amused to somber in an instant. "You were hit by a car."

Ohhhhhhhh. Not the best news a gal can get, but it triggers bits of a flashback: the puddle, the car, horizontal rain, the ambulance, glass in my mouth. Was it my fault? Like most people who grew up in New York, I'm a serial jaywalker. Did I get hit because I crossed against the light? What a dumbass. My windpipe closes up and there are more stupid tears. Stupid tears for stupid me.

"I'm sorry," I whisper.

"It's not your fault," my father tries to reassure. He wasn't there; how could he know?

I ask, "How bad?"

"Not as bad as it could've been," Sally says. "Nothing broken. You've got some sprains to your wrist and a couple of fingers. A concussion, but a mild one."

"They want to do an MRI to rule out a subdural hematoma," Robin adds.

My father the buzzkill, but yes, please let's rule out that horrific-sounding thing.

"Your spleen, though . . ." Sally chews on her lip. Oh come on, girl, don't trail off now.

What does the spleen do again? Isn't it one of those useless organs, like the appendix? No idea. I don't think I'd even be able to point out the general vicinity of the spleen.

"What about it?" I prod.

Sally tilts her chin one way, then another. "It's bleeding. If it doesn't stop, you'll have to have it removed."

"A spleenectomy?" The word sounds so silly it makes me chuckle. I wait for Sally and Robin to laugh with me, but they don't. Maybe if I make a joke about being really attached to my spleen?

"*Splen*ectomy. It's major surgery, a—" Sally catches the look of stop-scaring-the-shit-out-of-my-daughter from Robin and backtracks. "Not life-threatening or anything—"

"And there's still no telling whether they'll need to perform it or not," my father cuts in.

"Don't freak out." Sally takes my hand.

"Ow." I flinch. For a petite girl, she's got quite a deathgrip.

"Sorry." She releases my hand and pats it. "They're just monitoring you for now. The bleeding might stop on its own, in which case they won't need to operate."

I don't want to talk about it anymore. My injuries should take priority but it's so much nicer to focus on the TV, on Vanna flipping letters. Maybe Vanna can help me with this confusion and frustration, maybe she can help me recall . . . What? Something significant, elusive. I turn over the letters but they come up blank. This fog of consciousness sucks; I'm hurting too much to fall back asleep but am not alert enough to think and speak clearly.

"We must've made it to the bridge," I mutter.

Sally and Robin cock their heads, eyebrows knit. "What bridge?" they ask.

Bridge . . . What bridge? Why did I say bridge? The Brooklyn Bridge, the Verrazano, the Golden Gate (I've never even been to San Francisco), the Charles . . . Picture postcards of each bridge form an unfinished, wavering collage in my mind . . . Think harder. This bridge, it *means something* . . . but what?

"I don't know which one." My voice is small and pathetic. Sadness sweeps over me like a giant ocean wave, makes it hard to breathe. The images blur and fade into white, the flipside of an unused postcard, waiting for a message.

"Wish you were here," I whisper and sink my head deep into the pillow, eyes shut tight because I'm sick to death of these tears.

"Sally, get a nurse," Robin says with an air of panic. He's less familiar in the role of concerned father, but it suits him. I didn't know he had such range.

Eventually a goateed guy in green scrubs comes in and checks my chart. "How bad is the pain on a scale of one to ten?"

"Um . . ." I breathe hard, chew on my lip. "Seven." If my father weren't in the room, I would've said nine.

The nurse injects something into one of the intravenous tubes and leaves.

Forget Vanna White and wheels and puzzles and bridges and spleens. Focus on lovely Sally in her wedding dress and breathe. In. Out. Don't look so scared, Sally; there's no need when you make such a beautiful bride. Breathe in and hold it. Let it out slowly. Say something to ease their worry.

"But enough about me," I say. "Sally, why are you in your wedding dress?"

Her blue eyes spark; she's been holding in the story, waiting for her turn in the spotlight. "So here's what happened . . ."

Words spill out of her mouth and I want to keep up, but it's like trying to hold water in my hands: most of it slips through my fingers. She says something about getting a call in the middle of a fitting and her pretty mouth keeps moving, but this warmth in my veins is distracting. It's like my body is being filled with hot maple syrup. Is my temperature rising? It doesn't matter, because the aches are dissipating. Ah, much better.

"I'd love to hear all about it, but I don't think I can hold on long enough," I yawn.

Look at the two of them with their furrowed brows and nervous fingers. I wish I could reassure them. As long as I feel this warm and fuzzy, I know everything will be fine. I want to tell them, but I can't.

"Fucking bridge," I whisper, and close my eyes.

CHAPTER FOUR

9/9/99

Astrid was in the Harvard Book Store, browsing cookbooks for Sally's bridal shower gift. It was Thursday and she shouldn't have been taking a lunch hour, not with the countless Frankfurt Book Fair preparations she still had to make for the literary agents she worked for. Bad enough she was taking tomorrow off to attend the shower itself right after Labor Day weekend (Why choose a Friday night over a Saturday or Sunday afternoon for the event? That was Sally Logic; better not to question it). Astrid justified the outing by telling herself she'd work late again tonight, and she did need to get this gift. She'd put it off for too long.

It could be worse, it could be the overwhelming House & Home section of the local department store. Astrid never enjoyed shopping, especially for banal household items. The sight of glimmering silverware, crystal serving platters, and specialized kitchen gadgets disturbed her, reminded her of how far she was from true adulthood and domesticity. Though a couple of years out of college, the two-bedroom apartment she shared with her friend Cass still had traces of a low-budget, academic lifestyle. Packets of Ramen in the cupboard. Mismatching kitchen chairs taken from sidewalks on garbage days. Living room curtains that were swaths of olive green velour safety-pinned to the rod. Most shameful of all, Astrid's nightstand: two stacked milk crates, hidden beneath a section of leftover curtain fabric.

But never mind domestic trappings or failings. Today Astrid didn't have to be scared off by electronic pepper mills or hand-painted napkin holders or sterling silver toast racks. Sally had made it easy on her when they spoke earlier that week:

"Ignore the registry. Just get me some cookbooks."

"Really? What kind?"

"Any kind. I kinda exaggerated my cooking skills to Corey."

"In the ten months you've been dating, he never asked you to cook?"

"He did, but then he got this new client in Shanghai and was traveling a lot, and I was working twelve-hour days at Fairman's. It was easier when I broke my wrist—"

"Oh, you mean when you exaggerated your snowboarding skills to Corey?" Astrid suspected Corey exaggerated a few things, too; she didn't trust those buttoned up finance types. But after Sally's heart was broken by a Brazilian sculptor, she didn't trust free-spirited artistic types, so her rebound pendulum swung the other way.

Sally huffed into the phone. "Yeah, yeah, whatever. Anyway, the cast is coming off in a few weeks, and I know I'll be expected to dazzle with my long-promised cooking prowess."

"Or else what, he'll call off the wedding?"

"That's not funny."

"Neither is you lying to your fiancé about knowing how to cook or being in Mensa or having Pat Benatar as your godmother."

"I couldn't help it. He's a big fan of hers."

"And what are you going to do at Thanksgiving or Christmas or—I don't know—*your wedding* and dear old Pattycakes is a no show?"

"I haven't ruled out hiring an impersonator."

"You're killing me, Sal."

"Look, if you don't want to get me cookbooks—"

"You know I'll get them. I just don't want you to—"

"I don't want to hurt your feelings, but you aren't exactly in a position to give relationship advice."

"Ouch."

Astrid wasn't in a position to be picking out a cookbook, either, but she was trying. The bookstore's selection of recipe volumes was far from daunting, but offered enough choice to be challenging. Sally was of Scandinavian descent and Astrid wondered if she should get a book that celebrated one of those culinary heritages. Except she couldn't remember whether her friend was Norwegian, Swedish, Danish, maybe even Icelandic. It was one of those countries that produced fair-skinned, blue-eyed, elfin-looking people like her best friend. Maybe Sally would prefer a book of organic recipes, or quick ones, or low fat/low carb ones. Or maybe *The Gargantuan Gourmet*, a collection of over a thousand recipes "for the novice chef or seasoned expert." Maybe Pat Benatar had a cookbook . . .

The glossy covers depicting sumptuous-looking meals made Astrid's stomach grumble. She wanted to make her selection and be done with it. That would leave time for a quick browse of the remaindered books, then a muffin or bagel from *Au Bon Pain*, which she'd eat outside before returning to work. It was gorgeous out, possibly the last mild day the year would offer. The sun gave a special glow to the crimson brick facades of the Harvard buildings and cobblestone sidewalks, and the balmy air was woven through with soft breezes. She wished she didn't have to go back to work.

"That's not a very good one," a male voice called out.

Astrid blinked, her fantasy of sitting in a sun-dappled outdoor café replaced by the reality of the bookshop. Was he talking to her? She turned around to match the voice to its speaker.

He was a foot away, pointing at *The Gargantuan Gourmet*. Tall and broadly built, solid, with a lived-in, purposefully disheveled, rumpled look. Soft-looking hair, like the down on a baby duck. He looked like he was about to share a funny secret. Astrid bet he gave really good hugs.

She was about to return the book to the display pile, but held it close to her chest. "Why not? It says it has 'countless recipes for traditional dishes as well as innovative meal ideas sure to please the entire family.' Sounds fairly comprehensive."

"Comprehensive, sure, but what about actually *good*?" He held out his hands in a gimme gesture and she gave him the book, careful to avoid touching him. She wanted to, but she felt like a curious kid wielding a fork near a live electric socket. As he flipped through the pages, the hem of his beat-up suede jacket grazed her fingers and she got zapped anyway, static shock from the metal buckle. She dropped her hand.

He stopped at a recipe for rhubarb crumble. "See this? Looks like it would make a hearty dessert for a family gathering, maybe Thanksgiving, right? Wouldn't you agree that—"

"I've never had rhubarb crumble."

"Pretend."

"We usually have pumpkin pie."

"Well, if you ever decide to try rhubarb crumble, and I strongly encourage you to—it's delicious—but let's pretend we're in an alternate universe where *this* is what you make for Thanksgiving dessert—"

"We get the pies from a bakery." Sometimes Astrid confused being difficult with flirting.

"Wow, do you ever wish interrupting was a competitive sport so that you could win all the awards?" He gave her an exasperated smile, bright and perfect but for a single snaggletooth.

Zap. The ends of her hair should've been singed and her fingertips blackened. No skin or metal between them but electricity can travel in many ways.

"Sorry." Her eyes widened, illuminated. "Please go on. Tell me all about rhubarb crumble and why this recipe is *all wrong*," she said with exaggerated seriousness.

"Not just all wrong. A *disaster*." He echoed her pseudo-somber tone.

She held back a smile. "How so?"

"This calls for too much butter and not enough sugar, so you'll get greasy, bland rhubarb and even blander crumble topping which, I should add, will taste like wet sand."

"Okay. That's just one recipe, though." Her mouth twitched, working harder to restrain a grin.

He shook his head, as if her skepticism were a great burden and disappointment.

"It's more than one recipe. I really hoped it wouldn't come to this." He took a step closer and Astrid got a whiff of his cologne: clean and sharp, with hints of lemon and cedar, mixed with the apricot smell of his suede jacket. He kept turning the pages and Astrid inched toward him, wondering if his jacket was as soft as it looked. And his hair.

"See this?" He pointed to a recipe for lasagna. "You could buy frozen stuff that tastes better." He flipped to another page. "And this meatloaf? The only thing it's good for is filling in your bathroom tile." He kept turning pages. "Based on ingredient proportions, lack of seasoning, and other factors it would be *way* too complicated to explain, I know you'd be making a big mistake getting this book."

"A big mistake, huh?" It was a losing battle: she let loose a smile, and now struggled to hold in laughter.

"Trust me. You will only disappoint yourself and others if you try to cook anything from it." His face and voice remained stern, but his eyes, soft blue like worn-in denim, hinted at hijinks.

"Hm . . ." She pretended to consider what he said. Was she being too obvious, the way she kept inhaling his cologne? Getting caught smelling someone like this would be all kinds of creepy and embarrassing. Yet her nose wouldn't let up, and she became lightheaded. Could you get drunk on a scent?

"Why are you in the market for a cookbook, anyway?" he asked. "Did your boyfriend ask you to cook for him more?"

"I don't have . . . " she smirked. "Jeez, I walked right into that. I can't believe you guys still use that one."

"I can't believe you girls still fall for it." He set down the cookbook. "Actually, I've never used that line before in my life. I'm just cautious about flirting with girls who may have boyfriends, ever since a traumatic incident at the sandbox when I was six, which involved two nurses, a plastic bucket, and my head."

"Were you trying to give Sandbox Girl a piece of your rhubarb crumble?"

"Hey, I like the way you brought that around full circle."

Astrid smiled up at him, easy at first, then her mouth got tight. They stood before each other like they were about to slow dance. She took a small step back and he did the same. A different kind of dance.

She gestured to the stack of books. "This isn't for me, anyway. My friend is getting married, her bridal shower's this weekend, and she's been lying to her fiancé about being a good cook."

"How can you lie about—"

"That's what I wondered, too."

"Do you get really good at hiding take-out containers?"

"It's a long story. Well, not really, but it's a boring one. It involves a wayward snowboard."

"That sounds like the opposite of boring."

"Trust me, you don't want to know." Rather, she didn't want to talk about Sally. Or was the spotlight of his attention too bright on her?

"Sure I do. I like boring stories. They're some of my favorite kind. I think poor plot development and uneven pacing are underrated. How about this: I'll help you pick out a cookbook and you can tell me your boring story over tea at Algiers." He tilted his head down and raised his eyebrows, a look that asked, *is my offer as irresistible as I hope it is?*

Astrid's palms went damp. It wasn't that men never asked her out. She was pretty enough to attract *some* male attention, despite her perceived physical detractors (large ears, eyes set too far apart, a nose that veered slightly to the left, a refusal to starve the extra curves from her frame to waifish proportions). She kept her shiny hair long, which, according to one poetic ex-boyfriend, was "the color of sun-dappled chestnuts," and had eyes the same ex said gave her "an amber-hued expression of exotic wonder" (his poetry was terrible). Many complimented her sweet laugh. According to Cass, she had "a totally righteous energy." Even so, she wasn't the kind of girl men turned to look at on the street or bought drinks for in bars or clubs, even when she had the nerve to bare cleavage. Something about her shyness and delicacy. Despite attempts at being street wise or feigning cynicism, she still had the air of a girl with a fragile heart.

So what was this guy's deal? Did he cherish delicate things or enjoy breaking them?

And what was Astrid supposed to do with all this attention? It was like a warm blanket had been wrapped around her, but also like a grenade had been tossed at her feet.

"Look, I'll make it easy for you." He plucked an oversized volume from a high shelf and presented it to her with a flourish. The cover depicted piles of waffles sprinkled with powdered sugar and wild berries, garnished with sprigs of mint and magnolia blossoms.

"*The Big Book of Breakfast*?" Astrid took the tome and thumbed through it, her breathing steadier. Why couldn't people be as easy to handle as books?

"Pancakes, omelets, French toast, you name it. Your friend will secure her marriage for life if she makes her new husband a good breakfast. I've tried some of these recipes out myself and I swear they're awesome. My favorite is the baked eggs. That one always goes over well."

Astrid frowned. How irrational, to be annoyed at the thought of this stranger cooking breakfast for other . . . well, for dates, obviously. After a night of . . . obviously.

"I'm *sure* it does," she said. "Do you often make baked eggs for others?"

A disarmed chuckle, but he played along. "I can't help it. It's a very popular dish. But I only like to make it for special people . . . so I often end up eating alone."

"That's a lot of breakfast for one person."

"Are you calling me fat?"

"Don't try to twist things around." She almost reached out to swat his shoulder. "You just want me to buy the book."

"*I* didn't write it but . . . You're going to, right?"

Astrid couldn't think of a reason not to. She headed over to the sales counter, book in hand. He followed.

"See, now you're making me think that you might have tea with me, too."

She turned around. "Such wild optimism. Where might that be coming from?" She aimed at a playful tone. Did she miss the mark and come off as uptight?

He put a hand on her shoulder. Astrid felt his warm palm through two layers of clothing. She tried to keep her expression somewhere between cocky and neutral, but it faltered.

"I'm not optimistic. I just like how easy you are to get a rise out of. Nervous looks cute on you." He smiled his I-have-a-secret smile.

"I can help you over here," a salesclerk called out.

She approached the counter and fumbled with her wallet, a welcome diversion from coming up with an appropriate response.

When her purchase was rung up, the stranger followed Astrid outside and held out a hand.

"Nice to meet you . . .?"

"Astrid O'Malley." She shook his hand for a beat too long, thought of the defibrillator she'd need if she didn't let go.

"I'm Tom Collins."

"Like the drink?"

"Do you know anyone who drinks those?"

"I don't."

"Do you even know what's *in* a Tom Collins?"

"No."

"Then I think it's time to get rid of the connection with this obscure, old fashioned—but not as old fashioned as *the* Old Fashioned—cocktail and be recognized for my own merits. Do you think when Madonna meets someone, they say, 'Oh, Madonna? Like the woman in all those religious paintings?'"

"Probably not." She bit her lip, but it wasn't enough to suppress her grin's momentum. When was the last time someone made her smile this much? Probably never.

"I go by my middle name, anyway. Call me Theo."

"Wait, what?" She squinted up at him. "Why would you introduce yourself as Tom Collins, then? Who does that? Why not just say, 'I'm *Theo* Collins?'"

"And miss all that playful banter about cocktails?" He winked, then ducked when Astrid tried to swat him.

Her surge of boldness tapped out, she stiffened and shifted the plastic bag into her other hand.

Theo began to walk down Massachusetts Avenue. "You've been to Algiers before, right?"

His question went unanswered.

Astrid remained in front of the bookstore. He doubled back.

"Uh oh. Just when I thought this might be a good day," he said.

"I can't go. I have to be back at work in twenty minutes." The words were recited like lines in a script, weighed down with reluctance. She slipped into responsibility like a pair of stiff shoes, but she'd worn them for so long, she was used to the discomfort. What would it be like to go barefoot for once? Was being responsible in this moment her best idea?

"C'mon, twenty minutes is enough time for tea."

"By the time we sit down, get served . . ." She thought of the tasks awaiting her back at the agency: air and hotel reservations, a Staples order, a trip to FedEx, a call to the copier repairman.

"Okay, then how about I run into *Au Bon Pain*" — he pronounced it "pain" like many locals — "get us some tea to go, and we can hang out in The Pit with the gutter punks for a little while."

Astrid wasn't convinced, but was sensible enough to understand he wouldn't keep trying if she didn't give a little.

"I guess it wouldn't be the end of the world if I'm a few minutes late," she relented.

"And if it would be, I want to know all about your job."

While they walked, she kept her eyes to the ground. What would happen in less than half an hour, when she'd have to leave Theo and return to the office? She couldn't think about that right now. As they approached *Au Bon Pain*, she accidentally grazed his side with her arm.

"Sorry." She willed herself not to blush.

"You wanted to cop a feel. I understand."

Astrid laughed.

"I like your laugh. I'm sure that's something you've heard a lot."

It wasn't. She glanced over, but he was looking straight ahead. "Not in those exact words." *God, I hope he's not a poet.*

While Theo went into the coffee shop, Astrid waited outside, her back to the doors. She smiled into the trees and gave herself a cautionary you-just-met-him-and-he-might-be-a-serial-killer-so-don't-get-your-hopes-up anti-pep talk. It was no good. Her hopes rose with every passing second.

He came back out with a yellow and white paper bag. They crossed the street to the set of curved steps marking the entrance to the Harvard Square T-stop, nicknamed "The Pit." The bustle of the sunken space made it a good place to beg for money, show off skateboarding tricks, and put on impromptu concerts. Theo and Astrid chose a quieter spot by the public telephones.

"Don't you miss actual phone booths?" he asked. "They were so... I don't know... charming and insular."

"I guess." Astrid opened the lid of her paper cup and inhaled jasmine-infused steam. She closed her eyes.

"Muffin?"

She opened them. "Thanks."

"Lemon poppy seed. Pretty good, but nowhere near as good as the muffins in that book." He gestured to her plastic bag.

"I already bought it, so you can go easy on the sales pitch."

"Sorry." He said through a bite of raspberry Danish.

"Let me ask you something. Now that you have me here, be honest. Did you really know those recipes in *The Gargantuan Gourmet* would be terrible?"

"Nope. No idea."

"Then why were you so against me buying it?"

Theo brushed some crumbs off his lap. "Take a closer look at that book you just bought."

Astrid set aside her tea and opened the bag. She scanned the book cover. "Ah, Erin Collins. Your sister wrote a cookbook?"

"Half-sister. Same mom, different dads. Erin's dad was really tight with this religious group—a cult, according to my mom. He left on some kind of spiritual retreat before Erin could walk and never returned. When she started school, Mom began dating one of the construction guys repairing our leaky roof— but only after finding out he was an atheist—and eventually remarried and had me." Theo took a sip of tea, hissed as the hot liquid burned his tongue. "But enough of my boring stories. Though I did tell you I have a soft spot for them."

"That wasn't boring, not at all. And you're a good brother to pimp her book out . . . Do you commonly stalk bookstores and coerce people into buying it?" Astrid folded her arms across her chest.

"If you're asking whether I use it as an excuse to pick up chicks, no. But with you, I couldn't resist. You had pancakes written all over you."

A plummeting sensation came over her and she swallowed hard, forced herself to make eye contact. "Not baked eggs?"

Theo leaned back to take her in, looked at her with surprised tenderness. "No. Definitely pancakes."

For a moment, neither one spoke. Astrid looked away first.

"Anyway, I promise your friend really will love the book," he said. "Erin's recipes are too good. I spent a summer with her on the Cape and gained at least ten pounds helping her test them. Which is why I got offended when you called me fat."

Her eyes widened. "What! I never—"

"I know, I know. I'm just messin' with you."

Astrid smiled and stretched her toes. If only she could dismiss the ticking clock in the back of her head. She checked her watch. "Damn. I'm already five minutes late."

"You think you'd get fired if you didn't go back?"

She sighed. Contracts needed to be mailed, padded envelopes ordered, that stupid ancient Xerox machine fixed.

Theo persisted. "Look . . . How many more days like this are we going to have before we're complaining about the cold and the snow? We get maybe—what—three real days of fall?"

"It's technically still summer. Autumn doesn't—"

"You know what I mean. God! Go with the spirit of it, will ya? Today's the kind of day you should be doing exactly what *you* want. So, if you could be doing *anything* right now—within state borders—what would it be? Spending hours cooped up in an office?"

So much dread at the thought of it. "No, of course not."

"Then what?"

She considered the question.

"Hmm . . . Maybe . . . I've always wanted to walk across the Mass Ave Bridge."

"Hmm indeed." Theo twirled an invisible moustache. "Interesting."

"I always tell myself I'll do it when I'm on the T going over the Charles River and see it across the way. But I've been here for over a year and still haven't. And today really would be the perfect day for it."

"It would. Let's go."

"I don't do things like that." She pinched pieces off her muffin, but they never made it to her mouth.

He gave her an exaggerated pitying look, all lost puppies and dropped ice cream cones. "I bet you're one of those people who never calls in sick and uses up less than half your vacation days."

"And I'm never late." A reluctant nod. "But I did take tomorrow off to go to New York for my friend's bridal shower."

"Right, so what's the big deal extending your long weekend by a few hours?" He went over to the nearest pay phone and picked up the receiver. "What's your office number?"

"I still have so much to do." But couldn't it all wait? "You're going to get me in trouble."

"Wrong. I'm gonna get you *out* of trouble. If you go back to that office, you'll spend the rest of the afternoon—possibly your life—regretting it." He deposited some coins into the machine. "Number please."

If she walked away now, she'd always wonder what this day could've been.

Take off those shoes and go barefoot for once.

She gave him the number. As he spoke into the receiver, she was too intrigued to stop him.

"Hi, I'm calling on behalf of Astrid O'Malley, one of your employees . . . No, she's fine. This is Sam, her brother. Could you please tell her boss that she won't be coming in this afternoon? We've had a family emergency and she needs to come to New York immediately. Astrid will explain the rest when she returns on Monday."

He hung up the phone and offered an arm.

"Your bridge awaits, Madame."

"I'm not married, so it would technically be Mademoiselle."

"You're impossible, you know that?" He nudged her with an elbow. "C'mon."

"And how will I *explain the rest* on Monday?"

"I don't know. You have all weekend to think of something."

The mail, the office supplies, the reservations, every item on her to-do list vanished as the rest of the day opened before her.

She took Theo's arm, which was sturdy but with just enough give. It was a gateway drug to the rest of his body. This was an arm that promised it would pull her back from a building ledge. And the glimmer in his grin promised, once safe from danger, he'd crack a joke to take her mind off of the near-death-ness of it all.

An image projected itself on a blank wall of her mind: white curtains billowing, an expanse of crisp white sheets, the two of them in the heart of this pale oasis, lying in bed, fast asleep. She kept her head down as they walked, hair in front of her face to make sure he couldn't read it. She kept her grip on his sleeve loose, the suede shifting beneath her fingers.

Oh, and his jacket? Even softer than it looked.

CHAPTER FIVE

Tuesday, September 14, 1999

Groggy days at the hospital pass in a haze of pain, weird dreams, boredom, and medical tests.

A policeman comes to question me during one of my relatively lucid periods. He has this bushy red moustache, and I want to ask him if it tickles people when he kisses them, whether it feels like kissing a broom. Can morphine provoke uncontrolled fits of giggles? Because I have to keep apologizing to him for my inappropriate laughter, and for not being able to remember anything. Sorry I can't be of much use, Moustache Cop.

I get more details about the accident, but they don't gel into a memory that belongs to me, more like one that's implanted into my subconscious. Even the heavy rain that day, it's been mentioned so many times, I can almost feel the wet slant of it drench me as I mentally approach the four lane street where it happened. But is it my thirsty brain eager to fill in details or a true recollection?

Here's what I know secondhand: based on where the ambulance picked me up, I made it as far as Brooklyn, within blocks of my father's building. The car hit my left side. Most likely, I flew up onto the hood and knocked my head against the windshield. Hello, concussion and bleeding spleen. I probably landed in the street on my left hand. Greetings, sprained fingers. Judging by the tire tread, the car backed up, swerved around me, and kept going. The spleen trauma was the main reason I was kept for monitoring. And the hematoma, but I had the MRI, a noisy spaceship trip I hope to never take again . . . No blood on this girl's brain, thank you very much.

Here's what I know firsthand: everyone's trying to reassure me, says it could've been a lot worse. They use words like "good fortune" and "lucky" like some kind of dime-store tarot readers. I want to ask if they know what those words really mean. Yes, I should be more grateful that it wasn't worse, but being hit by a car at all is pretty shitty. I can't wait to go home.

Orange Man was taken away in the middle of the night. I don't know if he died or what. The only thing I'm sure of is, his bed is empty and soon mine will be, too. The doctor has declared my spleen fine and the rest of me ready for the outside world.

Robin is there for my discharge, taking notes as the doctor gives instructions. Between the blackouts and rotation of nurses treating me, I don't recall seeing him before, but find it comforting that he resembles a mental image I'd have for a doctor: beard, glasses, bald except for a middle-aged halo of hair above his ears.

He gives the usual pain management spiel, blah blah "get lots of rest" blah, and prescribes a muscle relaxant and codeine.

"If you have severe chest pains or see any black spots on your chest outside of the normal bruising, you *must* see me or another doctor immediately. Did I mention getting lots of rest?"

"You did." Robin underlines something on his notepad.

"It's worth repeating. Where will you continue your recovery?"

"She's going to stay with me for a few days," my father answers for me.

As eager as I was to leave this place, unexpected dread trickles in the second I step out of my room. I walk with a slight limp and there's a tightness in my lungs from the bruised ribs. It's all about baby steps and shallow breaths. The further I get away from the safety of my hospital bed, the more my uneasiness grows. Even something simple like the elevator ride feels fraught with danger and uncertainty—What if there's a power outage and we get stuck? What if the cord snaps and we plunge to our deaths? *Settle down, paranoia queen.*

I forgot my face is still bruised and cut up and it gets startled looks that run the spectrum of inquisitive to concerned to pitying. People are staring while trying not to and part of me wants to be confrontational ("Go ahead and have a good look"). Another part wants to be inappropriate ("It's the only way Daddy knows how to show his love"). But I keep my mouth shut.

Before long, I'm in my next recovery room: my old bedroom. Robin turned it into a home office years ago—replaced the bed with a high-end futon, added bookshelves to house numerous plays and scripts—but it's disconcerting, like being in a generic room with personalized adolescent traces. On the walls are little scotch tape rectangles, overlooked and painted over, from the horror movie posters I hung at crooked angles in high school. There's the windowsill, its ledge still splintered from the time I tried to remove an air conditioner by myself and ended up with a sprained foot. There are the tiny blue stars I etched into the closet doorjamb with ballpoint pen, one for every time I felt isolated or lost, a galaxy of loneliness tattooed on a skinny panel of wood. Then there's my dresser, its once pale oak now stained cherry and housing spare linens, but the inside panels still marked with the faint penciled names of everyone I ever met. I open the top drawer, remove a stack of folded sheets, and peer inside. Gregory Basets. Brenda Pazdyk. Reuben Weintraub. Cyndy Strach. Juan Manuel Hernandez . . .

I go by my middle name . . .

Wait.

"Astrid?"

Wait.

"Astrid, what are you looking for?" A hesitant hand on my back.

"I don't know." Whatever it was, it's gone. "I need to lie down."

"I already made up the futon. Unless you prefer to sleep in my room." Robin returns the linen to the drawer.

"No, this is fine." I lower myself onto the mattress, careful not to put weight on any tender areas. But even lying on my right side, my "good" side, triggers bitter twinges, radiating from the bones out. I feel like a box marked "FRAGILE" that's been thrown down the stairs.

"Were you able to reach my roommate?" I ask my father. "I hope Cass isn't worried."

"I tried, but the line was busy," he says. "Do you need something for the pain?"

"I'm fine," I say without thinking. My default response, but now's the wrong time to downplay my agony to minimize his concern. "Actually, I could use something. Maybe Tylenol?" Preferably with codeine. "What about work? Did you call the agency?" Did anybody mail those contracts, book those flights, fix the copier?

"I tried to get in touch with an office manager, but was told she wasn't in."

"That's me. *I'm* the office manager." I sigh, and the small motion causes a jolt in my ribs. "Can I have the phone, please?"

"I still don't have a cordless. Why don't I call again? Tell me the name of your boss and I'll explain everything."

I look out the window. Grey skies, no sun. "What is it, Tuesday?"

"Yes."

"They'll probably fire me," I blurt out before I can censor myself.

"They're not going to—"

"That's okay, a new job would do me good." I say this so he doesn't worry, but it's not okay, not at all. It's bad enough I don't have a real career, that the needle of my inner compass spins and spins without landing on a solid direction. Bad enough that I watched my father swap his acting dreams for a steady paycheck when he found himself a single parent twenty years ago. Where another child would've seen it as a cautionary tale, I saw it as permission to grow up independent but unambitious. I've worked odd jobs since I was a teenager, many of them crappy, but I've never been fired. I don't have a lot of money saved and the idea of being unemployed fills my head with thunder and doom, drains me of my last energy.

I change the subject. "Has it been raining the entire time?"

He leaves the room, either not hearing the question or choosing not to answer. Good talk, Robin.

By the time he returns with the pills and a glass of water, I'm halfway to sleep.

CHAPTER SIX

Briiiiiiiiiing!

The phone rings . . . and rings . . . and rings. Not in this room, but close enough to wake me.

I open my eyes. I'm back in the hospital. Sitting up, I expect to be pummeled by aches up and down my body, but I'm not sore at all.

Briiiiiiiiiing! Briiiiiiiiiiiiiiing!

Jesus, why is nobody picking up? Is there no one on duty who can get it? No? Really? I guess it'll have to be me.

I ease my legs out of bed and test the cold floor with my bare feet, not sure how many tries it'll take to get vertical. But there's no dizziness, no weakness in my limbs, no creaks in my joints from being in bed all this time. I'm up and at 'em in one go.

I grab hold of my IV stand like a dance partner, take care that the tubing doesn't snag on anything. I make my way out of the room and down the hall, follow the painted yellow stripe on the floor to the source of the sound. Whoever's calling is not letting up.

Though my body feels okay, I take slow, shuffling steps. Where is that ring coming from? Its tinny sound reminds me of old rotary phones.

Briiiiiiiiiing!

Any second now, somebody who works here will find me and shoo me back to my room. Up ahead is an administrative cubicle area, but it's empty. Doesn't anyone fucking work here?

Three quarters of the way down the hall, next to a painting of a pigtailed child holding balloons shaped like teddy bears, there it is: a payphone.

As I approach, the ringing gets so loud, the receiver vibrates.

I pick it up. "Hello?"

"I've been trying to call you. I haven't been able to get through." A male voice, static on the line.

"There's no one else here."

"I wasn't looking for anyone else. I wanted you to answer."

"Who is this?" I ask.

"You know who I am . . ." [static] " . . . thought you forgot . . ." [static] " . . . almost gave up . . ."

"I think you have the wrong number. You don't even know who this is."

The static grows louder. I strain to make out what he says. "I do know. I know but I can't reach you. This . . ." [static] " . . . Astrid? Where have you been?"

I shiver and look around. The hallway is empty.

"Astrid?" [static] " . . . let you go."

"Wait!" My knuckles go white gripping the receiver. "Do you go by your middle name?"

The line gets quiet. "Now is not the time for riddles."

"Please tell me who you are," I plead.

But the static rushes back in and eclipses his voice. The only thing I can make out is my name.

CHAPTER SEVEN

Friday, September 17, 1999

The days recuperating at Robin's are more comfortable than the hospital, considering I don't have a man dying two beds over or nurses interrupting my naps to bring in trays of unappetizing food. They're also less boring, since my father has cable and splashes out on the premium channels. And he's held onto all the books from my adolescence, so I can regress in comfort, reading Christopher Pike and V.C. Andrews novels in between mainlining HBO.

Every other day, I try to call Cass, but the line remains busy. I call the agency, but my boss is on vacation so I leave a message with the temp receptionist that I'll be back the following Monday.

I don't ask Robin to take any time off work to look after me, and he doesn't offer, so he continues going to his two jobs, teaching drama at a local high school and directing plays at a community theater. He's always preferred the stage world to the real one, anyway. Evenings keep him tied up in *West Side Story* rehearsals, but every night he brings something home for me: a gossip magazine, a bouquet of wildflowers, some scratch-off lottery tickets, a raspberry tart. He doesn't cook, but keeps a stack of delivery menus at the ready and leaves me cash to cover the sustenance. I'd gladly trade these creature comforts for one real conversation with him, but I'm enough of an imposition. I mean, he's already given me so much in my life, how could I ask for his time and attention on top of that?

Most nights, Sally comes over to watch movies, though she commandeers the remote if I suggest anything black-and-white or subtitled. I'm happy to put my inner film snob on hold for her mood-brightening presence.

Every day, I check on my bruises. When first discharged and back in my old room, I took off all my clothes to examine the damage. I gasped at the purple and brown patches that traced a mottled path up my left side. But then I looked in the mirror and caught myself smiling this fascinated smile. My body took a beating and showed all this *resilience*. It didn't break or stop working. It just changed colors here and there. It kept on ticking. *You go, body.*

A week later and my bruises still have dark cores, but are now ringed with yellow, and the cuts on my face are barely noticeable. The pain in my left side has gone from excruciating to tolerable, and my sprained fingers and wrist are nearly healed. There are still headaches, but I only take meds when they get really bad.

I sleep a lot and wake up from intense and complicated dreams. Yet I only retain random details: a white feather, a hat on the wind, a ringing phone, a fountain. Probably drug-addled nonsense, but something nags at me. It's like being at the market without a shopping list, unable to recall a key item. Other times it comes on stronger, a sinking panic like I'm about to miss a flight or a court date—something time-sensitive and crucial.

I don't leave the apartment and hope the days doing nothing will bore me into missing my life in Boston. They do, but only a little. I miss seeing movies at The Brattle with my friend Daphne, getting tea upstairs at Algiers after. I miss sitting with Cass on the deck of our apartment, eating marshmallow treats with M&Ms ("I'm gonna get baked, then I'm gonna bake," she liked to say). I miss going to The Garage on my lunch break and browsing at Newbury Comics. I don't miss my job, but I miss having a sense of purpose and daily tasks to accomplish.

Friday night, I'm watching *La Dolce Vita* when Sally buzzes from downstairs. Robin lets her in and shuffles back to his office.

On TV, a glamorous evening-gown-clad-Anita Ekberg frolics in the Trevi Fountain.

"It would be better with bubbles," I murmur.

Sally is wide-eyed and frenzied, ready to launch into her latest drama, but pauses to ask, "What would be better with bubbles?"

I blink a few times like I'm half asleep. "I have no idea. What's up?"

She throws herself down on the couch with a little too much force, takes the remote, and changes the channel to a tornado report. It's okay, their *vitas* weren't all that *dolce*, anyway. "I found . . . something disturbing. At Corey's."

"Were you snooping again while he was in the shower?" I *knew* he was sketchy. Something about his blank eyes and indistinct personality, like he was trying to blend into the world too much.

"That's beside the point, but yes." She chews her fingernails, which I haven't seen her do since high school.

"Are you going to tell me?"

"No. I'll show you." She pulls something out of her back pocket and tosses it into my lap.

A passport. I flip it open.

"You stole Corey's passport?"

"Take a closer look," Sally urges.

The words echo in my head, but a male voice speaks them.

Take a closer look . . .

Not now.

I scan the photo page and— "Oh!" I sit up straighter. "Daniel Mothersbaugh?"

"It's gotta be a nod to his musical heroes, Danny Elfman and Mark Mothersbaugh. But that's not all I found. There were a couple of photos tucked away in the back of his sock drawer."

"Polaroids of dead girls?" I blurt out.

"What is *wrong* with you?"

You don't want to know. I don't want to know.

"They were pictures of him . . ." she pauses to build suspense, " . . . of him with a *mohawk. Playing the drums.* I asked him about those."

"But not the passport?"

"No."

Sally Logic strikes again.

She leans in, scowling. "Turns out he was in a band in the '80s. Doesn't talk about it because one of his bandmates died before they released their first album . . . Just when I thought I found myself a stable, non-arty guy . . . a fucking band."

"Just so we're clear, the fake passport is the bigger deal here, right?" I wave it in front of her.

"Oh, and on top of everything, he wants to postpone the wedding."

The words "dodging" and "bullet" come to mind, but I don't speak them.

"When I showed him the photos, he got mad at me for going through his things, went on about trust and privacy . . . I don't know, all of a sudden he seems indifferent," Sally's low voice shifts down a note. "He talks about making sure our relationship is on more solid footing, but what does that even mean? It's the same as always. Now I wonder if he cares if the wedding *ever* happens. And I don't know what to make of this." She motions to the passport.

Why is she so hell-bent on marrying this thirty-something Wall Street cardboard cutout, anyway? I should get up the nerve to ask her. Sally's been different since the engagement, too; the spunky and irreverent girl I've known since first grade has diminished, deflated, a new insecurity stamped across her like an unflattering shade of lipstick. I miss my old friend.

Sally continues to bite her nails, eyes pleading for me to speak.

"I hate to say this, Sal, but I can't think of a good reason someone would have a fake passport." She's smarter than this. Deep down, she has to know.

"I thought . . . I made it so close to reaching this romantic ideal . . . and now it doesn't feel right." Her voice is small and trembling with the threat of tears. She moves her free hand toward me—the one with intact fingernails—and I give it a squeeze.

Is Sally's steady diet of chick flicks and women's magazines responsible for this damage? Or did her parents' unicorn of a happy marriage set an unrealistic romantic standard? That's one thing I'd never blame Robin for; I was too young to remember what his relationship with Mom was like before she died, and he gets cagey when I ask. Then again, he's only had casual girlfriends since, so I'm clueless when it comes to recognizing any kind of romantic standard.

My head gets tight; the pounding in my temples is eminent. "I'm sorry, Sally. What can I do to help?"

"Nothing. I don't want this to be a pity party . . . Let's talk about something else." She turns to the TV, sees a commercial's on, then back to me. "So are you still having those weird dreams?"

There's a jolt in my stomach. "Not so much." Why am I lying to her? "Maybe one here and there of doing random things around Boston. Nothing all that interesting, mostly walking." I hope my answer is benign enough that she changes the subject.

"Tell me more. Walking around where?"

Damn it, Sally, why won't you let it go?

Ever since ninth grade, when she bought a dream dictionary, she fancies herself an expert on the subject. She spent a semester mercilessly analyzing our dreams on subway rides to and from school and would get so disappointed when I couldn't remember any from the night before ("that's why you should always keep a notebook by your bed!"). More than once, I ended up inventing some to appease her.

I don't want to do that now, but I also don't want to tell her anything else about my dreams. Why am I so sensitive about them? So protective?

If I reveal any strong emotion, she'll sniff it out like a bloodhound and won't drop the subject, so I play it casual, hide my hands beneath a throw pillow so she won't see my tight, knotted fingers.

"I really don't remember, Sal. Mostly walking around where I work, Harvard Square and stuff."

"You probably miss your Boston life and want to go home." Luckily, at that moment, a massive lightning storm sweeps across the TV screen, taking Sally's attention with it. She turns her gaze forward, mesmerized by the beautiful-but-deadly natural phenomena on the screen.

I wonder what it would be like to frolic in a fountain. My eyes fill with tears and I don't know why.

CHAPTER EIGHT

I'm lying naked on a soft mattress that undulates beneath me like ocean waves. Someone nibbles along my collarbone, which makes me gasp and arch my back. I can't see who because I'm blindfolded. I also can't move my arms. Are my wrists bound? No, someone's holding them down on either side of me.

"I need to redeem myself a little here," a male voice murmurs.

A tongue runs down between my breasts. I squirm with pleasure, anticipation.

"You have nothing to prove," I say, between quick breaths.

"Does that mean you want me to stop?" He lifts his head from my body.

The absence of his mouth on my skin is agony. "No. Don't stop. Please don't stop."

His tongue resumes its downward path, now at the sternum, taking a slow, circular journey to my navel.

There's a loud, echoing sound above us, like typewriters clacking in a tin drum. I tense up.

"Don't worry about that, it's just the rain. It never seems to stop raining." He releases my hands, and I go to remove the blindfold. "No, leave it on. You won't remember this with your eyes open."

It shouldn't make sense, but I believe him. "Okay, but can I touch you?"

"No. Keep your arms where they are. Just focus on this. Enjoy it."

His tongue moves further south. Outside, the booming of thunder, the clatter of a shattering sky, far away, then closer, followed by sirens.

He says, "You have nothing to be afraid of, you're going to a safe place."

I can barely hear him over the din. The sirens are right above us now.

"Where are we going?"

He positions his body over mine, resumes his grip on my wrists. "You really want to know?"

I spread my legs for him and he is inside me.

"Tell me," I gasp.

"We're in an ambulance. Taking you to the hospital." His breath catches in his throat as he finds a slow, steady rhythm. "But we have to finish here first."

I have other questions, but he puts his mouth over mine, filling me above and below.

Our groans are loud, but the sirens drown us out.

CHAPTER NINE

Sunday, September 19, 1999

At the end of the week, after one more check-up, the bandages on my left hand are removed, I'm given a refill prescription for painkillers, and am finally permitted to return to Boston. I still have faint yellow remnants of a black eye and a map of violet-gray bruises along my left side, but I have enough energy to move around, so I book an afternoon bus ticket bound for South Station.

Sally springs for a taxi to Port Authority and rides with me.

"*Somebody* should see you off," she says in the car.

"Robin has a rehearsal."

"He always has a rehearsal."

I take out an envelope stuffed with twenties. "He left this for me."

She glances at the brief note on the envelope. "For incidentals?" Her sarcastic eyebrow matches her tone.

"Come on, that was nice of him." Her eyebrow remains raised. "Okay, okay, maybe it's to ease his guilt for not being around much during my recovery."

"You could've stopped at 'around much.'"

One unpleasant topic deserves another. "So you still haven't asked Corey about the passport?"

"Nope."

"Do you know what you're going to do about it?"

"Nope."

We spend the rest of the ride in prickly silence.

Once we reach the station, Sally insists on carrying my bag. A cloud of cheap fried food and urine hangs over us as we navigate the squalid bowels of Port Authority. I've never been so eager to board a musty Greyhound bus.

Sally waits with me until my bus arrives. As it pulls up, she takes my hand and gives it two squeezes, a code we've had since we were eight, when she had to board her first plane to visit her grandmother in St. Paul. I echo back with two squeezes of my own. *I am brave, you are brave.*

It's a relief to be going home, though a low hum of uneasiness still hounds me. I never did get through to Cass. Should I be worried? She's probably off in Vermont or Arizona on one of her spontaneous vision quests or some kind of hippie retreat—she's left before with no advance warning. A few days or a week later, she'll return with stories of healing circles, ley lines, hallucinogenic teas, and worshipping the forest or desert or whatever. Sometimes she'll bring me a trinket she swears is infused with special energy, like a woven belt or a wreath, or one time, a plain grey golf ball-sized rock. I hope she's home from wherever she's been. I miss her. And yeah, it may be selfish, but I don't want to spend my first night back in Boston alone.

The streets of Manhattan scroll past as we leave the city. It's not raining, but there's no sun and everything looks dimmer: the bodegas, the parking lots, the high-rises, all muted and gloomy. The people outside bend their heads against the driving wind and frown. The only creatures that don't look dejected are a pair of Dalmatians, who strain against their owner's leash in between pissing on parking meters.

There's already traffic. I close my eyes and settle in for a long ride.

The trip stretches from its usual four hours to five-and-a-half, and it's dark out when we reach Boston. I'm groggy from jolting in and out of sleep, and sore from twisting around in a cramped seat. When I finally exit the bus, my bag feels ten times heavier.

I board the T, switching at Park Street from the red to the green line, which will take me back to Allston. When the train goes above ground and starts its glacial journey down Commonwealth Avenue, it begins to rain. Surprise.

"Again?" I sigh.

"I know, never seems to stop raining, huh?" The woman who answers is stretched across the two seats in front of me. She has one of those gaunt faces whose age it's tough to pinpoint: could be hard-living 20s, well-preserved 40s or anything in between. She has hoops through her lower lip and both eyebrows, and most of her hair is shaved off, except for a dyed blue patch in front, cut into a V shape down her forehead. "It seems like it hasn't stopped for weeks now. It's worse than Seattle."

Normally, I would leave it there, but something about this woman makes me want to engage her. I find it flattering that someone so cool-looking wants to chat with someone so average-looking. But there's also a general comfort in talking to a stranger tonight, even if it's about weather.

"Doesn't it rain something like three hundred days out of the year there?" I ask.

"People say that all the time but it's not true." She brings a knee to her chest and plucks at the frayed denim on the cuffs of her jeans. "It's overcast a lot, and misty, but it isn't the non-stop rain-fest most think it is."

I like boring stories.

Shush.

"How long did you live there?" I ask.

"Most of my life. But I needed a change, so I relocated my business here."

"What kind of business?"

She reaches into her pocket and hands me a business card. "You should stop by some time. This is me." She stands. "I'm Minerva."

A screech as the train brakes, followed by a hiss as the doors open.

"Stay dry, Astrid." She pulls up the hood of her jacket before exiting.

Did I tell her my name?

I blink hard and turn over the card. Gothic black letters spell out *Curio City*. Located somewhere on Prospect Avenue. Probably in Cambridge.

I did tell her my name, right?

Doesn't matter, my stop is next. I put away the business card and search for my umbrella. It's gone. Either I left it in the taxi or on the bus. Oh well.

When I step off the train, I'm pelted with rain. I have the light and I should run across the street, but as I reach the curb, I can't step off of it. Can't move at all. The light changes. Something inside me lurches each time a car whizzes by.

Okay, okay, I can do this. Green light. I hold my breath and put a foot forward. The cars idle a foot away as I pass them. It should be easy, but it's like walking a tightrope. There's so much trust involved putting yourself into traffic, in front of large vehicles that can kill you.

Once safely on the opposite sidewalk, I hurry up the block. I expect my momentum to carry me through the next intersection, but nope. Another moment of panic. I want to get out of this cold rain, but I'm stuck on the curb. Get on with it. Go. Walk, dummy. I finally cross, but cast suspicious glances at the cars as I walk in front of them, am answered with indifferent windshield wipers batting their solo lashes at me.

By the time I reach my block I'm drenched.

Cass and I live in the top floor of a three-family house on a dead-end street with other identical clapboard houses. They were all probably painted different colors a while back but are now faded to beiges and grays. Here we are, second-to-last one on the right.

Once in the eave of the building, I take a minute to find my keys, wet fingers slipping around the insides of my pockets. Got 'em. Hey, what's with this padlock on the door? And the strange smell of smoke and wet wood, a soggy campfire only more acrid. I examine the doorframe, but it's not warped or singed. What's going on?

I squint at the padlock, bewildered. Why is the house boarded up? Has there been a fire? Just to be triple-sure, I check that I have the right house number. Of course I do; it hasn't been *that* long, not even two weeks. I step back out in the rain to see if there are any lights on inside the house or visible damage to the outside of it. Nope and nope. Back up the stairs and I ring all the buzzers repeatedly, but there's no answer. I *cannot* be locked out of my own home. A few frenzied tugs on the padlock, but it doesn't give.

Dread joins the rain trickling down my back. Welcome home, Astrid. Minus the home part.

Even though it's futile at this point, I go around the corner to a payphone and call my own number. Busy. I don't know any of my friends' numbers by heart, and my address book is inside the apartment, on the kitchen table. I can't decide if that's truly ironic or ironic in the Alanis Morissette sense, in which case it's merely unfortunate.

Looks like I have a big item on my To Do list: find a place to sleep tonight.

I'll have to take my chances, show up somewhere unannounced, and hope I'll be given crash space.

My best bet is going to be The Lab in Central Square, an apartment with a revolving door of residents (including my friend Daphne) and a spare room with a foldout couch that often houses strays. It was dubbed The Lab on account of all the computer science majors who lived there over the years, as well as the alcohol and drug experimentation that frequently took place, back in the day. Legend has it, a former resident working on a chemistry degree at MIT left his roommates a book of homemade acid as a parting gift when he moved out, which got passed along to further generations of roommates as more people came and went. Things have been a little complicated with Daphne, but under the circumstances, she couldn't turn me away, right?

I take the bus to Central Square and follow a side street to the rickety walk-up that houses The Lab. I'm so preoccupied with finding shelter, I don't freak out crossing streets like I did earlier, so that's something.

When I reach the house, the front door is ajar. Should I ring the bell? This windy rain is relentless, and I can't stand the idea of getting colder or wetter, so I go right in.

At the second-floor landing, I knock on the door. An Asian guy with glasses and a ponytail opens it as if expecting my arrival.

"That was fast," he says.

"You must be psychic." I try to smile through chattering teeth.

"Oh. You're not the paramedics." His shoulders drop. "It's not them!" he yells behind him.

"I'm sorry, I didn't mean to interrupt a medical crisis, I was here to see Daphne. Is everything ok?"

"You don't want to see her in the state she's in right now. Do you know if she's epileptic?" He opens the door wider.

Fear clamps my windpipe. Breathe. Answer the question. "No idea, she never mentioned it. What's going on?"

He scratches his chin. "Shit, it must be E then. Or acid. Eddie's usually so careful about cleaning up, but maybe she accidentally ingested a crystal and had a seizure. We'll have to think of a story for the hospital."

"Holy shit. How can I help?" I peer behind him but only see a coatrack. Is Daphne passed out? Is she breathing? *Seizure* is a scary fucking word. "Daphne's my friend. There has to be something I can do."

"Naw, she's pissed enough that I called 911 when she passed out. If I involve anyone else . . . you know Daphne. She's conscious now, and hasn't stopped giving me shit since she came to. I'll make sure she's taken care of." The buzzer rings. "That must be them."

I want to insist on staying, but I'd only be in the way.

As I turn to go, her vehement yelling from inside the apartment carries over. "Goddammit, Zak! You better send that ambulance away. I'm not getting in that thing."

"See what I mean?" he says. "She's going to be fine."

As I head back downstairs, I move aside for the two paramedics carrying a stretcher.

Back outside, I think about Daphne (even though a bigger, more daunting thought keeps trying to penetrate my brain and incite hysteria). I can't imagine being so blasé over a possible drug overdose, but Zak acted like he'd seen that kind of thing before. Living in The Lab, it wouldn't surprise me. Though Daphne's always been responsible in her drug use. She wouldn't be able to holler at him like that if she wasn't okay, right?

Psst, that other thought hisses at me, *I'm still here.*

There's no way to paraphrase it to make it less frightening. The words stomp through my head in a loop: I am homeless. I am homeless. I am . . .

It's only for the night. But what if it's for longer? Who knows why that padlock is there?

My breathing quickens and I pause under the awning of a brick house. I picture my charred apartment, Daphne in the midst of a seizure, and I can't catch my breath. I'm a soda can that's been shaken up and the panic is ready to overflow.

Get it together. You're an adult with a problem to solve. You got hit by a car and survived that. You'll survive this, too. Put on your big girl pants and figure this shit out.

I steady my breathing and return to Mass Ave, which feels familiar, safe.

Should I go back to South Station, get a bus back to New York?

No way. I'm not gonna let these setbacks run me out of town.

Outside a pizza place is a pay phone. Who else can I call? Hand on receiver, before I can decide, the phone rings. I pull back, like I've been burned.

Briiiiiing!!! Briiiiiing!!!

There's absolutely nobody around, no one who might be waiting for a call.

Briiiiiing!!!

"Hello?" Why am I answering the phone? It's not like—

"Astrid?"

If déjà vu is a feather down the spine, this sensation is a razor.

I must have misheard.

"Astrid, are you there?" The same male voice from my dream, the static now on my end in the form of the noisy downpour.

"Who is this?" I ask. "How did you know I would answer the phone?"

Before he replies, tranquility trickles into my veins like one of those lovely drugs pumped into me at the hospital. Of course. There's no need to worry about any of it. This is just another dream.

"You'll find out who I am soon enough," he says. "There are more important things you need to deal with first."

"Sure there are. Like what kind of snack I'll have when I wake up."

A pause on his end. "You're not dreaming, Astrid."

It stops raining, abruptly.

"The car accident, the fire, your friend's overdose," he continues, "All of those are real things."

"*Who are you?* You're scaring me." I look around, expect to see someone lurking in a dark trench coat.

"I'm sorry. Maybe I shouldn't have called. But I wanted . . . to reassure you, tell you you'll get through this. I'll be able to help you more later on."

"Do you . . ." My mouth is parched, my voice hoarse. "Do you go by your middle name?" I clear my throat, hold onto the phone with both hands. "Please tell me your name."

"You already know my name, Astrid. You just need to remember it. But first, you need to find a place to sleep."

"You mean a place to wake up. Right here would be perfect."

He sighs. "Don't do that. Don't deny what's real."

How am I supposed to tell the difference?

"Astrid, you're going to be fine. That's all I wanted to tell you. We'll speak again soon."

The line goes dead.

I hang up the phone and cross the street, continue to walk and walk and walk. My brain has short-circuited and I don't know what to make of anything that's happened tonight. All I can do is walk and look for a place to rest and ignore the kaleidoscopic whirl of the familiar and the strange.

I'm in a daze, and I don't know where to go and — did I just walk past a sign for a hotel? I circle back around. Yes, there it is. Hotel@MIT. I may not have a firm grip on reality, but I do have a barely used credit card that'll get me a bed for the night.

I cut through a small garden with manicured flowerbeds and curved brick footpaths. Moments later I'm at the hotel's entrance. Thank god. Through the revolving door, into the softly lit lobby, and a man in uniform smiles at me as if I'm a wealthy, important guest and not the soggy walking disaster I really am. He even uses the word "Ma'am" when greeting me.

The clerk at reception is just as courteous, and if he notices the small puddle my sleeve leaves on the counter as I sign whatever form he hands me, he doesn't react. Instead, he gives me the key card to my room and a compassionate smile.

In the elevator, my reflection in the mirrored doors is equal parts spooky and amusing, somewhere between escaped mental patient and swamp creature. I give my reflected doppelganger a shaky laugh and then ignore her all the way up to the seventh floor.

When I cross the threshold to my room, a lump forms in my throat, which I swallow down. I could collapse into a soggy pile on the floor and doze right here on the carpet, but I take a moment to admire my home for the next two nights. I could've been on another musty Greyhound bus. Instead, before me is a space decorated in pale yellows and olive greens, brocade curtains, polished mirrors, glossy wooden furniture. A double bed is piled high with thick pillows. All that hysteria about being homeless? Yeah, not so much. I'm the luckiest "homeless" girl alive.

I'm shaking from the cold rain and from everything that's transpired tonight. That phone call . . .

Making sense of that call, of everything else, can wait. Right now, I need a hot shower.

And oh, it is the best shower of my life. At first I just stand there and let the steamy water knead my clammy skin until I stop trembling. Eventually I muster enough energy to wash my hair with rosemary-mint shampoo and soap up my body. I exhale long breaths as I rinse off.

You're going to be fine.

The man on the payphone sounded so sure of it. I wish I had his confidence.

When I tuck myself into the giant bed, I can't stop his voice echoing through my mind, so I switch on the television to drown it out. I close my eyes and drift off to an entertainment news show profiling the newest "It" girl.

"Coming up, her breakout performance in *Other Peoples' Bedrooms* has critics calling her the next Julia Roberts, but before she was a leading lady, she overcame a heartbreaking struggle with dyslexia. Stephanie Hughes opens up about her disability, her rise in Hollywood, and what's in store for her after the success of *Other Peoples' Bedrooms* . . ."

CHAPTER TEN

9/9/99

"Can I carry that for you?" Theo asked.

"Nope." Astrid held on to the shopping bag, not out of stubbornness, but more a need to feel gravity pull on it, ground her.

The two walked down Mass Ave, past racks of used clothing outside Oona's thrift store and The Games People Play, a shop specializing in board and card games, then crossed the street to a block of basement-level businesses including Second Coming Records and Johnny Rockets ("That place has the *best* sweet potato fries," Theo proclaimed). They strolled in comfortable silence until they reached the outskirts of Central Square.

"So am I the only one missing work?" she asked.

A frown flashed across his face, which he replaced with an easy smile. "Be honest, do you actually miss it?"

"You know what I mean."

He didn't reply as they continued walking. Past the YMCA and the pyramidal steps of a post office. Past a cloud of cigarette smoke from a drunken man outside 7-11 and the waft of curry from an Indian restaurant.

Astrid tried to read Theo's face, but it was inscrutable. Who was this guy? Should she be uneasy, worried for her safety? Ted Bundy was charming and attractive, too . . .

She made another attempt. "I'm guessing you didn't call in sick to enjoy the weather."

"You could say . . . I've been given time off for good behavior." He folded his hands behind his back.

So aside from being a serial killer, he could be fresh out of prison. Lovely. She slowed her pace, threw him a shifty look. "Time off for good behavior," she repeated.

"Okay, you're looking at me like I'm an escaped convict or something. The prison thing was a metaphor."

She said nothing.

"For the record, I've never been arrested. Never even got a speeding ticket."

"I bet Ted Bundy never got one, either." She hadn't meant to say it aloud, but the words tumbled out.

Theo laughed so hard, he had to stop walking to brace himself against a glass storefront.

Was he laughing at her appreciatively or mockingly?

"Actually," he said as he straightened up, "Ted Bundy ended up getting arrested because he was stopped for a traffic violation."

"That's funny?" Astrid held the shopping bag with both hands, twisted the handles as if wringing water from them.

"No, but your paranoia is." His face grew serious. "I'm sorry, I shouldn't laugh. You have every right to be cautious. You've known me for ten seconds. And the bad guys are rarely gonna come out and tell you they're bad guys. But I'm not dangerous."

People can be dangerous in different ways, she wanted to reply. Instead, she said, "Okay."

"How about this. I say or do anything that makes you even a little uncomfortable, you tell me right away." He held out his hand to shake on it. "Deal?"

The concerned sincerity in his eyes, his physical proximity, the urge she had to touch his jacket again, the warm promise of his skin—all of it made her uncomfortable. But she shook on it anyway. His palm against hers sent another blistering current through her.

"Your face is bright red right now," he said.

"I feel silly."

"For thinking I might murder you?"

"No, for not remembering how Ted Bundy got arrested. I just read that Ann Rule book about him a few weeks ago." Why was he staring at her like that? Was that an odd thing to mention? Too late now. "I don't read too much stuff like that . . . but I enjoyed it."

"*The Stranger Beside Me* is a true crime classic. I don't read too much stuff like that either . . ." He smirked. "But if you liked that one, you should definitely read Graysmith's book on the Zodiac Killer."

Her face lit up. "Are you kidding? That's one of my favorites."

"I bet you've never seen the cheesy 1971 movie about the Zodiac."

"Not only have I seen it, I had the poster hanging in my room when I was in high school."

"Somebody really needs to make a better movie about him."

"Seriously."

They exchanged glimmering smiles over their shared interest in the macabre and resumed their walk, spending the next few blocks discussing theories over the Zodiac's real identity.

" . . . though I still think the evidence against Allan is circumstantial and . . ." Astrid went quiet as they approached a towering angel on the corner.

Or rather, a street performer dressed as an angel. She stood on a crate, covered by the hem of her silver toga, which gave her an imposing nine-foot height. A makeshift celestial beacon, a painted metallic face to match the dress and wings, dark hair pinned back with a garland of white feathers, a small basket in her hands. She watched an indeterminate point in the distance and blinked infrequently, convincing in the role of living statue.

The angel's stillness was contagious. Astrid froze in place, entranced.

Theo threw a quarter into the tin box at her feet and the woman began to move in slow, jerking motions, like a puppet whose strings were being tugged. She plucked something out of her basket and handed it to him with a sad smile: a white feather. When the sequence was complete, she resumed her motionless stance.

A few steps later, out of the performer's earshot, Theo asked, "Did we just witness art?"

Astrid giggled, though she'd been strangely moved by the scene.

"Maybe I'll put that in one of my scripts . . ." he mused.

"Oh boy, he's a writer."

"Oh, no, *worse*. He's an aspiring filmmaker. C'mon. You'd like me more if I was a corporate drone?"

"Who said I liked you at all?" She meant it tongue-in-cheek, but his hurt and confused face said she missed the mark. "Wait . . ." They paused in the street and Astrid held up her hand, tried to wave away her earlier words. "I do this sometimes, like, I try to do that thing where you playfully pick on the guy, and it's supposed to be flirting, only when I do it, it comes out all wrong." She winced, certain that the more she talked the less it helped.

Theo kept watching her, his face blank. He didn't reply, so she kept talking.

"Anyway, I wasn't trying to be bitchy, even though Sally says that would make me more appealing to guys, but what does she know, she's about to marry a man with a secret identity . . . I really want to stop talking now, so please say *something* before this becomes more embarrassing, even though right now that doesn't seem possible."

Theo held out the feather to her.

She took it between her thumb and forefinger.

"It's not flowers, but flowers are overrated," he said. "Feathers don't wilt."

She put the feather in her pocket and looked up through a pained smile. "Sorry for that crazy rambling."

"Eh, it was only about fifty percent crazy . . . but kinda cute, too."

"Well then . . . don't you have a bridge to sell me, or walk me across, or something?"

They continued into the heart of Central Square, past a shoe store whose main clientele was drag queens and cross-dressers, a fetish shop aptly named Hubba Hubba, an Irish pub, and The Middle East, whose downstairs was known for eclectic live shows and upstairs for tasty hummus.

"For the record, I *am* a corporate drone, by day," Theo confessed. "At a graphic and digital solutions agency. Trust me, that's all you want to know about it."

"Then tell me more about this script."

"Oh, so you like boring stories, too?"

"Sometimes."

"Uh, you were supposed to say, 'I'm sure it's not boring, I'm sure you have the makings of a cinematic masterpiece.'"

"Yeah, well, don't hate me for not taking your self-deprecating bait."

"Fair enough." He licked his lower lip and nodded. "Did you see *The Matrix*?"

"Of course."

"The whole premise of the world being one big computer program was brilliant. I also found that decision, where you choose the blue pill or the red pill—face reality or oblivion—*fascinating*. So I thought about other scenarios where you'd face a decision like that."

"Like . . .?"

"Death. What if you had the chance to know the exact date of your death? Would you find out? Or would you take the 'blue pill' and live out your life not knowing when it would end?"

"Hm . . ." Astrid's arm grazed Theo's as she veered to avoid a woman pushing a stroller; she rushed to continue before he could make a crack about it. "That's a good question. So what's the actual story?"

"It's the not-too-distant future, and we have technology to predict the exact date of your death. Society is split into two groups: the Death-Aware and the Death-Ignorant. Among the Death-Aware are two factions: the Early Diers, who have nothing to live for and go about wreaking havoc, and the Late Diers, who do everything possible to protect themselves and their livelihood. Then you have a rebel group who want to shut down the corporation that developed the lifespan predictive technology. They believe it's ruining society and want the next generation to live without that knowledge hanging over their heads."

"That sounds . . . really intriguing. I'd pay six bucks to see that."

"But would you choose to be part of the Death-Aware or Death-Ignorant?"

She tilted her head one way, then another. "I know you shouldn't willfully choose ignorance, that you're supposed to live every day like it was your last, blah blah blah . . . But I don't think I could handle having that kind of clock over my head."

"Right, because what if your clock was going to run out tomorrow?"

"Then I think I'm having a pretty good last day. So far." She winced at her earnestness.

Theo stopped walking and grasped her arm, nearly causing her to tumble.

"What is it?" Her neck grew warm, from her clumsiness, from his touch, and she hoped the flush didn't make a visible ascent to her face.

"You know how there are days you *expect* to be great?" he asked. "Maybe because of a vacation or holiday or something, but they usually turn out kinda disappointing?"

"Sure."

"And then you have these other days that do end up being great, but begin ordinarily and become unexpectedly awesome?"

"Yeah. Though I can't remember the last time I had one of those days." She kept her voice light, prayed no pathetic undertones crept through.

"Me neither, but guess what? *Today* is going to be one of those days."

"Are you saying you're unexpectedly awesome?"

"Maybe I'm saying you are."

A breeze blew her hair back and she closed her eyes. She could've been on a rollercoaster the way her insides flip-flopped, the way the ground beneath her vanished.

"I don't know, though. It's still too soon to tell." He nudged her with his hip.

They walked on.

CHAPTER ELEVEN

Monday, September 20, 1999

I open my eyes. Where am I? A quick rewind of yesterday: taxi, bus, T, fire, Lab, payphone, hotel. Jesus. Here's hoping today is less eventful.

What time is it? 9:07 a.m. Shit. I forgot to set a wake-up call, so I'm already late for work. Throwing on the first dry clothes I pull out of my bag, I dress quickly, and book it to the Central Square T stop.

A train comes right away, but less than a minute later, it jolts to a halt. A fire on the tracks causes further delay (more fire, causing more trouble). The Central Square taxi stand is right above my head, but the train doors don't open for ages, so a trip that should take me ten minutes takes forty-five. By the time I reach the office in Harvard Square, I'm over an hour late.

It's not until I rush into the building lobby that I realize I'm in jeans, sneakers, and a faded Bowie T-shirt—way too casual, even for a business casual dress code. I also forgot to put on deodorant or brush my hair or teeth. Awesome. In the elevator, I twist my hair into a quick bun and smooth the top of my head. A quick peek in a lobby mirror and—nope, still an unkempt mess.

The Spellman Rosenberg Literary Agency was set up ten years ago by Jonathan Spellman, a shark of an agent who left William Morris and the Upper East Side to start his own company after falling in love with a Boston-based caterer who refused to relocate. After a chance meeting with uber-agent Nellie Rosenberg while she was visiting her daughter at Harvard, it wasn't long before he convinced her to leave New York, too. Her list of award-winning authors gave the agency literary prestige and balanced Jonathan's commercially successful mystery and political thriller list. Both racked up six-figure book deals for their clients and on any given week, the *New York Times* best sellers list contains at least one book represented by Spellman or Rosenberg. They continued to expand and today, it's the eighth richest agency in the Northeast, with six agents, two junior agents, five assistants, a handful of interns, a revolving door of receptionists, and me.

I wave to the receptionist du jour and head to my office, which is filled with Staples boxes piled high on my desk and most of the floor space surrounding it.

Chloe, a junior agent and proud trust fund kid who favors tanning products and open-toed spike heels year-round walks by as I boot up my computer.

"Oh cool, you're back. The copier's been broken since last Wednesday. Jonathan's been having fits because of how expensive it is to have manuscripts copied at Kinko's." She fiddles with the zipper on a satin sheath that probably cost more than I make in a week.

"Nobody thought to call the repairman?"

She lifts a brown bony shoulder in a half-shrug. "You weren't here. We didn't have the number."

"It's written right above the machine."

Chloe gives a bored look, as if such matters are of no concern to her.

"I'll get it fixed right away," I promise.

"Thanks. We're also out of coffee." She walks off.

I make an appointment with the copier repairman and drag the Staples boxes into the mailroom, where I replenish the office supplies.

"Hey, Astrid." It's Peterson, Jonathan's sycophantic assistant. "We're out of number seven Jiffies."

I turn around, arms full of accordion folders. "They're in one of those boxes. Probably the one with the bright green sevens on it." I nod in their direction.

Peterson wrinkles his nose. "I'll wait until you're done in here. Also, the copier's broken."

"Since Wednesday, so I heard. The repairman's coming in an hour." His mouth opens to interrupt but I don't let him. "And I already ordered more coffee."

"Great. Could you get extra hazelnut next time? We always run out of that one first." He cracks his knuckles and leaves the mailroom.

"You're back!" A pair of skinny arms envelops me in a hug, which only hurts a little. It's Jasleen, half-Pakistani, half-Turkish, all-adorable, and my favorite person in the office. While she's been allowed to start developing her own list of writers, she's too good at being Nellie's assistant so her promotion keeps being put off. Jasleen always makes time for a friendly word no matter how busy, and practices thoughtful gestures, like giving interns birthday cards (whereas the rest of the staff barely remembers their names). She also has encyclopedic knowledge of the local music scene and writes occasional reviews for the smaller papers. Jasleen knows the schedule for local clubs like TT's and the Middle East as well as she knows Nellie's clients.

"How are you?" she asks.

"Not bad, considering I was hit by a car a week-and-a-half ago. Of course, that's a minor nuisance compared to the catastrophe of the broken Xerox machine and lack of coffee."

"Oh my god, are you ok? Nobody around here said anything." Jasleen's eyes get anime-character big. She clutches a piece of pink paper to her chest.

"Really? I left a message . . ." Am I that insignificant to the agency that the information wouldn't get passed on? "Anyway, I'm a lot better now. I appreciate the concern and would be glad to honor any office supply request you may have." I hold my hand out for the paper.

"Actually, this is for an upcoming show at TT's."

"The Blind Vultures." I read aloud from the flier.

"They're a really good post-grunge garage band, and I'm not just saying that because my boyfriend is their bassist."

The telephone intercom at my desk buzzes. "Astrid, are you there?"

It's Jonathan.

"Come see me in my office," he says.

Jasleen and I exchange a dark look.

"He probably just wants to welcome you back," she says.

Yeah, I'm not so sure. I doubt the big cheese is going to present me with flowers and balloons.

"Any idea what the weather in his office is like today?" I ask.

"A little stormy. I heard he lost an eBay auction on this musket . . ."

"Oh, boy."

I go down the hall to his corner office, nicknamed "The Museum" for its Civil War memorabilia. Dozens of framed coins, stamps, and medals line the walls, though it's only a fraction of his collection, the rest of which, rumor has it, takes up two rooms in his Newton mansion.

"Please close the door." Jonathan beckons me toward a ridiculous chrome and wicker chair. It's as uncomfortable to sit on as it looks.

"You look well." He nods up and down. "Like there's hardly a scratch on you."

I contain the flash of anger that seizes me. "Yes, well, I'm still pretty banged up under my clothes and I have a bump on my head the size of—"

"Yes, your clothes . . ."

" . . . an egg," I mutter.

"Interesting choice of ensemble." He fixes a cuff on his immaculate navy suit for emphasis.

"I can explain that. See, I was locked—"

"I had to call the front desk to even find out you were here, and the receptionist told me you were nearly two hours late. I suppose that's something else you can explain?" He pokes a Mont Blanc pen into the dimple on his chin.

"It wasn't two hours and I *will* explain, if you let me finish a sentence . . . please." I grip the metal bars of my chair, determined to retain some of my good manners.

"See, that's just the attitude I was telling Nellie about. To be clear, she is behind my decision."

I look into his eyes, pale and soulless as the rest of him, and ask, "What decision? Am I being fired?"

"You are."

I want to take the cannon-shaped paperweight on his desk and hurl it through the window behind him (even in my fantasies, I can't bear to cause bodily harm). Instead, I clench my hands into one large conjoined fist in my lap and ask, "Can you please explain why?"

"You call out in the middle of a Thursday on a family emergency—"

"Wait, *what*?"

"Please don't interrupt me. Then, you disappear the entire following week, and it's no longer a family emergency but a personal medical one. You'd have to agree it all sounds rather dubious. Meanwhile, we're all drowning in Frankfurt preparations."

"I don't know about Thursday, but I really *was* in the hospital. I can get you a doctor's note."

He dismisses me with a wave. "It's more than that, Astrid. It's also your performance. We've had three receptionists and one assistant leave in the last five months alone. It's your job to weed out the weak and find us the sharp ones who will show longevity on the job." Jonathan sighs. "This extended absence of yours has given me time to realize you don't care much about your work."

"That's not true. I care about my work. But I couldn't do it from a hospital bed doped up on morphine and waiting to see if I'd need to have my spleen removed."

Jonathan licks his lips and frowns. "I hope you're not hinting at filing any sort of wrongful termination suit against this agency. That would make things very tough on you, whereas I'm trying to keep things civil. Nellie is willing to provide a reference and we've even prepared a modest severance package, taking into account your . . . recent circumstances."

I stare at his glass desk, uncomforted, waiting for him to continue.

"All we ask is that you pack up your things in the next half hour and calmly leave the office. Someone from security will supervise you to make sure any sensitive material remains on the premises." He slides a manila envelope toward me.

I take it and stand up, clutching it hard enough to crumple the paper. "I've been here a year. I've worked very hard for this agency, Jonathan."

He turns to his computer and, not bothering to look up from the screen, shrugs. "The copier's been broken since Wednesday. Sorry, but I can't do business that way."

Jasleen is waiting at my desk.

"Are you here to make sure I don't smuggle my computer out?"

"I'm so sorry." She pats my shoulder. "I didn't know anything about it until I saw Peterson just now." She lowers her voice and leans in. "The smug bastard."

"Who, Jonathan or Peterson?"

"All of them, really." We laugh and exchange grim smiles. "Hey. You still have that flier I gave you?" Jasleen holds out her hand for it, writes her number on the back. "Please come to the show if you can, but either way, give me a call." Her kindness eases my own rising bitterness, but only a little, and only until a security guard appears behind her.

Fifteen minutes later, I leave Spellman Rosenberg Literary Agency armed with a cardboard box. Inside are a couple of framed photos, an umbrella, a pair of black flats, a plush lobster, some multivitamins, a box of Dayquil, a near-empty bottle of Pepto Bismol and — at Jasleen's insistence — a ream of heavy stock ivory paper and box of Pilot V5 pens. She drapes a tote bag full of free books over my shoulder before I go and wishes me luck.

When I step outside, all remaining traces of anger and indignation dissipate. A woman in a trench coat glances at me and smirks as she passes by. Can she tell I've been fired? How mortifying. I can't bear the idea of more appraising looks, more judgment that I've been found lacking. Even though I no longer have a source of income and need to stretch my remaining funds, I take a taxi back to the hotel.

When I return to my temporary room, the first thing I do is dial my apartment again.

"I'm sorry. The number you are trying to reach has been disconnected or is no longer in service."

Perfect.

Now what?

I drum my fingers on the desk.

What's the name of the management company Cass writes the rent checks to? It's two initials ... D&T ... T&E ... T&C? That's it.

I get their number from information, a woman actually picks up (victory!), and I explain the situation.

"I'm not sure who I should talk to, but there's a padlock on the front door."

"That's a precaution we had to take after the fire," she tells me.

Fire. My new least favorite word.

"I—I'm sorry, I've been out of town for a while. What happened?"

"Apparently, the fire originated from the third floor, which would be your apartment, correct?"

"Yes. Is Cass okay?" I swallow down the shrill note in my voice, the lump in my throat.

"No injuries were reported." There's a rustle of papers on the other end. "Let's see ... Cassiopeia Harris stated that she had people over to make candles. A few were left burning in the kitchen, which was the source of the blaze. It spread through much of the east side of the apartment before it was contained by fire workers."

The woman continues to talk and a fog settles over me, makes it tough to pay attention, though I get the key points. Luckily, the building was insured. Unluckily, the fire and water damage rendered the entire structure uninhabitable. Luckily (for me), Cass's was the only name on the lease. Unluckily (for her), the insurance company will probably sue her.

"Will I still be able to get my things?" I ask.

"I can arrange for someone to unlock the building, at . . ." There's a soft clack of pecking on a computer keyboard. "Wednesday morning at nine for a few hours."

"Thank you." It takes a few tries to put the receiver in its cradle because of how hard my hand is shaking.

Should I call Sally or Robin to update them on these developments? Sally would tell me to come home, probably let me stay with her, but she has enough to deal with at the moment. I leave her an innocuous voicemail letting her know I'm feeling better (a necessary lie) and will call again in a few days.

What about my father? I rarely share problems with him. He'd offer muted sympathy but urge me to make the most of this setback. Then I'd get his classic life lecture. It began with tales of his actor hardships and ended with a reiteration of his personal philosophy: there are leads and there are supporting players; everyone wants to be the star but most of us end up as secondary characters. Most only get a little bit of the spotlight or work behind the scenes. Maybe it was his way of reassuring me that it was okay to fail or how he made peace with his own life's disappointments. I get it. But once in a while it would've been nice to be told I have *some* star potential, to not feel like an understudy waiting for a part yet to be written. I can't handle hearing my father's "all the world's a stage and you're better off behind the curtain" manifesto again, so I leave him a generic voicemail, too.

Let's review my current predicament: I have no job, no apartment, and very few Boston friends (my ex Simon got most of them in the buddy custody battle). It's tempting to return to New York when I look at it that way. But how lame would that be? Things get a little tough and I cut and run?

A new determination flares up in me. I *will* find a new job and a new place to live around here. I *will* fix things with Daphne and make new friends. I will *not* run away from these setbacks.

How's that for star potential?

I call The Lab to check on Daphne, but get the machine. I'm about to hang up, but change my mind. Might as well begin the fixing now.

"Hey Daph, it's Astrid. I know it's been a while . . . I actually came by last night when . . . Zak told me . . . Anyway, I hope you're okay . . . I miss you and . . . I'll try you again tomorrow." And the award for Most Awkward Pauses in a Single Voicemail goes to . . .

I go downstairs and ask the clerk to extend my stay by two more nights. Sure, I could find a cheaper hotel or even a hostel, but this place is both comfortable and comforting. I'll allow myself a little bit of luxury, giving me forty-eight hours to get my shit together. Hopefully, I can at least find crash space by then.

With the basic need of shelter handled, my rumbling stomach demands food be next. I go to Star Market, conveniently located next door. At the top of the escalator, to my right, is a glassed-in flower shop with a purple and blue neon sign spelling out "Thora's Blooms."

Something pulls me toward it. I put my hand against the cold glass, over the letter "T."

My heart pounds a crescendo until I can hear my pulse in my ears.

The glass fogs under my hand, which glows indigo at the edges. My throat constricts; the neon blurs.

I urge my brain to make sense of it, but all I can think of is how lost and bereft I felt the first week after my father shipped me off to drama camp, when I was ten. All I want to do is go home.

Where are you?

A woman pokes her head out of the flower shop. "Can I help you?"

I wish.

No more lingering, I need to hustle here. I buy a newspaper, sandwich fixings, chips, and some tabloids, and return to the hotel.

Back in my room, I sit at the desk and flip open my paper. The apartment listings come up first, so I start with those. Now that school's back in session, there aren't as many roommate situations available, but I find a few promising leads. I make appointments to see three places tonight, two in Allston and one in Brighton.

The first viewing isn't until six, which leaves me plenty of time for job hunting. Admin jobs will be my best bet, but as I read the ads, the room gets smaller. I think of cubicles and pantyhose and stilted elevator small talk. I think of little plastic LEGO people with painted-on suits moving along a conveyor belt. Yeah, I could use a break from office work, even though a retail job will pay less and keep me on my feet more. I recall last summer working at the Tower Records on Newbury Street, where I first met Daphne. There was a simple satisfaction in stocking magazine racks or getting through the mayhem of a midnight CD release. Simple would be welcome in my life right now. And with my laptop currently trapped and possibly incinerated in my apartment, I don't have access to my resume, anyway. I'd much rather spend the afternoon pounding the pavement than recreating it in some Internet café.

So I do just that, beginning in Central Square. I fill out job applications at Blockbuster Video and Pearl Art & Crafts, and wind my way down Mass Ave to Harvard Square.

Something nags at me as I walk, a whisper I can't decipher. I've been on this street so many times, what's bothering me about it? As the businesses give way to pastel two-family houses, the whisper gets louder, though it's still unintelligible. When I reach the block with Second Coming Records and Johnny Rockets, it becomes louder still.

At the Harvard Book Store, it becomes a roar. This off-kilter vibe is now a spiral of tip-of-my-tongue confusion. Like when you walk into a room and forget why you're there in the first place. Except I know exactly why I'm here, so this feeling makes no sense. What is it? What is it?

This store is real. These books are real.

I force out a sharp breath and enter the bookstore.

A man behind the sales counter with wire-rim glasses and mutton chop sideburns informs me they're not hiring, but still lets me fill out an application.

Part of me wants to explore the shop and figure out why the hazy feeling is so strong here. But a bigger part demands I play Nancy Drew some other time, so I leave quickly.

My legs feel like popsicle sticks in the grubby hands of a kid about to snap them, so I make my way to the Pit and sit on one of the low walls.

A gutter punk with a green mohawk and suspiciously new-looking plaid bondage pants comes over and asks me for spare change.

"Let me see . . ." I stand and rummage in the pockets of my army jacket.

I pull out a white feather.

"Yeah, thanks for nothing," he grumbles and walks away.

The red bricks beneath my feet sway. Ground-level vertigo? This is new. I sit back down, but the movement continues, as if I'm at the center of a merry-go-round. Bits of scenery slow to a snapshot standstill before whooshing by me again: a newsstand, an antique streetlamp with twin bulbs like elongated onions, the information booth with its sombrero-esque dome, a brown building with ornate white trim. I stare at the feather in my palm, willing it to anchor me, but the lurching quickens. I close my eyes. Please let me off this ride.

Just when I think I'm going to be sick, the spinning slows, then stops.

When I open my eyes, the feather is gone.

Okay, that was freaky.

It's nothing. Probably dehydration. Buy a bottle of water and get on with the day.

I hit a few more stores, and fill out more applications. Here's hoping I make it back to the hotel with a stronger grasp on reality.

The apartment viewings that night are a disaster. One place in Allston needs a fifth roommate to take what must've been a converted walk-in closet, fitting no more than a bed and nightstand ("you can share one of our closets and put your dresser in the living room"). The other Allston listing is inhabited by members of a local band, who soundproofed the place so they could play into the late hours. These guys clearly care more about music than cleaning, as evidenced by the mold on stacks of unwashed dishes left on random surfaces and the brown ring around the toilet ("Our drummer kept the place spotless, but he OD'd last month; that's meth for ya"). The Brighton apartment is owned by a woman with at least six different species of pets, including large squawking cockatoos, two yappy Chihuahuas and a case full of hairy tarantulas the size of my palm ("I've only ever had one escape, but don't worry, they don't bite").

It's after ten when I return to the hotel, sapped of energy but not hope. I run a bath while I eat a turkey sandwich and try to block out the dreadful day I just had. Snapshots keep popping up like in one of those red View-Masters I had as a kid. *Click.* Jonathan fires me. *Click.* Fruitless job hunting. *Click.* Jail-cell room. *Click.* Squalor and rock 'n' roll. *Click.* Chihuahuas and spiders and birds, oh my. *Click.* Me back in Brooklyn, enduring Robin's absence and ambivalence.

No way. Today was a mess but tomorrow will be better. I have to believe that.

Loose thoughts float around my head. Who called that payphone in the rain last night and how did he know my name? Could I have imagined all that? And what did Jonathan mean about my calling out on Thursday for a family emergency? My only emergency was the following day. Not that it matters at this point.

When the tub is full, I bring in the tabloids, strip down, and sink into the foamy water. The magazine pages pucker beneath my wet fingers and it's nice to give my brain a rest.

After a little while, I toss the magazine on the floor and give my eyes a rest, too.

CHAPTER TWELVE

I'm sitting in the dark. There's murmuring around me.

A male voice behind me whispers in my ear, "Don't make any noise, don't stand up, and don't turn around."

"Are you going to hurt me?" I ask.

"No, the opposite."

"Then why can't I look at you?"

"Because you need to see this first. Here, have some."

Something is placed in my lap. I feel around the sides: a cardboard container with rounded edges, open at the top. Its contents have the consistency of packing peanuts. I bring a handful to my nose: popcorn.

His warm breath is against my ear. "I had them put M&Ms in the middle and on top. That's the way you like it, right?"

"How do you know that?"

My question is ignored. "The movie's about to start. I'll stay behind you, but you can't turn around. And again, you cannot make any noise or stand up."

"Or else . . . ?" I whisper.

"Or else you'll never remember."

A dim light illuminates my surroundings. I'm in a movie theater screening room, ten rows back, by the aisle. A handful of other seats are taken, but I can only make out dark silhouettes of their occupants.

Red velour curtains part to reveal a screen. A black-and-white film leader counts down from five, then the image switches to a rainy street. No opening credits, no music, only the booming clatter of thunder and rush of heavy rain. The camera zooms in on the back of a girl, blurry through the downpour. She walks down a residential street flanked with sand-colored apartment buildings and small houses with cemented front yards.

While I watch, there is hot breathing in my ear, followed by a nibble on my earlobe and a tongue tracing patterns along its curved edge. I squirm in pleasure, lick salt and chocolate off my fingers.

On screen, the rain intensifies and stains the pale buildings. The girl quickens her pace, her long hair drenched a muddy brown. There's a large puddle of water at the next crossing. She tries to hop it, but ends up shin-deep in water.

Staccato violins play over the images, dictate dread and impending doom.

"What are we watching?" I whisper, taking care not to turn my head, though I want to see the man behind me.

"Shhhhhh . . ." He runs kisses down my neck.

The soundtrack intensifies with nervous cellos. The camera moves in closer on the girl, who turns her head: she's me.

"What the hell is this?" I don't bother to whisper this time.

I'm shushed by everyone around me.

On screen, the girl continues to wade through the puddle, but the scene is intercut with shots of a car speeding toward her — me.

"I don't want to see this. I don't want to see this!" Now I am yelling.

The theatergoers hiss at me to keep quiet.

"You're making too much noise," he murmurs in my ear.

Meanwhile, my cinematic twin doesn't notice the light change or the dark sedan skidding around the corner. She doesn't hear the car horn over the thunderous rain.

I can't watch anymore.

"Turn it off!" I whip around to confront the mystery man but there's nobody behind me. All the rows are empty.

I throw my popcorn bucket to the floor and push off from the armrests to stand. My legs don't move. That's when I notice I'm not sitting in one of the regular seats; I'm in a wheelchair. I try to move the wheels but they're stuck in place.

I turn my gaze back to the screen, where my other self is being struck by the car. She lands on its hood and puts out a hand to grab at nothing before her head collides with the windshield.

A disembodied whisper fills the room:

"You'll never remember."

CHAPTER THIRTEEN

Tuesday, September 21, 1999

The next morning fills my window with sunshine and my brain with panic. I need to figure out this apartment situation right away.

I also need to see Daphne.

Leaving that voicemail was lame. I should've visited her yesterday, despite everything else going on. My guilt stems from more than that, though. When we worked together at Tower, we became friends instantly and grew close. She and Simon never got along, but we still hung out a couple of times a week outside of work. A few months later, when I got the job at the agency, Simon kept pressuring me to spend more time with his friends ("you should have grown-up friends to match your grown-up job") and I began drifting away from Daphne. Never mind that she was getting her master's in social work and volunteered at a battered women's shelter. I guess her cherry red hair, tattoos, and goth attire deemed her an unsuitable friend in his book. I should have told Simon to fuck off then and there but, you know, love. Instead, I obeyed our blossoming social calendar, and let him drag me to lectures, dinner parties, and wine tastings with his so-called grown-up friends. Meanwhile, I would've rather been with Daphne, going to the Roger Corman retrospective, or playing Scrabble, or hanging out in her room listening to Tom Waits albums. We saw each other less and less. I returned Daphne's calls less and less.

When I left Simon, I made every effort to repair my friendship with her, am making it still. We're getting back to a better place, but Daphne approaches me with an air of caution. Maybe she's expecting me to ditch her again. I won't, but I can't say I blame her.

Sometimes, I think I don't deserve the few friends I still have.

I circle more apartment and job listings to follow up on later and set out for The Lab. On the way, I stop to get a bouquet of white lilies, Daphne's favorite flower, and avocados, her favorite food. No idea if anyone will be home, but I figure I can have someone buzz me in and leave the gifts at her door with a note.

"Who is it?" Her voice sounds weary over the intercom.

"It's Astrid."

An "Oh" of surprise and a pause. "I look a mess, but come on up."

She opens the apartment door with the chain on and peers out suspiciously before unlatching it and letting me in. Barely glances at me. She's wearing a silk kimono and her curly hair is piled like a crimson bird's nest on top of her head. Her lips are pale and there are dark circles under her eyes.

"I'm making some coffee. Come join me."

I follow her to the kitchen at the end of the hall.

"Sorry to show up like this," I say. "I don't know if you got my message—"

"I got it. And Zak mentioned you came by."

"I wanted to see how you were." I hand her the flowers and avocados.

"I love lilies." She sticks her face so deep into the blossoms, the tip of her nose is yellow with pollen when she comes back up for air. "Thank you." I get a subdued smile. Progress?

"How are you feeling?"

"Knackered, but not terrible." Though she was born in South Boston, her father is from Manchester, and she spent many holidays abroad, so she's prone to the occasional British-ism. "Milk and sugar, right?" I nod as she fixes the coffee and hands me a mug. "I ingested so much MDMA it nearly put me in a coma. That fucker Eddie dosed me." She joins me at the kitchen table, sits ballerina-straight despite her exhaustion.

I fidget in my chair, glance at the doorway repeatedly until she says, "Don't worry, he's at work."

"Are you sure?"

"That he's at work or that he dosed me?" She doesn't wait for an answer. "Yes to both. He's been acting all bitter ever since we did E together and I wouldn't sleep with him." Daphne has a long string of platonic male acquaintances with unrequited crushes on her.

"Zak made it sound like it was an accident," I say.

"Zak doesn't like to believe real evil exists in the world. And I don't want those kinds of 'accidents' in my home. I told Eddie he needs to leave tonight. Wanted him gone yesterday, but he begged for one more day. Someone's coming to change the locks tomorrow." She crosses her arms over her chest.

"Wow."

"Yeah, I know it's a little extreme, but I don't trust the guy. Plus, I need to cut down on doing all this shit, and living with a dealer doesn't make it easy. Let me know if you hear of anyone looking for a place. It's a tiny room, no windows, but the rent is crazy cheap — three-fifty a month plus utilities — and, as you know, it's two blocks from the T."

"Oh my god, you have no idea . . ." I scoot my chair closer to Daphne and must get a wild look on my face, because she leans away from me. I tell her about the apartment fire. " . . . so I'd love the room and could even move in tomorrow."

She taps a fingernail against her coffee mug. "I don't know, living with friends could go either way . . . if that's what we still are."

"Of course we are."

"Until you get a new boyfriend who doesn't think I'm good enough?"

I suck air through my teeth. That one hurt. I deserve it.

"No, Daph. Until you get sick of me. You don't even have to rent me the room, I just want things with us to be good again."

She rolls her eyes. "What kind of asshole do you think I am that I'd let you go homeless? Of course you can have the room."

I reach out to hug her but she puts a hand out to block me.

"Uh-uh. We're not going to have a Lifetime-Television-for-Women moment. Not yet. I'm still a little pissed at you. But . . ." Her tone softens. "If you need any help moving, Zak's got a pick-up truck."

"That would be amazing. They're opening up the place for me tomorrow morning."

She calls Zak into the kitchen.

"Meet our new roommate, Astrid. Try not to make things weird by sleeping with her."

Pause for nervous laughter.

"I remember you." He tilts his head and smiles.

He's cute, but I'm not going to sleep with him. The last thing I need is for things to get any weirder.

CHAPTER FOURTEEN

9/9/99

Between Central Square and the MIT, a sugary scent pervaded the air. Not chocolate, not the doughy sweetness of a bakery, something else.

Astrid tilted her nose up, inhaled deeply. "Do you smell that?"

"We must be near the Necco factory."

"Like the wafers? I didn't know those were still around." She sniffed and sniffed.

"They also make those Valentine's Day conversation hearts."

"You know, I see bowls of those everywhere on Valentine's Day, but I never see anyone actually eat them. I think they're more decorative than anything at this point."

"Agreed. They might as well make them out of plastic now," Theo said.

"But then you wouldn't buy new ones, you'd just keep the ones you have and take them out every Valentine's Day, like Christmas decorations."

"Which might be bad for the conversation heart business."

The two exchanged quick smiles and Astrid got an irrational pang, a window into how much she would miss him when they parted.

Don't get carried away, she warned herself. *You don't know what this is yet.*

They passed pale grey MIT buildings set back from a lawn so perfectly manicured it looked artificial.

Astrid wondered what would happen when they crossed over into Boston. Would they turn around? Keep going? Would he say good-bye and leave her there? He was enjoying her company, right? But what if he was only being polite? What if he had other plans later and was killing time with her until then? She needed a back-up plan in case she ended up alone. Returning to Cambridge right away was no good; the walk would feel futile. She could take the green line back to Allston and pack for New York, but there was no fun in that. This clear, picturesque day begged not to be wasted. And sure, it was the ideal backdrop for something romantic to happen, but she couldn't rely on that outcome.

She'd continue walking, with or without Theo. She'd browse CDs at Strawberries and Nuggets, then books at Trident, where she'd pick up a card and wrapping paper for Sally's gift, along with some coffee and magazines. Then she'd head over to the Charles, find a bench along the tree-lined river, and read for a few hours.

Once she had a back-up plan in place, she was able to relax. A little.

Before long, they reached the bridge.

"How does it look?"

It was a postcard in motion: jeweled water, wispy clouds dusting a vivid blue sky, white triangles of sailboats clustered on the river, cyclists and rollerbladers gliding across the open bridge ahead. Astrid gave a wide smile, the wind filling her cheeks like air in a balloon. She resisted the temptation to lift her arms out to see if the swift breeze would lift her off the ground.

Theo accepted her grin as answer enough, took her hand, and led the way across. She curled her fingers around his and forgot to breathe. It didn't matter. Right then, oxygen was overrated.

"Will you let me take your bag now?"

Astrid handed it over. She hid her free hand in her jacket pocket, where she fiddled with the feather he'd given her earlier.

"Thank you," she said.

"It's not that heavy."

"No, I mean, for the bridge."

"I didn't build it."

"You know what I mean," she huffed in semi-exasperation. "For getting me to do something I've wanted to do for a long time." Her gratitude extended beyond the walk, but that was beyond articulation.

"So is it disappointing? Usually when you anticipate something, you build it up too much in your head and it's disappointing."

Astrid regarded Theo's profile: the Roman nose, prominent Adam's apple, faint stubble along the jawline. "Not at all. The opposite of disappointing. I don't know what took so long for it to happen." She looked away, felt his eyes on her.

"I guess everything had to line up a certain way. It wouldn't have been the same if it was some other day."

The tone of their voices was easy but the subtext pulsed between them like neon lights.

"I hope this isn't boring for you." Astrid cringed. Did she sound too vulnerable, too needy?

"Oh, I'm so bored, I'm practically sleepwalking." He gave her hand a short squeeze.

"Why were you at the bookstore?"

"You ever wake up with absolutely nothing to do?"

"I can't remember the last time, but sure."

"I thought it would be great to keep today open and have nothing lined up. No chores, no social obligations, nothing. It was nice for the first couple of hours. I enjoyed the quiet, but then it got too quiet. I found myself wandering around Harvard Square, hoping something interesting would turn up."

"Well it's barely two o'clock. There's still a chance that could happen."

He dropped her hand and took a step in front of her to block her way.

"This is where I'm supposed to say *'but it's already happened'*, right?" Theo asked. "And then gaze meaningfully into your eyes?"

Astrid searched for a sarcastic quip to offset the blush flooding her face. "I think a 'baby' would add a special smooth-guy touch. 'It's already happened, *baby*.' But you're right about the meaningful eye contact. I would, of course, counter with a look of awe and newfound adoration."

He stared at her in mock-intensity, and she looked back up at him in mock-adulation. There was a flutter and shift and the irony melted away from their respective gazes.

This is real. This is happening. Astrid felt a terrifying need to turn away but couldn't.

A rollerblader in a Clash T-shirt and black cut-offs passed them, then doubled back. "Hey, Theo!"

Astrid and Theo stepped away from each other.

Was she relieved or bothered by the diversion? She wasn't sure.

"Hey, Cole. I haven't seen you since Melina's going away party."

Astrid checked Theo's reaction to the interruption, but his poker face held steady.

"This is Astrid. Astrid, Cole."

They shook hands.

"Yeah, I wonder if they ever got those raspberry stains off the walls." Cole took off his shades and clipped them to his shirt. "Listen . . . I heard about—"

"I'm sure everyone's heard by now." A hand raised, friendly but also saying, *back off.*

"I'm sorry. That's rough, man."

"We need to get going, but I'll give you a call. Let's grab a beer at Phoenix Landing sometime."

"Sounds good, man." Cole backed away slowly on his blades, nodding.

Theo and Astrid resumed their stroll.

She wanted to pretend the air between them hadn't changed, hadn't grown heavier.

"Friend, acquaintance, or something in between?" she asked.

Theo shrugged. "In between, I guess. Cole's part of a group of friends I hang out with. Fun guy. Finds ways to rope us into these wacky stunts. Once, he talked a bunch of us into dressing in drag for a ladies' night in Faneuil Hall to see if we'd get free drinks."

"Did it work?"

"Cole was the only one able to pass for a woman. The rest of us just weren't pretty enough. Or maybe the bartender gave him free drinks as a way of flirting with him. She ended up dating him for a couple of months. You can imagine how much they loved to tell the story of how they met."

"And what was he . . . Why did he say he was sorry?"

Theo rubbed the back of his neck. "I don't know. Cole's a little strange."

Astrid knew she should drop it, but couldn't resist her inquiring mind's momentum. "If it's too personal, you can just say so. You don't have to lie because you think you might come off as rude."

"If you knew it might be too personal, why did you ask?" His voice was strained, politeness stretched thin.

"Obviously I'm curious."

"'Nosy' might be the better word." The politeness snapped. "I didn't want to talk about it with Cole and I've known him for three years. I met you an hour ago. What makes you think you're so special I'd want to talk about it with you?"

A kick to the stomach would've been preferable. Even a kick to the teeth. She stopped in her tracks. Those chanting kids on the playground, they're wrong. Sticks and stones may break your bones, but words can break your spirit.

"Astrid, I'm sorry, I—"

"I'm gonna head back." She turned around and began a retreat to Cambridge. He called after her, but the ringing in her ears drowned him out.

At least she learned it sooner this time, that he could lie, that he could fling words like knives. There was some twisted relief in abandoning Theo, in releasing the mystery at how their time together would play out. She'd be disappointed sooner or later, anyway; sooner was easier to deal with and dismiss.

What makes you think you're so special?

Variations on a question she'd heard before. At age nine, from Robin, when he refused to pay for a second year of cello lessons after the first didn't uncover prodigious talent. At age sixteen, from Mrs. Karpaty, when Astrid refused to dissect a cat in physiology lab the week after her own cat went missing, which earned her a C+ in the class. At age twenty-three, from Simon, after she caught him cheating on her.

What makes you think you're so special?

Nothing. Nothing at all.

That's what she got for trying to sneak into the spotlight. Boos and hisses telling her to get backstage where she belonged.

With every step, she fought the urge to turn around, to see if Theo had reversed his course. Would he follow her? Did she even want him to? Could anything remove this new sour edge to the afternoon? She didn't know how the rest of the day was supposed to go, but this was surely a glitch in the programming, a flub in the script. Or maybe not.

At least you know what this is now. It's nothing.

She looked straight ahead, expecting to feel a hand on her shoulder or hear her name called out.

Any second now . . .

Yet she continued on, alone, uninterrupted.

CHAPTER FIFTEEN

Wednesday, September 22, 1999

Early the next day, I check out of the hotel and meet Zak armed with garbage bags to pack up my apartment.

"You're really saving my life, you know that?"

He waves away my gratitude. His fingers are long, the kind that beg to play an instrument.

In the truck, he puts on an industrial CD and cranks up the volume. I don't complain about the heavy machine noises, even though they make my temples pound. Once he parks the car and switches off the ignition, I take a moment to enjoy the relative silence before the work begins.

The padlock has been removed from the front door. The damp campfire smell is more intense in the foyer.

"I hope you didn't have to take time off from work to do this." I'm trying too hard to be nice, but I can't help it.

"Don't worry about it. My hours are pretty flexible. Besides, after what you've been through, I wanted to help out." Zak raises a shoulder in a no-big-deal half-shrug.

"Sorry I didn't mention it's a third floor walk-up."

"That's too many stairs for me. I'm out." He pretends to turn around.

When we get to the top landing, I take in the sooty doorway before turning the key. "Shit, I don't even know how much will be left to move." My mouth goes dry. I want to go back downstairs.

It's just stuff. I can't afford to replace much until I find a new job, but I can't un-light those candles, either. Gotta get through this, get in so I can get out. I unlock the door.

A charred, damp smell greets us, more pungent than the smell in the foyer. Charcoal mixed with flooded basement.

The entire right side of the apartment is blackened and sealed off with caution tape. The floor is warped beneath our feet.

It's gruesome but fascinating, the habitat equivalent of roadkill; I don't want to look, but I do want to look.

"I guess I'll start by seeing what's salvageable in the living room," I say.

Not much is the answer. Even though the fire didn't reach that room, the couch and books are soaked through, broken glass covers the floor, and most of our video collection is melted at the edges. I throw a few unscathed VHS tapes into a garbage bag and point the way to my room.

My bedroom also has more water than fire damage. On my dresser is a piece of hemp paper with a short stack of hundred-dollar bills clipped to it. In her note, Cass apologizes for taking off so abruptly, says she needs to put some distance between herself and Allston, but promises to take full responsibility. The money is my deposit, plus a little extra to replace some of the damaged items. She's sorry she can't leave more and wishes me luck rebuilding. No forwarding address or number.

Zak holds out garbage bags, patient as I fill them with clothing, dry books, a photo album with most of the pictures stuck together, CDs, and a few toiletries. All of it smells of smoke. I grimace at the odor.

"Guess I'll need a new bed." I poke my damp mattress.

"Eddie left his behind. You might want to examine the box spring for drugs, but it should be fine to sleep on. There's also a dresser and desk that have been there for years."

My laptop is under the bed and when I pull it out, water leaks from the sides. That's what I get for being lazy and not using my desk.

"Bring it, anyway," says Zak. "I know so many other tech geeks, even if we can't repair the hard drive, we might be able to use some of the parts and build you a new one."

I'm tempted to peek into Cass's room, but it's on the charred side of the apartment that's sectioned off. Even though it would satisfy a morbid curiosity, it's probably not safe and would depress me more than anything. I keep that door closed.

"How long have you been living in The Lab?" I ask as we haul the bags downstairs.

"Almost two years. I was going to get my own place after graduating BU in January, but decided to save up for a condo."

"What did you study?"

He tosses the bags into the back of the truck. "Languages. Japanese, German, Spanish, Russian, Farsi. I had this dream of being one of those UN interpreters. Minored in computer science, though, which gives me more job options. You go to school around here?"

"No, I'm from New York. I studied Psych and English at a state school, thought about becoming a teacher or shrink . . . but that didn't happen."

"So what do you do instead?"

We stop at a red light and he looks over at me. His brown eyes are so dark, his pupils could be fully dilated.

"I *was* an office manager in a literary agency, but I recently . . . left. Don't worry, I won't have trouble paying rent or anything. It's just my boss—former boss—was such an . . ."

"Asshole?" He chuckles. "Is that why you left?"

I fiddle with the ashtray in my armrest. Should I tell the truth? Being unemployed by choice in this scenario makes me feel like less of a loser. "You could say that. He was the kind of person who wanted everything to run perfectly, but had no clue about how to keep the staff happy. For example, he blamed me for all the assistants and receptionists who left the company, while he was the one who extended the 'official' hours from five-thirty to six-thirty, cancelled the Christmas party on account of 'poor company spirit', and made everyone work New Year's Day."

"I know what you mean. I'm doing tech support for this university, and I get crucified if I don't fix a problem two seconds after it's reported. Nobody there has any idea how long *anything* takes. They think if they open an email with a virus, I can get their system running again within five minutes."

"Doesn't it feel like looking after children sometimes?" I pretend to be a crying baby. "Wah, the copier's broken."

"Wah, I spilled coffee on my keyboard."

We laugh as he pulls into a parking spot on Bishop Allen Drive.

When the garbage bags are piled on the bed in my new room, I thank Zak again. Blink hard as the walls around me blur. The horror of being displaced, the relief of finding a new home, the uncertainty of what I'm going to do for money . . . It would be easy to crumple into a mess of tears. I hold them at bay, but he registers my change in mood.

"Hey, don't worry." Zak gives me a one-armed hug. "You're lucky you weren't there when the fire happened."

"No, I was hit by a car and recovering in the hospital instead."

"Then I guess you're lucky to be standing here at all."

"That's what they tell me. At least I only had to be there for two of the three major disasters I've dealt with this month."

"What's the third?"

"I didn't leave my job. I was fired." I roll my eyes, embarrassed.

"It sounds like you're going to give Daphne a run for her money. She's the reigning drama queen here at The Lab."

"She can keep her crown. I'm usually pretty dull, I promise."

"Good, because I'm tired of calling ambulances around here."

My cheeks tingle, remembering the paramedic slapping my face, the glass in my mouth.

Zak looks at me closely. "You gonna be alright by yourself?"

"Yeah, yeah. You go on to work."

"I'll write my work number on the kitchen whiteboard, in case you need anything."

After he leaves, I sit on the bare mattress, surrounded by shiny black bags containing what's left of my possessions. My new room is tiny and painted a dark purple, somewhere between bruise and eggplant (parts of my body matched the walls perfectly after the accident). It's half the size of my Allston bedroom, but it's cheap, it's a place for me to sleep, and I couldn't be more grateful for it.

I pop an Advil and unpack. As I empty the duffle I brought to New York, something small and white flutters to the ground. A business card. Unadorned black letters spell out *Oliver Banks, Finder* above a phone number. I don't recognize the area code. Nothing on the back of the card. Where did this come from? Could it be Robin's or Sally's? Should I call the number?

The sensible thing would be to set the card aside and finish unpacking.

Sensible can go take a coffee break. Where's the phone around here?

I find a cordless in the kitchen.

"This is Oliver."

I gasp like I've been dunked in ice water.

"I've heard your voice before."

"That's because we've spoken before. Hello, Astrid."

It has to be the same guy, but how could it be? And how . . . "This may sound like an odd question, but did you call . . ."

"A payphone in Central Square last night? I did. Sorry if that scared you."

"Were you watching me?"

"God, no. I just got this strong feeling you needed . . . reassurance. Granted, I miscalculated that one. I'm glad you found my card." A thread of calm runs through his deep voice, but it doesn't soothe me.

I pace the short length of my room—four steps before I have to turn around. "How did I even get your card?"

"We've met before. A couple of weeks ago."

"I don't remember." I kick off my shoes, pull off my socks. Cool wood against my bare feet. *This floor is real.*

"You were reading *Memoirs of a Geisha* on the T. Long brown hair, green army jacket?"

"You're right about the hair and jacket, but I don't remember reading that book. And I *definitely* don't remember talking to you on the T."

"You thought I was hitting on you."

"Were you?"

"Maybe." A soft snicker. "You seemed distracted, but not by your book."

"I don't usually talk to strangers."

"Funny, considering you've been doing so much of it. It sounds like you're recovering from the accident okay. A little achy, though, right?"

I stop pacing, stand completely still. "You don't . . . This isn't . . ."

"I do. This is."

The bed creaks as I sit. Shaking my head clears none of the fog. " . . . How?"

"I just know certain things. Like I knew something terrible would happen to you after you got off the T. That's why I tried to keep you talking."

"Why don't I remember you?"

He doesn't answer the question. "It didn't happen in Boston, though, right? I thought if you missed your stop, you might also miss your train, plane, or whatever you were taking to wherever you were going."

Take the next one.

"It was a bus, to New York, and I didn't miss it." I feel like I'm having this conversation under water or in a dream or in a David Lynch movie.

"I wish you did. Maybe I didn't try hard enough. Or maybe some things are written in sand, but others in stone."

"Okay, Buddha." He laughs a goofy trill and, like a hypnotist snapping his fingers, my entire body relaxes. "Seriously, though. Did you really foresee my accident? And think you could prevent it? Is that why you allegedly talked to me on the T that day?"

"Yeah. Also, I thought you were cute. Was it a car?"

Hello, shivers and goose bumps.

"Yeah." I let out the word in one long breath.

Oliver Banks. The same questions orbit my head like goldfish in a bowl. Why I don't remember meeting him? How does he know what he knows? Is he some sort of stalker? Or worse?

"I'm sorry you had to go through all that," he says. "And that wasn't even the end of it, was it? Losing your apartment and job must've been awful."

No way. There's just no way.

"Look, I've always wanted a psychic friend, but this is starting to creep me out. Am I getting charged $4.95 a minute here?"

He replies with a throaty chuckle. Under other circumstances, I might find it sexy.

"Seriously," I continue. "How the hell do you know all this? Have you been following me?"

"No. I would never do that." His tone is surprised and vehement. "I'm not a creep, I just . . . sense things. I want to help you."

"Okay, then. Your card says you're a 'finder.' What exactly do you find? Can you help me find a new job?"

"You don't need me for that. A new job is right around the corner."

"I hate that expression. I mean, are you trying to be cute hinting that it's literally down the street or 'around the corner' as in soon?"

"I say whatever comes into my head. I'm sorry if it's not useful."

"What *can* you help me with, then?"

"Nothing right now. You called me too soon. You need to remember a little more. Call me again when you do. Oh—and you may not want to, but make sure you go to that moon party."

The line goes dead before I can ask any more questions. *Moon party*? Seriously? This is where the Rod Serling voiceover should kick in: "Her name is Astrid O'Malley, aged twenty-four. Jobless, nearly homeless, and recovering from an accident that could have taken her life—or spleen—she just had a most unusual phone call. Unbeknownst to Astrid, she has a direct line to another dimension, a dimension not only of sight and sound, but of mind . . ."

"Do-do-DO-do, do-do-DO-do," I sing the *The Twilight Zone* theme and laugh. It's not funny, but better to feign amusement than let the fear in.

I call Robin and Sally, leave them messages with my new number (without mentioning the fire; no need to worry them). Once I hang up, an ache twists through my left side, saps my remaining energy. Nap time?

Unfortunately, I no longer have sheets or pillows since the linen closet was in the charred part of the apartment. The prospect of lying on a bare mattress is gross so I search through my things for a makeshift sheet. No luck, but I do find a copy of *Memoirs of a Geisha*. The back of my neck tingles.

I wander into the living room where Maxfield Parrish prints hang on the crimson walls, with pewter sconces on either side. A large, black overstuffed velvet couch is set against the widest wall, flanked by armchairs draped in grey velvet.

"Looks like Daphne and Tim Burton share a decorator," I murmur as I curl up on the couch with a black chenille throw. Not that I can complain, because the cushions are so welcoming, marshmallows that embrace me and mold to my form (*charred* marshmallows—no, don't think of more burnt things). I'm only going to rest my eyes for a few minutes . . .

Of course, it's hours later when I wake up, well into the afternoon. I had more dreams, but can only recall eating noodles. Now I want something starchy for dinner. But food will have to wait until after errands.

First stop is the bank, where I deposit my severance check and some of the cash from Robin and Cass. Next is a visit to the local discount store for cheap pillows, scratchy sheets and several three-dollar T-shirts. On my way to the register, I pass a shelf of marked down candles in glass cylinders and shudder, thinking of Cass's misadventure with wax and fire.

The least I can do for Daphne and Zak to show my gratitude is make them dinner, so I go to Star Market and pick out ingredients for vegetable lasagna.

These small tasks help stave off the confusion and anxiety that's on the periphery of my mind. I still hold my breath and ball my fists at each crosswalk, but it's

more than that. A blind grasping for elusive memories.
A misplaced yearning. A distrust of the tangible. As I
perform these errands, I shoo away the earlier call with
Oliver, which lives in that grey area (a *moon party?*
Come on). Instead, I focus on my surroundings and
make ridiculous reassurances to myself. These white
plastic shopping bags are real. This lamppost covered
with fliers is real. The blue and yellow Blockbuster
Video sign is real. It's worrying, this need to emphasize
the distinction. Is it a byproduct of the physical
trauma? Maybe it's the kaleidoscope of dreams
rotating through my sleep, the ordinary entwined with
the surreal, the frayed threads of each I'm left with
upon waking.

"You need to remember a little more," he said. How
can I know what I'm supposed to remember if I forgot
it in the first place? What kind of Möbius strip logic is
that?

A better question: How much did hitting my head
fuck me up?

Back at the apartment, I stash my non-perishable
purchases and set about slicing vegetables. I preheat
the oven, open a bottle of white wine, find a small
radio behind the toaster, and tune in to an oldies
station. Hey look, it's possible to act like a normal
person.

Then Frank Sinatra's "Fly Me to the Moon" comes
on and the knife slips out of my hand and falls to the
floor as I'm engulfed by a warped sense of
homesickness. It's so intense, I grab onto the counter
until I ride it out.

I take a big gulp of wine and rinse off the knife. Shake it off and keep chopping.

The lasagna is in the oven and I'm cleaning up food scraps, when Daphne comes into the kitchen. "What is that *gorgeous* smell?"

"Just a little something to say thank you," I say.

She collapses into a chair and lights a cigarette. "Don't be daft, you're doing me a big favor here, too. God knows how long it would've taken me to find someone for that room and even then it probably would've been a friend of a friend of a friend, which would still make them a stranger to me. I hate living with strangers. Mind if I help myself?" She points to the wine.

"Not at all. There's another one chilling in the fridge."

"Good thing, seeing as you've done a bang-up job on this one. Not that I blame you. If there had been a fire here, I'd be at the Phoenix Landing, knocking back whiskeys for days. Were you able to salvage any of your stuff?"

I shrug. "Enough, I guess. I didn't live there long, so I didn't accumulate much. It was more the shock of seeing the place like that."

Daphne taps ash into the now-empty wine bottle. "Zak mentioned you're between jobs at the moment."

At least he didn't tell her I was fired. "I am, but I have money saved up, so I'm good for rent and bills, and I'm already looking for something new. Oh, I left you a check on the fridge." I point to where it's clipped beneath the wings of a bat-shaped magnet.

"Well, you can stay as long as you don't sell any of our major appliances to buy drugs. There I was, thinking I'd moved up the chain by living with a dealer instead of an addict, but oh well."

Zak comes in a little while later, carrying a white plastic bag. He sniffs the air. "Who sabotaged my plan to cook dinner?"

"All my fault." I knock back the last inch of wine in my glass and refill it, even though my tongue and lips are numb. Numb is nice, numb can pull up a seat and stay awhile.

"Whatever you had planned can't be better than this veggie lasagna Astrid's got on." Daphne lights another cigarette.

"What are we, a bunch of rabbits? I got steaks. Astrid, please don't break my heart and tell me you don't eat meat, just when I was starting to like you."

"Zak, what is wrong with you?" Daphne asks. "Did you overdo it with the coffee today?"

He looks at the floor. "Maybe a little."

She clucks her tongue and explains, "He becomes a bit of a wanker when he has too much caffeine. I've never seen anything like it, it's almost a Jekyll and Hyde thing."

Zak turns to me. "And she becomes extra British when her Southie accent starts to slip through. I've never heard anything like it, it's almost a Cliff Clavin and Mary Poppins thing."

"There were no convincing Boston accents on *Cheers*. But thanks for proving my point, *Zakuro*." Daphne blows smoke in his direction, then stage-whispers to me, "You ever want to piss him off, call him by his full Japanese name."

We serve the steaks along with the lasagna, and Zak joins in on a third bottle of wine.

Daphne ignores her food. "So, Astrid," she claps her hands, "after all the crap you've been through, you need to have a bit of fun. Zak and I have a couple of friends that live out in JP and throw the most incredible parties. They're having one next week. You should come with us."

I mentally shuffle through potential excuses to say no like going through a deck of cards.

Zak chimes in, "This is not something you want to miss. Daphne is not kidding about the Lunar Haus parties, they're—"

"Lunar Haus?" I ask.

"Yeah, they live in this weird stone house—I forget, Daph, did it get its nickname because it's shaped like the lunar module or because it looks like it belongs on the moon or—"

Giggles bubble out of my mouth before I can restrain them. Daphne and Zak swivel their heads at me, faces suspended in cautious amusement.

"The moon party," I blurt out, before another fit of laughter overtakes me.

CHAPTER SIXTEEN

I'm in my Allston apartment, on the rickety balcony, looking out. Above the trees, dark clouds on the horizon spread out like a pool of spilled ink. Sharp darts of wind make me pull the sides of my army jacket closed.

Cass appears in the doorway. "Someone left a message for you, but the answering machine melted before I could write down his name and number."

I barely give her a glance; I'm too captivated with the approaching storm. "What do you mean, it melted?"

"It melted in the fire."

I'm distracted, only peripherally part of the conversation. "The fire from the other week?"

"No, the fire happening right now."

I look at her. The hem of her floor-length lavender cotton skirt is in flames. This does not alarm either of us as much as it should.

"Looks like you're burning up, Cass."

She looks down at the wreath of fire around her ankles and nods. "I was hoping the rain would come in time."

"It might. Come out here so you can catch it." The roiling sky inches closer, jagged slivers of lightning cutting through it.

Cass steps out onto the balcony, the fire now at her knees.

"It's chilly here," she says. "At least the fire will keep us warm."

The beams of the balcony's railing hiss as they ignite. They pass the blaze around like an Olympic torch until we are surrounded by it on three sides, in the heart of a sizzling peninsula.

Cass's skirt is now entirely engulfed in flames. It's terribly beautiful, though the smoke from it makes my eyes water.

"I don't think the rain is going to come in time," I say.

"At least we're not cold anymore. And hey, you know fire has great cleansing powers, right?" She gives a loopy smile, and the tips of her long curls burst into flames. The singed smell of it is acrid.

"Maybe I should go inside."

"No, stay out here and keep me company," she says. "It's going to rain any second now."

My arm grows hot. I look down at the sleeve of my jacket. It's on fire. "I hope so."

CHAPTER SEVENTEEN

Friday, September 24, 1999

On Friday, I come home from another fruitless day of job-hunting. The *Dirty Dancing* soundtrack is blasting from the living room. Daphne dusts picture frames as she sways her hips and sings along.

"Oops, sorry, didn't realize it was so loud," she says when she sees me, and turns down the volume with no trace of embarrassment. "One of my not-so guilty pleasures."

"Mine too." My fingertips go numb. That sensation again, of trying to bring something blurry into focus or scratch a deep-rooted itch just out of reach. I'm desperate to figure this out, but I need help.

You need help alright.

"Hey, are you okay?" she asks. "You have a just-seen-a-ghost look on your face."

"No, I'm fine . . . I need to make a call. Do you mind if I use the phone?"

Daphne digs the cordless out from between two sofa cushions and tosses it to me. I take it into my room, fish out Oliver's card from my wallet.

"This perpetual déjà vu is starting to get to me," I say when he picks up the phone.

"Don't give up, that new job is really close." He sounds like he's smiling on the other end.

"Yeah, right around the corner, right? I hope I don't go broke or crazy first."

"You won't."

"And what's the deal with this so-called 'moon party'?"

"All I know is, you shouldn't miss it."

I lie back in bed and stare at the ceiling. "I suppose I shouldn't bother asking again how you know all this."

"Astrid, if I could figure out where this knowledge comes from, I wouldn't be living in a fourth floor walk-up in Brighton. I'd record some tapes, get a 900 number, maybe do an infomercial, make a fortune, and get a brownstone on Beacon Hill."

I chuckle. "I bet my friend Sally would be one of your first customers." This conversation should be frustrating, fraught with hurdles, yet I find it so easy to talk to him. "Couldn't you still make money from going on TV and dazzling people with your psychic prowess, like that guy who talks to dead people?"

"I can't switch it on whenever I want to. Some days I don't get any impressions, which would make for boring TV."

"So I guess helping the police find missing kids is also out of the question?"

"Same issue. I get hazy with dates and places, so I'd probably do them more harm than good. And certain premonitions are draining, so sometimes I have to actively close myself off to them. It's rarely fun. But when I know I might be able to help, I have to."

"Like with me?"

"Like with you. When you called me the other week, I knew things would start falling into place for you, so I was happy about that." His voice deepens. "But when I had the vision of you getting hit by a car, I had nightmares for a week."

My stomach churns at the mention of the accident. "I'm still having them."

I need to find a way to ask him without asking. "I hope you don't see any other catastrophes in my future. I've had my fill for a while."

"Nothing you can't handle."

"Don't even." In the other room, Daphne has turned the volume back up on the music, swapping *Dirty Dancing* for the perky synthesizers of an early Depeche Mode album.

"Relax, Astrid. You're in for an adventure. A quest of sorts."

I pull the phone away from my ear and stare at it, baffled. "What is *that* supposed to mean? You make it sound like I'm going to be slaying dragons."

"Now that you mention it, I do see dragons in your future."

"Not funny. Quest implies search. I'm going to be looking for something? Do you know what?"

He doesn't answer.

"You either do or you don't," I prompt.

"I do *and* I don't."

"I'm hanging up."

"I know you're eager. But it's still too soon."

"Because I haven't gotten a new job yet?"

" . . . *Yes* . . ." He makes the word sound so loaded, but I know I won't get much more out of him.

"So I should call you when I'm employed again?"

"You can call me before then. You're a little impatient, but I like talking to you." There's a flirtatious lilt to his voice that makes me nervous. In a good way? Hard to say.

"I don't know how much I believe any of this." I scan the eggplant walls, as if they'll provide an answer.

"I don't blame you. I'd have trouble believing me, too."

"Then why should I?"

"Because." He pauses, lets out an audible breath. "Because you know it goes beyond remembering. You feel out of sync with everything, not sure what's real. You don't have a lot of people close by who you can trust. But that'll change soon, too." His voice is like a cool towel on my hot forehead, a focus knob on a blurry image. "What I can tell you is, you're not ready to give this all your attention yet. You're still adjusting, rebuilding. You also need to have a little fun. Like tomorrow. You—"

The line goes dead. The battery light on the phone blinks red.

"No warning beep or anything? Okay then." I return to the living room and set it back in its cradle. Should I call him back? What if he was going to tell me something important about the party?

Or I could navigate a simple party like the grown-up I am, without the help of my new psychic friend. That sounds like a more sensible plan.

There's more talk of the party at dinner that night.

"You're still coming, right?" Zak asks me.

"I sure am."

"We'll need to get you a costume." Daphne spears a piece of plain chicken, sniffs it, and sets it back on her plate.

"Wait, a *costume*? Isn't it too early for Halloween?"

"You sound like the frat boys who mock Daphne's outfits," Zak says.

Daphne rolls her eyes. "The Lunar Haus parties always have a theme. This one is 'A Midsummer Night's Wonderland.' Think fairies, Mad Hatters, elves, mushrooms, leaves, glitter, yada yada. Enchanted forest via rabbit hole."

"Oh boy." Sounds like a party I'd much rather see in a movie than attend. "Are costumes mandatory?"

"You won't get turned away at the door if you don't have one, but dressing up is part of the fun. Lunar Haus parties are the dog's bollocks," she says.

Zak slumps in his chair. "Jesus, Daph, you didn't even grow up in England."

She gives him the finger.

"Dog's bollocks means good?" I squint.

"Better than good. Wait until you see this house." She spreads her fingers wide, as if trying to conjure it out of the air.

"What's up with all these nicknames for houses and apartments, anyway? Is that a Boston thing or something you and your friends do?" I ask.

"There was an apartment dubbed the Netgoth Shelter and it grew out of that," Zak explains. "Maybe it's a little pretentious, but it's easier to refer to a place by a nickname when a group of people we know all live there. And it's still not as pretentious as, say, putting on a British accent." He ducks as Daphne throws a balled-up napkin at his head. "And you really don't have to dress up if you don't—"

"Ignore Zakuro," Daphne interjects. "We'll go to Garment District tomorrow. I'm sure we'll find something in Dollar-a-Pound."

Before I can argue, the phone rings.

"It's for you." Zak hands me the receiver.

There's sniffling on the other end of the line.

"Hello?"

"Astrid?"

"Sally?"

A hiccup. "Corey's gone. There's a warrant out for his arrest."

"Holy shit, *what*? Are you okay? Are you safe?" Also, who did he murder?

"Safe? Yeah, why wouldn't I be? He's wanted for embezzlement. Some detectives came by earlier. They think he's fled the country." Sally takes a jagged breath. I wait for her to say more, but she remains silent.

"Oh man . . . I'm so sorry, Sal."

"At least that explains the passport. And why he wanted to postpone the wedding."

Daphne and Zak raise synchronized eyebrows, and I give them an I'll-explain-later wave.

Sally continues, "I just finished giving a statement to the police. The cops searched his place and found a break-up letter he started writing to me, dated yesterday. The detectives made a copy of it for me, wasn't that nice of them?" An ironic laugh gets stuck in her throat. "I haven't read it yet."

I put the phone to my chest. "My friend's fiancé just left her . . . and the country. He's got police looking for him, he's using a fake passport, I don't even know the whole story."

"Poor girl. How soap opera. Tell her to come here," Daphne urges.

"She's in New York."

"So what? I'll pick her up from South Station," Zak says. "Whatever time she gets in, no problem. Tomorrow's Saturday, we can all sleep in."

"But—"

"She shouldn't be by herself right now. And it'll be good for her to leave town for a little while, at least for the weekend." Daphne is adamant; her tone conveys she knows what's good for a personal crisis.

"Plus, there's plenty of space," Zak adds. "This place doesn't seem right without somebody crashing on the futon in the spare room."

"Astrid, are you still there?" Sally blows her nose, a sound like an out-of-tune tuba.

"Why don't you come up here for a while? My roommate Zak and I could meet you at the station."

"I wouldn't be good company right now. And I don't want to ruin your Friday night plans."

"You *are* my Friday night plans. And I don't care what kind of company you are."

There's silence on the other end.

"Sally?"

"I'm thinking."

"Don't think. Get on the first bus out here."

"Let me see how I feel tomorrow morning."

Sally was by my side at the hospital, then at Robin's apartment, and I want to be as essential to her recovery as she was to mine. "Come on, Sal, it's not like you're gonna get any sleep tonight. Why wait? I don't want you to be alone right now. Just get over to the Port Authority, call to let us know what time you'll be arriving, and sleep on the bus."

Some sniffles on the line, then, "Ah, screw it. And screw the bus. I don't have a wedding to pay for anymore. I'm taking the train up." That's my girl.

Several hours later, we greet a shell-shocked Sally at the station. Her light hair is in tangles around her shoulders, her eyes glassy, her lips dry and cracked. She holds a crumpled sheet of paper in her fist.

"His unfinished note. It's as awful as you probably think it is."

I brace myself for tears, but she just falls into me and gives me a zombie hug.

She tosses the note in the nearest trashcan.

The three of us are quiet on the drive to The Lab.

Daphne's in bed by the time we get home, but left Sally a welcome message on the kitchen whiteboard, saying she can stay as long as she likes.

"You can sleep in my room. I'll be in the spare room next door," I say.

"No way, I'm not taking your bed."

"Up to you. The futon's already made up." I point down the hall. "Bathroom's the second door on the right. I'll leave a clean towel for you. Can I get you anything else?"

"A shot."

"A shot?" I echo.

"Of anything. Robitussin. Peppermint schnapps, Jager . . . I don't care."

Zak gives her the list. "We have Jack Daniels, Bombay Sapphire, Goldschläger, some kind of tequila, vodka—though I think it's the cheap stuff—"

"Vodka, please." She presses her fingertips into her eyes.

Zak returns with the drink and a box of tissues.

"Nice meeting you, Sally. Sorry about . . ." A grim smile and he leaves us.

"I like him. Is he always this nice?" she asks.

"He does seem to be pretty good in a crisis."

"Is he a good lay?"

"Sally!"

"What? He's cute in a dorky way."

"He's not my type."

"Right, you have a thing for blue eyes. I don't know who my type is anymore." A bitter laugh. "Remind me to get the number here so I can give it to Detective Manis in case he has any follow up questions. Did I tell you his full name is Yannis Manis?"

"Like Julia Guglia?" Sally dragged me to see *The Wedding Singer* with her six times when it came out last year. The rhyming name scene made us laugh every time. Call it cinematic Stockholm syndrome, but I now have a soft spot for the movie. I should rent it this weekend to cheer her up.

"Julia Guglia! Yannis Manis!" Sally falls back on the futon in giggles. I wait for them to turn into sobs, but they don't, though her eyes are shiny.

"You know what the worst part is?" she says when she catches her breath.

"What?"

"He misspelled 'engagement' in the letter. He wrote, 'engagment.' And he spelled 'fiancée' with a 'y.' I almost married an idiot." The corners of her mouth twitch.

"A criminal idiot."

There's a dark edge to her laugh this time.

"Sal, I'm so sorry. What else can I do?"

"This is plenty. Maybe there's something I can do for you."

"What do you mean?" I try to keep the unease out of my voice. What does she know? Could Oliver have found a way to reach her?

"You. Home on a Friday night." She makes sloppy circles with her hand. "You went from being cooped up in Brooklyn to being cooped up in Boston. You've been through shit, now I'm going through shit . . . We need to get out there and forget our shit for a while."

Forgetting my shit is the problem, not the solution, but I nod in pretend-agreement.

"I'm gonna make sure we have some adventures while I'm here," she says.

Uh-oh.

CHAPTER EIGHTEEN

9/9/99

"Wait—Astrid . . . Will you *stop*?"

An imploring hand between her shoulder blades.

She turned, her face a flashing yellow light.

Theo was flushed and breathing heavily. "You forgot your bag."

"Thanks," she uttered the word like snapping a whip and took the bag from him.

That was something, right? That he went to the trouble of returning it to her?

It wasn't enough.

She resumed a brisk pace.

"I thought you were going to come back." He took quick steps to keep up.

"Uh, no. Not after you talked to me like that."

"I was an asshole. I'm sorry. Please turn around. We didn't even make it halfway across."

Her resolution wavered, a trickle of relief snuck through. But still, no. It wasn't enough. She didn't reply, continued on back to Cambridge.

"Astrid, come on. Say something."

She halted. Faced him. Indecision twisted her mouth. She hadn't spoken up to Robin, or her teachers, or her exes. But it wasn't about being special anymore. It was about being heard, if only by a stranger she'd never see again.

"People show you who they are," she said. "Hell, you just *told* me who you are. You're all charm and spontaneity until shit gets real. Then you're a dick. I get it. You want to build yourself up by making someone else feel small. But I won't be that someone."

Theo's face went queasy. He grabbed onto the bridge's shoulder-high railing like he was on a lurching ship. "That's not who I am. Cole was trying to offer his condolences. A good friend of mine died recently. I've been—it's been . . ." he sank his teeth into his lip, composed himself. "It's still no excuse to be so rude to you. I feel awful about it. I want to punch the guy who talked to you like that. You shouldn't be made to feel small, you should be . . . and I know this is cheesy to say, but you should be on a pedestal."

What could she say to that? Was this enough? Her hurt simmered away into sympathy, anger softened into forgiveness. "Well . . ." She stood close enough that their arms brushed together. "There's a street performer back there who has a pedestal. Maybe she'd let me borrow hers?"

Tentative smiles and the needle found its groove. The song resumed.

"Let's make it all the way across this time?" He offered an arm.

She took it.

For a while neither said anything as they walked and the air was still strange between them.

Astrid pretended to look straight ahead, eyed Theo peripherally. "I don't know about you, but I think this awkwardness sucks," she said. "I mean, there's been a little weirdness from the moment we started talking, but it was the good kind and I'd like to go back to that."

"And how do you suggest we do that?"

"I have a few ideas, all of them probably terrible."

"Let's hear 'em."

"The first is, we keep talking, non-stop, about any minor, inconsequential thing that pops into our heads."

"And the second?"

"Completely the opposite. We don't say a word until enough time passes and things are back to the good kind of weird."

"I have a third idea," he offered.

"Let's hear it."

"How about we don't script it and let things be whatever kind of weird they're gonna be?"

"I guess that could work, too."

They continued in silence. She ran her thumb across the suede of his sleeve as softly as she could to evade notice.

Halfway across the bridge, they passed a couple in their thirties looking over the railing. The woman wore a bright blue straw hat, which perfectly matched the sky and her sundress. She kept one hand firmly on her head to keep it from blowing away.

The man pointed to something on the water.

Astrid and Theo stopped to look. A group of kayakers crossed the river pulling a long plastic banner behind them. Red letters spelled out, *SUZANNE, WILL YOU MARRY ME?*

The man got down on one knee and took the woman's hand. She nodded, brushed tears off her face with her free hand, didn't even notice when her hat blew off and sailed over the water like a miniature UFO.

It was a lovely scene to witness, but also filled Astrid with suspicion. Wasn't this the kind of thing that only happened in movies? But even Theo seemed charmed by the moment. His face momentarily dropped its mask of mischief and relaxed into the role of pleased bystander.

Neither of them mentioned the proposal as they passed the happy couple.

Theo pointed at the ground. "Hey, do you know about these numbers?"

Astrid looked down at a yellow line with '124' painted beneath it. "Is it some kind of measurement?"

"It's a Smoot."

"A Smoot?" she echoed and raised an eyebrow.

"Allow me to play tour guide. The story goes, Smoot was an MIT student pledging some fraternity. One night, he was carried here and used to measure the entire length of the bridge. Hence, Smoots. I can't remember exactly how many make up the bridge, three hundred and something. And one ear."

"And *one ear*?"

"That's what it says on the other side, where the numbers descend. Next time you walk across, have a look. Oh, and there's also 'Halfway to Hell' painted in the middle with an arrow pointing toward MIT, and 'Heaven' painted under the 69 Smoot. You know, college kids."

"Huh." Astrid watched for the next Smoot, a few steps away.

"It's become such a popular local thing, when the markers start to fade they get repainted. We're talking decades now. The Smoot is here to stay."

"It's also a fun word to say. Smoot." Astrid pursed her lips to let the vowels hang in the air. "Thanks for that."

"For educating you on a bit of Cambridge trivia?"

"No. For getting us back to the good kind of weird."

"Don't jinx it, missy."

Eventually, the Boston tree lines and Citgo sign of Kenmore Square grew larger, they passed the final Smoot, and the bridge gave way to tidy residential streets.

Theo and Astrid stopped at a corner beneath an overpass and shared a synchronized look that asked, *now what?*

"Well, I hope that was worth missing work for," he said.

"Definitely." She nodded, kept bobbing her head until she became aware of it and stopped.

He glanced at his feet and put his hands behind his back like a shy little kid. Astrid's stomach flipped as opposing impulses duked it out inside her—one to lunge toward him, the other to run away and spare herself future disappointment. She resisted both urges.

"So now that you've had your walk across the bridge, are you done with me?" he asked.

Something about his directness took the wind out of her.

"No. Are you . . . done with me?" She didn't have the guts for eye contact, so instead she watched an old lady emerge from a brownstone a few doors down, pulled along by a giant Dalmation.

"No," he answered.

"Well . . . that's good."

She braved a look at him and a timid smile, which he reflected back at her.

Her ribcage a slingshot, her heart a stone shot across the city. *Please be one of the good ones.*

"Where to next?" he asked.

"Your turn."

"My turn to what?"

"To choose. The bridge was my idea, so now it's up to you to decide where we go next."

He pressed a finger into his upper lip. "Hmm . . . Well, you barely touched that muffin I got you. Either you don't like lemon poppy seed or maybe you thought I was trying to poison you, but either way I'd guess you're pretty hungry. So how about some food?"

"Sounds good."

"I'm thinking someplace right around here, really fancy and exotic . . ."

"Deli Haus?"

"You stole my punch line."

"You know what they say about great minds."

Deli Haus it was.

The small Kenmore Square diner was at basement-level. A short set of crooked steps led to a narrow doorway plastered with fliers for upcoming punk, ska, and indie rock shows. Inside, a petite brunette with a nose-ring and barbed wire belly button tattoo greeted them. She showed them to a booth, set down a couple of menus, poured them coffee, and returned to the front counter.

"I love this place." Astrid sighed and inhaled the smell of frying meat and burnt coffee. She took in the cracked pale green vinyl booths, the peach Formica tables. "I haven't been here in so long."

"Sounds like you haven't done a lot of things in so long."

"Um . . ."

"I didn't mean . . ."

Eyes widened, she waited for him to continue, but he hid behind his laminated menu.

"Maybe," Astrid leaned across the table, flicked his menu, "I'm selective about who I do a 'lot of things' with."

"I'm sure you are," came the muffled reply. A short cough and he slowly lowered his menu. "So you were saying? About not being here in a while?"

"Right. Anyway, the thing I love about this place is that it always feels the same. The only thing that changes is the art." She gestured to the walls dotted with a local photographer's black-and-white snapshots of abandoned houses. "And the music." She made a face at the noise coming over the speakers, female voices caterwauling in German accompanied by bongos.

"Sounds like angry beatnik kittens," he said. "So, Miss Astrid O'Malley, how hungry are you?"

"Not starving."

"Why won't girls ever admit they're hungry on dates? Not that I'm saying this is a date," Theo quickly continued. "I've just always wondered. Hypothetically."

It was Astrid's turn to hide behind her menu. "Different reasons. Could be nerves, which can wreck an appetite. Or they might be scared to eat something that'll give them bad breath or indigestion or make a mess. There's also . . ." She took a long sip of coffee as she found her words. " . . . something, I don't know . . . kinda intimate about eating with someone. You're in close proximity to this other person while putting food in your body, watching each other perform this basic life function."

"So . . . does that mean you won't share a Velvet Elvis with me?" he asked.

"Of course I'll share a Velvet Elvis with you."

They both lowered their menus.

"And, of course, we have to get fries," he said.

"Absolutely. Salty to balance out the sweet."

While they waited for their food, a tall curvy woman with purple hair came into the diner. A flash of recognition and she rushed over to Astrid.

"I'm so glad I ran into you. I have the *best* news. Simon just got fired from Cinemania!"

Astrid breathed in and was overwhelmed with the scent of sandalwood oil.

"Nadia, oh my god! Hi . . . This is Theo."

Nadia mumbled a hello and turned back to Astrid. "Can you believe it? First a sex scandal gets him booted from teaching and now the loser can't even hold down a shitty job in retail." Her green eyes, tilted at a feline angle and rimmed in thick black liner, widened with malicious glee.

"That's too bad, I thought he was getting back on his feet."

"Oh stop, you know you love seeing that smug bastard fail. Apparently, his boss caught him trying to smuggle a rare Polish *Suspiria* poster and fired him on the spot." She sneered. "Guess he'll have to find another naïve girlfriend to freeload off of." Nadia checked her watch and looked around. "You haven't seen Cujo, have you?"

"I haven't."

"Okay. I'll check Nuggets. He said he wanted to get the new Switchblade Symphony CD."

She turned around, trailing black lace, the metal tips of her pointy boots clicking against the floor tiles as she left.

Theo leaned back and let out a low whistle. "What's the deal with Spooky Girl?"

"My friend Daphne's close with her, both kinda big into the goth scene here. Nadia can be nice, she just gets . . . passionate about certain things."

"Such as others' misfortunes?"

"Not everybody's. Just Simon's."

"And Simon is . . ."

She cleared her throat and fidgeted in her seat. "Someone Nadia and I both dated. Not a good guy. Let's leave it at that."

"It's nice of Queen Schadenfreude to give you progress reports of his suffering."

Astrid scratched at a dried coffee stain on the table. "I don't ask her for them, but she thinks I'm as pleased to hear about Simon's misery as she is, so she passes on every piece of negative gossip about him. I guess she gets a morbid thrill out of it. If it helps her deal with the break-up, I figure it would be mean to tell her to stop . . . though I wish she would."

"You're such a good friend."

"Oh stop being sarcastic."

"I wasn't being sarcastic. That's the whole problem with our generation. We can no longer recognize sincerity . . . Be honest, though. If this guy was such a tool he was involved in a sex scandal—" His nose twitched in distaste.

"According to Nadia. I don't know the details."

"Either way, you have to enjoy getting her updates at least a little."

Her mouth fought a smirk. "No comment."

Theo changed the subject. "Have you ever noticed it's impossible to walk around this city without running into someone you know?"

"I have noticed that, yes. Especially today."

"It's like Boston's the world's biggest small town."

"Yeah, that sort of thing rarely happens in New York, I guess because it's so much larger and spread out."

"I think it's more than just size. Something about this city lends itself to synchronicity."

"Velvet Elvis." A thick white plate with a fried peanut butter and banana sandwich was set between them, followed by a platter of fries.

"You better grab your half fast, because I am *hungry*," Theo warned.

Despite not admitting it, so was Astrid.

"Salt on the fries?" she asked.

"As much as you can handle." His eyes gleamed with innuendo.

"I can handle plenty, don't you worry." She coated the plate in a sodium flurry.

They took large bites, sipping water out of frosted plastic tumblers, and finished the food in a matter of minutes.

"That was *good*. Oh, you have some peanut butter on your face. Here, let me get it." Theo reached across and smeared something on the tip of her nose.

"Thanks." She laughed, wiping at it.

The waitress came back over, all jutting hipbones and bored sulkiness.

"More coffee?" she asked.

"I'm all set. Astrid?"

"No, thanks."

She picked up their plates and tilted her head at Astrid. "You have something on your nose."

Astrid kicked Theo under the table.

Their check was brought over, the square of paper floating down like a feather.

Theo reached for his wallet, but Astrid held out her arm, palm facing him. "Stop."

" . . . in the name of love?" he asked.

"Let me get this." She took out her own wallet. "You can get the movie."

"What movie?"

"It's my turn again. I think we should see something at the Copley."

Astrid counted out some bills and left them on top of the check.

A dark room with Theo. Her nerves nearly short-circuited at the very thought of it.

CHAPTER NINETEEN

Saturday, September 25, 1999

Sally and I have this odd connection: we always wake up simultaneously when we sleep under the same roof. Every time, our eyes open within a few minutes of each other. We discovered this as kids after a few sleepovers ("we have special powers!"). Which made us think we might have other special powers ("maybe we can read each other's minds!"). This wasn't the case, but it didn't stop us from playing countless iterations of The Psychic Hour in which one of us would try to guess what the other was thinking ("It's a two-digit number." "71?" "No, but almost! 73!" "We're psychic!"). Though we never had any moments that would've been featured in a Time-Life book, we still continued to wake in unison.

Sally's first morning in Cambridge is no exception. Despite being up late the night before, we both shuffle into the kitchen just after nine, where Zak is arranging a spread of Dunkin' Donuts coffee and bagels.

"Zak, if you're doing this to get me into bed," Sally says with her mouth full, "it's probably going to work."

He chokes on his coffee mid-sip, dabs at the spilled liquid camouflaged by his black T-shirt.

Daphne pokes her face in the doorway, looking like a disembodied head, her cherry hair in two buns held together by chopsticks. "Almost done eating? Good. Time for our field trip."

"Where are we going?" Sally asks.

"Allegedly, to get costumes for Willy Wonka's Magic Christmas," I reply.

"'A Midsummer Night's Wonderland,'" Daphne corrects. She explains the party and its theme to Sally.

"If you don't feel up to it I'll stay home with you," I say.

Sally shoots me an *as if* look. "Will I be able to get good and fucked up at this party?"

"It's practically required," Daphne assures her.

"Then I'm in." Sally abandons her half-eaten bagel and pushes her chair back. "Let's go."

Yay?

Garment District is housed in two floors of an anonymous brick building in a desolate section of Kendall Square, near the MIT campus. Inside are endless color-coded racks of previously worn clothing, shoes, hats, wigs, knickknacks, dishware, and used records. The ground floor is less organized, offers a giant room filled with mounds of clothes. A chalkboard on the wall proclaims anything retrieved from these piles costs a Dollar a Pound. This is where we look for our costumes.

The four of us start at opposite ends of the room.

"Think gauzy, sparkly, forest-y, elfin, earth tones, nudes, that sort of thing," Daphne directs, sifting through clothing. "Unless you're going more for a Wonderland look. Then it depends on the character. But you know the story."

"What about this?" Sally holds up a beige silk blouse.

"Not sheer or shiny enough," Daphne dismisses.

I point to a silver tulle and lamé monstrosity. "This?"

"Better."

We find enough odds and ends to meet Daphne's criteria and spend the afternoon assembling our costumes. It's easiest for Sally, who's petite and doe-eyed, and digs up a blue mini-dress and white apron to make the perfect Alice. The rest of us opt for *Midsummer Night's Dream* looks, with varying degrees of success. Zak resembles something between a centaur and figure skater, in a brown Lycra vest, leggings, and small horns glued beneath his hairline. My cheap butterfly wings and metallic tutu make me look more like a cracked-out ballerina who's been attacked by glitter and silver body paint than any elegant nymphish creature. Daphne trumps us all, naturally, in an ensemble that's little more than leaves of green and bronze taffeta strung together with glass-beaded wire, strategically wound around her body.

We go into Libby's Liquor to get a few six packs for the party. Despite our jackets flapping open to reveal our ludicrous outfits, the clerk barely glances at us.

The Lunar Haus is a stone cottage set at the top of a steep hill that looks like it would be more at home in Middle Earth than in Jamaica Plain. The hosts have taken the party theme seriously: walking in is like being transported to an enchanted garden whose decorators were overly fond of hallucinogens. The living room ceiling is a canopy of twigs dotted with tiny colored lights, the walls are covered in antlers and ornate gilded mirrors of varying sizes, the floor is a carpet of fake grass. Most furniture has been pushed to the sides of the room to leave the center free for a mound of flower-shaped cushions surrounded by stools padded to look like mushrooms. The air is thick with the smell of lemongrass incense and weed.

"Welcome to a beautiful evening, beautiful people," Kaya, one of the Lunar Haus residents, greets us. She's in an iridescent bikini, her pale skin speckled with pink glitter, and wears a wreath woven through with ribbons trailing down to the floor.

"You have to try some punch," she says. "We have two kinds, red and blue." She points to a table with placards in front of each punchbowl, one labeled, 'DRINK ME' the other, 'DRINK ME TOO.' That's helpful. There are also platters of small cakes that say 'EAT ME' and lollipops tagged, 'LICK ME.'

"Before you drink either of those, you should know something," Daphne warns us.

"Let me guess, the punches are spiked?" Sally laughs and helps herself to a ladleful of crimson liquid.

"Indeed they are. Is this the trippy one?" Daphne asks Kaya.

"No, the touchy-feely one."

"Even better." Sally grins at Zak and pours him a cup.

"Are you sure you're okay doing this?" he asks her.

"I don't know, you might want to keep an eye on me." She links her arm through his. "Who knows what kind of things I might decide to touch and feel?" He throws a nervous glance over his shoulder at us, and they go off to explore the party together. Sally is such a different person when she's single . . . especially suddenly single, when her wilder self rushes in to make up for lost time.

I turn to Daphne. "I don't know how she gets away with it. If I said that to a guy, he'd think I was trying too hard to be sexy. She says stuff like that all the time and guys find it charming."

"Probably not the kind of guys you'd want to be with. Except for Zak, but he's got a soft spot for off-kilter, bitchy girls. No offense to your friend. Takes one to know one." She shrugs, at peace with her prickly nature.

"None taken. I should probably worry more about Zak than her. If you're weird about it, I can make sure Sally behaves." That's a lie. I can rarely make her behave.

"Eh, Zak and I hook up once in a while, but it's a no strings/no jealousy arrangement. You know the deal." Actually, I don't. I'd never agree to such a deal. I prefer strings. "Don't worry, I'm sure he'll smother her with his affection before she knows it." She holds up an empty plastic cup. "Red or blue?"

I wave my finger between the two bowls. Eeny, meeny, miney, mo. "Let's go with the blue."

We make small talk for a few minutes before a trio of girls in bronze-colored sarongs whisks Daphne away, giggling and pulling her down the hall.

I stay by the punchbowl and try to stave off an awkward unease. How do normal people mingle so easily? If this were a movie, it would be the scene where the attractive stranger comes up beside me, says something witty, and helps ease my social discomfort. But this is my humdrum life, not some silver screen fiction, so it's not gonna go that way. Besides, I've grown up with enough reminders that I'm not leading lady material. At this party, I wouldn't even make the end credits. I'm an extra. I stand at the table and have no lines for the partygoers who stop by for punch and sweets. Booze isn't putting me at ease so maybe candy will? I sort through the lollipops, take way too long choosing, finally settle on a green one with white spiraling on its curved edges like a miniature galaxy.

It's going to be a long night.

I take a seat on a sofa next to a couple of guys in Mad Hatter outfits, talking intently. *The Last Unicorn* is projected on the wall in front of us. Before long, the pair beside me is in the throes of heavy foreplay. They nudge me with careless knees and elbows, cause my punch to slosh in its cup. Here's hoping the lollipop will undercut my drink's bitterness. Nope, it's sour apple-flavored. Not the best choice.

It's painfully clear the living room won't offer any potential for social interaction, so I set off down a long hallway to explore the rest of the party. I find Sally in the dining room with Zak and several others, hunched over a giant hookah pipe, exhaling puffs of apricot-tinged smoke.

"You okay?" I ask her.

"The shrooms won't kick in for another half hour, so I'm killing time before my trip." She smiles an easy, unfocused smile. "Have you been to the naked room yet?"

"What's the naked room?"

She gives me a look that says, 'duh' and sways her head back and forth like it's on a spring. "What it sounds like."

Zak gently puts his hands on Sally's ears to cease the motion of her head. "Anybody's welcome, but you have to take off all your clothes as soon as you come in," he says.

I hope there's a sign on the door.

Zak offers me the hookah.

"No thanks." They exchange a glance, puzzlement with traces of sympathy. I bet they think, *poor Astrid, why isn't she having fun? Why is she so awkward?*

I reach for the punchbowl in the middle of the glass table, this one filled with a purple liquid. "I thought there were only two kinds."

"Maybe they mixed the red and blue together? Careful, I have no idea what that one does," Zak warns.

"Hey, you wanna do shotguns?" Sally offers him the hookah.

"What's a shotgun?" he asks.

"Do you seriously not know? Okay, I'll show you."

Their voices trail off as I leave the room, armed with another drink.

Next stop, the kitchen for some ice. Not that I care about having a colder beverage; I just want something to do. A paralyzing dread prickles at me that I have nothing to say to anyone at this party, not even the people I came with. I've fallen into an antisocial rabbit hole and I don't know how to climb out.

Maybe drinking more will help? You know, because alcohol has been proven to solve so many problems. Whenever I drink, I hope it'll make me more extroverted, even temporarily. Like when I went with Simon and his academia friends to wine bars, where I always felt underdressed and under-informed. They could've been sommeliers-in-training with their encyclopedic knowledge of wine, and would spend hours discussing things like primary aromas and body profiles. Each sip was described in terms of weight and structure, and when they'd ask for my thoughts on a particular bottle, I felt like a six-year-old being given a pop quiz on thermonuclear physics. My simple answers always garnered condescending smiles. So I'd keep quiet and take large sips of whatever was in my glass until things took on a soft blur, and it didn't matter how out of place I felt.

It would be nice to find that same level of alcohol-induced indifference now, but the more I drink, the more shyness cripples me. The crowd's sparse, glimmering costumes are all better than my own; even when mine receives a compliment, I have a conversational block that renders me mute and nervously smiling.

I walk up and down the hall, pretend I have a direction.

There's shrieking and singing coming from behind one of the closed doors. The pounding bass from the music inside drowns my knock, so I hold my breath and turn the knob.

I should have known. The first thing I see is Daphne's nipples, then the outline of her ribs and the rest of her bare torso, stretched in a curve as her head tilts back in wild laughter. A short, portly man, defying the room's rules by keeping his hat and socks on, waves me inside. I shake my head and close the door.

Things are getting fuzzy, which means the calm that usually accompanies the blur of getting fucked up should soon follow . . . but it doesn't. Instead, my jaw twitches, and I start seeing things through jagged jump cuts and double images.

Have I been in this room yet? No. The floor in here is covered with golden leaves and long cushions shaped like logs. I choose one near the corner, squirming on the hard foam beneath me, and put my head back against the wall. A ceiling light casts the room in rotating yellow and orange autumnal circles, but watching them spin makes me queasy, so I close my eyes. It even sounds like a forest in here, with sounds of chirping birds and a babbling brook piped through hidden speakers. It's actually kind of relaxing.

"Have you seen the white rabbit?" a raspy male voice asks me.

So much for relaxing.

"I have no idea how to answer that question." Maybe if I keep my eyes closed he'll take a hint.

"There's a white rabbit here with special treats. I haven't seen him yet, though."

Maybe not.

"I think I've had enough treats for one night," I say.

"Are you rolling?"

"I think so." I part my eyelids slightly and see odd features—buck teeth, flared nostrils, a pointy chin— but not a face as a whole.

"Are you loving it?"

I'm really not. Especially how articulating words takes longer than my brain thinks them up. It's like driving with the parking brake on. It reminds me of when I first got to the hospital. But I don't want to be a bad sport by admitting all this. "It's okay," I say.

"Do you mind if I kiss you?" A waft of artificial cherry candy hits me as he leans in.

I do mind, and I want to say so, but I'm too tired to resist. Not smart. Sharp teeth press into my lips and a small tongue probes the inside of my mouth, like something that doesn't belong there, something I want to spit out. I shouldn't have let him near my face. I turn my head but he still doesn't get it. He runs clammy hands down my bare arms, tries to touch the skin beneath my waistband. I sit up sharply, hold out a finger.

"Please, don't."

"Oh . . . okay then . . . Don't forget to drink water." He hands me a plastic bottle and, moments later, crouches beside another girl across the room.

"Have you seen the white rabbit?" I hear him ask.

I want to warn this girl of the party predator, but she shoos him away as I get up.

Where else can I go?

Mixing punches was a bad idea; they've filled me with ambivalence and contradiction. My mouth is a desert, my stomach a sloshing, flimsy boat on a stormy sea. I'm sleepy, yet agitated. I don't want to talk to anyone, but also don't want to spend the rest of the party alone.

In the doorway are two figures wearing identical black cloaks and rabbit masks.

"Would you like to join me for a tea party upstairs?" asks one.

"Or me for a game of chess downstairs?" asks the other.

They both hold out white-gloved hands, expecting me to choose one.

"I'd like to get past, please," I say.

"Care for a treat?" They point to candy necklaces around their necks strung with plastic pouches containing colorful baubles I assume are more than sugar.

"No, thank you."

They step aside to let me through.

"Are you sure?" one of them whispers in my ear. "Maybe it'll help you remember."

"Wait, what?" I sharply spin around but the rabbits have gone off in different directions, and I'm not sure which one to follow, so I go after neither.

There's a tap on my shoulder.

"Hey. I know you!"

Where have I seen this woman? The blue bangs, the shaved head, the facial piercings are familiar, but I can't remember the context.

"We met on the T. I'm Minerva. You're Astrid, right?"

"That's right. Good memory." Wish I could say the same.

"You look like you're having a bad trip." She offers me a red plastic cup.

"You could say that. What's in this?" I take it and sniff the clear contents.

"Water. If it starts out bad, adding more drugs will only make it worse."

"You know what they say, don't throw good drugs after bad." I gulp down the water.

"You wanna get some air?"

I follow her out to the deck. Thankfully, the brisk weather has deterred most of the underdressed guests, except for a couple entwined in a shadowy corner, their whispers and low laughs easy enough to tune out.

Minerva leads me to a short set of wooden steps, and we sit facing the dark backyard. There's a rustle in the bushes followed by a sigh. The party noises gradually fade into the background.

I sip more water. "Ugh, this creepy guy just tried to make out with me and I can't get the cough syrup taste of him out of my mouth."

"Well don't worry, I'm not gonna try to make out with you. I like girls, but you're not my type." She takes a pack of clove cigarettes out of her pocket. "I'd never take advantage of someone in your condition, anyway."

"I thought E was literally a happy pill. Everyone here but me seems so . . . orgiastic." I'm getting my verbal bearings, but my tongue is still fat and lazy in my mouth.

"E *can* be a happy pill. But you can only bury your feelings with drugs for so long."

"Or, in my case, not at all."

"Eh, most of the people in there are miserable, and it'll catch up with them. We're better off having a head start on dealing with the suckage." Her face briefly glows, all angles and shadows, as she bends her head to light a clove.

I drink more water and inhale the bracing air, now interwoven with spicy smoke. "I was all set to have a good time tonight. I don't know why I couldn't. Sorry I'm being so whiny."

"Some philosopher said you're only happy when you're anticipating future happiness. Maybe now that you're here, you don't have the next thing to anticipate. I mean, the real thing rarely pans out, anyway."

"Don't they say you should live in the moment, though?" It's nice to form words more easily but my jaw aches like crazy. I wish I'd brought gum like Daphne suggested.

Minerva leans back on her elbows and stretches her legs out. "That's what they say, right? Live in the now. But it's hardly ever as good as looking forward to something, when it's perfect because it hasn't happened yet. Or looking back on it, when our memories can give it a rosy glow and smooth out any sharp edges. Life as it's happening is no glow and all edges. The moment is overrated. You just gotta realize the moment sucks more often than not. Accept what you get and don't hope for a lot. Build up a thick skin so you don't feel those sharp edges as much."

"Wow, you'd make a great demotivational speaker. Minerva the Miserable. Become a Cynic in 30 Days."

"It's not cynicism, it's realism."

I snort. "That's what all jaded people say. Hope takes work. I've definitely hit a few sharp edges recently, but I like to think there's still potential for the . . . *unexpectedly awesome.*" A jolt, lightning down my spine, a burst of static in my ears. Come on, tune into it, find the right frequency. I jerk my head to clear the noise.

Minerva tilts her head back to blow out a plume of smoke, and I'm mesmerized by the spiral patterns of it against the night sky. "Hope in careful doses, kiddo," she says.

This buzz in my head is distracting, like a single lost bee doing laps inside my cranium. The smoke, too, which my drug-addled mind creates filigree out of each time Minerva exhales.

If I chase it too hard it won't come to me. I change the subject. "So are you new to Boston? On the T, you mentioned being from the west coast."

"Yeah, I moved from Seattle a few months ago."

"How are you liking it so far?"

"Too crowded with college kids, but it's okay. I've got some friends here, so it doesn't totally feel like starting from scratch. Not that I get to see them much because the shop keeps me so busy."

"Curio something, right?" I try to recall the store's name from her business card.

"Curio City. Sells all kinds of death-related stuff. So far, it seems like there's a market for the bizarre here. But I really need to get someone in to help me run things. I've been so swamped, I haven't even had a chance to interview anyone yet." She puts out her cigarette on the porch railing, throws it into the darkness.

"You should interview me." Could this be the job around the corner Oliver hinted at? "I have retail experience and I've been looking for work. It's perfect."

I laugh, then lean over and vomit between my feet. Minerva holds my hair back while I heave a few more times.

"Wow, that was totally unprofessional." I should be embarrassed, but it felt really satisfying to get something not belonging in my body out. I wonder if this is how a cat feels after coughing up a big hairball. "I hope you won't hold that against me as a potential employee. I'm organized and a hard worker."

"That was . . . oddly amusing. I bet you feel at least marginally better."

"I do. Good enough to find a mushroom or log to nap on until my friends decide they've debauched themselves enough for the night."

"It might be a while if they're into it. But I can give you a ride home now if you want. I haven't touched the punch or anything else that's been passed around here, so I'm fine to drive. You could even crash at my place. This stuff won't be out of your system for a while, so you might not want to be alone. And we can talk job stuff in the morning."

A sleepover with my possible new boss? Why the hell not. "That would be great, if you don't mind."

"I wouldn't have offered if I did. Let's get you some more water on our way out." Minerva helps me to my feet. As we head back into the house, I look over my shoulder into the dark yard. A white blur catches my eye. Just as I make out the shape of a rabbit, it hops away and sneaks under a neighboring bush. Okay then.

We cross the threshold, return to the fairy lights and garlands and glittery eyes and sloppy smiles.

"Where do you live, anyway?" I ask.

"Inman Square."

"And you really haven't taken any drugs?"

She shakes her head. "I know the hosts, and I supplied the antlers. Also, not everyone here is on drugs. I think some came just to hang out and enjoy the eye candy. But I don't do drugs, anyway."

"Maybe I shouldn't have, either. I thought it would make it a better party for me."

"You were hoping it would be the fairy tale it's trying to look like."

She's right, but I don't reply. Hey, at least there's a possibility of a new job. Probably why Oliver was so keen on my attending this "moon party."

I find Daphne on my way out and let her know I have another ride. The leaves of her costume are back on, but wound crookedly. She plants a kiss on my forehead, tells me not to worry about Sally, and twirls into another room.

Minerva doesn't seek anyone out, only says goodbye to people in the path of her trajectory to the front door.

As soon as I'm inside her car, a sharp odor makes my nostrils sting and my eyes water. The smell is thick, medicinal, and cloying, like nail polish remover and rotting pickles.

"Whoa."

"Yeah, sorry about that. I had a jar with a preserved pig fetus shatter in the front seat," Minerva says. "The car's been cleaned a few times, but I can't get rid of the formaldehyde smell. I'll need to replace the carpet. Let me know if you start to feel sick again so I can pull over."

I take slow breaths to keep my jumpy stomach in check. Having all the windows open helps and, as we wind around the hilly streets of Jamaica Plain, my nausea ebbs. A few minutes into the ride, I begin to see trails in the streetlights, little white comets dotting the roads, red, yellow and green ones at the intersections. Wow. When I move my hand in front of my face, same thing happens, as if the image has a visual echo. What was I feeling so terrible about earlier? Who knows, who cares? There are so many small things to feel good about right now, like these velvet tights under my tutu, so ridiculously soft, stroking them is like petting kittens. I get a mental image of pants made out of kittens and giggle.

"Well at least you'll get to enjoy some of it," Minerva says, bemused.

Why haven't I noticed these amazing textures before? I pull a finger along the line of my jaw, across my forehead, down my nose. It feels like someone else's hand touching me, one wearing a silk glove.

"Hey, are you bleeding?"

I check my face in the passenger mirror. It's streaked with red, painted like I'm a fanatic at a football game or going to battle in an ancient war.

"Oh." Hey look at that, the pad of my right middle finger is cut. How did that happen? I hold it up, entranced by the crimson streaks pooling at the webbing between my fingers. "I don't even remember cutting it."

"There should be a Band-Aid in the glove box."

Let's see if I can avoid bleeding on anything while I search. As I pull open the glove compartment, a small object falls to the ground. I reach under my seat to retrieve what turns out to be a coin. Bronze, with a square cutout in the center. I peek through the hole at the stoplight, which dilates and contracts like the crimson pupil of an eye. Back to the coin itself and it's got Chinese symbols carved on one side, scaly creatures on the other.

"Are these fish or snakes?" I hold it up to get a closer look.

"They're actually dragons."

Dragons.

Wait.

I know this. I know this. The coin blurs in my shaking hand.

"I'm pretty sure they're dragons. But I don't know why she gave these to us."

"Hey, are you okay?" Minerva glances over, slows the car. "Do you need me to pull over?"

"Yes. No. No, I'm fine. I just need to . . . What can you tell me about this coin?" I press it between my thumb and forefinger, tighten my muscles to keep from trembling.

"A friend of mine gave it to me for Chinese New Year. It's supposed to be good luck or some shit. You sure you're not gonna be sick again?"

"Maybe she thought we looked like we could use some luck?"

I'm so close. Almost there.

"I'm sure," I say.

I close my eyes, bring my left hand to my velvety knee, soft soft, think think. A second later, I'm not touching fabric anymore, I'm touching hair. Soft, like a baby duck's.

"Theo." My eyes fly open.

"Did you say something?" Minerva asks.

I did, didn't I?

Theo.

"I need a pen," I say.

"Should be one of those in the glove box, too."

There's no paper, so I write the name on my arm, which takes forever to scrawl and still comes out a mess of squiggles. It doesn't help that the ballpoint tickles my bare skin and makes me want to jerk my arm away from myself. Damn it, these stupid drugs are murder on my motor skills.

Other words come to me and by the time we reach Inman Square, I'm still trying to jot them down. Minerva doesn't say anything to distract me, just makes sure I don't trip up the stairs to her apartment.

Once inside, she hands me a blank notepad and a spare pen. I curl up on her couch to transcribe the words on my arm. Paper is easier than skin, but I still feel like a first grader learning the written alphabet. Especially considering some of these words, which are out of a child's early vocabulary: "coin," "bubbles," "bear." Time passes and my fingers cramp from holding the pen so tightly, but I keep my head down, keep going. I don't touch the glass of water set beside me, though I'm thirsty, and I don't move my body, though my knees are cramped from sitting cross-legged for so long. I keep writing. I add new words: "bookstore," "kiss," "Chinatown," "popcorn," "diner," "karaoke." What else . . .? "Bridge."

I put the pen down. That's all of them. So let's see . . . I scan the list. Yeah, I have no clue what any of it means.

But I have a place to start.

I have a name.

Theo.

Who the hell is Theo?

CHAPTER TWENTY

I'm in the passenger seat of a car driving through what looks like a video game version of Chinatown. Red neon everywhere. Lucky cats wave their lucky paws in every window. Glowing paper lanterns float in midair. Multicolored LED dragons flicker across the fronts of buildings covered in busy, indecipherable signs.

"Where are we going?" I ask.

"Where do you want to go?" The driver replies.

When I turn my head to look at him, one of the dragons breathes out a big digital breath and the inside of the car fills with a blinding light.

"You're Theo, aren't you? You're the one who called me in the hospital. The one in the movie theater?"

"If you ask too many questions, you won't enjoy the ride."

"I just want to know who you are, how I know you."

"I'm a stranger taking you for a drive."

I notice we're looping around the same block over and over again.

"We're going in circles," I say.

"Yes, but it's never the same twice. Look closer."

I scan the streets and he's right. The spidery letters on shop signs flicker and morph into new characters I still can't decipher. The bricks of the buildings rearrange themselves into pagodas before returning to their original boxy forms. The lucky cats continue their winked waves in unison but grow to fill their window frames, then shrink back down. The dragons shape-shift into kaleidoscopic fish and undulate from façade to façade.

I try to get another look at the driver but there's that flash of light again, violent as a sun flare. It forces my eyes shut.

"You keep doing that, and we're gonna end up in an accident," he says.

"Can you please stop the car? I want to talk to you."

"We are talking."

"I want to see you."

"Hey, it's not my fault you're blinded by my good looks."

The car accelerates. Our surroundings become a vortex of color.

"Theo, please slow down. Please." I grip the armrests, expect a collision any second now.

"I'm a very good driver. Never even got a speeding ticket."

"I'm scared."

"I wouldn't hurt you."

"Then please slow down. And take us somewhere else."

He reduces his speed. "I can try a new route, but I don't know where we'll end up. You game?"

"Yes."

He veers left, and then we're driving through a tunnel, ivy creeping along its curved edges, dried leaves crunching beneath the tires.

"Is this better?" he asks.

"We'll see."

CHAPTER TWENTY-ONE

Sunday, September 26, 1999

The following morning, I should be hungover from last night's mystery party punches, but other than a stiff neck from the sofa, I feel fine.

I check the armrest to make sure my notes are still intact. The pages are there, but making sense of the scrawls is another story. Up and down my left arm are squiggles of smudged ink that I can vaguely make out.

What do these lopsided words mean? Is it random babble from being under the influence or something more?

"Hello? Anybody home?" I call out.

There's a note from Minerva on the fridge held in place by a scarab magnet:

> *Help yourself to coffee, juice or food (sorry I don't have anything better than PopTarts).*
> *The front door locks from the inside. My store is a few blocks away. Come visit. —M.*

Beneath the note is a hand-drawn map to Curio City.

I don't feel the slightest pull for caffeine or food, but I'm acutely thirsty so I pour myself some orange juice. I take a sip and—holy shit, it's the best juice I've ever tasted. The sweetness and acidity from the citrus hits my tongue just so. I take a larger gulp and check the container. Tropicana. Did they change their recipe? I could spend an hour savoring the entire carton, but I've got to start the day so I force myself to drink it down and not linger.

Hang on, am I sure I don't need to scare up some aspirin? Nope, my head is still ache-free. Am I sure I don't need coffee? No grogginess here, either. I'm energized by something new ignited within me, a fierce motivation.

I have to find Theo.

I don't know who he is or why I need to find him, but I do. Simple as that. Correction: it's the furthest thing from simple. Having no last name or physical description poses a challenge (hair softness notwithstanding). But maybe I can decode some of the gibberish I wrote down last night and begin to make some sense of it.

And there's always Oliver . . .

This so-called quest will have to wait a little longer. First up, I need to secure a new job.

I find Curio City easily, and stop to admire the window display. Behind a sheet of plate glass, a giant unicorn skull is nestled on a bed of teal velvet, surrounded by gold-plated scorpions. I love this store already.

A bell rings as I cross the threshold. Minerva waves from behind the register, setting aside a leather-bound ledger.

"How are you feeling?" she asks.

I take in my surroundings before answering. It's like being in the attic of a crazy aunt married to a taxidermist (and possible serial killer), both of whom were hoarders. There are walls of glassed-in shelves filled with skulls, fossils, shrunken heads, and taxidermy. Then there are racks of gold and silver jewelry made of bones, small stands with antique postcards and daguerreotypes, and various odds and ends I can't begin to figure out, some of which seem innocuous, objects like bottles and bowls, and others that resemble rusted instruments of torture.

"Much better than last night," I finally answer. "Pretty awesome, actually. Thanks for looking out for me like that."

"First time on E?"

I nod.

"Enjoy the after-effects today, maybe tomorrow, too," she says. "You'll find food tastes especially amazing. But be prepared for the comedown—a little depression here, some moodiness there—and remember your fried egg of a brain is recovering from the drugs. Next time, be careful about mixing your punches, so to speak."

"Yeah, that'll be the last time I drink anything without knowing exactly what's in it." I gaze at some ornate oval frames housing portraits of Victorian-era zombies in various states of decay and motion to the space around me. "This place is incredible, by the way.

My friend Daphne would also go nuts over this stuff. I feel like I could live here. Or at least, um . . . work here," I add. It doesn't come out as assertive as I hoped.

Minerva takes out a rack of skull rings and begins to polish them. "I do need someone. But I don't know . . ."

"What you saw last night, that wasn't me. I'm not usually a socially awkward weirdo prone to puking and writing on myself." Half of that statement is false but hopefully she won't call me out on it.

She glances up at me, doubtful. "Actually, I think you *are* a socially awkward weirdo. But I like that. And last night you were having a bad trip but kept it together. That says something about you." Minerva holds out a hand, each finger stacked with three skull rings apiece. "Too much?"

"I think you could pull it off." My tone veers into obsequious. Whatever, I need her to hire me.

"I just worry you're too shy to handle a place like this."

Damn it.

I lean forward and brace my hands on the counter, causing her to drop a skull ring and step back. "I can handle a place like this. In high school, I spent summers working at Claire's Boutique. I handled girls freaking out over getting their ears pierced, shoplifting like it was an Olympic sport, and making a general mess. More recently I worked at Tower Records, the one on Newbury Street. I handled midnight releases for Megadeath and the Backstreet Boys. I handled a guy who got so mad the Chumbawumba single was

out of stock, he threw a Mariah Carey CD at my head."
I'm not sure if her eyes are widening at my stories or
my intensity so I straighten up and force some
tranquility into my voice. "My shyness—which I'm
working on—is not going to get in the way of this job.
I'll do whatever you need me to do. Clean up a broken
jar full of preserved pig fetus? Done. Prevent someone
from stealing that two-headed stuffed goose?" I point
to one of the shelves. "You got it. Give me a chance to
show—"

"Okay."

"Okay? I'm hired?" Come on come on come on.

She folds her arms and looks at me like a stern
teacher reluctantly impressed by a student's answer. "I
wanted to see if you'd fight for it. You did. I can offer
you twelve bucks an hour, plus five percent
commission on anything you sell over a hundred
bucks. And some of the taxidermy can get pricey—like
that two-headed goose—so it's not a bad deal." She
takes out a dog-eared catalog from beneath the
register. "I'll need you to study this so you can speak
knowledgeably about the merchandise. You'll get a lot
of questions, especially from tourists and gawkers.
They'll want to know all about animal skulls and
lobotomy ice picks, spend an hour pestering you with
questions only to buy a frog change purse or nothing at
all. And you'll get sick of telling people not to touch
things or take pictures. But the pay is more than you'll
typically get at a retail gig. You in?"

I do another sweep of the room. Could I really
spend my days surrounded by these bizarre artifacts?
Would being in the company of all the dead things and

antique oddities creep me out, give me nightmares? I couldn't handle a new roster of bad dreams, but I can't handle poverty, either.

Except that I'm already used to the space, comfortable even. Before Corey, Sally briefly dated a guy training to be a mortician. The three of us met for drinks one night, and I asked if he was uncomfortable being surrounded by so much death.

He said, "Dead people don't bother me. They can't hurt you. Dead is dead. It's the living you need to watch out for."

I take the catalog. "I'm in."

It's quiet back at The Lab. Maybe they're still sleeping it off. I'm buzzing from all these new developments and I have to share them with somebody right away, so I take the phone into my room and call Oliver.

"I think I've begun to remember," I say.

"Hello to you, too."

"Sorry. Hi. It's Astrid."

"I know who it is." His voice is on the cusp of laughter.

"Right. Because you're psychic."

"No, because I've spoken to you enough times that I recognize your voice now. And your endearing lack of niceties. Basic deduction, not supernatural ability."

I hold back a sigh of impatience. "Good afternoon, Oliver. How is your Saturday going?" I say in a robotic voice.

"Fake niceties are worse than none at all."

"I can't win with you." I let out the sigh.

"You are so easy to get a rise out of, anyone ever tell you that?"

"Yeah, and that nervous looks cute on me." My breath catches in a short gasp.

I just like how easy you are to get a rise out of. Nervous looks cute on you.

"I think *he* told me," I say.

"Who?"

"Theo. The name I remembered last night. I think I need to find him."

Oliver chuckles. "And so it begins. Congratulations on the new job, by the way."

Man, this guy takes The Psychic Hour to a whole other level.

"Thank you," I reply with caution.

"Why don't you tell me all about it over lunch?"

"With a complete stranger? Shall I bring the ax for you to chop me up with, too?"

"Hey, you can be all flippant about it, but I think I've proven myself enough to at least merit a cup of coffee."

"You could still be some kind of creepy stalker."

"You're the one who keeps calling *me*, remember?"

Fair point. I may not have his extrasensory powers (if that's even a real thing), but I need his help to put these pieces together. I need to figure out who this Theo guy is and why it's important to find him. Based on Oliver's track record so far, meeting in person—in a public place—might not be the worst idea.

"Okay," I concede. "But I don't have a lot of money, if that's what you're after."

"So now I'm a gold digger, too? I thought I was just a creepy stalker. And possible ax murderer."

"I haven't decided."

"I can't wait for you to label me some more in person. You pick the place."

I look at the list I made last night.

Diner.

There's only one diner worth anything to me.

"Meet me at Deli Haus in two hours," I say.

It's not until I'm at the diner, in a booth, and spooning sugar in my coffee, that I realize I have no idea what Oliver looks like. It's unsettling, like waiting for a blind date that might stand me up if he doesn't like what he sees. Except it's only blind on my side. And it's not a date. And the guy actually wants to meet me, so any apprehension that he might reject me is ludicrous. So why do I still get the feeling that I'm the one who has something to lose here?

It was easier when I thought he might be a stalker/ax murderer.

I'm in one of the smaller booths by the door, facing the entrance. Before I left, I jotted a note on the Lab's kitchen whiteboard saying where I'd be as a paranoid precaution, but I don't think I'm in any real danger here. Just trying to stay afloat on this wave of unfamiliar everything that's been carrying me along. I don't like being taken out of my comfort zone to begin with and these last few weeks have been one giant *dis*comfort zone.

Am I making a face? Do I look anxious? Gotta stop jerking my head up every time someone comes through the door. Instead, I'll squeeze this coffee cup when I get nervous . . . bad idea; I'm going to shatter this cup.

A better idea is to study my surroundings and try to coax another memory, a scrap of a detail, *something* that'll reveal why this place is on my list. So let's see. The booth's pale green vinyl, the Formica counter, the chipped floor tiles, all looks the same as always. The only thing different is the photography on the walls, black-and-white prints of hands double exposed with close-ups of eyes in the center of the palms. They don't remind me of anything; they look like student work.

Nevertheless, I crane my neck to get a peek at a photo behind me in a far corner.

"You can't force it all to come back to you. It doesn't work that way."

When I turn back, there he is, sitting across from me. He could play Clark Kent's ganglier, slightly nerdier brother, with long limbs, thickly-framed glasses and dark hair that falls into his blue eyes. The kind of attractive that sneaks up on you before it gives you a good wallop. Allegedly, I've met him before, but he doesn't look familiar.

"You're name isn't actually Theo, right?" I ask.

"You really like to get right to it, huh? It's good to meet you again, Astrid." He holds out a hand and I shake it, tentatively, expecting a flood of recognition or even a twinge of *something*. There's nothing. Stupid memory.

"It's okay if you don't remember me. Maybe it'll come to you later. And no, my name isn't Theo. You have my business card, but if you need me to supplement it with additional forms of ID . . ."

I stare at him, open and close my mouth a few times without replying.

"Go ahead and say whatever it is you want to say." He makes circles with his hand.

"Can I be totally honest?"

"I prefer it," he says.

"I'm a little weirded out that you're here. That you're this eager to help me, this . . . available."

A waiter comes over with a pot of coffee and a second mug. "You guys need a minute?"

"I don't suppose you'd want to share a plate of fries . . .?" I ask Oliver.

"I'm more about mashed potatoes today, sorry. Burger and mash, please," he orders.

"Okay then. I'll just have a BLT. Thanks." I hand over our menus.

"You could've still ordered the fries on your own," he points out. "If that's what you wanted, you should've gotten them."

"They're just potatoes, no need to read too much into it."

"I like to think I read just the right amount into things." Oliver smiles with one side of his mouth and reaches for the sugar. "So you were saying, something about being creeped out that I was here."

"Not creeped, weirded."

"And the difference is . . .?"

"Weirded is less harsh. I don't mean to come off as ungrateful, I just want to be straight with you." My hands need something to do, so I fiddle with a packet of Sweet'N Low.

"You have every right to be suspicious," he says.

"Okay . . . So, why *are* you helping me?"

He leans forward and drops his voice. "At the risk of weirding you out further, it's because I feel like I have to. I can't explain it beyond that." He sits back, gives a take-it-or-leave-it shrug.

"Well, that was thoroughly illuminating. I'm so glad you cleared that up."

"You're very welcome."

His faux smugness pulls a bewildered smile out of me.

"Let me put it this way," he says. "Now that you're starting to remember, don't you feel this compulsive need to piece it together even though you don't really know what 'it' is?"

"Big time."

"Well I have that same compulsive need to assist you. And at the risk of sounding full-on creepy, I've felt that way since we first met, but couldn't do anything about it until now."

I watch him, uncertain of how to react to his intensity. "You do realize I'm looking for a guy, right? Which means it's possible there was something romantic between Theo and me? Likely, even, because a string of random words come back to me, like 'Chinatown' and 'bookstore' and one of them was . . ." Why can't I say '*kiss*'? God, I'm shy about the most ridiculous things sometimes.

Oliver gives me a your-secret-is-safe-with-me smirk. "I think I can guess the word."

A rush of heat from my collarbone up. "No no, not that." Let's pretend this coffee cup is riveting, because I can't look at him right now. I finally mumble, "It was 'kiss.'" But, I mean . . . Who knows?

I hazard a glance back up. Was that a hint of a smirk? Is he hiding annoyance or jealousy?

"Is that supposed to scare me off?" he asks.

"I just . . . not that I'm questioning your motives here . . . but, maybe you're looking to 'slay my dragon.'" It comes out sounding so dirty, I cover my mouth.

A rat-a-tat-tat snicker fires out of him. "Is that what the kids are calling it these days?"

I could slither right down and hide under this table. At the same time, our banter is giving me a fizzy lightheadedness that I don't mind.

"I don't have an answer that'll satisfy you, Astrid. You're looking for Theo Collins, and I'm supposed to help you find him. So do you want to keep talking in circles or do you want to start this search?"

Did I hear him correctly?

"Who did you just say I was looking for?" I draw out every word of the question.

"Theo Collins. You said so yourself."

"I never told you his last name."

"Didn't you?" He blinks and tilts his chin like he's trying to make out the lyrics to the punk song coming out of the speakers.

I put my palms flat on the table. This table is real. My coffee is real. I look across at Oliver. This guy is . . . I don't know what he is.

"I didn't," I say. "But it *is* Collins. No doubt about that. What else can you tell me?"

"Nothing." A quick cobweb-clearing jerk of his head. "I mean, this? Just now? Rarely happens. Usually the impressions I get are less specific. But I might be able to prompt you to recall more."

"Great. So how do we begin?"

"Hmm . . . Let's see . . . Close your eyes and tell me everything you remember."

"Right here, in the middle of Deli Haus?" Even though I'm sitting with my back to the main dining area, the idea of shutting my eyes like that makes me feel exposed.

"I'd normally pick somewhere more private, but I think you chose this place for a reason," he explains.

It's not like he's asking me to get on the table and do a dance. No big deal, right?

"I have a list." I reach for my pocket, but one of his abnormally long arms stops me. Man, he must have no trouble reaching things on high shelves.

"Forget the list. Close your eyes. Tell me what you remember. Tell me how you started to remember."

Okay, here goes. I do as he says, fidgeting my shoulders as I block out the diner. "I found a Chinese coin in Minerva's car—Minerva is this woman—"

"That doesn't matter. Tell me about the coin."

"Right. So it had these animals etched into it. I asked her if they were snakes or fish and she said, 'dragons.' That's when I knew."

196 ASLEEP FROM DAY

"Knew what?"

"I had that conversation before. With Theo. After his name popped into my head, it was followed by all these random words. 'Popcorn.' 'Chinatown.' 'Kiss.' 'Bridge.' 'Bear.' 'Diner.' There were others, but I'd have to check my list. I don't know, some of this stuff might be from the dreams I've been having since my accident."

"Let's stay on Theo. Focus on his name and think about that Chinese coin. Imagine holding it your hand. Turn it over, feel the weight of it, feel its texture. Now make sure you keep your eyes closed for this part." His voice has a depth and richness that envelops me, puts me in a soundproof booth that shuts everything else out. "Keep looking at the coin, but imagine you're sitting across from Theo. Move your eyes from the coin to the table. From the table over to him. He's right there in front of you. Tell me what you see."

Holy shit. He's right there behind my closed eyes.

"BLT, burger and mash." A dish is set in front of me with a light clatter and I open my eyes. The image is gone.

When the waiter leaves, Oliver says, "Close your eyes again. He's still there."

I do, and it takes a moment to bring him into focus, but I see him. This is Theo.

"Tell me what you see."

Out loud I describe Theo in broad strokes: fair bedhead hair, light eyes a faded blue, solid build verging on stocky. But as I go into his main features, other details come back to me, which I leave out. I don't mention how strangely perfect his ears are, how I could (and maybe did) run my fingertips around their curves. I don't tell him about the enticing softness of his hair. I don't tell him how Theo's eyes go from mischievous to guarded and back again depending on how he blinks and tilts his head. I recall the exact dip of his downy cheeks and firmness of his lower lip, but I don't say any of this out loud.

In fact, I could reach out and touch Theo's face right now, and I do, and his cheek is warm and I move down his face only this mouth is a little wider, a little fuller.

I open my eyes and pull my hand back, as if from a fire. "I'm so sorry."

Oliver looks down and takes hold of his burger. "Don't be. I'm glad something came back to you. That's why I'm here."

I don't think he's entirely glad. As I chew a mouthful of my sandwich, I frown. Shouldn't I be reassured recalling Theo's face? Satisfied that the tugging at the back of my mind alluded to something tangible? So why am I not happier about it? Why this confusion, discomfort, even vague guilt?

We don't speak for a few minutes. I pretend to focus on my food and guess he's doing the same.

"Tell me something." Oliver breaks the silence, and I let out a breath I've been holding too long. "What's the last thing you remember before your accident?"

"Before coming to New York?"

"Do you even remember the trip to New York?" he asks.

"Sure, I . . ."

Hang on a second. Time out. Rewind to the Friday I left town. I *thought* I . . . Well, isn't that odd . . . When I search my mental file folders for any details of the trip, they come up empty. "Shit . . . That can't be . . . I don't . . . Let's see . . . I remember the day before the accident, I went to work, had a busy morning. Then I must've taken lunch . . . and the rest of my day would have been ordinary."

"That's a lot of speculation. What do you actually *remember*?"

"Calling hotels in Frankfurt. Ordering coffee and soda for the office. Talking to Jasleen about an open mic night she wanted me to go to in the Back Bay. Leaving the office around twelve thirty . . ." Wait, is that it? That can't be right. "Um . . ." It's like travelling through a long dark tunnel of my memory, searching for a patch of light. "Wow. The next thing I can remember is waking up in an ambulance with glass in my mouth."

"And when was that, again?"

"Friday, September ninth. Sometime in the early afternoon."

"Friday, September ninth?" Oliver does some mental arithmetic. "Friday was September *tenth*."

"Why did I think it was the ninth?"

"Because you can't remember much of the ninth, so maybe your brain is trying to fill in the gaps. Looks like you're missing about twenty-four hours."

"That's insane. Why—How—" I stammer. Is it possible I tricked my brain into covering up a hole in my timeline? If my mind is that susceptible to misdirection, what other mental glitches might I be experiencing? "How did I not realize I was missing a *full day*? Why did it take me so long to realize?" I push my plate away. I can't sit here anymore. The smell of the grease, the loud background punk music, the people around us, it's too much. I stand up.

"What do you need?" Oliver asks.

"Air."

Outside, I find a nearby stoop and sit heavily, elbows on knees, head in hands.

A minute later, Oliver joins me. He drapes my jacket over my shoulders but doesn't say anything, doesn't touch me, just sits beside me.

"I know it's stupid," I say. "It's just time. It's not even like I lost a *year* of my life or anything. I mean, that accident . . . I was lucky. It could've been so much worse," I regurgitate the platitudes from the hospital as I try to buy into them. "Losing a day shouldn't be such a big deal in the grand scheme of things."

"And yet . . ."

"And yet, in my own not-so-grand scheme, it was an important day. Maybe my best day. What if that's it? I can't say how I know this—hey, I'm starting to sound like you—but what if it was the best day of my life, and now it's been wiped clean?" I look up at the sky, anemic white with dark grey clouds moving in. A cold wind infiltrates the open spaces of my jacket. I shiver and move closer to Oliver.

"It hasn't been." A cautious hand pats my back. "You remembered his name, what he looks like. You have a whole list of other things. The rest will come back to you."

But will Theo come back? Will I ever see him again? And what if that list is meaningless, a byproduct of the drugs I took at the party? Should I tell Oliver what might've been the real catalyst for that chain of words, besides the coin? Because anything could have actually happened that day, or *nothing* could have happened. Theo could be a figment. Would Oliver still help me if he knew we might be chasing down a hallucination? Or does he already know? Is he enabling me, giving a last name to my lunacy? If so, why would he do that?

The sensible thing would be to level with Oliver, but there's something deeply embarrassing about questioning your sense of reality—sanity, even—out loud. Whether or not he already senses my tenuous hold on the waking world, right now he believes me, and he could possibly help me figure out what's real. I'm not sure I'll ever get that day back but I can't afford him doubting me by adding more confusion to the mix. So I chicken out and don't say anything else. Maybe his motives should matter more to me or maybe each of us is turning a blind eye on the situation. For now, I can live with that.

"So what happens next?" I ask.

"What happens next is, it rains."

The skies open right up as if waiting for Oliver's cue, a cold rain that partially soaks us in the time it takes to scramble up the stairs to the entrance of a nearby brownstone.

"The psychic who doesn't carry an umbrella," I admonish through chattering teeth.

Across the way, cars slow to accommodate the sheets of rain that blur sightlines. The rushing water builds to a din, and I know this is exactly how it rained when I was hit by the car, a twin downpour that derailed my mediocre but perfectly acceptable life. The first domino that sent the rest toppling. If only I could've been a little more careful at the crosswalk. I wouldn't have lost my job. I might've been able to prevent Cass from torching our apartment. I definitely wouldn't have forgotten Theo. I might be with him right now. Instead, I'm cold and weighed down with pointless alternate reality scenarios. Full of remorse and fear that no matter how much I try to stay on the edges of life, keep my head down and stick to my little routines, I could step off the curb and have them wiped out just like that. And now I'm dwelling on unchangeable consequences and grieving over a little bit of lost time. How petty of me. How ungrateful.

My shudder is fifty-fifty self-loathing and frigid rain.

"Come here," Oliver says. When I hesitate, he adds, "I'm not making a pass at you. Stop being so suspicious."

I move in and—how is this much heat emanating from his lean body? When he hugs me ("shut up and let me get you warm") it's like being encased in one of those space-age foil blankets marathon runners and trauma victims get: thin but surprisingly effective. My head rests on his shoulder. He smells like towels fresh out of the dryer. We stand there, inches from the downpour, and my deluge of bad feelings gradually ebbs away. A better sensation comes over me: of being

202 ASLEEP FROM DAY

cozy under the covers, of not wanting to go out in the rain, of being pressed against a body, inhaling the smell of skin and feeling drunk off of it.

"Hmm . . ."

"Did you remember something?" Oliver asks.

"Kind of," I murmur.

"Are you warm?"

"Getting there."

I want to keep my eyes closed, to keep pretending, but it's not fair to him.

"It's almost over," he reassures.

Maybe I don't want it to be.

Moments later, the rain stops. Even though I'm still cold, it's time to step away.

"Now what?" I ask.

"Now you go home."

"Wait, what do you mean? What about the new memories and my list and this big quest I'm supposed to be on? I thought you were going to help me."

"I am, but you're sad right now, and your thoughts are muddled. It's not the right time."

It never is.

I want to keep going, but he's right. Despite this brief respite, the melancholy is seeping back in, and my skull warns of another headache on the horizon.

"I don't understand," I say. "I have a new job, and we're making some progress here . . . but I feel awful about everything."

"It'll pass. Maybe it's the weather." Oliver shrugs.

Maybe it's the drugs.

"I'm sorry I've been such terrible company today."

"For the record, I'm not here for you to entertain me. I don't care what kind of company you are. I kinda figured this would be a tough process for you."

An inner switch is flipped and I bristle with irritation. The smug act is getting old. "Does anything ever surprise you?"

He steps away from me as if from the business end of a ledge. "Yeah, of course."

"Well, maybe you could be a little less self-help guru about it all." I'm doing that unfair thing, when your emotions get unhinged and you take it out on the person in front of you. Time to extricate him from my crazy. "Yeah, home is probably my best bet now."

"My car's in the shop or I'd drive you, but let me at least walk you to the T."

"It's fine. I'll walk. Thanks for lunch."

I take off down the stairs without looking at him or saying goodbye.

The rain has thinned into a misty drizzle. Doesn't matter, right now, I'd walk through a hurricane. I can't take the thought of being hemmed in by a doorway or a subway car or a taxi.

We forget things all the time. My memory isn't sharp to begin with, and there are countless days I can't remember well, if at all. But they've been forgettable because they were unremarkable. September ninth wasn't lost to me because it was as ordinary as the days that preceded it. It might've been a day in my mental calendar I would've circled and replayed, a day set apart, noteworthy. I don't get many days like that—I don't think most of us do—and I want it back.

I reach the Mass Ave Bridge and begin to cross it.

If meeting Theo was so special, it'll come back to me, right? If it won't, then either it doesn't matter . . . or it never really happened.

The wind whips hard with no buildings to buffer it, and my hair goes Medusa wild. A fine rain trickles down the back of my neck and even though I'm shivering again, I no longer feel the cold. Maybe I've calmed down or maybe I'm tired, hungover. But no, that's not it.

I blink.

I feel nothing. It's a blessing to take a break from emotions, even for a little while.

Ahead of me is the rest of the bridge and the path back home and I don't think about what I'll do the rest of the day or tomorrow. All I have to do is keep walking.

I glance at my feet as I step over something painted on the ground: "364 SMOOTS PLUS 1 EAR."

I can't remember exactly how many make up the bridge, three hundred and something. And one ear . . . That's what it says on the other side, where the numbers descend. Next time you walk across, have a look.

I keep watching the numbers at my feet. They do descend.

It's become such a popular local thing, when the markers start to fade they get repainted. We're talking decades now. The Smoot is here to stay.

And it's also a fun word to say.

"Smoot!" I call out. A passing jogger turns back to give me a queer look.

I didn't know anything about Smoots before Theo. This isn't a conversation I had with myself. It's not the drugs and it's not my imagination.

I'm remembering.

CHAPTER TWENTY-TWO

9/9/99

"What do you want to see?" Theo asked.

"I don't even know what's playing," Astrid replied. "Do you ever have this urge to go to a movie, regardless of what's out? Just to have that popcorn-smell, feet-sticking-to-the-floor, sitting-in-a-dark-room-with-dozens-of-strangers experience?" One of his eyebrows headed north and she rushed to cover up her embarrassment. "And don't place too much emphasis on the dark-room-with-strangers part. You know what I mean."

He looked at her, sleepy-eyed, and said, "I'm a wannabe filmmaker. Of course I know that urge. Let's check out our options."

The Copley Theater was in a small shopping center that catered to the upper classes. Astrid always wondered why a run-down movie house would share a roof with a gourmet chocolatier, an antique furniture shop, and several designer clothing stores. It didn't seem like the same people who shopped there would want to see movies there, too.

"Just a warning in case you haven't been here before, but this place has pretty bad screens," she said.

"Hey, I *like* watching movies on a postage stamp from the end of a long tunnel."

"Ah, so you *have* been here before. What should we see, hotshot?"

They considered the selection.

"I have a rule about sequels, so we can't see *Timebomber 2: The Escape*."

"That's okay, I never saw the first *Timebomber*, anyway." She paused. "Hang on. You have a *rule* about sequels?"

"It's pretty simple. I won't watch them."

"Not any? Not even *Star Wars*?"

"That was a single story told over the course of three movies, so it's different."

"Didn't a fourth one just come out?"

He shook his head. "We shall not speak of it."

"Okay then. What about *Aliens* or *Terminator 2*? Some would regard those as superior to the originals."

"I agree with what William Goldman said about sequels being whores' movies."

She made a gagging noise. "Oh no. You're not one of *those* guys are you?"

"Uh, maybe. What do you mean?"

"You know, one of those guys who watches a movie and goes on about stuff like the cinematography and denouement and mise-en-scene. And worships obscure-ish directors like Jodorowsky and Tarnofsky."

"Tarkovsky?"

"Whatever." She inhaled the buttery popcorn smell emanating from the theater.

"*Andre Rublev* is only one of the greatest movies ever made."

"I'm sure it is. Oh look, there's something starting in fifteen minutes. It's not in black-and-white or subtitled, though. Are you sure you'll be able to handle it?"

A reluctant sigh. "I guess I can restrain my inner film snob for a couple of hours."

"Your inner film snob makes my inner film snob look like an Adam Sandler fan," she said.

"I actually didn't mind *The Wedding Singer*."

Her smile was pleased but she wedged irony into it.

They approached the sales counter. Theo bent down to speak into the silver circle embedded in the Plexiglas. "Two tickets to the five-thirty screening of . . ." he turned to Astrid to fill in the blanks.

"*Other People's Bedrooms*."

"*Other People's Bedrooms*—hey, this better not be a sappy romantic comedy."

She gave a faux-innocent, wide-eyed shrug.

Tickets in hand, Theo led the way to the concession stand. "It's not a movie without the popcorn, right?"

"Right. Oh, but could we get M&M's and put them in the middle and on top?"

"And how do you get them in the middle?"

"I ask them to fill the carton halfway, put in some M&M's, then fill up the rest."

"The snack counter people must *love* you."

"Hey, I add the ones on top myself," she defended.

They made it in time for the previews. The theater was only half-full, but they still chose seats in the back row.

Theo leaned over and whispered, "Listen, I know there's usually awkwardness when seeing a movie on a first date, or whatever you want to call it. To begin with, there's the issue of the armrest. I'm happy to share it, unless you want it all for yourself, in which case feel free to push my elbow off. Then there's the question of whether I'm going to try to put my arm around you"—Astrid's eyes widened in the dark—"or worse, try to kiss you."

She held her breath until he continued.

"But I won't. First of all, I don't know if you want me to. Even though you have no poker face, you still seem a little nervous, and I don't know if it's a hey-I-like-this-guy nervous or a I'll-hang-out-with-this-guy-but-still-don't-trust-him-not-to-be-a-psycho nervous. Second of all, I don't think a movie theater is the best place for a first kiss. Too expected. I also don't know if putting my arm around you would make you uncomfortable, so how about this: if you decide at any point that it would be okay for me to do that, nudge my knee with yours. That'll be the signal. What do you think?"

She missed half of what he said because she was paying too much attention to his warm breath on her ear and his tangy cologne—an intoxicating combo. For all she knew he might've been asking her to join him on a murder spree after the movie.

Theo moved his head so that she could answer. Her lips grazed his earlobe as she whispered, "Sounds good." She'd find a way to get out of the murder spree later if need be.

The movie was indeed a romantic comedy, about a gorgeous-but-kooky, unlucky-in-love real estate agent who develops a crush on a client, a handsome-but-reserved architect. The architect is purposefully indecisive in choosing an apartment because he's smitten with the agent.

Astrid took in every frame with thorough enjoyment, though it had little to do with the movie's formulaic plot. Anticipation rose in her every time she reached for the popcorn and her fingers brushed against Theo's. During the movie's second act, right after the agent bumps into a woman claiming to be the architect's wife, Astrid shifted in her seat and accidentally bumped knees with Theo. He put a sturdy arm around her and her anxiety dissolved in a puddle of relief. Emboldened, she put her head on his shoulder and they watched the rest of the film in that position. Who cared if the picture was tilted for her? Who cared about the eventual pins and needles in her arm from being pressed against the armrest? She barely felt them anyway.

On screen, numerous twists and misunderstandings keep the agent and architect apart, until the inevitable Big Romantic Moment, in which they reunite and close out the film with a kiss on a penthouse balcony. When the credits rolled and people started leaving their seats, Theo and Astrid moved with the lazy gestures of kittens waking up from a long nap.

"You hated it, didn't you," she said as they walked through the crimson-carpeted lobby.

"Are you kidding? I thought it was pretty good."

"Really?"

"Yeah. Though the movie itself was atrocious."

Astrid bumped him with her hip, and he responded by grabbing her hand.

Outside, they separated and faced each other.

Theo scraped the sidewalk with his toe, once more appearing like a shy little boy. "So . . ."

"So . . .?"

CHAPTER TWENTY-THREE

Sunday, September 26, 1999

Hurry, hurry, hurry. Quickened steps until I return to The Lab. I impatiently pull off my wet clothes—which insist on sticking to my skin—and pat my hair down with a towel. In the kitchen, a stack of phone books props up a basket of fruit. I find the current one and flip open to the C's. There are three listings for Theodore Collins, six for Ted Collins and fifteen for T. Collins. No Theos specifically, but that doesn't mean he's not among those names.

I sit at the kitchen table with the listings, the cordless, and a pen.

I'm ready. Except . . . What should I say when I call these numbers? What if someone other than Theo picks up the phone, or I get an answering machine? What kind of message could I leave? "If this is the same Theo Collins who met a girl named Astrid a few weeks ago and spent the day with her—me—please give me a call. Unless it was a one-time thing for you, which is fine. It would still be nice to get a call back, though, so I know I got the right number, and also where things stand. Thanks." Yeah, that would rival the answering machine scene in *Swingers* for champion of awkward.

Gotta think this through some more before I start dialing.

Sally pads into the kitchen full of yawns, stretching her fists to the ceiling like a cartoon little girl.

"Is there any orange juice?" she asks. "Someone at the party told me to make sure I have juice today. Something about it being an orgasm for my mouth."

"I don't know if we have any, but if we don't, I'll get some because that someone wasn't lying."

She finds a carton in the fridge and fills a mug.

"Oh my god," she says after the first mouthful.

"I know, right? Pour me one?"

"So what happened to you last night?" She hands me a mug of juice.

I tell her about Minerva, her store, and the job offer. I don't tell her about Oliver or anything else that happened today. I can't, not yet. It needs to be mine to obsess over for now.

"What about you and Zak? Did you two hook up?" I ask.

"I don't remember. There was a room at the party filled with pillows, and one person in the center would be blindfolded and hold up a number with their fingers and that many different people would take turns kissing them. I was in the middle a few times, so who knows."

I think of germs, of that toothy stranger who kissed me, and I must pull a face because Sally says, "I just had my wedding called off. Last night took my mind off that for a few hours, so I really need you to not judge me right now. You know I'd never judge you."

This is a variation on what Sally always says after an episode of outlandish behavior. In high school, she set her hair on fire in the science lab on a dare, then shaved her head, "because the smoky smell was annoying." In college, she dated a performance artist who she allowed to pierce her nipples onstage as part of his act. Her first job out of college? Personal assistant to a porn director. She does things that could elicit all kinds of judgment, but won't stand for it. Maybe that's also why she rarely slings it back.

I should tell her. At least some of it.

"Sally, I think I met someone."

"At the party? I hope I didn't accidentally make out with him in the pillow room."

"No, before that. Before the hospital."

She puts down the mug and slides her chair forward, instantly less bleary-eyed. "Wait, what do you mean, you *think* you met someone? You either did or you didn't."

I tell her the bits I recall, but I leave out Oliver, even though there's no good reason for me to do so. Instead, I stitch together the story around him and keep vague on the other memory triggers. But I tell her about the coin, the ensuing list of words, Theo's face, the rain, the Smoots.

"Are you kidding me? I can't believe you're only starting to remember all this stuff now. What if he's your soul mate? What if he's been calling your apartment nonstop and getting a disconnected number, not realizing your dippy roommate incinerated the place?"

This is why I love Sally, my insta-accomplice.

She zeroes in on the phone book. "Were you about to call him?"

"I was gonna try. But I don't know what I'd say to all the wrong Theos . . . and especially not to the right one."

"Let me think . . . Get me some more juice?" She holds out her mug.

"Yes, boss." I pour myself another glass, too, draining the last of the carton, but pleased to see another in the fridge. Zak or Daphne must have known and prepared ahead of time.

"Okay, I think I have a plan." Sally's face is fierce with concentration. "Where's this new place you're working?"

"Inman Square."

"This is what we're going to do." Her fingers waggle in the air the way they do when she's plotting. "You call up all the Collins guys and tell them an expensive purchase was made with their credit card to—what's the name of the store? Spooky City?"

"Curio City."

"Right. Tell them they need to come to Curio City to verify the purchase as an extra security measure blah-blah-their-credit-card-company-tried-to-dispute-the-charge-or-something-blah."

"Uh, first off, you're missing some pretty vital steps in those blahs. Second, I just got this job. Lying to not one but over a dozen people about a credit card charge seems potentially illegal and something that could piss people off and get me fired. Again."

"Hmph." That was as close as she'd get to admitting she was wrong. "Fine, new plan," she shifts gears. "We go completely the other way. No bells, no whistles. Call up each person and tell them you're looking for Theo Collins, who you met last month before you got into an accident and lost your memory. Say you need to speak to him to find out what happened that day."

I consider playing it straight once again . . . There's no way it'll work. "Aside from sounding like a soap opera, if the Theo I'm looking for is behind one of these numbers, there's a chance he's not gonna want to talk to me. What if it was a one-night stand?"

"You don't have one-night stands."

"What if I made an exception? If we hooked up, it could've been a one-time thing. And if it wasn't, blurting out the real story like that might make him think I'm a nutjob—which I haven't entirely ruled out, either. Oh—and what if I call one of the wrong Theos and the guy's wife answers? Or if the right Theo turns out to be married? So many things could go wrong. No, it can't be the truth right now. There needs to be a different way to find the real Theo and rule out the others." If there *is* a "real" Theo. The Smoots memory bolstered my confidence, but I'm still not totally persuaded.

"Do you think you'd recognize his voice?"

"After all this time? Considering how little I remember, probably not. I'd need to see him to know for sure."

"Then we have to find a way to lure him to the store."

"Sounds like you two are plotting something nefarious." Zak appears in the doorway, carrying an armful of computer equipment. "Who are you luring where, or is it safer for me not to know?"

"Nobody, nowhere." I point to the bundle he's carrying. "What's all that?"

"Gear for your new laptop and some Y2K stuff. Please tell me you're not planning a murder."

"Of course not," Sally jumps in. "Just helping Astrid with some boy trouble. So is this Y2K thing real? Are there going to be blackouts and airplanes falling out of the sky and other catastrophes when the calendar changes over to 2000?"

"Oh please. Don't listen to those alarmists." Zak sets down the equipment on the table. "There's been a major Y2K-compliance program for years. It's just the media inciting a panic. We made it through September ninth with no problems and the Millennium Bug is going to prove just as inconsequential. Is there any juice left?"

"If there is, could you bring over the carton?" Sally waves her empty mug.

"Wait, what was supposed to happen on September ninth?" I ask. A spider of unease scurries down my back.

"Some systems use 9999 to mark the end of a file, so there was concern that computers would freak out on September ninth, 1999 and stop processing, in accordance with the code. But the day came, and computers and other communications systems ran without any glitches. The same thing is going to happen with Y2K—a lot of fuss over nothing. More juice?"

I wish *my* internal processer ran without any glitches.

"No thanks. I'm going to lie down for a little while." I take the cordless and phone book with me.

"Can I come?" Sally asks.

"It's okay, I'll figure something out. But thanks."

I settle at my desk and turn to the Cs in the phone book again. But when I dial, it's a different number, one I now know by heart.

"Hello?"

"Oliver?"

"Speaking. Who's this?" He sounds tired.

"Astrid. I'm surprised you didn't recognize me."

"I'll try to do better next time. What do you need?"

"Is this a bad time? I can call back." I didn't expect such a frosty tone from him, but then again, I was far from cordial when we parted.

"It's fine. What's going on?"

"I'm sorry for snapping at you like that. I don't know what got into me, and I'm not going to use my stupid accident or memory loss as an excuse. I still should've been nicer."

Silence on the other end of the line.

"Are you there?" I ask.

"I'm here."

Another pause. Am I getting on his nerves or did I really hurt his feelings? I hate the thought of either being true.

"I don't want you to think I'm not grateful," I continue. "I am. And even though you said I should take some time and process, I wanted to talk to you, and I don't really know why." It could have something to do with how safe I felt when he was keeping me warm in that doorway. "Should I leave you alone? Maybe you need more time to be mad at me? Or maybe you've had enough?"

"There's something you can do for me." Still guarded, but there's a softening.

"Sure."

"Have dinner with me tomorrow."

I blink rapidly and put a hand to my throat. "That sounds like a date."

"Maybe because it is—or would be."

"Um . . . I was awful to you, why would you ask me out after that?" Maybe all that nonsense Sally tells me about guys liking bitches isn't such nonsense after all.

"You were shaken up. I'll give you a do-over. Dinner. Tomorrow."

"So would this be any different from our lunch today? Apart from my being less of a jerk at the end of it."

"Yes. It won't be about solving the mystery of your missing day or missing guy. It'll just be us getting to know each other."

"Hmm . . ." I run my fingertips over a page of the phone book, as if the letters and numbers will rise up like Braille, but only find a dry, smooth sheet. "Not that I'm insecure or fishing or anything . . ." Except that I'm both insecure *and* fishing. "But why do you want to go out with me?"

"The usual reasons. You're cute, and I like you."

My heart gives a little drumroll, but I press on. "That's it?"

"Now you *are* fishing. But . . . okay." His voice takes on the intimate hush of letting me in on a secret; it's like being immersed in a pool of warm water. "You have a certain tenacity I don't see often. You're endearingly stubborn, but there's also a sweetness there. Something more vulnerable. And a potential to do great things you haven't started tapping into yet. Enough about you," his voice adopts a livelier inflection. "I'm not too shabby either, you know, and dinner with me would give you a chance to discover that. So if you ever do track down this so-called dream guy, I'm confident you'll be won over by my charms and none of that will matter."

His words are sweet with a touch of grit, cotton candy sprinkled with sand. The compliments are a nice ego boost, but what's up with that phrasing? Does he question Theo's existence like I do? The certainty I had earlier on the bridge continues to waver, thin out. I could've come across information about Smoots a different way, heard about them from someone else. How do I know for sure this came from my missing day? Add Oliver's involvement in all this, and the situation could get even weirder and more confusing.

"Astrid? Are you there?"

"Yeah, sorry, I was thinking . . . I don't know . . . Things could get complicated."

"Sometimes that's not so bad."

I laugh a sharp, humorless laugh. "I think I'm all set on complicated for a while. I . . . I'm just—I don't . . ."

"You don't trust me yet," he finishes for me. "I get that. I can accept that."

"I'm not asking you to prove yourself or anything." Aren't I?

"You don't have to ask. I'll do it anyway."

Do I even want to know how? "You really don't have to."

"Don't sound so nervous. I'm not going to do anything over-the-top. I'll give you a chance to get to know me better, somewhere you're comfortable."

"When?"

"Soon. You'll see."

"Okaaaaay . . . but in the meantime, there's something else I want to ask you about."

I swear I hear him smile on the other end of the line. "Okay. But he's not listed."

"You must be the worst person to plan a surprise party for." I huff into the line.

"I'm serious, put away the phone book and don't waste your time."

"Bossy much? How do I know you're not saying that to sabotage my efforts?"

"I'm not. I'll even give you a plausible phone script for the would-be Theos. Like . . . say someone ordered a gift for him from that store where you work, but his number and mailing address was misplaced so he needs to pick it up in person to verify his identity."

Hm. Better to stay skeptical. It's in his best interests to steer me wrong. And I want to doubt him, even contradict him, if only to prove to myself that I can be rational, that I'm not a sucker. I want to be more Scully than Mulder, but I might as well have my own "I Want to Believe" poster hanging above my desk. I'm already giving Oliver's words too much weight, even as I tell myself to question them.

"It's fine, I'll figure it out." I try to keep the sulk out of my voice.

"You're making progress, but you can't force it. You need to let things happen at their own pace."

"Yeah yeah yeah. So I guess I'll talk to you soon?"

He laughs again, low and flirty. "You definitely will. Goodbye, Astrid."

Back to that damn phone book.

I start with the listings for T. Collins. Those'll be easiest to rule out while I practice my spiel.

A woman answers the first call. Great.

"Hi. I'm looking for Theo Collins. This is Astrid from Curio City. Someone ordered a gift for him that we need him to pick up in person. I'm afraid our clerk made a mistake on the paperwork, so I don't have a current phone number or address on file for him."

"This is Theresa Collins. I think you have the wrong number."

She hangs up before I can apologize for disturbing her.

I get a Timothy, a few Thomases, a Tamara, a Tracy, a Todd, a Ted, a couple of answering machines with no names (I leave messages with the store address and hours), a couple of people who hang up on me before I finish speaking (I don't call back), two disconnected numbers, and a few that keep ringing unanswered.

The Ted numbers are next, though I don't think Theo would be listed under that first name. They don't fare any better. There are uncomfortable exchanges with more non-Theos and two suspicious wives, more answering machines, and an elderly lady who says her Ted passed away four months ago.

Now it's down to the three Theodores; these count the most. Everything up to this has been practice, but I still haven't rehearsed enough. Something I hadn't considered before: if I get the right Theo, he might actually remember me as the same Astrid he met last month, see through my ruse and—it could get painfully awkward.

But awkward would still be better than this pile of question marks, so it's time to shake off the shyness and go after some clarity. Oh, comfort zone, how I miss you.

I take a breath and hold it while I dial the first Theodore. Not sure if I'm hoping more for a familiar voice or a wrong number. This is a bad idea and I know it, but now I have to see it through.

The numbers lead to answering machines or disconnected numbers. All but the last one.

A woman picks up that call.

"Is Theodore there?"

"Just a minute," she says through chomping gum. I hear her shout his name.

"This is Theodore."

"Hi, I'm looking for Theo Collins—"

"It's Theodore. Never Theo."

"Oh. Then you're not the person I'm looking for. Sorry to bother you." I hurry through the words but he lets me finish without hanging up.

"No trouble."

The line goes dead. And that's that.

CHAPTER TWENTY-FOUR

The nighttime sky is salmon pink, which means it's going to snow. There's no clock in sight, but I know it's late, middle of the night late.

I can't sit up, can't move my arms or legs. I'm strapped to a long board being carried by two people, one at each end. To my left are several lanes of traffic, with few cars going by. To my right is a metal railing.

I'm on the Mass Ave Bridge.

"Okay, let's set her down here," a male voice calls out.

They place me on the ground and a large metal can is set near my head. A paintbrush is dipped into it then brought out dripping red.

"Careful, try not to get any on her," says the same voice. I know it but I can't place it. Theo?

"This makes 192 Astrids," a different male voice responds. This one I know: Oliver.

"We're gonna be here all night."

"Excuse me? Guys? Can you get me out of this thing?" I writhe against the straps.

"You shouldn't move," says maybe-Theo. "You might have a subdural hematoma."

"You're lucky to even be alive," adds Oliver. "We're on the way to the hospital, but we need to do this first."

Small particles fall from the sky, glittering in the streetlights. The way it hits me, at first I think it's sleet. But this precipitation cuts at my bare arms, gets into my mouth, and doesn't melt. It's glass. A familiar metallic taste as the small pieces cut my tongue and the insides of my cheeks. My mouth fills with blood. I try to spit it out.

"Look what you did, you got paint all over her," says Oliver.

I try to explain. "It's not paint—"

"This will go a lot faster if you don't talk," maybe-Theo cuts me off.

"193 Astrids," Oliver says. "Halfway to hell."

CHAPTER TWENTY-FIVE

Monday, September 27, 1999

My first day at the new job. It takes me ten minutes to walk to Curio City from The Lab. Minerva greets me with coffee and donuts. As she talks, it's tough not to get distracted by all the bizarre objects around me. I also keep glancing at the front door, expecting some version of Theo Collins to walk in at any moment. And hopefully not get me in trouble. Why did I have to be a moron and put my new job at risk?

"It'll be easy to get the hang of this. I'll show you the register, how to look up inventory in the computer, take special orders, etc. Pretty straightforward stuff. Just make sure you keep an eye out for the photographers and shoplifters."

"Why aren't people allowed to take pictures in here?" I ask.

"These types of shops get lots of tourists, goths, artists—or some combination of the three. You can end up with a store crowded with people who have no intention of buying anything, which also makes it easier for them to shoplift. I don't mind the browsers—you'll still get plenty of those—but they'll have less excuse to linger if they can't take photos."

She goes through other aspects of the job, concludes with, "And despite the signs telling people not to touch the glass, the cases get covered in fingerprints, so it's good to wipe them down every once in a while. Any questions?"

"I think I'm all set." I steal another peek at the entrance.

"Expecting someone?"

"No, just a little nervous for the first customers. I don't want to mess anything up."

"Don't worry, Mondays are pretty quiet, and I'll be in the back all day. I won't ask you to fly solo until you have a good grasp on everything. Did you read any of the catalog?"

"Almost half of it." I take the binder out of my messenger bag.

"Great. Keep it handy to get up to speed on the merch. You'll want to be able to give people the background on most of it after a while. There are also some magazines if it gets really slow. Oh, right, can't forget about atmosphere."

Minerva sifts through a stack of CDs on a shelf behind the register and puts on music that sounds like Gregorian chants backed by synthesizers. She also lights some Nag Champa incense and fits it into a holder shaped like a miniature spinal cord. An earthy floral scent wafts over us.

"That should do it. I'll be in the back making some calls, give a shout if you need me."

My main task today is to go through a new batch of jewelry, log each piece in the computer database, then place it into a corresponding display cabinet. I sift through the small plastic bags, surprised to find innocuous crystals and cameos among the more macabre items like animal claw pendants, bracelets fashioned from teeth and bones, insects in amber, and all kinds of skull, scorpion, and spider accessories. Even though there's a bell above the door to announce customers, I keep swiveling my head toward it and the street beyond.

"He's unlisted." Oliver's words come back to me, over and over, but I'm still keyed up with the possibility that one of my messages reached the right Theo.

There isn't much foot traffic outside the store this morning. A dozen or so customers come in while I sort through the new stock, but only a couple of them purchase anything. I expect Curio City's patrons to be unusual-looking, but they're mostly nondescript, apart from a few low-key goths. On the whole, the first half of the day passes uneventfully.

After lunch, a middle-aged man with salt-and-pepper hair and tortoiseshell glasses stops outside the store. He checks a slip of paper, studies the awning, squints inside, reaches a tentative hand to the doorknob, and enters.

"Pardon me," he begins in a thick, upper-crust British accent, "I received a most unusual message from one Astrid O'Malley about an item here for me. My name is Theodore Collins."

Damn.

"I'm Astrid. Um, there was a slight mix-up and we actually found the Theodore Collins we were looking for. I'm so sorry for any inconvenience."

"Yes, well, I did think it a bit odd, but you could have done me the courtesy of phoning back to let me know the matter had been cleared up. I drove in from Charlestown."

Of course this is the moment Minerva chooses to come out of the back room.

"Everything alright in here?" she asks.

"Yes, just a slight misunderstanding." I turn back to the wrong Theo. "You're absolutely right, Mr. Collins, and I apologize again for the trouble."

His mouth curls in disdain, but he says nothing more and leaves with a shake of his head.

I hurry to think of a reasonable explanation for Minerva, who doesn't demand one, just waits for me to say something.

"It's . . ." I begin, but that's all I can think of. Nothing beyond that seems right. Not "complicated" or "a long story" or even "dumb."

The phone rings.

I reach for it but Minerva slides in behind me before I can get to the receiver. Oh boy.

"Curio City, this is Minerva." She keeps her eyes on me, mouth pursed in an ominous mix of suspicion and disappointment. "Astrid is indisposed at the moment, but I'm the owner. Anything I can help you with? . . . I can imagine. That must've been a pretty strange message to get . . . Yes, I'll make sure we keep more careful records moving forward . . . No, you won't be getting any more calls from us . . . It wasn't a prank, just a mix-up on our end . . . I will . . . I will . . . Have a good day."

I step around to the other side of the counter, ready to make a quick exit if she fires me.

Minerva stands there, long and lean with eyebrows arched, poised like a cartoon villain ready to strike. She silently prompts me to speak.

There's no reasonable excuse I can think of and even if there were, I wouldn't want to lie to her, not after she took a chance on hiring me. Might as well spill out the convoluted truth.

"Okay . . . I was hit by a car last month and it turns out that there's this twenty-four-hour period I can't account for. All I can remember about it—vaguely—is that I met someone named Theo Collins. I was trying to track him down, so I called a bunch of people in the phone book that might be him. I'm hoping he'll help fill me in on what happened that day, and also because I think—I don't know, there might have been some kind of romantic thing . . ." Great, now I'm blushing like a little girl. "And if I had given him my number and he tried to call . . ." I explain about the fire at my Allston place.

"Jesus . . ." She rubs her eyes like my confession has thoroughly confused and exhausted her. "But why couldn't you tell these people the truth? Why come up with this convoluted story and involve my store?"

Better yet, why not listen to Oliver and forget the whole stupid plan to begin with? "At the time, it seemed more complicated to go into what really happened. I was hoping that seeing Theo in person would jog my memory. If he ever showed up." If he ever existed. "I realize it's a terrible impression to make on my first day and, I promise, I'm not a drama queen. I'm a hard worker. I'm just going through some strange shit right now, but I'm getting it together, and I *swear* it won't affect my work here."

"Except it kinda already has." Her entire face seems to narrow as she considers what to do with me.

There's nothing else I can say to persuade her, so I chew on the inside of my cheek and stand perfectly quiet, perfectly still. Have I started sucking at life so badly, I'm going to get fired from two jobs in one month? Being responsible was one of the few things I actually took some pride in. How humiliating if I can't even hold on to that.

I plead with my eyes for another chance.

She reaches under the counter and hands me a cloth.

"Wipe down those front cabinets. And leave my store out of any other madcap plots, please." She turns to go, changes her mind. "I've been through some shit, too, Astrid. Pretty dark shit. But you know what? You deal and then you get on with it."

So many questions on the tip of my tongue. I open my mouth, about to release one of them, but her face says, *not now*. Instead, I thank her and get to polishing cabinets.

Minerva changes the CD to some kind of medieval chamber music.

"Oh, and I don't think the guy on the phone was the one you're looking for," she says. "He sounded about a hundred."

When I get home from work, Sally accosts me in the kitchen. The Lunar Haus party raised her spirits more than I expected it would. Her inconsistent heart has always baffled me; she's had one-night stands that left her in mourning for months and long-term relationships she bounced back from seemingly overnight. Not that I think she's recovered from Corey, but she's decided Cambridge is the best place to do so. Daphne said she could use the spare room as long as necessary, so Sally's taken a leave of absence from her job in New York, where she's a furniture buyer for an upscale store that sells things like chairs made of mirrors and chandeliers fashioned from old pipes. Life is never boring when Sally is around, and while I could use more boring in my life right now, I *am* glad she's here.

"You must be hungry, let me heat up something up for you." She pulls out a chair and gestures for me to sit. "We ate early tonight, but there's lots of chicken curry and rice left over."

"Did you make it?"

"No."

"Then sure, I'll have some."

She shoots me a lighter version of her signature pouty scowl and prepares a plate for the microwave.

"Why are you doting on me?" I ask. "Shouldn't I be getting you bowls of ice cream and boxes of tissues and helping you cut Corey's face out of photographs?"

"I'm fine. But there's something else you can do for me. With me."

"What's up?"

"Daphne and Zak are having a *Buffy* marathon to get ready for the new season, and I can't watch any more teens running around killing monsters. I have to get out of the apartment."

"Weren't you out all day?" I've spent hours on my feet and hoped for a quiet night with *Memoirs of a Geisha*, but trying to read with Sally around is like building a house of cards in an earthquake. I'm better off making sure she's entertained. And I owe her some best friend time besides.

"Yeah, but playing tourist this afternoon doesn't count. I want to go *out* out. But not alone. *Please* tell me there's something going on tonight."

She sets down a plate of curry before me; steam tinged with cardamom and coriander reminds me how hungry I am.

"I don't care where we go. As long as it's somewhere I can get a drink to forget about my sham of a life for an hour or two," she says.

I grab the latest issue of the *Phoenix* to see what's listed for tonight.

"There's a goth night near the Fenway. We could see if Daphne and Zak are interested," I suggest.

"Okay, maybe I care a *little* where we go. No offense, but I'm looking for something to cheer me up. Droning music and mopey people dancing like they're caught in spiderwebs might not do the trick. Plus, those two are so wrapped up in their silly show, I don't think they're going to leave Sunnyvale any time soon."

"Sunny*dale*," I correct her on *Buffy*'s fictional setting. "And it's actually a really good show. You should give it a chance."

"Whatever." She points to a triangle of pink paper peeking out of my jacket pocket. "What's that?"

"You're our resident snoop, why don't you find out?"

She unfolds a pink flier with Jasleen's number scrawled on the back of it.

"Oh right, a friend I worked with gave me that. Some showcase for local bands. Her boyfriend's in one of them. It's not tonight, is it?"

Please don't let it be tonight. Please don't make me spend more time on my feet, listening to the plonking and wailing of wannabe rock stars.

She checks for a date and grins. "It's fate. Is TT The Bear's far from here?"

I force my grimace into a grin. It can't be about me tonight, it's gotta be about what Sally needs. "TT's is walking distance. I don't know if these bands are any good, but we can go if you want." *If?* Like there's any question.

"Sweet! What should I wear?" she asks.

"A ball gown. It's basically a bar, Sal. What you have on is fine."

She points down to her baggy jeans and baby doll T-shirt. "Are you crazy? You know I never wear pants to a club."

I finish eating while Sally Logic dictates a wardrobe change. She comes back wearing a slip dress and combat boots.

"It's not too much, is it?" She does a twirl.

"The red lipstick and body glitter might be too much on someone else, but not on you."

"Is that what you're wearing?"

I actually made an effort for my first day at Curio City with a plaid grey jumper dress over a white shirt. "This is probably overdressed for TT's, but I don't feel like changing. Is my outfit a problem?"

The purse of her lips says it is but out loud, she shows more tact. "It's a little plain Jane schoolgirl, but I guess it's fine. *Please* wear some of my lipstick?" A pleading sigh. She holds out the gold tube.

The sooner I comply, the sooner we'll be out of here, and the sooner we'll be home, so I paint my mouth like a '40s starlet, which makes the rest of me feel frumpy by comparison.

As we walk over to the club, I blot the lipstick on the back of my hand.

We reach the purple building of the Middle East and go around the corner to TT's. A bouncer wider than the doorway checks our IDs, we go in, and I pay the cover for both of us.

"I'll take care of drinks," Sally promises.

There are a couple dozen people in the cozy club, and they all look like they're stuck in the earlier grunge part of the decade: lots of torn jeans, plaid shirts, and unwashed hair. The band playing is all fuzzy guitars and choleric female shrieking, the lead singer a pale redhead in a lacy nightgown and torn fishnets who clutches at her chest like she's trying to tear the flesh from her body.

"If Courtney Love and Shirley Manson had a love child . . ." Sally says as I lead us to the bar, where she gets a rum and Coke for me and a Long Island Iced Tea for herself.

A square-jawed guy with artful stubble and a forced squint I presume is his attempt at sexy gives us a drowsy smile. "It's too bad you didn't get here earlier, you already missed the best act," he says.

"Let me guess: yours," I reply. "And you're the lead singer."

"Hey, how'd you know? You see us play before?"

Sally steps in front of me. "A lucky guess. What kind of music do you play?"

I turn my back to them, leave her to flirt in peace.

"Astrid!" Jasleen bounds over to me. She stands on her toes to give me a hug, smelling of pear body spray. "You're just in time, The Blind Vultures are going on next. How are you doing? Any luck finding a new job?"

"Actually, yeah, I'm working in retail until I figure out what I want to do next. Needed a break from the office scene."

"If you change your mind about that anytime soon, I've been talking to an editor at Houghton Mifflin whose assistant just gave notice. She'll be interviewing replacements over the next few weeks and I could put in a good word for you." She waves to the bartender, who slides over a drink and doesn't charge her.

I think of my new old room in Allston lined with stacks of books, and my new room down the street bereft of them. The free books were great, but more than that, working in publishing, even on an administrative level, gave me a sense of purpose and satisfaction I never had in any other job. The idea of returning to that industry fills me with odd longing.

"I don't think I'm ready to go back to publishing yet." Why did I say that? I want to go back. "I think . . . I think I need to miss it more. Figure some other things out first."

"Hey, I get it." The way Jasleen moves her head, I can't tell if she's nodding at me or bobbing to the music.

"What's been going on at the agency since I left?" I ask.

"Jonathan had some obsolete currency go missing from his office and is installing security cameras. He was so livid, we thought we were going to have to take lie detector tests. The new office manager is like some evil old lady out of a Dickens novel. I keep expecting her to hit us with a ruler if we take too many paperclips. Nellie's been a crab because she just found out her assistant is pregnant and probably quitting. But Nellie also . . ." She offers a modest shoulder twitch. "She recommended me for a promotion. I have to wait for all the paperwork to go through before it's official, but as of next month, I'll be a junior agent at Spellman Rosenberg."

"Finally! It's about time. Congratulations." I squint at her. "Why don't you look happier about it?"

"I just . . . I still feel really bad about what happened to you. Like I should've said something." She slides her empty glass across the counter and won't look at me. "Like maybe I didn't say anything because I didn't want to mess up getting promoted. I was hoping I could help you get that job at Houghton to make up for it."

"Nothing you could've said would've changed Jonathan's mind." Jasleen doesn't look convinced. "Really, it's sweet of you, but it's not like I was in a coma for two weeks. I should've called the office myself and explained the situation. None of this is on you."

Jasleen's attention is diverted by someone who just walked in. "Damn, Charlie Chameleon is here. He writes for *Boston* magazine and I've been talking to him about doing a book proposal on influential musicians from New England."

"Go, go." I playfully shoo her away.

"Come by after the Vultures set. I'll introduce you to my boyfriend. And let me know if you change your mind about the job stuff."

Another quick hug and she's off, taking spring-loaded steps toward the door.

I turn back to Sally, but she's no longer at the bar. Did she already run off with Stubble Singer? I look around and—there she is, pressed up against an amp, half-dancing/half-making out with him. Good for her. I take a big sip of my drink. It's not like I'm jealous, not at all, no really . . . Okay, maybe a little.

Is that somebody waving at me from the other end of the bar? I crane my neck, but a tall dreadlocked man approaches to order a drink and blocks my view. Okay, let's be cool in case the wave was meant for someone else. I walk over, trying to adopt a veneer of nonchalance.

"Hey, stranger."

It's Oliver, elbows out at sharp angles as he leans on the bar and sips a bottled beer. Like me, he's overdressed, wearing grey suit pants and an untucked black button-down. Unlike me, he appears perfectly at ease in his surroundings.

"Did you follow me?" I don't mean to be so direct, but I'm too bewildered for a filter.

"Of course not. I've been here for an hour, and I've heard two other equally mediocre bands before this one."

"I don't believe you." Except that I do.

"Ask the bartender. I've been entertaining her with my doodles." He gestures to a stack of napkins; sloppy stick figures adorn the top one.

"How'd you know I'd be here?" I ask.

"What makes you think I'm here to see you? Maybe I'm out to support some of my musical friends."

"Are you?"

"Well . . . no."

"So what, your Spidey sense told you you'd find me here?"

His shoulders pause in mid-shrug. "If that's what you want to call it. I can leave if you want."

I should be unnerved, disturbed, and yet . . . "It's okay. I don't hate it that you're here."

"That's exactly the reluctant reaction I was hoping for when I was making myself all handsome for you."

"Every girl's crazy for a sharp-dressed stalker." How does he do it? How does he manage to crack me up even when I'm still suspicious of him? "I guess neither of us got the memo to dress grunge," I say.

"Thank god. I spent enough time looking like an ill-washed lumberjack in college. Hey, what happened to your hand?"

I hold it up; it's covered in red smudges from Sally's lipstick.

"My friend tried to give me a makeover." I grab a cocktail napkin and wipe at the stains on my hand, then take a second one to blot my lips again.

Oliver leans in close to my ear and says, "You know, avoiding red lipstick isn't going to make you invisible. Your friend tries too hard to be noticed, but you try too hard to blend into the background. It works for her but it doesn't work for you."

"Not all of us want the spotlight, Oliver." I give him a tight smile. "Some of us prefer to be behind the curtain."

"Or that's how you justify it because nobody's ever let you have center stage."

The way he zeroes in his attention on me is both thrilling and unnerving. "I'm fine where I am."

He looks at me like he's multiplying a long string of numbers in his head. A pause and he has the answer. "Nope. I don't buy it."

I need another drink. Before I say anything, Oliver signals to the bartender.

"What are you having?" he points at me.

"Doesn't your sixth sense tell you?" I nudge him with my elbow.

"I don't actually read minds, contrary to what you may think." He leans down and sniffs the remains in my plastic cup. "But my regular sense of smell tells me you had something with rum. Help a guy out?"

"Captain and Coke. Thanks."

While he's paying for the drinks, Sally comes over. Her lipstick is smeared around her mouth and she's holding hands with Stubble Singer, who wears the rest of it.

"I'm taking off with Marshall. See you tomorrow."

"Wait. You don't even know this guy. No offense," I say in case Marshall can hear me. He doesn't react.

"That's what I like about him. Don't worry, we're going to get condoms at CVS first."

She kisses my cheek and is pulled away before I can say anything else.

"She'll be fine. It's only a harmless one-night stand. It's what she came here to find." Oliver hands me my drink.

"Is that what *you* came here to find?" Oh god, I really said that. Why is my inner-censor broken around this guy?

He gives me a you-should-know-better look. "Do I really need to answer that?"

As I scramble for a response, The Blind Vultures begin their set, pausing further conversation. They play their instruments like they're angry at them, filling the space with melodious grit and reverb. A male and female guitarist take turns speak-singing into the microphone, until the chorus, when they tunefully shout.

"Not bad," Oliver assesses after the first song. "Kind of a poor man's Pixies."

"Agreed." I pick up my drink as the second song begins. Before I can take a sip, the edges of my vision go dark. The pain at the base of my skull is so instant and acute, it's like someone threw a brick at my head. The plastic cup slips through my fingers and my knees start to give way. Determined hands on my upper arms keep me from collapsing to the floor.

"Astrid. Astrid." Oliver continues to repeat my name as he leads me to a chair.

"Don't move. I'll be right back," he says.

My vision narrows to pinholes, and my skull is ready to crack wide open any second now.

Someone places a cold towel on the back of my neck. I breathe in. I breathe out.

Oliver kneels down beside me. "Do you want me to call for help?"

I shake my head. An echo of the pain remains, still loud, but diminishing.

"Can you walk?"

"I think so." He helps me stand, and I take his arm as we leave the club.

Outside, the gusty air slaps my cheeks and helps revive me. I put a palm to my forehead, even though the pain is on the opposite side.

"Do you get migraines a lot?" Oliver asks.

"No, but since the accident . . ."

"I want to make sure you get home okay. Can you make it to the taxi stand?"

"I'm only a few blocks away." I point in the general direction.

"We'll take it slow."

I'm stable enough to walk on my own, but I don't let go of his arm the entire way to The Lab. It's like nothing can hurt me as long as I hold onto him.

"This is me." I point to the house, but I'm too tapped out to make it up to the landing. Instead, I do this graceless slither onto the front steps and pat the seat next to me.

Oliver sits like he's hovering above the step, like he might leap up at any moment. "What else can I do? Maybe get you coffee or aspirin or something?"

I hold up a palm. "I'll be fine, really. I'm mostly used to the headaches, just never had one that snuck up on me this bad before. It's almost gone now. The air is helping." The alarm on Oliver's face doesn't diminish. "Seriously, I'm gonna be okay. I'm even well enough to be a little embarrassed about it now. Thanks for being all Jane-Austen-hero-like and—"

"Coming to your rescue? It's cool, I'm used to having women swoon at my feet. One of the hazards of being this charismatic." He rolls his eyes at his own false arrogance.

"Oh yeah, what are the other hazards?" My words carry an unexpected weight and the look that passes between is pensive, deep.

Instead of answering my question, he asks, "Will you have dinner with me tomorrow night?"

I surreptitiously hold my fingertips to the tail of Oliver's shirt, press the fabric against the stone step.

This shirt is real. This stone is real. Oliver is real.

"Okay," I say. "But I still . . ."

"Need my help finding Theo. I get that. I can work around that."

"So does that mean I'm not allowed to bring him up tomorrow?"

"I won't tell you what you can and can't talk about on our date," he says. "Who knows, maybe we'll have more interesting things to discuss. How about dinner in Chinatown?"

He writes down the name and address of a restaurant, and I agree to meet him there.

When we stand, there's an awkward beat.

"See you tomorrow." Oliver gives me a hug and kisses my temple. Both gestures are too brief for me to extrapolate any deeper feeling from them.

I take the steps slowly, turning back once when I unlock the door.

He doesn't leave until I am safely inside.

CHAPTER TWENTY-SIX

9/9/99

It was dark when Astrid and Theo came out of the movie theater.

"Do you want to keep going?" he asked.

"Only if you do."

"I do."

"Then it's your turn, kiddo." Astrid kept her eyes lowered, unable too look at him, though she wanted to. She smiled at his footwear: black Converse All Stars. She had a pair like that in high school.

What would he suggest they do next? She was scared that she'd agree to just about anything at this point.

"How about dinner in Chinatown?" he offered.

"Sure. Can we walk there?"

"I was hoping you'd be up for walking. Taking the T when it's this nice out would be criminal. Especially after spending the last couple of hours inside. Not that I'm complaining about any of it. Except for the movie itself, which, c'mon, you have to admit was *the worst*."

Astrid held up both hands in an exaggerated I-give-up pose.

They started down Boylston Street and soon reached the fountain and church of Copley Square. Perfect wedges of grass stretched out to the next avenue over.

"It's so weird how there are buildings all up and down Boylston, but when you get to Copley, all of a sudden the block opens up and there's all this *space*." Astrid resisted the temptation to do a Mary Tyler Moore twirl; it helped that she had no hat to toss in the air. "I heard that's because of the Trinity Church. It's considered a historic landmark or something and it's against the law to build anything around it within a certain radius, to let the sun shine through the stained glass windows."

"Which is funny, because when it was built, all the windows were made of regular glass. The stained glass came later. But you're right about it being a historic landmark. It was declared one in 1970. Also, did you know it's one of the Ten Most Significant Buildings in the United States according to the AIA?"

"The AIA?" Astrid cocked her head.

"American Institute of Architects. The clay roof, stone arches, and tall tower makes it look European, but the American architect, HH Richardson, lent his own distinct style to it, which went on to be known as 'Richardson Romanesque' and influenced other architecture throughout the country."

"Well that's the last time I try to impress *you* with my limited local knowledge."

248 ASLEEP FROM DAY

Theo cracked a crooked smile. "I like that you're trying to impress me, but it's not exactly a fair competition. I was a tour guide for a couple of years out of college. Don't ask. I thought it might help me get ideas for movie settings and stories. It didn't, not really. But I could tell you a lot about the other historic buildings around here: the Boston Public Library, Museum of Fine Arts, John Hancock Building—hey, what's going on over there?" He pointed to the fountain.

From further away, it looked like it was filled with snow, but as they got closer, they saw mounds of white foam between the two obelisks.

"What happened here?" Astrid scooped up a handful of bubbles and blew them into the air like a small cloud.

"Looks like somebody put detergent in the fountain again. This happened a couple of years ago. Let's check out the other side."

They walked around to the broad, rectangular basin of the fountain, which was the size of a large swimming pool. The spigots had been turned off, but not before massive quantities of suds had accumulated. Despite the weather cooling after sundown, many of the younger crowd—likely college students—had taken off their shoes and were playing in the froth.

"It looks like a bubble bath for a giant. This is insane!" Astrid laughed.

A group of guys in fraternity T-shirts stripped down to their boxers, waded around, and threw foam at each other as if having a snowball fight in slow motion. A toddler in a far corner squealed and clapped his hands as his parents—a gaunt duo wearing sunglasses—blew sudsy handfuls at him. Adding to the scene was an overweight man with a shaved head and hairy chest who tried to cover his entire upper body with the bubbles and jogged around the perimeter of the fountain like a deranged abominable snowman.

The crowd grew larger as more people stopped to watch the fountain hijinks, most gathering at its perimeter. Random camera flashes lit up the darkened basin.

A laughing couple came out of the fountain toward Astrid and Theo, bubbles in their hair, slipping on the stone steps and holding onto each other to keep from falling.

"Astrid! Theo!" The woman ran over and took turns hugging them. She was small and tan, with big curly hair, her proportions similar to a mushroom's.

"Jen?" Astrid called out.

"I didn't know you guys knew each other." Jen stepped back, beckoned to her companion, a stocky man with a horse-like face and wire-rimmed glasses. "Steve, I don't think you met Astrid. She moved in with Simon—when was that, last summer?"

"Um, actually, I'm not living with Simon anymore. I've been subletting in Allston."

Mortification flickered across Jen's face. She quickly turned her attention to Theo. "And where have *you* been? I used to run into you at the Phoenix Landing just about every week. Did you move out of Cambridge?"

"I'm over in Davis Square now. I've been tied up at work . . ."

"I think the last time I saw you was Melina's going away party." Jen brushed bubbles off the hem of her shirt.

"Probably. How's San Francisco treating her?" Theo asked.

"Not very well. The dot-com she was working for went bust, so she returned last week. In fact, I think we're gonna have a welcome back party for her soon. Which is also gonna be a farewell party for us. Steve just got a job in Singapore, so we're moving out there next month."

"What'll you be doing in Singapore?" Astrid directed the question at Steve, but Jen answered for both of them.

"Systems support for a large investment firm, and I'll get my scuba certification and figure it out from there. They're giving him an amazing relocation package, and I have all this money saved up from the freelance web design I've been doing. Maybe I'll take up sailing, who knows?"

"Congratulations. Sounds really exciting." Astrid felt a tug on her jacket. "I wish we could catch up more, but we're running late for our movie."

Jen waved them off. "Of course, of course. What are you seeing?"

"*Other People's Bedrooms*." Theo and Astrid answered in unison.

"Ooh, that looks really good." She turned to Steve. "You and I should go see that before we move. Who knows what movies we'll get out there."

Steve pulled a face.

Jen cupped the side of her mouth and said in a stage whisper, "Steve doesn't like movies unless they have lasers in them."

"That's not what I said. What I said was, any movie can be made *better* with the addition of lasers."

"Laser *Citizen Kane*, I can only imagine. Anyway, I'll send you guys Evites to the party. You should totally come." She shook her head free of stray suds and pulled her boyfriend onward.

Theo and Astrid exchanged raised eyebrows and continued down Boylston Street.

"So . . . The plot thickens," he said.

"How so?"

"Simon . . .?" A tone of stating the obvious.

"How does Simon thicken the plot?" Maybe if she kept her voice casual, he wouldn't dig any deeper.

"First your spooky friend mentioned him and now Jen, and you got all tense both times. You and Simon lived together, so he's obviously a part of the story."

"There's no story." A note of defensiveness in her breezy response.

"Maybe not now, but there was. I'm guessing it didn't have a happy ending."

"It ended, that's it. The end. Roll credits."

"You're a hard person to get information from."

"And you're not?" She nearly missed a step, and Theo put a hand on her lower back to steady her.

"Eh, I thought maybe you could be coerced into sharing, since you're too shy to volunteer personal details."

"I'm not shy." Astrid's arms stiffened, and she nearly pulled away when he tried to take her hand, but she gave in, though her mouth remained in a grim line.

"Relax. Shyness is not such a bad thing," he said. "Unless it's stopping you from doing all the things you want to, like wise old Morrissey once said."

"My friend Daphne loves quoting that song to me." She sighed.

"Sorry to be unoriginal."

"You're forgiven. Anyway, remember how you got all weird on the bridge when I got too nosy asking you personal questions?"

They approached a sculpture of a giant bronze teddy bear with oversized toy blocks, which marked the entrance to FAO Schwarz on the corner of Berkeley Street. Theo let go of Astrid's hand, instead placed it on one of the bear's enormous paws as if to catch his balance.

"Fair enough. It wasn't about it being personal, though, just . . . something I didn't want to think about right then. I was having a really good time with you and didn't want anything to spoil it."

"Was?"

There it was, that gleam of mischief, the dare in his eyes. "I mean, you have to admit the rest of the day has gone totally downhill."

"Totally," she echoed.

"Totally." He stepped closer.

They matched grins, and something finally snapped into place, a derailed train returning to its rightful track. Theo took another step closer and Astrid lifted her head. He touched her hair, leaned down and brushed his cheek against hers. She thought he might whisper something in her ear, a sweet sentiment expressing surprise or desire, something perfect to hear at that moment, but he only breathed and that was fine too, probably better. She put tentative palms on his waist, like an uncertain grade-schooler at a dance, and waited for the natural moment when their faces would shift by degrees, realign for the inevitable. A minute passed like that, frozen in utter silence. No cars or people going by, just Theo's mouth warm against her ear, then jaw, then cheek, then an inch from her lips. They paused, not debating or deciding, just basking in that second before, which you can never get back no matter how many kisses follow, because there's only ever one moment of anticipation leading to the first. Gradually, both leaned in and their mouths fit into place, a hungry breath of air passing between them. He squeezed the back of her neck, and she slipped her hands beneath his jacket, no longer tentative, wanting to slip in further, under his shirt, under his skin. Their mouths still tasted like popcorn and chocolate, salty and sweet.

It was impossible to determine how long they stood beside that statue, wrapped around each other. It was like being under sedation; it could've been a few minutes or a few hours. The wind picked up around them, but neither felt the cold, or heard the fire trucks that clanged past. The only sound they heard was breathing, back and forth, back and forth.

CHAPTER TWENTY-SEVEN

Tuesday, September 28, 1999

I meet Oliver at a small corner restaurant with no sign at the edge of Chinatown near the Mass Pike, where cars audibly whizz by. Inside are four curved booths and a handful of tables that could've been rescued from a garage sale. He waits for me in one of the booths, stands to greet me. We hug, and what is that fresh powdery smell? Is it his cologne or detergent or his natural scent? And why didn't I notice—*really* notice—his eyes before? They're so persistently blue, if it weren't for the glasses I'd think he was wearing colored contacts.

Despite my reluctance to break the hug, I'm careful to keep some distance between us when I slide into the booth.

"How's the head?" he asks.

"Like it never happened."

"And the new job?"

"You tell me." It was meant to come out guarded, but it sounds flirtatious instead. I can live with that.

"Hmm, well, let's see . . . You set a new record for selling two-headed chicken taxidermy, found a mistake in the books saving the store thousands of dollars, and negotiated a deal on a bird skull earring line, so obviously you've been promoted to store manager?"

"Some psychic you are. I nearly got fired thanks to your terrible idea. I meant to tell you about it yesterday, but then my head decided to implode."

A middle-aged Asian man with an Elvis pompadour and sideburns comes over to take our order. I glance at my menu: none of it's in English, though there are blurry photographs of the food.

"Do you want me to order for us?" Oliver asks me.

"Okay. But would you mind getting something with noodles?"

"Sure thing."

He points out a few things on the menu to the waiter and smiles his thanks.

"So remind me of this terrible idea of mine?" He twists toward me and drapes an arm over the top edge of the booth, closing the distance between us.

"I'm not supposed to talk about it tonight. But it had to do with the phone book."

"Ah, you mean the phone book that was your idea to begin with? The one I also told you would be a waste of time, Miss Smirky?"

"I'm not . . ." But I am, so I shut up.

"So how was your day? How are you feeling?" he asks.

"If I'm Miss Smirky, you are Mr. Questions tonight."

"Sorry, nervous habit." A little-boy bashful smile sneaks across his face. I find both the fleeting grin and his nerves endearing.

"Let's talk about you for a change. What did you do today? What do you do *any* day?" I ask.

Bowls of soup are placed before us, wafting of ginger and scallions. My mouth waters.

"Real estate. Mostly rentals for college kids. Mostly around Allston."

"That's where I lived before the fire. Hang on . . ." After rooting around in my pocket, I bring out his business card. "*That's* what 'Finder' means? I could've used your services when I was homeless the other week." I put away the card and try the soup. It's even better than it smells. "Funny, I thought 'Finder' had something to do with your special abilities."

"I know." He wiggles his eyebrows Groucho Marx-style, takes his soup bowl into both hands, and tilts the contents back into his mouth. "So tell me about this fire."

There's some yelling coming from the kitchen, and I wait for it to die down before I respond. "I feel like— part of me thinks you already know about it, like you already know all about *me*, but you're humoring me."

"Why would I do that?"

"So that I forget that you're not . . ."

"Normal?" His smile is self-effacing.

"Normal," I agree, with reluctance.

"It's okay. I like that you can be straightforward with me."

"Is that why you look at me like that?" I poke his shoulder.

"Like what?"

"Like you find everything I say a little bit funny, but not laugh-out-loud funny."

Oval platters of food are slid across our table and we pause to eat. I spoon a little bit of everything into my bowl. The chopsticks are the plastic kind, which makes it tough to keep shiny lo mein noodles, string beans, and pieces of roast pork from sliding through them.

Oliver scoops some fried rice from his bowl into his mouth in a deft move that would've made me turn the rice into confetti had I tried to copy it. "You know why I look at you like that?" he asks.

"Because you don't find anything I say surprising since you can see into the future?"

"A lot of what you say surprises me. I may have premonitions, but it's not like there's script in front of me and I can predict every line. No, I look at you like that because when a lot of people speak, they're trying to be impressive or endearing. You don't do that." His direct gaze makes me squirm.

Maybe that's because I don't believe I can be either of those things. He makes it sound like a compliment, but it's hard to take it that way. I take a sip of green tea, hope it dissolves the lump in my throat. "Doesn't it worry you that I might only be here tonight so that you keep helping me?"

"See, that's exactly what I mean." Amused bafflement lights up his face. "And no, it doesn't worry me. I think you're here because you want to be here. I think you like hanging out with me, but you're still a slave to your fantasy. You're torn. It's okay."

The chopsticks slip out of my fingers, clatter onto the table. Does this mean he doubts my memories as much as I do? Or does he mean 'fantasy' figuratively?

Ask him.

I can't.

Instead, I change the subject. "So tell me something about yourself. How did you first discover you had special powers?"

He snickers. "Special powers? It's not like I was bitten by a radioactive spider or anything. I think of it more as a stronger sense of intuition. The earliest memory I have of it is being six or seven, on vacation with my parents in the Poconos. I had just learned to swim, and, every day, as soon as I woke up, I hurried to the pool. But one morning, I refused to put my trunks on and when my mother asked why, I said I didn't want to go into the red water."

"Oh god, don't tell me there was some kind of grisly murder."

"There wasn't, but when Mom pulled back the curtain to show me the pool, she screamed because she thought there *had* been. Some kids thought it would be funny to dye the water red and throw in a few inflatable sharks into the pool."

"And you really hadn't seen it earlier?"

"That's how my father explained it away. As I got older, there were things he wasn't able to explain so easily, but eventually I learned to keep quiet about the premonitions. When one of them came true, it was followed by extra visits to church, which I found really boring."

"So, your family was that religious?"

"I think having a son like me made them more so. Though when my older sister started getting into trouble, they shifted their prayers over to her." He moves food around his bowl, not eating any of it, then pushes the bowl aside.

"What kind of trouble?"

"The usual kind. Sneaking out of the house, staying out late, getting drunk . . . on top of which, she liked girls, which they didn't approve of. Older girls at that. She got thrown out of summer camp for hooking up with one of her counselors, then got fired from her job at Chess King when the boss caught her with his wife. She was a minor at the time. There was almost a lawsuit."

"Did your parents ever accept her being gay?"

"No. She ran off to Colorado to be with some woman she met in a chat room while I was still in high school. None of us have heard from her since. It's been . . . nearly ten years now."

The way he chews on his lower lip as his face grows downcast makes me wish I had the perfect thing to say to comfort him. But the best I can come up with is, "Wow, I'm sorry . . . I can't imagine." I slide my hand across the table, stop short of touching his fingers, which are tense and spread out. "Do you sense that she's . . . okay?"

"I hope so." His grim tone closes the door on the subject.

Our waiter comes over with a small tray bearing our check, two fortune cookies, and some orange slices speared by toothpicks.

I crack open my cookie and read the fortune aloud: "*A ship in harbor is safe, but that's not why ships are built.* I think that's the only one I've ever heard of where adding 'in bed' doesn't make sense."

Oliver reads his: "*Today is probably a huge improvement over yesterday.* Hmm . . ."

"Well, is it?"

"We'll see. Day's not over yet. Want to go for a walk, see if anything around here jogs your memory?"

I nod and he pays the check, refusing any cash from me.

Outside, we turn the corner and follow narrow streets lined with swollen garbage bags and flotsam from the day: loose pages of Chinese newspapers, chicken bones, soda cans, cigarette butts. There's a high-pitched laugh in the distance and the air smells of exhaust and cat piss.

"Thanks for dinner, it was really good," I say.

"I know it wasn't anything fancy, but the most nondescript places around here often have the best food."

I know this. Did Theo tell me? There's that eerie tingle again at the base of my neck. I must've been somewhere in the vicinity on that lost night, but where exactly?

We pass a storefront for a fortuneteller, pink neon in the window forming a pair of eyes inside a crystal ball.

Oliver nods toward it. "Want a second opinion?"

"I'm fine with one psychic friend, thankyouverymuch."

"Uh oh, she called me a friend."

"Well you're not my psychic enemy, I hope," I say, ignoring his intended meaning.

There's a metallic rattle, and a man in a shabby fur coat pushing a shopping cart rounds the corner. On his head is a cavalier hat trimmed with a giant red ostrich feather, which he tips to me as he stops in front of us.

"Have either of you fine people spied my pet rooster? Every few weeks he goes missing and makes me search for him. I must find him soon for fear he may meet his demise in a plate of chow mein."

"Sorry, we haven't seen any roosters come through," Oliver says.

"He answers to the name Porthos. If you see him, do be so kind as to tell him, loudly and firmly, 'Go home, Porthos! Go home!' He is a smart rooster and will know where to find me."

We agree to do so and Oliver offers him a dollar, which the man waves away.

"I am already a fortunate fellow, with a mouth full of riches." He smiles to reveal a row of gold upper teeth.

"I hope you find your rooster," I tell him.

"You are kind to say so." He tips his hat to me once more. "He is my dear companion but there is only so long I can contain him before I am no longer a friend to him. A ship in harbor is safe, but that is not why ships are built."

"What did you say?" I ask, but he's already down the block, the tinny staccato of his shopping cart the only reply. My skin goes icy.

I turn to Oliver, my mouth wide open.

"Did you hear what he said?"

"I did. Do you want to get some bubble tea?" He resumes walking, unfazed.

"Wait. Stop." I catch up and tug on his hand, expect him to turn around easily, but that lanky frame hides a surprisingly solid build, as if his bones are made of steel. When he does turn around, it's because he chooses to, not because of any exertion on my part. And when I try to take my hand back, I can't, because his fingers have closed firmly around mine. There are sirens in the distance; I can't tell if it's an ambulance or fire engine.

"What's wrong, Astrid?"

"You don't find it just a bit eerie that he quoted the fortune in my cookie word for word back there?"

"I don't."

"Then what was it to you?"

The sirens get louder. A series of three fire trucks rumble past us. Oliver tilts his head as if listening to a catchy melody.

"So come on, what do you think that was all about?" I persist.

"Synchronicity and a nice example of the unexpected people you'll come across in a city like this."

"That's it?" I try to shake my hand out of his grip, but he holds on, then takes a step toward me. I take one step back.

"You're not always going to find meaning where there is none. The fortune cookie thing is meaningless."

"I disagree."

He blinks rapidly and shakes his head. "It's funny . . . there's something so contradictory about you. You let life carry you along, but when you try to exert some kind of control, it's with this unrelenting stubbornness. You become unreasonably disappointed if people don't say or do exactly what you expect."

He's right, but it's never pleasant to hear people talk about your faults, so I'm justified in a bit of resentment here, right? I pull my hand violently, finally free it from his.

"Don't walk away, Astrid. It's what you do, but don't do it with me."

It *is* what I do. It's what I did before. With Oliver, but also with Theo.

Also with Theo.

I walked away from Theo. And Theo followed.

Maybe if I walk away from Oliver and he follows, too . . . maybe I'll remember more.

I go at a fast clip, zip by a strip club with a girl in a leopard print leotard smoking a cigarette in the doorway, around the corner past a boarded-up adult movie theater, up Tremont Street where I can see the green of the Boston Common up ahead. I'm like a frenetic character in a Greek myth, chasing something ephemeral, hoping I'm also being chased as I scurry up a grassy hill. I walk as fast as I can without breaking into a run.

Please please please let him be behind me. Let him know I need him to follow, need him to stop me.

And then there's a hand on my shoulder and I turn around and it's Oliver, and I laugh and I keep walking backwards, again on that torturous precipice of remembering, as if on the cusp of a sneeze or orgasm. So very close, almost there, maybe one more step and—

I stumble over a section of uneven ground and grab Oliver's shirt for balance, but that throws him off, too, and we tumble onto the grass sideways. And I'm laughing harder now and I'm almost there, I just need . . . I need . . .

I lean in and take off his glasses and kiss him, full on, eyes closed. My arm curls around his neck to bring him closer to get me there, and he kisses back and the electricity surges—let there be light—and finally, *finally*, I am not lost at all. I know exactly where I am: on the corner of Boylston and Berkley Street. This isn't grass at my back, but the cool bronze of the teddy bear statue outside FAO Schwarz. And the hands at my face are Theo's hands, and I don't know how I could've forgotten any of this, the plummeting, the moving through space at light speed while our bodies hover in one spot. As long as I keep my eyes closed, I've found him. But I need to know more, because there's so much more to know and these lips against mine are my direct line to him, a light illuminating a long dark hallway, step by step. We walked down Boylston, and we must've kept going to Chinatown. Something happened before and after, but those parts of the hallway are still dark. After another minute of kissing, they remain dark, so I loosen my hold, take a breath, open my eyes, and remind myself I'm here with Oliver.

"Sorry I dragged you down with me like that," I murmur. "Are you okay?"

Oliver looks like he's computing a lot of information all at once. "No broken bones. And hopefully no broken glasses." He retrieves the frames from a nearby patch of grass.

"Do you want to come home with me?" I blurt out.

"Look at that, maybe there *is* something to these fortune cookies after all." He wipes his glasses on the hem of his shirt, puts them back on, and blinks me into focus. "I don't . . . No. Not tonight."

"Oh."

"Do you want to know why?" he asks.

Definitely not. "I don't know, do I?"

"There's no question I'm attracted to you, in case that was in doubt."

"Not anymore, but that kinda makes your refusal more puzzling."

"Let's just say . . . I think it might get a little crowded up there for you." He taps my forehead.

But it's not enough, I want to tell him. I want it crowded up here. Invite the whole neighborhood, let's throw a rager. If he spends the night, I *know* more lost memories will come back to me. There's no question about it. Except . . .

God, I'm such an asshole.

I can't use Oliver like that. How could I even make him such an offer? I should be ashamed of myself, not for the boldness of it, but for the motive behind it. It was so easy to get carried away and forget there's another person involved here, one with feelings and boundaries.

"This was a pretty good date, right?" he asks.

"It was." I stare at the ground, hope I'm able to mask my confusion and contrition.

"You'll let me walk you to the T?"

"I will."

We stand and brush stray grass from our clothing, and then, just a few feet away, we both see it at the same time: a rooster.

Go home, Porthos. Go home.

CHAPTER TWENTY-EIGHT

I'm at Curio City, reading the product catalog. I'm so engrossed, it takes me a minute to notice someone has come into the store. He's hunched over a display shelf of bat skeletons with his back to me.

"They're real, in case you're wondering," I say.

"They're also under glass, so basically, I have to take your word for it." *I've heard that voice before. His slouchy build is also familiar.*

"We wouldn't charge hundreds of dollars for a knockoff."

"If the imitation is done well, you can set whatever price you want."

"Not if people don't buy it," I say.

Turn around turn around turn around. *He doesn't.*

"Would you buy it?" *he asks.*

"If I was, you know, an animal skeleton aficionado or something, sure."

"Do you get a lot of those types in here?" *He moves on to a neighboring display of insects in resin.*

"Sometimes. Are you looking for anything in particular? We can special order items if you . . ."

He turns so his profile is visible. I go numb. I open my mouth but words vaporize on my tongue.

"So if I was looking for a specific fossilized lizard, you could track it down for me?" Is he smirking?

Finally, my lips move. "Are you Theo?"

He briefly glances my way and turns back to the display. The glimpse of his face is startling. Like I slipped on ice and quickly righted myself before falling.

It has to be him.

"Theo?" I repeat.

"No," he answers.

"You look like someone I know."

"Do I?" He tilts his gaze to a higher shelf of taxidermy birds.

If only I could go over to him, get closer . . . but I'm stuck behind the counter, limbs frozen, mouth dry.

"I'm pretty sure we've met before," I say.

He checks his watch. "I have to go."

Another sliver of his profile as he leaves the store. It's definitely Theo.

I finally get my legs to obey and hurry out, down Cambridge Street after him.

"Wait! Please, wait," I call out, but he keeps walking. I run to catch up, grab hold of his sleeve. "I need to talk to you. It's . . . complicated, but I was gone for a while."

He looks down on me, his blue eyes cloudy and reserved.

"I'm not who you think I am." He pulls out of my grasp.

But he is. Isn't he?

Around the corner, he unlocks a red hatchback and gets behind the wheel.

I knock on the passenger window from the sidewalk but he ignores me as he starts the engine. He backs out of the parking spot, and I squeeze between cars to pound on the driver's side window from the street.

"Theo, please. Just give me two minutes."

But he drives away and leaves me in the middle of the street.

I watch his car until it turns and is out of sight. There's a roar of an engine behind me. Loud honking.

I turn around. A black van barrels toward me, leaves me no time to get out of the—

CHAPTER TWENTY-NINE

Friday, October 1, 1999

The next couple of days pass in a state of limbo. There's no contact with Oliver. I guess he's letting me process, and I really should be processing. Instead, I go to work, catalogue and sell oddities, then go home, where Daphne and Zak talk cheerfully about nothing important over dinner, and Sally considers whether she'll resume her furniture buying career or toy with "whatever jobs" like the one I have. After dinner, Zak tries to get us to watch *Doctor Who*, but we're never in the mood so we watch horror movies or VHS tapes of *The X-Files* instead. Then Daphne and Zak go to their rooms, and, as much as I want to go to mine, to read or do some of this "processing," Sally keeps me up talking. She brings up the broken engagement now, and sometimes cries a little (but not a lot) over Corey and how close she thought she came to having the perfect life (perfect lie?). She wonders if hooking up with more strangers will get Corey out of her system, and I reply, "probably not," but she says it's worth a try. Sometimes she complains of going through a quarter-life crisis, except that she has no secretary to sleep with and doesn't want to buy a sports car because she'll have nowhere to park it in Manhattan. Sometimes I'd like to trade problems with Sally.

During our nightly chats, there's always a point when she gets tired of talking about herself and asks about me. I tell her about noteworthy moments of my retail day, like the local artist/dominatrix who bought all our antique glass eyes, and the man who asked—"hypothetically"—if the antlers were hygienically safe to use as sex toys. But none of my work stories hold her attention for long and invariably we return to Theo. She prods at the subject like a child poking a beached jellyfish with a stick, believing her nudges may bring new life to it. I'm not ready to talk about Oliver or my recent breakthrough on the Common, but I humor her as best as I can for the first few days. By the end of the week, I'm out of new things to say.

"So, did anybody else from the phone book call or stop by today?" she asks.

"Nope." I wrap a chenille throw around my legs against the frost sneaking in through the drafty living room windows. "A few more people called but nobody came by since that woman, Theodora, late last week. I think that misadventure is over. I'm lucky Minerva didn't get more pissed off about it." It helped that Theodora was so effusive about the store's "haunting charm" and bought a pricy vintage holy water bottle.

"And you haven't remembered anything else?" Sally is cross-legged on the couch beside me. She hugs a pillow to her chest, squeezing it the way I imagine she's trying to squeeze information out of me.

"No." I hate lying to her.

Oliver was right: it's getting crowded in my head with both him and Theo. I need to untangle these feelings and questions, but can't verbalize them right now, not even to my best friend.

"Nothing at all?" Suspicion crinkles the corner of her eyes.

Enough of this withholding. I have to give her something. "Okay, I kind of remembered . . . I know Theo and I . . . We kissed," I finally offer.

I fend off pillow swats from her as she makes a noise that's between a gasp and a shriek. "You bitch, how could you not tell me sooner? Where did this magical memory come from?"

"I had a flashback, out of nowhere . . . a couple of days ago." I try to duck, but this time the pillow gets me on the ear. "I didn't tell you because . . . it felt like it just happened and . . . did you ever have an experience that you needed to keep private for a little bit, so it could be yours? Like, as soon as you start telling anyone, it doesn't fully belong to you anymore?"

Sally's face reads Does Not Compute. She's of the shout-it-from-the-rooftops ilk, so this will take some finessing.

"I needed to sit with it for a while, Sal. I can't explain it any better than that."

Pseudo-betrayal gives way to curiosity. "You better tell me everything about this kiss right now."

Here we go. "Um . . . it happened at night, outside FAO Schwarz."

"You kissed outside a toy store?" she asks. "What were you doing there?"

"Good question. I don't know."

"And was he a good kisser?"

"There are no words."

"There are *always* words." Of course. With Sally, there's an abundance of them, even if they're the wrong ones. Even when silence is preferable. But in this case, my friend is right. Let's find some words.

"Okay," I relent. "It was . . . singularly the most breathtaking, heart-stopping, time-bending, universe-pausing kiss of my life. Is that better?" It's not better for me, because I don't know who that kiss truly belongs to. Is it Theo projected onto Oliver or vice-versa?

"So . . .?"

"So what?"

"So what happens next?" she asks. "Obviously, you've got to put all your energy into finding this guy. Especially now that you know there was a romantic connection."

"If my Swiss cheese brain gave me something more to go on, that might be possible."

Sally lets go of the pillow and takes both of her hands into mine. Oh boy. She gazes at me intensely, the way she did when we played The Psychic Hour as kids, as if she truly believes she has supernatural powers and can will recollection into my faulty mind. If Oliver could only see her.

"Listen to me, Astrid. If you recalled this much, you *have* to be able to remember the rest. Or *something* else. A place, a smell, a sentence, a word."

This isn't about me as much as it is enlivening her unencumbered days with something tantalizing. But if that's what she needs, I'll give a little more.

"Karaoke."

"Karaoke?" She draws the word out, as if summoning a spirit.

"I don't know how, but karaoke is somehow connected." I retrieve my hands and pull the blanket higher around me.

"So that's what we do next," she says.

Daphne comes into the living room. "Did I leave my specs in here?"

"On top of the TV," Sally says. "Hey, where's a good place to go for karaoke around here?"

Daphne grimaces as she puts on her glasses. "There's no good place for karaoke *anywhere*, because karaoke is *horrible* and the bars that host it tend to be dodgy. Why would you want to hear a bunch of drunk people singing bad songs badly?"

A quick shake of my head at Sally. *Don't tell her.* "Eh, Astrid's dad did some musical theater back in the day, so once in a while we like to go and sing some show tunes."

"I'm not the right person to ask, but I think Zak had a crush on a waitress who worked in some Irish pub with a karaoke night." She sticks her head into the hallway and calls out to him. He returns a muffled response. "Will you get in here for a second?" she hollers.

He leans his upper body into the doorway.

"Can you come into the room like a normal person?" Daphne shakes her head.

He does, and we get a good look at the Darth Vader pajama bottoms he was trying to conceal.

"First of all, how old are you?" Daphne asks.

"Did you need something, other than to mock me?" Zak's neck turns pink, and I try not to make it worse for him by laughing. I better not look at Sally, either, who loves nothing more than to crack me up at inopportune times.

Hands on hips, Daphne asks, "Where did Belly Button Ring work when you were stalking her over the summer?"

"I wasn't stalking, that place had the best Guinness—"

"Yeah, yeah. Whatever. What's the name of the place?"

"Dark Heretic Taproom, near Kenmore."

"Oh right, we thought it was going to be a goth bar, which is why we went there in the first place. Don't they have a karaoke night?"

"Fridays. Anything else?" His glare is murderous.

"No, you can go back to destroying Jedis now." Daphne waves him off.

He says good night through clenched teeth and leaves the room.

"There you go, we have a plan now." Sally looks like she's expecting heaps of praise.

"I don't see that as much of a plan, but I don't have anything better to do, so why the hell not. Let's go get drunk with a bunch of tone-deaf BU kids."

The Dark Heretic Taproom doesn't look like any Irish pub I've ever been to, apart from the requisite wood paneling and mirrored bar signs. There are stone archways and sandy brick walls, with stained glass light fixtures spread across the high ceiling. The bar itself is covered entirely in bronze coins with a curved harp on them (Irish pennies?).

We get there as a short man with an '80s-era-Bono mullet is setting up in a far corner on a small platform. He adjusts the television that will serve as the lyric prompt and a microphone stand, then distributes stacks of song binders among the low round tables.

"You ladies singin' tonight?" He asks in an Irish brogue. Even though his face is pockmarked with acne scars and one of his brown eyes veers off to the side when he looks at us, the accent makes him instantly more attractive.

"I don't know if—" I start to say, but Sally cuts me off.

"Of course we will. Thank you." She flashes a man-eater smile as she takes the binder from him. Seriously, Sally?

"Sign up sheet is on that wall there, and someone will be comin' 'round to take your drink order if you want to take a seat." He winks with his wandering eye and leaves us to it.

There are fewer than twenty people here and most are clustered around the bar, so we have our choice of tables.

"Maybe eight is a little early for this crowd?" I speculate.

"Between midterms and the Sox game, I suppose it'll be pretty dead tonight." A waitress, who looks like someone plucked her from an Irish fairy garden and plunked her in the middle of Boston, hands us menus. I check to see if she has pointed ears while my friend hones in on her pierced navel.

"Do you know Zak?" Sally, all tact all the time.

Her freckled, heart-shaped face registers recognition. "Red hair, right? He hasn't come around in a while."

"He's busy saving the world from some massive computer meltdown that's supposed to happen on New Year's Day," Sally says. "But he raved about this place and the excellent servers. And also the Guinness."

"Ah, isn't he the sweetheart. Will you be wantin' a couple o' pints then?"

We nod and she goes off to get them.

"Did you see her eyes light up when I mentioned Zak?" Sally gushes. "Remind me to write down his number on the check. I think she's into him."

Yeah, I will *definitely* not forget to remind her. I pretend to study the menu, even though we just came from dinner.

"So? Are you getting flashes of anything?" She flutters her fingers as if trying to procure something mystical from the air.

"Sal, I've never been here before in my life. Do you know how many karaoke nights there must be in Boston?"

"Fine. Let's see if singing will bring on a flashback. What song, what song . . ." She thumbs through the binder pages, and I take a second book for myself from a nearby table.

The songs are alphabetized by artist, but somewhere around Aerosmith, I stop paying attention. Something about the crinkle of the pages . . . the way the plastic sleeves stick together and come apart with a faint noise like a tearing or Velcro being pulled apart. This urgent sense of—

"What, what is it? You're remembering something, aren't you?"

"Not anymore. Maybe a little less with the pouncing?"

"*Sorry.*" She stretches the word to four syllables. "So do you think that host guy is single?"

I slump back in my chair. A moment of silence with this one is futile. "Really?"

"You're right, that lazy eye would probably get to me after a while. Eye contact is so important. But that accent . . ."

"Hey, it's not like you're looking for a new husband." What is *wrong* with me?

The hopeful glimmer in her eyes dims, but fortunately our pints arrive at that moment. Thank you, Pixie Cocktail Waitress. At least one of us can brighten up Sally.

"Alrighty, folks, we're going to get started in a moment." The microphone screeches as the host speaks into it. "Let me make some final tweaks here. Not many sign-ups so far, so don't be shy. We promise not to boo . . . unless you're *really* terrible. Only kidding."

Sally takes a long swig of Guinness and stands. "I'm going to put us down for a song."

"Is it going to be a corny girl anthem like 'Girls Just Wanna Have Fun' or something by the Spice Girls?"

"You can be a real killjoy, you know that, O'Malley? It's not like there are tons of karaoke songs by Tom Waits or Nick Cave or whatever other gloomy singer you're depressing your ears with these days."

"Sorry, I'm not in a rah-rah Girl Power mood."

"Too bad. Maybe you'd be more fun if you were." She heads to the sign-up sheet before I can say anything else. Whatever flashback I might've been on the cusp of earlier is gone. Serves me right for being a jerk to Sally.

"Okay, let's get this party goin'. I'm gonna lean on you for a little help here." The host launches into a rendition of Bon Jovi's "Livin' On A Prayer" and holds out the mic during the chorus for the audience to fill in the "OHHH-ohs."

Next is a fresh-faced coed duo who sing a song from *Grease* surprisingly on-key, followed by a middle-aged man in a rumpled suit who mumbles his way through Elton John's "Tiny Dancer." Then our names are called and Sally pulls me toward the platform as if there's no question that I'll join her.

A brief guitar jangle opening and—Oh! It's "California Dreamin'." Not what I expected. When we were high school sophomores, Robin started auditioning again and was cast as John Phillips in an Off-Off-Broadway musical about The Mamas & The Papas. Sally would come over and we'd all make tuna melts, then Robin would take out his guitar, teach us the harmonies, and let us sing back-up on the songs as he practiced. He ended our sessions with "California Dreamin'," which he let us sing on our own. Sally always took the male lead part, of course, relegating me as her backup. She and I fell in love with the music and plotted a cross-country trip after graduation; we'd rent a convertible and drive with the top down, blasting The Mamas & The Papas non-stop until we reached the Pacific Highway. We planned to visit Mt. Sinai Cemetery where Mama Cass was buried, put sunflowers on her grave, and sing her our version of "California Dreamin'." It never happened, but the opening notes of that song always make me imagine riding in a convertible with Sally, on our way to somewhere sunny and warm.

I smile at her and her smile back says, *apology accepted*, and we do a pitch-perfect rendition. It gets applause and cheers from the small crowd that's gathered since our arrival. As we leave the stage, my ears hum and my body feels like a helium balloon levitating up and up and up.

This is why Robin loves the stage. It's only a tiny taste of what he must've experienced, but it's a high better than alcohol, better than anything I took at the Lunar Haus party —

Tinsel curtain.

Purple and blue neon.

Bending backwards, backwards . . .

I make it to my chair before my legs give way. Take a big swig of Guinness (shudder at the creamy bitterness). What just happened? What did I see?

Sally is too busy basking in the remnants of applause to notice me.

"Let's hear it for Sally and Astrid! Next up we have Aurora singing one of the classics."

A pale plump woman in her forties makes her way forward. She's dressed in what looks like a navy satin bed sheet, pinned at her shoulder. Her curly hair is pulled into a topknot, emphasizing the roundness of her face and her eyes, which roll around in her head like a porcelain doll's.

"What the hell is going on with this one?" Sally mutters.

"Be nice," I whisper.

"Yeah yeah yeah."

The woman sings Jo Stafford's "You Belong To Me." Her voice is a record that's been left out in the sun to warp: mostly on key but with a wobble.

"Isn't this, like, the original stalking song?" Sally asks in a low voice. I flash a warning with my eyes. "Okay, okay." She remains quiet for the rest of the song.

Why does this woman keep looking over at me as she sings? Not like she's serenading or trying to recognize me, more like she's urging me to *listen*, not to the song, but something beneath the song. I'm probably imagining it. When she's finished, I'm one of a handful of people who clap.

Aurora approaches our table.

I swear, if she starts quoting my fortune cookie like that Musketeer guy in Chinatown, I'm gonna freak out.

She puts a hand on my shoulder. "Do what I do, my dear. Sing to bring him closer to you. Sing it by heart, with your eyes closed, and he will find his way back to you."

I start to get up, but she puts weight into her palm to keep me in my seat. "No questions, dearie. Keep your bewilderment in its proper home, to its rightful owner."

As she walks away, I reach out to touch her but only graze the cold satin of her dress.

Sally twirls her finger in circles. "What rabbit hole did we fall into?"

Good question. I open the songbook and turn the binder pages, strain to make out that faint tearing noise of plastic separating, but it's no use. Someone is howling "Don't Stop Believin'" a few feet away, which drowns everything out.

Sing to bring him closer.

Might as well try, right?

I add my name to the sign up list. When I'm called forward, I move as if walking through water and take hold of the microphone. I keep my eyes closed the entire time I sing the dark lullaby of Mazzy Star's "Fade Into You." I sing of strangers and strangeness and shadows and smiles. It takes everything out of me but gives nothing back. The curtain behind my eyes remains black, the stage empty.

When the music ends, I step off the platform and some girl tries to grab my arm, but I walk past her, past our table, until I'm outside.

I put my face against the side of the building, feel the grit of the brick under my skin.

A couple of guys in Red Sox caps are smoking nearby and laugh at me. One says to the other, "Looks like someone should be cut off."

"Don't you have a frat party you're late to, asshole?" Sally hisses at them. She shoos them away and pats my back with caution.

"You're going to find him, Astrid. I know it. I *promise*. You'll find him."

CHAPTER THIRTY

9/9/99

Theo and Astrid held hands the rest of the way down Boylston Street, the silence between them lush and charged. They passed the majestic red brick building of the Four Seasons hotel, a couple of piano showrooms, an antique bookstore, a luggage shop, and a college dormitory. The streets grew darker and more uneven as they entered the periphery of Chinatown.

"Welcome to the Combat Zone," Theo announced.

"And me without my camo. Why Combat Zone?"

"That's what they started calling this area in the '60s because of the crime and because it's where soldiers on leave would go for ... adult entertainment."

"Nice to see some businesses carrying on the legacy." Astrid gestured to a storefront advertising XXX videos and peep shows.

"Yeah, but it's not as rough and tumble anymore, don't worry. Have you been to the Eatery?"

"What's that?"

"Only the place for some of the best Asian food you'll ever have."

"As long as it doesn't come with a lap dance."

Past a bakery and a sooty parking lot was a building with papered-over windows and a dirty cement façade.

"Is this place even open?" she asked.

Theo held open the door and waved her in. Up a flight of stairs, they entered a dusty cafeteria with food stands lining opposite walls. A handful of patrons dotted the communal tables, hunched over steaming bowls and colorful plates of food. The place smelled of sesame oil, garlic, and simmering meats.

"We're talking cheap and no frills, but the pad thai here is going to blow your mind." Theo led them to a far corner of the room.

"I don't mind a little squalor now and again."

They placed their order from one of the stalls and took Styrofoam cups of Thai iced tea to a nearby table. Astrid lifted the plastic lid and stirred the condensed milk until the liquid turned a bright creamy orange.

"My friends and I call this place the Blade Runner Café." Theo shook his own cup, the ice cubes producing a muffled rattle.

"I can see why. It does remind me of the food stands Deckard goes to. And you don't have to look so surprised."

Theo's eyebrows remained raised. "More . . . impressed than surprised."

"Give a girl a little credit. I know Ridley Scott's voiceover-free director's cut is considered the superior version, and I agree. You're not the only film snob at the table. I just keep quiet about it because it's impossible not to sound annoyingly pretentious when discussing Fellini, who happens to be my favorite director. And I'm sure I don't know about movies as much as you in general, since you probably went to film school and all that good stuff."

"There might have been a year or two of film school in my past. But then I came to my senses and switched to marketing."

She leaned back to accept the large plate of noodles set before her. "Sounds like the opposite of coming to your senses."

"Depends on whether you want to be an artist or want to pay the rent." He speared a piece of chicken and blew on it before taking a bite.

"Plenty of artists out there are able to pay their rent. If you have the talent, luck, and perseverance . . ."

"Yeah, I don't know if I can nail that trifecta."

Astrid squeezed a wedge of lime over her noodles and spread the crushed peanuts around with her chopsticks. "I'd be happy with one out of three."

"Sounds like you're still figuring out what you want to be when you grow up."

"I just can't decide between ballerina and astronaut."

He waved away her faux Miss America earnestness. "What did you study in school? Besides astrophysics and dance."

"I was an English and psych double major. Psychology was my safety net. Figured it would be more useful to learn how to read and analyze people than books."

"But let me guess, you prefer books to people."

"Pretty much. Hey, at least I ended up working at a literary agency, even though the most I do is unpack or mail the actual books."

Theo offered a you-gotta-start-somewhere shrug. "Hey, maybe you'll become an agent one day."

"Naw, I don't have the hustle for it. I'll probably stay on as an office manager until . . ." Astrid stared at her plate. "I don't know."

"See, I bet you've got all three." Theo picked the bean sprouts out of his noodles, making a little white pile of them in the corner of his plate. "I bet you have the luck, talent, *and* perseverance, but for whatever reason, you're standing in your own way."

She put down her chopsticks and looked past him, over at a group of middle-aged Asian men smoking and playing cards in the corner.

"Uh-oh." Theo put a hand on her wrist. "You aren't gonna walk off in a huff again, are you?"

"No, I'm thinking about something Robin—my father—told me when I was a kid. I came home one day after learning about snowflakes, how no two are alike, and told him the teacher said we're snowflakes, too, each one of us unique. Robin said it's only a matter of time until science proves snowflakes actually *are* alike. He believed the whole thing was a fallacy society latched onto as a bad metaphor for individuality. He thought it was more important for me to accept being ordinary than delude myself about being . . ."

"Special?"

She nodded.

Theo moved their plates aside and took both of her hands. "No offense to your dad, but that's a shitty thing to say to a kid. And now I feel like an even bigger asshole for what I said on the bridge."

"The thing is, when he said stuff like that to me, I saw it as his way to take pressure off me to be an achiever. Not that I didn't try, but . . ." *Maybe if I tried harder, he'd be more interested in me as a person. Maybe we'd be closer.* She shook her head. "I figured I wasn't different, I wasn't born to do anything great, or stand out in any way, and that was fine."

"That's not fine. How could you know if he discouraged you from trying? It's like he stopped you from . . . *dreaming*." He smiled a crooked smile. "But I bet it didn't stop you from feeling different."

"You could say that," she replied, her voice tired. "But don't most people feel different, anyway? And if it's such a universal thing, doesn't that make it ordinary?" *Doesn't it make* me *ordinary?*

As if reading her mind, he said, "You're not ordinary. Your father is wrong. There's definitely something special about you." He squeezed her fingers for emphasis. "I wouldn't be sitting here if I didn't think you were somehow . . ."

"Snowflake-like?" She rattled the ice in her cup for emphasis.

"Until science proves otherwise, anyway." He winked.

Astrid's face clouded over. Her gaze shifted to a far corner, but what she really saw was much further away. "Robin wasn't trying to be shitty to me. He wanted to protect me."

"From what?"

"From ending up like my mother. She died when I was four, and he always told me it was from a brain aneurism. A couple of years ago, while I was visiting him in Brooklyn, I came across a newspaper article among his things. I wasn't snooping, just looking for— it doesn't even matter. Anyway, the article was from 1979, around the time Mom died. About a woman who was stabbed in the neck when she got in the way of a guy trying to mug a couple of girls on the subway. She stopped the mugging, but the guy was never caught and she bled to death before she got to the hospital. There was no aneurism."

"I don't get it." Theo rubbed his forehead. "Why wouldn't your father have wanted you to know she died doing something heroic?"

"He probably thought what she did was reckless and dumb. That's what he always said when he saw news stories of local heroes."

"And what do you think about it?"

A melancholy determination settled across Astrid's face. "Some days I agree with him and get angry that she put herself in harm's way like that. Other days, I think what she did was brave and selfless, trying to help those girls. And it makes me hope I inherited some of her courage. Anyway, I'm oversharing and making things the bad kind of weird again." She twisted her hips in her chair, wished she could redo the last few minutes of their conversation.

His face didn't betray any unease at the disclosure; his eyes were full of sincerity and compassion. He held her hands tighter and said, "Nothing weird here."

An elderly woman in an embroidered forest green silk robe came out from behind the giant fish tank marking one of the Chinese food stands. She walked over to Astrid and Theo's table and started speaking to them in fervent Cantonese. Her skin sagged and liver spots marked her thickly veined hands, which she waved around as she talked, her mouth smiling, her voice shrill and urgent.

She took two small objects out of her pocket, placed them on the table, and shuffled back around the fish tank. Theo and Astrid leaned in and each took a trinket to examine. They were bronze coins with square holes in the center; Chinese symbols carved on one side and scaled creatures on the other.

"Are these fish or snakes?" Astrid held up one to the light to get a closer look.

"I'm pretty sure they're dragons."

"They're probably good luck charms. Why do you think she gave them to us?" She peered at the fish tank but only saw the dark murk of the water.

"Maybe she thought we looked like we could use some luck?"

"We make our own luck," she said.

Theo held his coin in the center of his palm and looked down on it, brow furrowed. "Is that from the O'Malley School of Hard Knocks and Tough Love?"

"Yep. It's carved right above the entrance."

When he looked back up, traces of worry remained in his eyes, which he blinked away. "I'm going to keep this anyway." He pocketed the coin.

They pushed their chairs back and stood.

"Ready to go?" He held out an arm.

"Where to?"

"That's for you to decide."

"I don't even know what's around here or what might still be open," she said.

"Well, then let's go make our own luck."

Astrid left her own Chinese coin on the table.

Outside, a couple of prostitutes in white patent leather mini-dresses asked for the time ("ten thirty") and a toothless man with a garbage bag tied around his neck asked for spare change (Theo gave him a few quarters).

Astrid and Theo followed the narrow, twisted roads lit a dirty amber by dim streetlights, up to Downtown Crossing.

"Have you ever been *there*?" Astrid pointed at a low building whose second floor bore a giant purple and blue neon sign spelling out 'TKO Karaoke'.

"I haven't. Let's check it out."

"You sure?"

"It's lady's choice, remember?"

They stopped in the building's crooked doorway, which smelled of cigarette smoke and bleach. Theo grabbed the sides of Astrid's army jacket and pulled her in for another kiss. She leaned in and ran a thumb over the stubble on his chin and across his jaw. She pulled up the back of his shirt and touched a small patch of his bare skin, wanting to explore the rest of it, feeling hindered by the boundaries of his clothing.

A group of drunken Asian men in tuxedos stumbled out of the door and knocked Theo and Astrid apart. They held unlit cigars and sang Frank Sinatra's "Fly Me to the Moon," the song trailing them as they wove an uneven path down the street.

"Your eyes glow like a cat's in this light, you know that?" Theo moved his face in close to look at them.

"I can, with all confidence, say that nobody's ever told me that before." She ruffled his hair. "So . . . can you sing?"

"Let's find out." He opened the door and held it out for her.

"How gentlemanly." A mock-curtsy and she walked through.

The stairwell was foggy, as if filled with dry ice, and lit red. Astrid held on to the railing as she climbed.

"You better not be checking out my rear view," she said over her shoulder.

"Why do you think men *really* open doors for women?"

She turned around to stick her tongue out and shrieked when he replied with a short spank.

"Hey!"

"Come on, we've got some bad singing to do."

"Speak for yourself. I can carry a tune."

At the entrance, a Japanese woman in a white pageboy wig and opera gloves greeted the couple and informed them of a two-drink minimum. They were led to a tiny square table next to a plate glass window illuminated by the back end of the neon sign. Astrid barely recognized her reflection in the glass: hair tousled, the corners of her mouth turned up, eyes bright and a little wild.

They ordered whiskey and Cokes and leaned over a shared binder to consider the song list.

"Do you think they have anything in English?" Astrid asked. They turned page after page of titles handwritten in neat cursive, housed in sticky plastic sheaths that made a tearing noise when pried apart.

"I don't even want to know what might've made these pages so sticky." Theo made a face.

"Oh." she grimaced. "Let's not even think about that."

"Okay. But too late."

The hostess returned with their drinks, a couple of slips of paper, and a chewed-up pencil.

"I also hate to think where this has been." He examined the tooth marks on the writing implement.

"After The Eatery, I'd think you wouldn't mind a little seediness with your karaoke." Astrid nudged his knee with hers, was about to reach for the pencil, but reconsidered. "Actually, I think I have a pen." She checked her jacket pocket.

"Now all we need is a song." He flipped through the pages until they found some English titles.

"'Islands in the Stream'?" she suggested.

"Sorry, Dolly, I'm not sure I can wrangle that one."

"'Love Lift Us Up Where We Belong'?"

"I'd need a lot more whiskey and about a carton of smokes before I could attempt a Joe Cocker impersonation. Not that I doubt your chops to sing the Linda Ronstadt part."

"Jennifer Warnes," Astrid corrected.

"Ah, Jennifer. That's right. Is it me, or did she sing on every film soundtrack duet in the '80s?"

"Just about, but she was also friends with Leonard Cohen, and collaborated and toured with him a lot, too."

"Sounds like she had the time of her life." Theo pointed at himself with two thumbs, overly pleased with his joke.

"That was horrendous." She swayed into him.

"I know, but I like getting a rise out of you because you get so physical when you're annoyed." He put an arm around her waist.

"How about 'Somewhere Out There' from that mouse cartoon?" Astrid was distracted by Theo's proximity but still wanted to choose a song.

"First of all, that 'mouse cartoon' is *An American Tail*. Second of all, I think I'd feel like a cornball singing about wishing on the same star."

"You sure seem to know a lot about it."

"Let's just say, watching that animated feature was a particularly emotional experience for me as a kid."

"We're still talking about a cartoon mouse here, right?"

"Fievel. A little respect, please. His name was Fievel."

"Wow." She looked at him like he was a pile of tangled puppies then turned back to the binder. "How about 'Don't You Want Me'?"

"Poor grammar notwithstanding, that's a pretty bold question for such a shy lady. I think you already know the answer to that one."

A flash of free fall exhilaration and fear. "Could you *be* any cheesier?" She shoved him with her shoulder and he held her tighter.

"Only if it makes you act out more," he whispered in her ear. The hairs on the back of her neck and arms rose.

On stage, a bald man in thick-rimmed glasses sang a poignant song in Japanese or maybe Korean, based on the songbook categories. A younger Asian man nearby in a T-shirt with iron-on decals spelling out "The Greatest Love of All" screamed along. When the song ended, there were happy shouts and something came sailing from the back of the room that looked like underwear but turned out to be a doily. A bow from the singer, and then a cluster of inebriated women in jeans and sequined tops stumbled and giggled through a rendition of "It's Rainin' Men."

It was tacky and noisy and smoky, and just about everyone there was far drunker than Astrid and Theo, but a pleasant hush settled over the duo. During the hostess's rendition of "Blue Velvet," they smiled the same secret smile, twisted their fingers around the loose fabric of each other's clothing and kissed, not stopping even when the next table over began to hoot at them. Astrid could've been submerged in water; all surrounding sound gradually became low and garbled, until everything felt slow and muted. The whiskey added a tart flavor to their kisses, but dissipated as they continued to embrace, their bodies lit blue-purple, blue-purple, neon lights echoing off their oblivious forms.

More drinks followed more kisses; they got tipsy but not sloppy. Soon it was their turn to sing.

They got up on the low stage, which had a tinsel curtain backdrop and TVs mounted at each corner.

On the screens, pink dotted lines counted them down to the opening and the lyrics to "(I've Had) The Time of My Life" appeared at the bottom: in green for the male part, pink for female.

Theo hammed it up as he sang, swiveling his hips and pulling melodramatic somber faces, while Astrid reached out an earnest hand to him during her portions of the song.

The girls in the sequined tops got up and danced to the *Dirty Dancing* anthem, using their bottles of beer as makeshift Patrick Swayzes.

After the last chorus, Theo wrapped his arms around Astrid, dipped her, and planted a big one right on her lips. There was the fervent applause that only a crowd of twelve can create, then a man in overalls came up to sing Patsy Cline's "Crazy."

"I think it's time to go," Theo spoke in her ear.

Astrid nodded. "Okay."

CHAPTER THIRTY-ONE

Saturday, October 2, 1999

Oliver calls me at the store on Saturday.

"What time do you go to lunch?"

"I was going to leave in a few minutes," I say.

"I'm a few blocks away. Do you mind if I stop by?"

"I don't mind." What I *do* mind is this new caution and formality in his voice.

He waves through the front window when he arrives, but doesn't come inside.

A ripple of relief is followed by a wave of uncertainty.

I call to Minerva and ask if she minds taking over for a half hour. She comes out from the back and says it's no problem.

"Hi," I greet him outside. Neither of us moves in for a hug.

"Hi." His smile is flat, his blue eyes sharpened like they're trying to cut through me.

"So there's a diner a few blocks—"

"We're actually not going to eat," he interrupts. "I hope that's okay."

"Where are we going?"

"Down the street."

I've been so preoccupied at Curio City that I haven't had a chance to explore the neighborhood, so I'm surprised when he leads me to a store selling new and used books tucked away next to a vintage clothing shop.

"Are we looking for something in particular?" I ask as we go in.

"Yes and no." Typical Oliver answer.

A woman with a silver-streaked brown bob barely looks up from the giant hardcover in her lap as we enter.

He leads me to the back, where the sunlight doesn't quite reach the double-stacked shelves.

I'm about to ask why we're here when the reason pinches the back of my eyes and causes an ache in my throat. "You remembered 'bookstore' was on that list of words I wrote down after the party. But I never even told you the full list, I think I only mentioned a couple of the words."

"'Bookstore' and 'Chinatown.' Why do you think I took you there for dinner?" His voice, his eyes, maddeningly neutral.

Inside me, everything is twisting, my organs a damp towel being wrung out.

"That makes sense. Though if I went to a bookstore on September ninth, I don't think it was this one. Nothing about it is familiar."

"I thought maybe the smell of the books would remind you of something."

We speak in low voices, and there's a strange energy between us, like an off-key violin, its strings about to snap. Like we're more concerned with being polite than saying what we really want to say. I hate it.

I take a paperback off the shelf and fan the pages in front of my face. The scent is powdery and sweet, with musty, faint rotting undertones. It brings to mind comfort and escape and ever-so-slow decay but that's about it.

"Nothing?"

I shake my head.

He squints at me and tilts his head to one side then the other, the way a painter or photographer might regard their subject. A plummeting sensation overtakes me, but I stand as still as I can, afraid that any small movement might dissuade him from coming closer. I take in a breath but forget to let it out.

He moves his mouth to my ear and whispers, "I know what you want from me. But why do you want it? Because it might lead to Theo?" His warm breath tickles my ear and the side of my neck in a way that is both glorious and excruciating. He exhales and a spark travels down my spine, down the sides of my body and back up until it's inside me.

I turn my head by careful degrees until our cheeks are pressed together.

"I don't know," I say in a low voice. Neither of us moves. Maybe he's waiting for me to say something more but there's nothing else I can say.

The store clerk approaches with a stack of books. "Are you looking for something in particular or browsing?"

I take a step back, embarrassed, disappointed.

"Cookbooks." The word slips out, startles me. "I'm looking for a cookbook . . . for my friend's wedding shower."

Oliver nods, encourages me to continue.

Something slides into place in my hazy brain. "Do you have *The Big Book of Breakfast*?"

My favorite is the recipe for baked eggs.

"Let me see if we have that one in stock." She goes off in search of the book.

"I'm sorry," I tell Oliver.

His face is maddeningly pleasant and blank, like a bank teller's. "What for? That's why we're here. That's why *I'm* here, right?"

"No, it's not. I mean—"

"*Big Book of Breakfast*, here we go. Lightly used, but overall in very good condition."

I take the book, which feels like a cinder block in my arms, and follow the clerk to the register.

Oliver and I don't speak during the short walk back to Curio City, not until we get to the store.

"Oliver . . ."

"I got you something." He reaches into his pocket and takes out a small bundle encased in thick white paper. "Since I figured you might not have time to get food. I remembered you like BLTs."

"Wow. Thank you . . . But wait."

"Ask me what you really want to ask me, Astrid."

I chew on my lower lip, mustering up the nerve to be honest. I have no right to ask, and yet . . . "Are we ever going to go on a second date? I mean, I know I have some baggage . . ."

"Baggage?" A dry chuckle. "Lost luggage, more like."

"Is that a no?"

"It's not a no. But before anything else can happen, you need to talk to the city."

"Did you just say . . .?" Yeah, of course he did.

He won't say anything else, either, just waves and walks off. I watch his back and mentally urge him to turn around. He doesn't.

Talk to the city. What the hell . . .? The only remotely applicable thing I can think of is taking an ad out in the paper, but that would feel too foolish, frantic, futile.

Back at The Lab, I study *The Big Book of Breakfast* for clues. It's nothing but recipes and glossy photos of attractive eggs, stacks of immaculate pancakes and other morning foods. At best, the only thing this book will help me with is learning how to poach an egg. But I know this is the second copy I bought. What happened to the first? And what does it have to do with Theo?

Take a closer look at that book you just bought.

Of course. The author. Erin Collins. His sister?

Half-sister. Same mom, different dads.

All this panning for memories and a nugget finally rattles in my brain.

Erin's recipes are too good. I spent a summer with her on the Cape . . .

If I can't find Theo, maybe I can find Erin.

There's nobody on Zak's spare computer in the den so I boot it up and search for "Erin Collins cookbook" in Alta Vista. I find out she lives in Atlanta, Georgia, but there's no contact info listed for her, and I'm done with phone book shenanigans. I'm not deluded enough to think I could call up Delicious Books and magically get her phone number, but the publisher's address is listed inside, and she names her editor and agent in the acknowledgments, so I could try to get a letter to Erin through one of them.

I get out a spiral notebook and a pen. What the hell am I supposed to say to this cookbook author anyway? *Dear Erin, I think I hooked up with your half-brother and we lost touch for a bunch of reasons I won't go into. Help me find him, pretty please?* Or I could make up something extreme to make sure she puts us in touch. *Dear Erin, Your half-brother Theo knocked me up and then disappeared. I need to find him pronto to tell him he's going to be a dad.* Yeah, no. I need a good balance of honest but not preposterous, urgent but not pathetic . . . or crazy. Might as well just tell it straight.

> *Dear Erin,*
>
> *I'm hoping you can help me find your half-brother, Theo. I met him last month and spent some time with him. Soon after, I was hit by a car and suffered some minor memory loss. I recently moved and have misplaced Theo's contact info* [a minor fib, but for the greater good]. *I'd appreciate it if you could put us in touch. I know this sounds unusual, but he*

should be able to help fill in some of the blank spots in my memory. Theo actually recommended your breakfast cookbook to me, and I love it. He spoke fondly of spending a summer on the Cape with you when you were developing the recipes . . .

I finish out the letter with my address, number, and gratitude for her time.

Next, I run out to the CVS on Mass Ave for stamps and envelopes, because the letters have to be mailed today. I wish they could've been mailed yesterday, the day before, the very day I started to remember those missing twenty-four hours.

I address the envelopes right in the store and I drop them in a corner mailbox.

That's when I see her.

A tall woman, standing on a carton that makes her taller, wearing long satin robes the color of shiny dimes. Her face is painted silver; grey wings are attached to her back. She holds a basket and there's an open tin box at her feet, one that may have once contained cookies or other sweets, but now houses spare change and a few loose bills. She stares at a spot above my head, completely immobile.

I'm eye level with her basket. Even though I can't see its contents, I know there are feathers inside.

Flowers wilt. Feathers don't.

I drop a quarter into the tin box. She comes to life in herky-jerky motions and offers me a feather.

"Um, I don't mean to disturb you," I say as I take it. "I'm sure this is a long shot, but do you remember seeing me before?"

She returns to her frozen pose and says nothing.

"Really, I hate to interrupt your act here, but this is important. Do you remember seeing me with somebody a few weeks ago?"

No answer.

Maybe a quarter was too chintzy. I take out a five-dollar bill, wave it in her line of sight, and drop it in the box at her feet.

She begins to move in stiff mechanical jerks again. There's a brief graze of eye contact and a sad smile as she hands me another feather.

"So . . . Now can you tell me if you've seen me before?"

She doesn't speak. Doesn't look at me again.

I release the feathers, let them float to the ground, and go home.

CHAPTER THIRTY-TWO

I'm in the back of a church whose walls and ceiling are made entirely of stained glass. The sun beams down bands of color, which reflect on my bare skin. My arms look like they're tattooed with rainbows.

Theo stands beside the pulpit on a low stage, behind which is a tinsel curtain that belongs more at an amateur talent show than a place of worship. He's wearing a silver tuxedo, and his face is painted to match. He stands still and holds a basket with both hands. At his feet is a metal tin.

"Theo." I hurry down the aisle to him. "It's Astrid. Do you remember me?"

He says nothing, looks straight ahead.

I stand before him but don't climb up on stage. "Don't do this. Talk to me."

Silence.

There's loose change and a few bills in the tin. I search my pockets, but all I find is a black feather. I drop it in.

He moves like a marionette whose strings are being tugged, reaches into the basket, bends down, and hands me a

Chinese coin. I grab his hand before he can pull his arm back, hold onto it tightly.

"You know me, Theo. Please look at me."

He watches the space above my head, jerks his arm away, but I won't let go.

After a few moments of this tug-of-war, his body convulses and large black wings sprout from his back. Startled, I release his hand and the wings begin to flap. They sound like the snap of a sheet over a newly made bed.

Theo flies up, and I snatch at his ankle, but he's moving too quickly for me. I can't hold onto him.

He makes a swift ascent to the ceiling. A high-pitched shatter as he bursts through it, leaving a jagged hole in the colored glass.

"Astrid, you have to get out of here," says a voice from the back of the church.

I turn around. Oliver beckons to me.

But I can't get out of anywhere; my legs are rooted in place. I can only look up at the hole in the ceiling and down at the pool of yellow sunlight on the stage.

"You're not safe here," Oliver calls out.

A sound like thin ice cracking under too much weight, and a few large shards of glass fall at my feet. They crumble into smaller pieces, glitter like worthless gems.

A louder noise fills the church, a din akin to a thunderclap. All the ceiling glass goes at once, a chromatic downpour aimed at my head, which is tilted up, aimed at my exposed throat.

CHAPTER THIRTY-THREE

Sunday, October 10, 1999

Another week passes. Nothing from Oliver and no new memories.

Sunday is my day off. I try out the baked eggs recipe for Sally, Daphne, and Zak, to have something to do and make me less of a liar to Erin Collins. They enjoy the food and praise it, but I eat in preoccupied silence, wondering what thread I can untangle next.

After brunch Robin calls, and I let him know I'm pretty much healed, settled into my new apartment, and enjoying my new job. I leave out the fire and the firing, the headaches and nightmares. It would be so nice to go beyond the headlines and give him the full story, but there's no reason to worry him. Considering the sacrifices he's made to provide for me as a single father, the least I can do is not burden him further with my shortcomings and failures. Instead, I ask about the new musical he's working on. While he tells me his plans for directing a community theater production of *Rent*, I pull out the list of words I put together at

Minerva's. The day after the Lunar Haus party, I'd rewritten it on a single sheet of paper, but now I go through it and add notes:

Diner – Has to be Deli Haus. Did Theo and I go there?

Bear/Kiss – Statue outside FAO Schwarz, where we had our first kiss. Why there?

Bridge – Mass Ave Bridge. We must've walked across it, since Theo told me about Smoots.

Bookstore – Where I bought the cookbook. But where? Did Theo help me pick it out? Or sell it to me?

Chinatown/Coin – Presumably, these are connected. Did Theo and I go there, too?

Karaoke – Not sure. Did we do karaoke together? If so, where?

Bubbles – No idea.

Popcorn – Ditto.

" . . . so I think it's going to be a strong production, if I can keep a couple of the divas in line. Are you still there, Astrid?"

"I'm here."

I keep him chatting a few minutes longer, until he's satisfied he put in enough father time and has a solid idea of what I'm up to, even though he doesn't, not even a little. Maybe one of these days . . .

After I hang up, I turn over the annotated list and draw a rough map, bottom up, beginning in Central Square. Two lines for Mass Ave, a break for the bridge and Charles River, then a section off to the right representing Kenmore Square, with a small square for Deli Haus. Back on Mass Ave, I extend the lines up until they're roughly where Boylston Street should be, then veer left until Berkley. Another square for FAO Schwarz. More lines until Boylston hits Tremont and then I Chinatown all the way on the left (*"Welcome to the Combat Zone"*).

I try to piece it together like one of those activity book logic puzzles. The bridge came either before or after Deli Haus. Ditto FAO Schwarz. Chinatown would've been before or after FAO Schwarz. But how does the bookstore and karaoke fit into all this? Did we actually go to all these places? Covering that much of Boston in a single day seems unlikely.

I always sucked at solving those logic puzzles. My temples tighten like a giant rubber band has been twisted around my head.

Should I call Oliver?

I pick up the phone, but instead of a dial tone, I hear Sally's voice: "We'll definitely be there at four o'clock. Thank you so, *so* much."

Something tells me she wasn't using the royal "we." Frenetic knocking on my door a minute later confirms the suspicion.

"Do I even want to know?" I ask through the door before opening it to a Sally full of dangerous energy.

"Don't give me that look. Just hear me out."

I could nap in the dramatic pause that follows. Good lord. "I'm listening."

"The world is full of mysteries. We may never know what came before the Big Bang or who killed JFK or what happened to Amelia Earhart . . . but finding Theo and figuring out what happened on September ninth is a mystery I *know* we can solve." She sits on my bed, crushes my list/map.

"Are you seriously comparing my missing day with the origins of the universe and the assassination of a president?"

"Well . . ."

"And Earhart's disappearance is considered one of the greatest unsolved mysteries of the twentieth century."

"You know what I mean. We can figure this out."

There it is again. "We?" I cross my arms.

"Yes, we. You know how Zak does IT stuff for Gardner College?"

"What kind of mad caper did you sign us up for this time?"

Of course it won't be as simple as that. First we've got to have Story Hour.

"So they have this local radio station, WGCA, which has a decent listenership outside of the Gardner students. I've been really into their Girl Power Hour, where they play all these great female singer-songwriters. And not the typical Lilith Fair stuff, either, though they do throw in some Jewel and Natalie Merchant once in a while, but also Kate Bush, Suzanne Vega, Marianne Faithfull, Tori—"

"I get the idea. What does this have to do with anything?" I pull out the now-crumpled paper from under Sally, fold it, and stash it beneath a copy of the *Improper Bostonian* on my desk.

"The station also does this weekly show called *Bizarre Beantown*, where they interview some of the city's weirdoes and locals. It's great. Like, on the last show, they featured a woman who's had all these creepy sexual extraterrestrial encounters, and this ninety-three-year-old man who has the world's biggest collection of movie stubs, and some biochemist dude who came up with a formula for a liquid food alternative he lives off now, and someone else—I don't remember. Anyway, I asked Zak to put me in touch with the show's producer and host, Renatta Johnson, a grad student there. Turns out he recently helped fix her laptop so she kind of owes him a favor."

"Oh god, don't even tell me."

Sally jumps up and holds my upper arms, possibly so that I don't flee, because she knows me well.

"Astrid, this is your chance to get a real lead on Theo. I mean, maybe someone who knows him will be listening, maybe even Theo himself! And—get this— normally, they wouldn't book someone so late, but they had a last minute cancellation for today's show. You're going to be a replacement guest! It's win-win for everyone."

"Not for me. I'd make a fool of myself on the radio."

"Don't you see? This is your chance to ask the universe for what you need—okay, if not the universe, then Boston. You'll get to tell the whole city your story, or at least a couple of hundred people—if not thousands."

"You could even say . . ." Oh Oliver, how do you keep doing this? "I'd get to talk to the city."

"Exactly! My gut tells me this is what you need to get a step closer to finding Theo."

"*My* gut tells me it's going to lose its breakfast. Sal, you know how much I hate public speaking. Don't you remember I used to throw up before every presentation in school?"

"But you do karaoke no problem," she reasons.

"Singing in front of drunken strangers is not the same thing. It's easy when you can carry a tune and have the words in front of you. I can't believe you signed me up for something like this without asking me first." Who am I kidding? This is classic Sally.

She gives my arms a squeeze. "Then pretend it's karaoke. Imagine you're in some dingy bar, singing one of your depressing songs."

What other options do I have left? There's no telling if I'll ever hear back from Erin Collins' agent or editor and Oliver . . . Well, he steered me directly into the path of this radio show. And as tangled up as things are with him, the volatility in my heart is rooted in the puzzle of Theo. The only way to get any resolution is to solve it. Talking to the city may offer another clue. A rational conclusion, but the idea of broadcasting myself like that to countless people still fills me with unbearable queasiness.

Grimacing, I pull myself out of Sally's grip. "You gotta let me get by."

I barely make it to the toilet before I vomit.

We take a taxi to the Back Bay, passing quaint historic streets lined with brownstones and trees modeling their fall colors under a cold sun. My nausea persists despite my now-empty stomach. We're dropped off on a corner of Beacon Street and Sally leads the way to a brownstone with a bright blue door. She rings the bell.

A woman with golden-brown skin and dark hair woven into fine cornrows answers the door.

"I'm Renatta. Thanks for coming." She leads us downstairs to a cramped office, where she offers us folding chairs and bottles of water.

"I usually like to have more time to prep guests, but since we've had a last-minute dropout, we'll have to be quick and dirty about it, so to speak."

She hands me a blank legal pad and a ballpoint pen, and begins to scrawl something on a clipboard.

"Sally told me your story, but I'd like to hear the way you tell it and go over key talking points. Feel free to take notes as we chat in case there are specifics you'd like to cover when we're live. Have you been on the radio before?"

I shake my head.

"So when we're on the air, don't give nonverbal answers. The listeners can't see you nod or shake your head, so make sure you speak up. Seems obvious but you'd be surprised how many guests forget." She takes me through more prep and ends with, "Best thing to do is forget you're talking to an audience at all. Think of it as a conversation you and I are having."

"I told Astrid to think of it like karaoke," Sally interjects.

"Whatever makes you more comfortable." Renatta checks her clipboard and continues, "Do you want to take call-in questions or only questions from me?"

Sally grabs my arm. "You *have* to take call-ins. What if Theo calls in?"

Renatta directs her reply to me. "We have an intern screening calls who can take down any info from him or anyone who may know him. Some guests choose not to talk to callers to avoid the surprise element. But, as you can imagine, that's often the best part of the show and live calls *do* make it more interesting."

More interesting for the listeners, sure, but how might such unpredictability affect me? What if people call in to mock me, tell me I'm desperate, crazy, pathetic? What if someone calls to tell me Theo is married or in a coma or dead? I'm drowning in horrifying variables and clutch the legal pad on my lap like it's a flotation device.

"Hey." Renatta waves a hand in front of my face. When I don't look at her or say anything, she gets up from behind her desk and crouches beside me. "I understand your hesitation, but I promise I got your back. I will shut down anyone who's inappropriate right away. And if at any time, a caller makes you uncomfortable for *any* reason, you can signal to me, and I'll cut them off. You're here to share something personal, so I'll do everything I can to make sure you get to speak freely. If you don't feel at ease, that's not good for anyone."

Light strokes from Sally on my upper back. Her mouth is open like she wants to speak but worries it'll come out wrong.

"Go ahead and say what you need to say, Sal."

"You know I'd talk to callers in a heartbeat. I wouldn't be able to resist. But you're different. I'm just happy you're doing this show. Anything else is up to you." She takes my hand and squeezes twice.

I reciprocate the squeezes. *I am brave, you are brave.*

"Okay . . . I'll take call-ins," I relent and turn to Renatta. "But I'll hold you to keeping them in line."

Renatta gives me an atta-girl smile and makes a note on the clipboard. "Great. Now let's go over some of the questions I've prepared . . ."

We do a dry run and then it's time to head into the studio. I swallow, tell my stomach to behave, and follow Renatta to the end of the hall. The walls of the studio are lined with textured gray foam, like the inside of an egg carton.

Guess I was meant for a padded room sooner or later.

I'm fitted with headphones and seated at a small, round table with a switchboard. Another bottle of water is set before me. Sally bends down to give me a hug and is sent to an adjoining room where she'll be able to listen to the show.

"Remember, it's just you and me having a conversation. You're going to be great."

A thumbs up from Renatta and then it's time. She pushes some buttons on the switchboard and speaks in a mellifluous voice as she introduces the show and gives an overview of the day's guests and topics.

"Please welcome our first guest, Astrid, who has found herself in the middle of a search after an unusual turn of events. Maybe one of you listening can help her find who she's looking for. Thanks for joining us today, Astrid."

"Thanks for having me, Renatta." Oh god, it's like somebody poured sand down my throat. I take a gulp of water.

"Astrid, tell us what happened to you last month."

"Sure. So last month . . ." I speak about the car accident and then the apartment fire, offer a few details but not too many. God, how many people are tuned in and judging me right now?

"It sounds like you've had quite a run of bad luck," Renatta sympathizes.

I shrug and she points to the mic. Right, I'm on air, nobody can see me. I force a chuckle. "Yeah, it was kinda like my life turned into a country song—I lost my job, I lost my apartment, I *almost* lost my spleen . . . But I recovered and things turned around. New place to live, new job—I'm lucky I got back on my feet so quickly. Except I recently realized I lost something else: I'm missing a day."

"How do you mean?"

"The accident happened on a Friday afternoon, September tenth. But I don't remember anything that happened in the twenty-four hours before that. And . . . This is going to sound strange . . ."

"*Bizarre Beantown* listeners live for strange. Go on."

I describe finding the Chinese coin and the fragments it triggered, of course leaving out the part where I drank drug-laced punch beforehand.

"Then other details started coming back to me and I realized I'd met someone that Thursday, and I'm pretty sure I spent a good part of that day with him. And then I remembered his name and what he looks like."

Renatta gestures for me to continue and I do. I give Theo's name and description and go into the list of words that I was trying to make sense of, which I now know by heart. I falter at "kiss" and almost don't mention it, but Renatta is so damn good at what she does, her compassionate doe eyes coax it out of me.

"So you remember kissing him?"

I fidget and slouch down in my seat. "Um . . . I do remember that part now. And this wasn't a friendly peck or anything."

"So there was obviously something romantic between the two of you, some kind of spark."

"I guess so. I mean, I don't go around kissing strangers, so presumably we spent some time getting to know each other first."

She holds up a finger. "Astrid, we have a caller. You're on *Bizarre Beantown* on WGCA. What's your name and neighborhood?"

"This is Pamela from Brighton. Astrid, did you have sex with this guy?"

The question hits me like cold water thrown in my face. Wow, blunt much? "I . . . don't know . . . I don't remember."

But Pamela isn't done with me yet. "Are you worried he might've, like, raped you? And you're suppressing, like, the trauma of it?"

This time it's like being splashed with boiling water. "Um . . . I'm pretty sure that didn't happen."

"How can you be sure?" the caller persists.

"Because every memory I have associated with Theo is . . . *good*. Happy. I know he was kind and funny and that we had a great time together. I'm sure anything that happened between us was consensual."

I give Renatta a get-me-out-of-here look, and she pushes a button on the switchboard. "Thanks for your call, Pamela. And that's really why you want to find him again, isn't it, Astrid? To see if there was something genuine between you two?"

"Let's not scare the guy off after one date. First and foremost, I just want to know what Theo remembers about that day. I'd be happy getting coffee and talking to him."

"Well, let's hope somebody listening can help put the two of you in touch. We have another call. Please tell us your name and neighborhood."

There's a lot of coughing on the other line. "Gosh, I'm so sorry about that," says a woman with a thick Boston accent. "I'm Jennifer, proud Southie." She drops the "r" from her name: *Jennifah*. "Astrid, I think it's wicked awesome you've overcome all the crap you been through without bein' all woe-is-me about it. You got some guts to tell us all this personal stuff—I *mean* it, good for you. But let's say you hooked up and it was a one-time thing for him. What if you're chasing a guy who's not into it?"

Or not even real?

"That's the thing. I don't know. If I gave him my number and he tried to get in touch, he wouldn't have been able to, because my phone was disconnected after the fire. But sure, it's possible that it was a one-time thing . . ."

"You do whatcha gotta do, but I'd be pretty friggin' embarrassed if that was the case," the caller replies.

"I have to agree with Jennifer about how brave you are putting yourself on the line like this," Renatta interjects.

"Brave or foolish?" A lame laugh and I clear my throat. "My friend Sally told me something earlier that stuck with me. She said there are all these mysteries in the world and questions we may never be able to answer. Like what really happened to Amelia Earhart or who really killed JFK. Not that my lost day is *anywhere* on that scale of importance. My personal mystery is much smaller, but it might actually be solvable. Will it kill me not to find out what happened on September ninth? Of course not. But if I can find Theo, I can fill in some of the gaps. If it was a one-time hook-up, okay, but at least I'll know for sure. And if it was something more . . . Well, we'll see what happens."

"I hope you find him, Astrid, I really, really do," says Jennifer. "And I hope he doesn't turn out to be a lowlife or a player." She pronounces it *play-uh*.

"Thanks, Jennifer. I hope so too."

Renatta smiles and gives me a thumbs-up. "We have time for one more call. Who do we have on the line?"

"This is Mike from Dorchester."

"Thanks for calling, Mike. Do you have a question for Astrid?"

"I don't . . . but I do know Theo."

There's a jolt in my throat and a crashing in my ears, as if I've been woken out of a deep sleep with a sharp noise. "Are you serious? Is he a friend of yours?" I press my mouth closed to prevent a stream of other questions: *When did you last see him? Has he ever mentioned me? Is he seeing anyone? Is he a lowlife or a player?*

"He's more of an acquaintance," Mike says. "We have a couple of friends in common, so I see him out once in a while." He sounds so reluctant, like he might change his mind about talking and hang up at any second.

I flash an SOS at Renatta with my eyes, because I need her radio magic to help get more out of this guy. She gives me an I-got-this wink.

"Mike, do you think you'd be able to put Theo in touch with Astrid?"

"I don't even have his number, and . . . I mean, I could probably get it, but I don't know, I think I'd feel funny about it . . . it's kinda weird, you know?"

"Even an email address would be fine." Whoa, gotta ease up on the desperate, gotta tread carefully here. "Or I could give you my Hotmail address to pass on to him. I know this whole thing is . . . unconventional, but I would *so* appreciate any help with this."

Silence.

Come on, Mike, *say something*.

I'm ready to scream like Lola in the casino scene from *Run Lola Run*: a scream that shatters glass, slows time, a scream to will the roulette wheel to stop where it absolutely has to.

The silence continues. Did Mike hang up? The twitch in Renatta's eyebrows echoes my thought.

Please please please please please please *please*.

"Mike, are you still on the line?" she asks.

"Yeah," he says. "I'm thinking. I mean, I don't want to invade Theo's privacy or create an uncomfortable scene for him. But I have something that could help. I'd just rather not say on the air."

Exclamation marks fill my head like confetti.

"That's fine," Renatta says. "We're just about wrapping up our time with Astrid. If you could hang on, she'll be able to talk with you one-on-one. Could you do that for us?"

"Yeah, I guess so."

Renatta waves a triumphant fist. "Terrific. Astrid, thank you again for joining us on *Bizarre Beantown* and sharing your story. Good luck and I hope you'll let us know how things turn out."

"Sure. Thanks for having me." It's all I can do not to run out of the room.

"We'll take a short break and when we return, we'll talk to Travis, a millionaire who spends a week out of every year living as a homeless person. You're listening to WGCA."

Renatta hustles me back to the small office. "Nice job in there. I'll have Mike transferred to this phone. Sit tight."

But I can't sit at all, I can only stand beside the desk with a hand hovering over the phone. If this call gets disconnected, I don't know what I'll—

Briiiii—

I snatch up the receiver.

"Mike?"

"Yeah. Astrid?"

Thank you thank you thank you. "I'm here."

"Okay . . ."

Man, I thought Sally's dramatic pauses were epic, but Mike's are on a whole other level.

"You mentioned you had some info about Theo," I prompt.

"We have a mutual friend who's a performance artist, and she's gonna be in some kind of skit at ManRay on Friday. You know, the goth club?"

"I know ManRay."

"They do this monthly party called Hell and the theme for October is Dead Stars in Hell. You gotta dress up as a dead celebrity or historical figure or some shit. Not really our scene, but we're going to support our friend. They can be strict about the dress code, so we have to wear costumes. Theo is dressing up as Andy Warhol. If you go to the club on Friday, you should be able to find him there."

"Mike, you have no idea how much I appreciate this."

"Please don't turn out to be some kind of psycho stalker."

"I promise I'm not." Before I can thank him again, the line goes dead.

When I tell Sally about Mike and this event at ManRay, she looks like a kid at Disney World who's been invited to live in the Magic Castle. I brace myself for much gushing.

"Can you believe you're going to see Theo again? And to be reunited like *this*—it's like something out of a movie. Dead Stars in Hell? Oh my god. How come we never went to such cool parties in New York? Who are you going to go as?" Her eyes widen. "Who am *I* going to go as? I've always wanted to dress up like Cleopatra. Do you think I could pull off a white toga and black wig?" She looks at a strand of her buttery hair and squints at it, then turns an appraising gaze on me. "Maybe you should go as Marilyn Monroe. Maybe *I* should go as Marilyn."

If only I could have Sally's fearless enthusiasm. She plunges headfirst through her world like it's strung with balloons and welcome banners whereas I tiptoe around mine like it's a maze of traffic cones. Always inside me, this seesaw to be more elastic like Sally and fight my rigidity, to float like she does even as lead boots weigh me down.

We walk through the Boston Garden toward the Park Street T, past a large statue of an angel with an inscription on its granite base that reads: "Cast thy bread upon the waters, for thou shalt find it after many days." What exactly am I going to find after all these days?

As we cross the bridge over the lagoon, absent of the swan boats that take tourists around during warmer months, I look out at the willow trees along the water's periphery. I could curl up under one of those trees right now, even though it's overcast and the wind is picking up, heavy with the threat of rain.

Sally's been talking this entire time. "Hey, you're not listening." There's a pout in her voice.

"Sorry, I was replaying what just happened, on the show and after, on the phone with that guy. I think you'd be an amazing Marilyn. I have no idea about my costume, but I don't want to wear a wig or anything else that could make me difficult to recognize. I want to keep it simple."

"So then you agree with my plan?"

"I don't know if I can handle another Sally plan right now."

"It's nothing that thrilling." She pulls out a map of the city. "I was saying, we're not far from the Downtown Crossing shopping center. We should see if we can find anything for our costumes there."

"If that's what you want."

"What's gotten into you? You've just had a major breakthrough in the Theo mystery. You're going to see him again in only five days. Why aren't you more excited?"

Because there's a nagging in the back of my head that says I'd be dumb to hope for a happy outcome and questions whether chasing this lost memory is worth it. Because I want to call Oliver and tell him about this new development, but I also want to see him again and maybe kiss him again, too. Because as we walk through the Common and pass the spot where Oliver and I kissed, there's no maybe about it—I miss him. Because I know these trees and benches are real, but not much more than that, and there's a pounding right behind my eyes, and I'd give anything for a quiet, unlit room, a big blanket, and maybe a warm body next to me. Because I'm jealous of Sally's energy and resilience, and I can't match it, and I'll never be able to.

"It's this stupid headache, Sal. I haven't been getting them as often, but when they hit, they're pretty bad."

"Oh." Her tone is deflated, but grows more concerned. "You want to go home and save shopping for another day?"

"No, we're already here. We might as well see what we can find." I force a smile. "It'll be fun."

Sally narrows her eyes, registers my lie, and offers a sympathetic sigh. "We'll make it quick."

We follow a side street off Tremont and find a sliver of a shop that sells flamboyant accessories: candy-colored wigs, feather boas, velvet chokers studded with rhinestones, the works. While Sally fingers a rack of marabou, I find a pair of oversized goggles and a leather cap with earflaps.

That was easy. I bring the items to the counter.

"What are you going to do with those?" she asks.

"Wear them to ManRay. When I go as a poor man's Amelia Earhart."

"Ooh, I love it! Doesn't Zak have a brown leather jacket? I bet he'd let you borrow it. But you should also get this." She fishes out a gauzy white scarf from a nearby rack with a magician's flourish and wraps it around my neck.

"Perfect." I pay for the items and wear the scarf out.

Next, we head over to Filene's Basement, at the heart of Downtown Crossing. The area is retail heaven, built for commerce with numerous pedestrian walkways and minimal room for cars; shopping-bag-laden foot traffic is preferred here. There's a faint layer of grime over everything and . . . something else. Hold still. Everyone around me keeps moving, but I tune them out and try to dress up the streets in the darkness and silence of evening. At the edges I can almost—

"Are you coming?" Sally calls out.

I twitch and teeter as if on the edge of a precipice. Maybe it was nothing. Maybe I'm trying too hard, am too susceptible to déjà vu these days. Maybe I've lowered my immunity to coincidence and the quotidian.

At Filene's, Sally finds a white halter dress in the clearance racks, and I pay more than I should for a pair of brown leather boots, but hey, you only try to circumnavigate the globe and disappear over the Pacific Ocean once.

At the make-up counter, Sally spends an inordinate amount of time selecting the perfect red lipstick. I swallow my exasperation every time she holds one up and wonders if it's "Marilyn-y enough." She finally settles on a shade sufficiently reminiscent of the platinum-haired starlet and we head home.

On the T platform, while waiting for the red line, Sally burbles an endless stream of conversation.

" . . . And Zak and Daphne go to ManRay all the time, so we should ask if they're going to this party—no, *insist* they come if they weren't already planning on it."

"Hey Sal, I'm all for having them join us, but can we keep the Theo thing between us?"

"Really? A couple of hours ago, you went on a radio show and told god-knows-how-many strangers about it. But you want to keep it from your friends?"

"Actually, yeah, I do." Her raised eyebrows and hands-on-hips Wonder Woman pose demands an explanation, but I don't offer one.

"And what if one of them heard the show and asks you about it?"

"Well, I'm obviously not going to deny it. I just don't want Friday to turn into some kind of big drama. Having you involved is drama enough," I tease.

Sally pretends to pout for a moment then, like a magpie catching sight of something shiny, gets distracted by a passing thought and resumes her chatter.

Back at The Lab, Sally heads to the spare room to do Marilyn research on Zak's computer, and I go to the kitchen, where Daphne is making a smoothie the color of grass.

"Apple, spinach, avocado, celery and ginger. Want some?"

"No thanks. But have fun living longer than me." I grab a Coke from the fridge. "I'm glad to see you being all healthy. You, uh . . . you haven't been eating a lot lately. I didn't know if . . ."

"If I have an eating disorder? Don't be daft." She smells the contents of the blender as if it's a bouquet of flowers and pours herself a glass.

We sit at the kitchen table and sip our respective drinks.

"It's Zak," she says.

"What about him?"

Daphne emits a frustrated sigh and rolls her eyes. "I'm in love with the wanker. Can't eat, can't sleep. It's horrible."

"Does he know?"

"I haven't told him. Better to let these things play out." She moves aside her glass and lights a cigarette. "Listen, can we have a quick chat about something else?"

Uh oh. Her tone is forced casual. I brace myself for bad things.

"Sure, what's up?"

"I know Sally's going through a tough time and needed to get away. It was my idea she stay here, and I think she's smashing, really lovely."

"Oh god, it's been weeks now. I'm sorry, you must feel like you have a fourth roommate."

The smell of Daphne's concoction wafts my way and makes my stomach clench.

"We love having Sally here but . . . it *can* feel a bit crowded sometimes. If she needs to stay another week—even two—that's okay, but it would be helpful to have some idea . . ."

"Of when she'll be leaving. Of course. I totally understand. I mean, she's talking about going to ManRay on Friday, so it doesn't seem like she's thought about when she'll return to New York."

"She can return to New York right after that—next weekend—if that wouldn't be too much extra time to stay," Sally says from the threshold.

Shit.

"Sal, I'm sorry, it's not like that," I stand up, expect her to dash away and make me chase after her.

But she remains still, clear-eyed. Right, I'm the one who dashes. "There's no need for you to apologize." She turns to Daphne. "I didn't expect to be here for this long, honest. Being away made it so easy to think about my life in New York like it was happening to someone else. Look at that girl whose fiancé is on the lam, who was crazy enough to consider marriage when her taste in men is so questionable." Her husky voice catches, but she swallows and continues, "You've been so generous to let me stay this long. But you're right, I need to set a return date for myself. So if you don't mind putting up with me for one more week, I'd really appreciate it."

Daphne bites the side of her mouth and nods. "Whatever you need."

Oh, Sally. Regardless of how demanding being her friend can be, I'm gonna miss the hell out of her when she leaves.

CHAPTER THIRTY-FOUR

9/9/99

Back outside, the sound of a motorcycle in the distance mingled with the leftover karaoke din in Astrid's ears. The wind picked up speed, made her a little dizzy. Was the night over? This couldn't be it, could it?

They bumped into each other on purpose as they walked back toward Chinatown.

"Whose turn is it now?" she asked.

"Mine."

"Our choices might be limited at this hour."

"Not *my* choice."

"Oh?" Her mouth went dry and her pulse surged. She studied a dustbin across the street.

"How about . . . my place?" The words bold, their delivery tentative.

"Your place?" she stalled.

"Yeah. We can still get the T out to Davis Square."

"I have to be up early to catch a bus to New York. But . . ." How were other people so good at articulating their desires? All of them skydivers and she the only one who couldn't jump out of the plane.

"But . . .?"

So high up now, she had to try, she had to leap.

"You can come over to my place." If her chute didn't open, so be it.

"Sure. That would be—sure. You . . . uh . . . you can kick me out any time you want."

Delight lit up her face. "Wow, nervous stammering looks cute on you."

"I'm not nervous."

"Anyway, who says I'm gonna *want* to kick you out?"

"You probably won't."

"Confident much?"

"It's more of a pseudo-confidence-slash-overcompensation thing. Let's go."

She couldn't tell whose palm was sweaty as they held hands all the way up to Tremont, to the border of the Commons. Leaves had begun their scatter at the base of the trees. A couple of students smoked outside the giant Emerson College dorm building and, next door, a man in a patchwork coat painted a clown face on the Dunkin' Donuts storefront.

Down the wide stairs of the Boylston Street T station, they waited on a C and E train to pass before a B finally arrived, one of the last of the night. They boarded the narrow, rickety train, and took seats near a cluster of frat boys wearing bedsheet togas and tinfoil halos, their faces and bodies covered in glitter. The low-rent angels swayed, grinned, and held themselves in an overly stiff way to belie their inebriation. Their conversation was so loud, eavesdropping was inevitable.

"Oh, come on, dude. You wanna tell me you think your entire existence might be a dream? Is that what you're really saying?"

"No, I'm saying consciousness is some convoluted bullshit that a dead French guy can't explain away." One of the guys stumbled as the train took a turn and bumped onto Theo's leg. "Sorry, man." He turned back to his friend. "Maybe it's like that Chinese guy who dreamed he was a butterfly, but then wondered whether it was the butterfly who was dreaming him."

"It's all the same thing," a third guy interjected. "According to Parmenides, the universe is a single eternal action and all events are part of it, including time. The problem is the duality of our mind, appearance versus reality. We can't trust our logical, mathematical minds because we confuse the real flow of events with our attempts to interpret them. Even experiments in quantum mechanics show particle behavior changes based on whether it's being observed or not. So if the observation gives it substance, what if the external world is actually an internal experience? It's all taking place in our brain, so maybe the universe is a giant electromagnetic blank canvas and we just plug in and project our own reality onto it."

The haloed men swayed in silence for a moment, then one said, "This is why I fucking love Davy. You get enough beer in him and he'll go off on these philosophical rants that'll melt your brain."

Theo and Astrid exchanged bewildered smiles. As the train made its ascent above ground and crawled along Commonwealth Avenue, they caught more snatches of the group's chatter ("But what about Kierkegaard?" "Kierkegaard was a miserable prick") until it approached a major intersection with a CVS on one corner and Pizzeria Uno on another.

"This is us," Astrid said.

They sidestepped the drunken angels as they got off the T.

"Wow," Astrid said. "That was . . ."

"Yes." Theo draped an arm around her. "That was."

Down Harvard Avenue there were still a couple of bars open, but most of the shops and restaurants that lined the street were dark. They walked past the giant sign for Blanchard's Liquors, its neon switched off, but Astrid was lit from within, charged with enough voltage to illuminate the sign, the street, the whole city.

They didn't speak as they walked, a low hum between them, a shared frequency.

As she unlocked her apartment door, Theo tugged on her hair. When she turned around, he kissed the tip of her nose. "Thanks for having me over," he said. "Even though it was my brilliant idea."

He caught her playful punch before it landed.

Inside, a short hallway opened up to a large foyer whose only furniture was a sewing table with an old computer monitor. A mantle covered with smiley face stickers held multiple incense holders and the walls were shrouded in aqua- and salmon-colored tapestries. A shag rug shaped like a daisy spread out from the middle of the room, which served as a nucleus to the rest of the apartment: kitchen, Cass's room, and bathroom on one side, living room and Astrid's room on the other. Beaded curtains that faintly rattled marked the entrances to the living room and kitchen. The air was heavy with the scent of marijuana and patchouli.

"It's nice to see that The Grateful Dead, apart from being iconic musicians, are also such . . . unique decorators," Theo said.

"Shh, Cass might hear you. Her parents were big-time hippies. You know what they say about the apple and the tree."

"This apple was obviously turned into a bong."

She snickered and led them to her room, where she cracked open a window. "Hope you don't mind if I air out the smell, I've never been a fan. Though we won't get a contact high now."

"Depends on your definition."

Theo took a slow lap around the room. There wasn't much to see. Her walls were bare, painted a pearly gray, which matched the makeshift silver curtains (fabric safety pinned to the rod, as in the living room). An overstuffed navy couch and card-table-turned-desk took up one wall, while an Ikea dresser, on top of which was a small TV/VCR combo, and a bed took up the other. Teetering stacks of books lined a third wall. She straightened one that looked about to fall over.

"I know I still need to get some grown-up furniture like bookshelves and a nightstand. Cass keeps trying to get me out to Salem with her to visit some carpenter she knows who makes furniture out of shipwrecks."

"How'd you meet this Cass, anyway? At a Phish concert? *High Times* convention?"

Astrid smirked and pushed him down on the sofa. "Drama camp, when we were ten." She sat beside him. "This was before I discovered I didn't inherit my father's acting chops. Cass was really good, though, even ended up starring in a Nickelodeon show for a couple of years. A few months ago, she called me out of nowhere and said she was moving to Boston to attend massage school. I was looking for a new place and she needed a roommate, so it worked out for both of us."

A fidgety energy overtook her and she stood up. "You want some water?" Beside her bed was a case of Poland Spring. She took two bottles, lit a cinnamon-scented candle, and switched off the light.

"Mood lighting, I like it."

She looked around the room, thinking of other ways to create ambiance. "Music?" she asked.

"Come here." He beckoned her to the couch and gently took both bottles of water from her, setting them on the floor. "I don't need music and I don't need water. I'm good."

"Okay." She positioned her knees on opposite sides of his legs, and he placed his hands below her hips. He traced the backs of her legs, stopped midway, and pulled her closer until she was kneeling on the couch over his body.

Her shyness evaporating, Astrid cradled his neck and leaned forward, planted her lips on his, opened his mouth with hers. Already this was plenty, more than she'd expected or hoped for, but she wanted more. She wanted to soar higher, she wanted all of him. It was a moment to savor, yet she was too consumed to do anything but devour. She pulled up his shirt, which he helped her take off by raising his arms. His shoulders were pale and broad, he had a sparse triangle of blond chest hair, and through each one of his nipples was a small silver hoop.

"Huh. Didn't expect these." She gave each one a light tug. "Did—"

"Yes, getting them hurt. That's always the first thing people ask. Both of them hurt. Like hell."

"Then why get them?"

"Pain and pleasure are two sides of the same coin. The more something hurts, the more amazing you feel when the pain goes away. Avoid one and you might not experience the other."

"Wow, I've never heard someone get so deep about nipple piercings."

She kissed his neck. His smell, the lemon and cedar mixed with secondhand smoke and whisky, quickened her breath, added to her buzz. She bit the area where his neck and shoulder met, and he let out a happy murmur. The cause and effect fascinated her, inspired her to elicit more positive responses from him. She stroked the V of his collarbone, then swept her fingers out like conducting a symphony in slow motion, to his shoulders and down his upper arms. Everywhere she touched, his skin grew warmer, as if her hands had the power to ignite him.

His fingers crept beneath her shirt, up along her spine to her bra, which he unlatched. He was about to take her shirt off when she said, "Hang on. Not to be presumptuous, but do you have any condoms?"

"Let me see." She moved aside so he could check his pockets. "Apparently, I wasn't feeling very optimistic today. Do you have any?"

"No. I, um . . . haven't been feeling optimistic for a while now. Let me see if Cass has any."

"Don't let her give you any of those hemp condoms. One word: chafing."

She giggled as she left the room.

A strip of light glowed under Cass's door. Astrid knocked.

"Who is it?"

"Cass, I'm the only other person who lives here." Astrid slipped into the room, closed the door behind her, and paused to take in the scene.

Her roommate was on the floor in the lotus position with a broad sheet of white paper before her. Surrounding it were little pots of paint. Her arms and curly hair were dotted with specks of yellow and red.

"What are you doing?"

Cass held her palms out, which were completely green, and gave her a patronizing look. "Finger painting."

"Of course you are. Listen, do you have any condoms?"

"You got back together with Simon?" Cass tilted her head and grinned, eyes sleepy and bloodshot.

"No, I have somebody over. Not Simon."

"Oh . . ." It took her a long moment to register this fact. "Oh, wow . . ." Her eyes began to close, and her body swayed like it might topple over.

"Cass!"

"Yeah. Mmm . . ." Eyelids back open to their usual half-mast position.

"Condoms."

"Sure, sure." She pointed to her dresser. "Middle drawer. Take as many as you need. The night is long."

Astrid searched through striped rainbow socks and tasseled knit caps until she found a strip of foil squares.

"Thank you!"

She hurried back to Theo, who was standing beside the sewing table.

"Where's your bathroom?"

She pointed the way.

Back in her room, Astrid scrambled to find something more alluring than the beige cotton panties and mismatched white bra she had on, swapped them for a dark and lacy set. A quick swipe of deodorant, comb through the hair, swig of water, and she was ready. Almost. Perfume? All she could find was the vanilla oil Cass had given her for Christmas, so she dabbed some on the insides of her wrists and behind her ears.

The second he closed the door behind him, they came at each other with a new ferocity. This was going to happen. Theo navigated her to the bed and on the way, Astrid tripped over a stray shoe and sent them tumbling onto the mattress. They laughed low, deep-throated laughs, their ankles dangling off the edge, and undressed each other with a greedy impatience. When they were down to their underwear, Theo paused.

"Hey, weren't you wearing a different bra?"

"Um, no."

"Huh. It didn't feel so lacy earlier. You sure you didn't get all sexy for me while I was gone?" He teased.

"You're asking too many questions." She reached for his nipple rings, fingered the area where skin was stretched over metal, and gave the rings a light tug. A happy sigh greeted her, so she tugged again.

He shifted her over so she was completely on top of him, their bodies parallel. Astrid tensed for a moment, prayed for an even distribution of weight, but when she felt him pressing up against her, noticeably aroused, she relaxed and kissed him with no reservations.

"I have another question," he whispered when they stopped to catch their breaths. "Why do you smell like cookies?"

"It's the scented candle."

"The candle is cinnamon. You smell like my favorite Christmas cookies and it's kinda making me crazy."

"Oh yeah? What are you going to do about it?"

He laughed a low dirty laugh and unfastened her bra. Before she could toss it aside, he caught a strap and gave it another look. "Definitely not the same one as earlier."

"Will you please shut up and finish undressing me?"

He complied, and in a surge of boldness she reciprocated, adding his boxers to the pile of discarded clothing beside the bed.

Once they were naked, Astrid felt a contradicting mixture of curiosity and bashfulness. She could only see his body peripherally or up close, as she was touching and kissing it, but she wanted to zoom out and take in his form as a whole. At the same time, a stronger urge pulled her against him, made her wish she could move through him like water.

She got a condom ready, climbed on top of him.

A hush at their joining, an orchestra of synapses firing, even through the veil of tipsiness. She moved against him while his hands navigated her body, their hipbones meeting and softly grinding against each other. It was an ascent with no end, a labyrinth of skin and light and heat.

After a while, Theo said, "This feels great, but I don't think it's gonna happen for me. The alcohol . . ."

"Same here. Let's take a break." She stopped moving and carefully withdrew her body from his. His stomach was damp with sweat, and she licked it as she rolled off. He took off the condom and dropped it in the wastebasket beside her bed.

They lay on their sides facing each other, legs tangled, hands smoothing each other's backs.

"I'm glad you're here," she whispered.

"Me too. This started off as a really bad day."

"It did?"

He closed his eyes, took a long beat before he answered. "That friend of mine who died recently? Well, it happened on Sunday. The funeral was yesterday. I *was* working an intense schedule up to then and I wasn't going to tell my bosses about it, but I needed the day off for the funeral. They told me to take the rest of the week off."

Astrid opened her mouth, but couldn't think of a decent thing to say that wasn't obvious and trite, like *I'm sorry* or *my condolences*. Instead, she stroked his hair, watched his face with utter concentration.

Theo looked past her, breathed in heavy sighs.

"Chris and I went to college together, met in a film class. We were gonna collaborate on a movie script. He was riding his motorcycle and a truck hit him, throwing him off an overpass. He didn't die right away, he was in a coma for a month. So all that time he was here, and he wasn't here."

"Oh my god."

"The funeral was in Rhode Island. There must've been two or three hundred people there." He talked in a low monotone. Astrid massaged the back of his head while he found his words. "After the service, I was at the end of the procession and lost sight of the cars in front of me. I made a few wrong turns and got lost. It took me an extra half hour to reach the cemetery, which was almost funny, like he was fucking with me from the beyond. Practical jokes were his thing. Anyway, his coffin was in a separate room, but I only stayed in there for a few seconds. Chris's brother was there, talking to the coffin, and I couldn't interfere with that. I didn't get my own private moment, but that's okay. I guess I had enough chances to say goodbye at the hospital." He closed his eyes again and took in a ragged breath. He opened them and they were calm, brighter blue, a little bit tired. "So will you tell me about this Simon guy now?"

Astrid frowned and stammered, "Uh . . . You're kidding, right?"

"It'll take my mind off of my drama."

"But . . . my drama is nothing compared to what you've been through. It's so minor, commonplace. It's nowhere near as tragic . . . I mean, nobody *died*."

"Fair enough, but somebody is out of your life, right?"

"Yes . . . Obviously Simon is an ex." She raked her teeth across her lower lip.

"So what happened?"

It wasn't that the story was too personal or even too painful, not anymore. If anything, she worried it was merely too *ordinary*. She told him, anyway:

"Simon was doing a PhD in microbiology at Harvard, and I met him when he was in New York on a visit. He took me to the planetarium on our first date. It was instant whatever-you-want-to-call-it, then we did the long distance thing for a year, alternated Boston and New York visits every other weekend. Eventually I decided to move up here to be with him. I was working as a secretary in a dentist's office back then, so I had no career keeping me in New York, and Boston wasn't so far that I couldn't regularly come back to see friends. He found us an apartment, and I worked at Tower Records for a couple of months before getting the job at the lit agency."

"So what went wrong? He cheated?" Theo twisted his fingers through her hair.

"Yup. The entire time we were dating. I found a box with women's . . . um . . . 'keepsakes' in different sizes a couple of months after moving in. I thought maybe he was a sentimental perv, that they belonged to his exes, but there were also all the late nights at the lab . . . Such a cliché, I know. So I followed him one night and caught him making out with some girl in a library. I thought maybe that was a fluke, so . . ." She looked over at her stacks of books, wished one of them would fall over to create a diversion. If only she and Sally had played The Telekinesis Hour instead of The Psychic Hour. " . . . I didn't say anything."

"Seriously?"

"I know, so dumb. But I was in the thick of it, emotionally. And we had a lease together. A week later I followed him again and . . . saw more. This time in the back seat of his car. Different girl, too. This time I said something. When I confronted him, he got weirdly scientific about the whole thing. He actually tried to rationalize that men aren't monogamous creatures, that their chemistry dictates they should spread their seed."

Theo's eyebrows shot upward. "In other words, he wanted to sleep around and have you be cool with it. Why not tell you all that upfront?"

"That's what I asked him."

"And?"

"Get this. He said it was a biological fact he thought everyone was aware of. He assumed I was smarter than the average woman and didn't go in for all that misleading monogamy propaganda."

"Then why bother to lie and sneak around?"

"Simon believed in privacy, and in keeping part of yourself separate from others to maintain your identity's integrity," she said in a low mocking voice. "His words, not mine."

"What a douchelord. Did you believe all that garbage?"

"Of course not. I moved out the following week."

"Smart girl. He was right about that, at least."

Theo rubbed the back of her neck; she'd tell him just about anything to keep his hands on her.

"He was *that* good at hiding that side of himself, huh?" he asked.

She closed her eyes. "Or maybe I was that good at not seeing it."

"You're too trusting."

"Said the serial killer before claiming his next victim?"

Theo nuzzled her nose. "Come on. I don't murder anyone before the third date. I'm old fashioned that way."

"But not as old fashioned as *the* Old Fashioned."

Low snickers and their faces came in again. Why had kissing never felt so exhilarating before? It was like walking a high wire, falling off, and floating right back up again. Their heated fingertips pressed into each other's smooth skin, and there it was again, that intense current passing back and forth between them.

"I wish we had another condom," he whispered, "so I could redeem myself a little here."

"We do, but let's enjoy this until it starts to make us completely crazy."

"Too late."

But they held out, building anticipation until there was nothing to do but satiate it. This time with Theo on top and Astrid breathing out her affirmation, pulling him in deeper until he found a rhythm in the friction that brought her over. He worked with a quiet ferocity, breath catching in his throat, let out a muted gasp when he was finished.

On his back, he took a moment to catch his breath. "I know I shouldn't ask, but—"

"You have nothing to worry about. Consider yourself redeemed."

They periodically slept, waking up for patches of conversation that evolved into an entirely other language spoken with tongues and hands and limbs entwined, teasing, demanding. Each time an itch that could be scratched but quieted for only so long.

It was dawn, and Astrid kept her eyes half-closed against the silver light, tracing her finger across the smooth arc of Theo's ear, memorizing every curve and bump.

"Do you think you'll ever make your movie?"

"I don't know . . . I'd like to," he said.

"What's standing in the way?"

"Money, time, the usual culprits . . . you need a cast, locations, a solid script—and now I need a new writing partner. But apart from that . . ." He let out a dry laugh.

"Still, I bet you can see the whole movie play out in your head. I bet it's all there."

"It is. But it feels too big to tackle. Every time I start thinking about it . . . I just can't right now."

She smoothed his hair back and kissed the furrowed groove between his eyebrows. He closed his eyes, his breath slow and even. They breathed in sync and drifted off to sleep again.

After what felt like hours, she woke up, checked the clock, and hurriedly began getting dressed.

"What's going on?" he asked through a yawn.

"I'm going to miss my bus."

He found his pants in a crumpled pile of discarded clothing. "What time does it leave?"

"Noon."

He checked his watch. "I don't think you need to rush. It's barely seven."

She stopped short of putting her top on and sat down on the mattress. "Are you kidding? I must've mixed up the hour and second hands on the clock. What is wrong with me?" She flopped back on the bed and he tickled her exposed neck.

"That's a pretty goofy thing to do, Miss O'Malley. Clearly, somebody wasn't paying attention in kindergarten. If it makes you feel any better, I was out sick the day they taught us how to tie our shoes. I still suck at it."

"I'm such a dope."

"So does this mean we can get back in bed?"

"Oh, yeah."

They got under the covers, partially clothed, just as a rainstorm began outside. Astrid hid her face against Theo's chest, inhaling the last traces of his cologne, a lone lemon left in an abandoned log cabin. She curled up against him, sandwiched a knee between his legs, and sighed as his arms closed firmly around her. Her first impression had been spot-on: he did give good hugs.

Astrid slept as if diving under water: deeply but coming up for air often, waking every half hour to check the clock. Each time, she stretched her neck, watched the flicker of Theo's closed eyelids, and curled back into position. Throughout her disjointed slumber, the rain pounded against the window with ferocity, water hitting glass like hailstones, filling the room with its rush and rattle, an alarming lullaby.

Eventually, she couldn't put off getting out of bed any longer. She threw some clothes and toiletries into a small bag while he continued to sleep, brushed her teeth, put on a little make-up, and combed her hair. When she was nearly ready, she kneeled on the mattress and gave him a gentle shake.

Theo opened one eye and grabbed her by the wrists to pull her back down.

"I can't. I have to get to South Station in the next hour and I still need to finish packing. But I'll only be gone for the weekend."

"Can I call you when you get back?"

"Yeah, let me write down my number."

She took the first things that were at hand, an envelope from a piece of junk mail and a vial of liquid eyeliner. She painted her number in fast strokes, waving the envelope until the liner dried.

At the door, she wanted to tell him he was right: the day had been unexpectedly awesome. But she didn't.

They shared an extended kiss on the threshold. Every time they paused, she thought he'd pull away, but he only took another breath and kept kissing her. She didn't want to, but she eventually loosened her arms and stepped back.

They smiled and held hands until he was too far across the threshold and had to let go. She watched him descend the first flight of stairs. When he got to the bottom, he looked up and gave a little wave.

CHAPTER THIRTY-FIVE

Thursday, October 14, 1999

I don't know what to do about Oliver. Maybe I should've called him before the radio show, but I didn't. And as the week goes on, I pick up the phone many times, but don't follow through with his number. At Curio City, I steal hopeful glances through the front window, wondering if he'll turn up again, but he never does.

The ambivalent days pass and my confused resolve holds out until the night before Hell.

If nothing else, I need to hear his voice.

"Oliver? It's Astrid."

"Ah, the prodigal amnesiac returns."

I brush off a twinge of resentment at the comment. Should I open with small talk? Yeah, as if casual conversation is ever possible between us.

"I have another lead on Theo," I say.

"Mazel tov?"

"You sound agitated."

"Do I?"

He definitely does. "Are you upset with me?"

"What's this new lead?" Now he sounds bored.

I tell him about the radio show and the upcoming party at ManRay.

"Don't go," he says.

"Why not?"

"Just don't."

"Is it because you think I won't find him there? Or because you're worried I will?"

"Because I don't want to be the cleanup crew."

"What is *that* supposed to mean?"

"It means that I always take your calls, but I don't know how long I'll be able to do that."

"Oliver, I—"

He hangs up on me. Ouch.

As I return the phone to its cradle, I notice the blinking red light of the answering machine. One unheard message.

BEEP!

"Hi, this is Erin Collins for Astrid O'Malley. Thanks for your letter and the kind words about my cookbook. I'm glad you're enjoying the recipes. As for Theo . . . I wish I could be of more help here, but . . . I have no idea who he is. I'm an only child, so . . . no brother, no half-brother. I don't even know anybody named Theo. I'm not sure what kind of story you were told, but I did want to clear that up. Hope that helps and thanks again."

So . . .

A sick feeling, an oozing, like my insides are being coated in slime. Just as I'm trusting my mind, my memory, and finding balance in the waking world, the floor tilts and I slip sideways.

Sally's in the den, playing Solitaire. I beckon her to my room and bring her up to speed on the cookbook development.

"You had another lead and didn't tell me?"

I stop her potential histrionics short. "Sal, please, *please* can we not make this about you right now?"

She folds her arms across her chest and drops on my bed with only a small huff. "Fine. So what does this mean? That he lied?"

"It could mean that, yeah."

"So what? He was trying to impress you and used that as an excuse to keep flirting with you. Big deal."

"Not all of us are so comfortable with lying." The purse of her mouth tells me to tread lightly. If I'm going to be honest with her, now is the time.

"It's . . ." I rub my temples. "Sometimes I wonder if all of these memories are real. If maybe I didn't . . ."

Spit it out. Say it out loud.

My lips tremble. Oh god, no, please no, not now.

Sally's face is all enthrallment and confusion. "If maybe you didn't what?"

I ball my hands into fists and swallow hard. "I mean . . . what if this is all just . . . what if I . . . imagined Theo? Created him in my mind?"

Airing out my potential lunacy should make me feel better. It doesn't.

"Don't be silly, of course Theo is real." Sally blinks too fast when she says it.

"How do you know that?"

"I just do. And you will too, at the club tomorrow. We're almost there, Astrid. Don't give up on this now. Tomorrow. You'll see."

CHAPTER THIRTY-SIX

I'm standing in front of the angel statue in the public garden. Before me, in a horseshoe formation is a group of reporters gripping microphones, accompanied by cameramen and photographers. Continuous flashbulbs go off, and I can barely see anything.

"Astrid, do you think he's going to show up?"

"Astrid, what outcome are you hoping for when you and Theo are reunited?"

"Astrid, what will you do if Theo doesn't actually exist?"

I have no answers.

I crane my neck, try to see past the crowd.

"Have any of you seen Oliver?" I ask.

One of the reporters steps toward me and thrusts a padded microphone in my face. "Astrid, who's Oliver? You're supposed to be looking for Theo."

"I know," I answer. "But . . ."

There he is, way in the back. Oliver leans against the wrought iron fence of the garden's entrance, arms folded, light glinting off his glasses so I can't make out his expression.

Another microphone held up to my face. "Astrid, you need to answer our questions before it rains or nobody will show up. What does this second man have to do with any of this?"

I try to wave over Oliver but he shakes his head. More blinding flashbulbs go off.

A man dressed in a white wig, dark glasses and black turtleneck steps forward. "Astrid, what would you say if I told you I'm Theo Collins?"

The crowd erupts in murmurs and gasps.

He's impossible to recognize in the Andy Warhol costume. "Take off your wig and sunglasses," I say. "Let me see."

"No, you have to take my word for it," he replies.

A crack of thunder in the distance. I check the spot where Oliver was standing but he's gone now.

"Pack it up, everyone," somebody calls out. "This whole thing is a hoax. There is no Theo."

The crowd disperses as a dark cloud moves in, casts a shadow over me.

The man claiming to be Theo shrugs. "I guess none of it mattered." He turns to walk away. I can't speak, can't move, so I let him.

Another crack of thunder and the skies open up. White feathers rain down on me.

CHAPTER THIRTY-SEVEN

Friday, October 15, 1999

I'm tying the scarf of my Amelia Earhart costume when there's a knock on my door.

Sally does a pirouette in the doorway. She doesn't resemble Marilyn Monroe at all, despite having all the right elements to her visual homage, but she does look sexy as hell.

"Is it too much?" she asks.

"Since when does 'too much' apply to you? You look amazing. It doesn't even look like you're wearing a wig."

"I'm not." She takes my hand and has me fluff her hair, which has been transformed from golden to platinum blonde. "I went to some salon in Davis Square called Judy Jetson, had it cut and dyed. I mean, it's not a proper traumatic breakup unless you do something major to your hair, right?"

"I didn't do anything to mine after I left Simon, but then I guess I've always had it pretty much the same. Yours looks great, though."

"You think so?" She squints at her reflection in the mirror hanging on my closet door. "I thought I should go back to New York somehow different."

"Sal, if you want to stay longer—"

"I do, but I need to go home and deal with things. The police want me to come in for a follow-up interview about Corey. And my boss has been cool about my absence so far, but if I don't leave soon, I won't have a job when I get back, and you know how much that sucks."

"I sure do."

Her eyes are shiny with tears, but she blinks them back. "Anyway, tonight is not about me. For once." She turns around, appraising my ensemble. "The clothes are decent, but let me help you with the makeup."

"I was thinking I'd keep it low key."

She puts a finger over my lips. "Shut up and let me make you beautiful."

I do and this time, I don't wipe away the red lipstick.

"I'm sorry, Sally," I say.

"For what?"

"For not being there for you as much as I should be."

"What are you talking about? You're the best. Always." She gives me a wink that would've done Marilyn proud.

The four of us head to ManRay, a short walk from The Lab, down the street from TT's. Zak and Daphne have dressed up as John F. Kennedy and Jackie post-shooting, replete with fake blood spatters ("I was going to get a fake brain and cover that in blood, too, but I didn't want to carry it around all night," Daphne says).

We turn down Brookline Street and on the next corner, our destination: a low building with no windows painted entirely in black.

A bouncer checks our IDs and lets us in. Sally pays the cover for all of us, waving away any argument.

"It's the least I can do for you all putting up with me this long. Now let's find a bar so I can also buy you drinks."

We trail her to a large, barely lit room with a sunken dance floor and red leather banquets lining the walls. There's a mist of dry ice, which makes dark silhouettes of the five people dancing. Sally was right: they *do* look like they're caught in spiderwebs. The song is one I recognize, an upbeat hit from the '80s, only it's a cover done as funeral march, clanging and dirge-like, low vocals growling the lyrics.

"What's good to drink here?" Sally asks.

"The frozen margaritas pack a punch, but we usually start the night with a mind eraser. It's something of a tradition," Daphne says.

Sally's red mouth opens in a grin of delight. "That sounds completely perfect. What's in it? Never mind, doesn't matter."

"Get one with four straws," she instructs.

The drink is poured, and Daphne has us gather in a small circle. "On the count of three, drink as quickly as possible. One. Two. Three."

We suck down mouthfuls of brown fizzy liquid until only ice is left.

"Welcome to ManRay." Daphne sets down the glass.

Sally buys a proper round of drinks, and a new song begins with a woman shrieking. Daphne and Zak recognize it and go off to dance.

"How are you feeling? Nervous?" Sally shouts over the music.

My drink glows under the black light, and I take a long sip before answering.

Whatever this feeling is, it's not nervous and it doesn't look cute on me. It's more frenetic, and I have to keep tamping down a sense that there's too much hinging on this. "Yeah. I guess. I'm not really sure what I'm going to say to him."

"Well, I wouldn't mention that you've been on this big quest to find him. Hopefully, that Mike guy didn't tell him about the radio show. Say you've been out of town for a while."

"I tried that already," I say. Wait, that didn't really happen, it was one of my dreams. Which didn't end well.

Thankfully she doesn't hear me over the caterwauling. "What?"

"I'll try that. If I even find him."

"You will. Now let's go hunt down Andy Warhol."

She takes my hand and pulls me forward. *I am brave. You are brave.*

We start in the room across the hall, a lounge area with a phone booth, pool table, and some brocaded couches. It's quieter in here, a welcome respite from the industrial clanking in the other room, and my fried nerves begin to settle. Until I see the man perched on the armrest of one of the couches. He's in dark jeans, a black-and-white striped shirt, a shaggy white wig, and opaque sunglasses. I turn so he can't see my face.

It's like I just stepped into an elevator only to find an empty shaft.

"Sally, I think that's him."

"Do you want me to ask for you or do you want to do this yourself?" She peeks over my shoulder conspicuously.

I should be the one to approach him. Sending Sally in my place would reek of schoolgirl hijinks. But I think back to that nightmare of seeing Theo at Curio City and the way he denied being Theo and wouldn't talk to me, would barely even look at me.

"How about this," Sally suggests, "I'll ask, 'Are you Theo?' If he confirms, I'll tug on my earlobe. If he denies, I'll scratch my chin. Got that? Earlobe, yes. Chin, no."

"Why don't you just ask him and wave me over if it's Theo? I don't think I can deal with complicated signals."

"Well, if you're going to be all boring about it . . ."

A few vendors have set up tables on the other side of the room, and I pretend I'm interested in chainmail jewelry while glancing over at Sally and the faux Warhol. I won't need any signals from her after all, because the shake of his head tells me all I need to know.

"Sorry, A," she says when she returns.

"I thought he might've been skinnier than I remember." I'm a seesaw of disappointment and relief.

"We still have the rest of the club to explore, and he might not even be here yet." Sally fingers a large chest piece on a display bust that resembles something you'd wear jousting. The woman behind the table, in a corset that pushes her ample assets nearly to her chin, smiles at us.

"Excuse me. Do you know what time the performances are?" Sally asks her.

"The first one's usually close to midnight, and the second one about an hour after that. They're not very precise about timekeeping, though."

"So he might not even get here for another hour," she says to me.

"That's fine. It's been a month. What's another hour?" I take another sip of my frothy drink to level out the seesaw.

"Let's see what's in the next room." She leads the way once again.

We pass through a doorway beside the phone booth into the main space of the club. At the four corners of the dance floor are oversized black blocks which, along with the stage, provide some of the more attention-seeking patrons space to show off their moves. There's a giant cobweb made of chains strung between two columns; a woman in a black vinyl catsuit dancing on the front blocks holds onto it while she writhes to the music.

Even though I'm halfway done with my drink, I'm already considering a refill, and thankfully there are two bars in here, one along the left wall and a square island by the dance floor. Switching to something nonalcoholic would probably be wise, but tonight I need courage in any form I can get it.

The crowd is split between those in costumes that fit the theme and those dressed in various degrees of goth, referencing Victoriana (top hats, corsets, bustles), fetish (patent leather, fishnet, dog collars), Tim Burton (striped tights, black veils, shredded-on-purpose fabric) and all the shades of black in between. Some have opted for elaborate getups: there's a King Henry VIII and two of his wives (one with a bloody slash across her throat to indicate beheading), and a Marie Antoinette (pre-beheading). Others have taken the dead theme literally, including a zombie Elvis, lifeless Abe Lincoln, and a duo dressed as a post-mortem Janis Joplin and Kurt Cobain. There's a man in tight pants, no shirt and a leather jacket with wavy shoulder length hair but I'm not sure if he's supposed to be dead Jim Morrison or dead Michael Hutchence.

And there, standing at the corner of the island bar, is another Andy Warhol. He also has the wig and dark glasses, but is in a black turtleneck instead of a striped shirt.

Coincidence, right?

"You ready for this one or should I take him?" Sally asks.

"I can do it."

He's paying for a beer as I approach him.

"Um, excuse me," I say. He tilts his head. It's disconcerting not to be able to see his eyes and read his expression. "Is your name Theo?"

"Nope, James. Nice Earhart costume. Buy you a drink?" His eyebrows flicker over the sunglasses.

"Thanks, but I have to find my friend."

I walk back to Sally, shaking my head. "Kind of strange there are two guys dressed as Warhol, don't you think?"

"Not as strange as three." Sally points with her chin at a couple dancing.

This Warhol is also in a turtleneck, but taller than the one I just spoke to. The woman he's with has on heavy eye make-up, chandelier earrings and a leopard coat, presumably his Edie Sedgwick. They dance to a Gary Numan song and make awkward geometric shapes with their bodies. When the song ends, he puts an arm around her waist and kisses the side of her neck as he leads her to a nearby sofa.

"I need another drink." I turn away.

"We have to find out for sure." Sally's mouth forms a grim line. "I'll ask him."

We agree to meet by the pool table in a few minutes.

I return to the front room with the sunken dance floor and take small comfort in the dim lighting and dry ice obscuring forms. This time it's male shrieking over the sound system, a song that thumps and pounds as his gravelly voice begs for a drink. He has the right idea. I get another frozen margarita, cold and sweet and a little tart as it goes down. I walk a few feet and—

No. This can't . . .

I stop so abruptly someone bumps into me from behind.

A visibly peeved dead Brandon Lee in full Crow regalia steps around me, but I'm still locked in place. A few feet away, sitting at the end of a banquette, is yet *another* Andy Warhol. This one has a Polaroid camera suspended around his neck. He slouches back, ankle draped over knee, and looks around at the crowd.

What the hell is going on here?

I take one step toward him, then another. When I stand right in front of him, he lifts the camera, takes aim, and a light flashes in my face. He pats the seat beside him. I take it.

The script is obvious, but stage fright has a hand around my throat and I can't say my lines.

"Um . . . Can I see the picture?" I finally ask.

"You can see it, but you can't keep it."

I hold it by the bottom white border and flap it back and forth to develop it faster.

"That's a myth, you know." The music is too loud to tell whether his voice is familiar.

"What is?"

"That shaking a Polaroid speeds up the development. It doesn't. Doing so can actually damage the picture."

"Oh." I stop waving the photo. "Sorry. I had no idea. Are you a photographer?"

"Tonight I am."

An image of me emerges in the white square, eyes uncertain and a little scared, a novice pilot about to fly treacherous skies.

"What's your name?" I ask.

"Andy."

"Haha, and I'm Amelia. But seriously . . ."

"It's Andy."

"And your last name?"

"Warhol. I would think you'd know who I am."

I cannot believe this guy.

"Would you mind taking off your sunglasses for a second?"

"I would mind, yes." His smile is smug, final.

Okayyyy. Time for a different tactic. "I'm looking for someone dressed as Andy Warhol."

"And so you have found him."

"I mean someone I know. Kind of know."

"We've been chatting for a few minutes now so you could say you 'kind of know' me."

I want to rip the wig right off his head. Instead, I hand him back the Polaroid.

"Have we met before?" I ask.

"Have we?" he echoes.

"Okay, you obviously don't want to be straight with me here."

"'Give a man a mask and he'll tell you the truth.'"

I raise my voice over the music. "I thought you were Andy Warhol, not Oscar Wilde. Way to butcher that quote, by the way."

"I like to think I would've gotten along quite well with Wilde. In some ways we're cut from the same cloth."

"So if a mask will make you honest, why don't you tell *me* the truth?"

"I don't think I need to tell you the truth when this photo does it for me." He holds it out for me to see again.

"And what does this photo tell you?"

"Isn't it rather obvious?" An exaggerated sigh, so put-upon. "If you need it spelled out, the image says, here is a scared girl who does not know what she is seeking."

"I do know." I stand. "I know it's not this."

I walk off and return to the lounge across the way.

Sally is at a vendor display, examining riding crops, ball gags, and various other BDSM toys.

"Something's not right here," I say.

She turns and tickles me with a feather attached to a rod. "It's not my scene, but if people want to bring these into the bedroom, who am I to judge?"

"I mean the Andy Warhol situation. I saw another one just now, and he wouldn't even tell me his name."

Her playful smile fades and she nods. "I saw another Andy in here, too, playing pool. Said his name was John. Wouldn't tell me anything else and played dumb when I asked about Theo. What does that make now, five? What are the odds?"

"Is that the one you talked to?" I point to a wannabe Warhol in the phone booth, this one wearing a leather jacket.

Sally's eyes and mouth make big O's. "That makes *six*. This is so crazy."

My skin, which was pleasantly numb from alcohol, now burns, like it's been rubbed raw with sandpaper. "I'll go talk to this one."

Before I can, Daphne and Zak appear before us, foreheads shiny, sweat mingling with rivulets of fake blood running down their faces. They smile crooked, boozy smiles.

"Sorry we left for a while," Zak says, not looking at all sorry.

"Come to the other room, we want you to meet some of our friends," Daphne urges.

Sally goes to follow, but I hold back. "I'll join you in a few minutes. Need to run to the ladies' first."

"Down those stairs." Daphne points the way. "We'll be in the main room."

I take a few slow steps in the direction of the staircase until they're out of sight, then circle back. The sixth Warhol is stepping out of the phone booth.

"Hi there." I try to keep my voice and smile friendly, but both feel tight, brittle.

"*Hello,*" His deep baritone draws out the word, slowly, with uncertainty.

"You're not Theo by any chance, are you?"

"I am not."

"Are you Mike?"

"Nope."

"Are you friends with Mike?"

"Doesn't everyone have a friend named Mike?" I can just make out his eyes behind his sunglasses; he's looking at me dubiously, he wants to get away from me.

"Look, there are a lot of guys here tonight dressed as Andy Warhol," I say.

"So? I saw at least two guys dressed like The Crow. Excuse me." He turns away.

This is ridiculous. I grab one of his leather sleeves.

"Wait. Just hang on." He turns back. "Is this some big joke? Did Mike put you all up to this? Or Theo? I *have* to know." My eyes get wet with big, baffled tears. I will *not* lose it in the middle of this club, so I blink them away.

The man sighs and takes off his sunglasses. His eyes are brown. He's nobody I recognize. "I don't know why you're getting so fired up about this. Mike thought it would be cool for a bunch of us to dress up as Andy Warhol, that's all. I don't know this Theo guy or what he has to do with anything. *Okay*?"

"Okay." I nod.

He walks off and I blink and breathe rapidly. Hold steady. I step into the phone booth, rest my head on the glass door, and pick up the receiver.

Before I can dial, a male voice on the other end answers.

"How can I help you?" He's hard to hear over the cheery, booming OMD song in the background on his end.

"Who is this?" I ask.

"Evan, the DJ. You have a request?"

"Oh. No. Sorry." I hang up and notice the phone has no dial pad.

I have to get out of here.

"Astrid? Hey, Astrid," a voice calls out from across the room.

It's Nadia, who comes barreling toward me before I can escape.

"You look great," she says. "Amelia Earhart, right?"

I can't do this right now. But I also can't be rude. "Yeah. And you . . ." I survey her prim puffy-sleeved dress and old-timey updo.

"Lizzie Borden." She holds up a bloody plastic ax. "Wait until you hear the new dirt I got on Simon."

"Listen, I'd love to get all the gossip but—hold on, I ran into you last month. At Deli Haus." *With Theo.* "Do you remember?"

She tilts her head and squints. "Last month . . ."

If she can place me with Theo, it means I have a witness. It means Theo is real.

"You told me all about Simon getting fired from that movie poster store," I prompt.

"Right! And check this out, he's so broke he had to *move back in with his mother.* At thirty-two!"

I grasp the ends of my scarf in tight fists and shake my head. "I can't believe it. That's . . ."

"Karma in action is what it is." She holds up the ax in triumph.

"So when you saw me at Deli Haus last month, I was there with someone, right?"

"Huh?"

"Do you remember the guy I was with?" That last flame of maybe flickers. *Come on, Nadia.*

"I remember talking to you . . ." She lowers the ax and gives me an apologetic face. "But I thought you were there alone. Why?"

And just like that, it's extinguished. The edges of the room grow dim, the air seeps out of it.

"I could be remembering wrong," she says. "Hey, are you alright? They're mixing the drinks strong tonight, huh? Do you need—"

"I'm fine. I'm just—I'll be . . ." My voice so high and pinched, my smile hard and tight as everything behind it collapses. "I gotta go."

That's it. I'm done. I've already been here too long.

Outside, I pass a couple of goths in velvet capes smoking cloves, and the spicy, earthy scent follows me up the block. Across the street a cluster of people gathers outside TT's and their shrill laughs pierce through me like spikes. I head toward Mass Ave, arms wrapped around my middle as if I'm a ragdoll and my stitching is coming loose. One misstep and my guts will spill to the ground. This headache is late to the party but makes up for lost time with precise bludgeons to the base of my skull. I take off the aviator hat, toss it into the nearest trashcan, and push the pain back with clueless determination.

I did my best, Amelia, but my plane is going down.

I can't go back, and I can't go home.

Why did I waste my time with this search? I became so fixated; I took the tangible for granted, fenced off the people around me who actually gave a shit. How much of my waking life did I nearly sabotage by pursuing this figment? How much did I fuck things up with Oliver?

I thought I was being intrepid. What a joke. After all these years, I still can't tell the difference between brave and foolish.

Ahead of me is a pay phone. The same one Oliver called on that rainy night when things were scary and strange but not slipping away from me at such an alarming rate. I pick up the receiver and . . . There's only a dial tone. My laugh tastes as bitter as it sounds. Did I really think he'd be on the other end, that it would be so easy? At least I have a quarter, so small mercies and all that.

Oliver picks up on the third ring.

This blockade that tames the mess of me is ready to crash forward; it's at the back of my throat and it's tight and it's cracking. The invaders are at the door with their battering rams and there is so little defense and so very much splintering.

"It's . . . me." I have no right to identify myself this way, but two syllables is all I can manage. I swallow. I hold it all back. It's not going to last.

"What's wrong? Are you hurt? Where are you?" His voice has no trace of the detachment from our last conversation. It's softer, concerned. The goddamn civility of it is enough to release my tears.

Fuck.

"I'm fine." And then it's a race to beat the sobbing, which is coming up fast. "I'm at the payphone you called me on before, outside Hi-Fi Pizza. Can you please come get me?" If he asks me to explain, my insides will avalanche and I'll be on my knees and he won't be able to hear through my whimpers and I don't have enough quarters for that.

"I'll be there as soon as I can. Where do you want me to meet you?"

He's coming. *Breathe.*

The fact of his imminent arrival clears enough space in my airway to answer. "Here."

"It's going to rain and I don't want you on the street. At least wait in the pizza place. Can you do that?"

I nod, take in gulps of air.

"Astrid?"

That's right, the rules of radio also apply to the rules of the telephone. No nonverbal answers.

"Yes. I'll wait inside."

The dam is fortified, my lungs resume their job, and I wipe my face free of tears. I fish out another quarter and call The Lab. Keep my voice steady as I leave a message saying I had a headache, ran into Minerva, and am crashing at her place again. Only partly a lie, because the throbbing at the apex of my neck is still there. One novel thing about it, I never know what part of my head the pain will invade, like a nasty intruder that sometimes comes in through the front door, sometimes through the back, and sometimes through a window.

Inside Hi-Fi, the light is too bright; it bounces off the pale floor tiles and anemic walls. I buy a soda and don't drink it, instead let the condensation drip down the waxy side of the cup as I sit hunched over at a table by the door. Hopefully, my friends are sufficiently distracted that they don't come looking for me.

It begins to drizzle while I wait, and the passersby quicken their pace and tuck their heads into their shoulders like turtles, most unprepared for the weather. The drizzle turns to rain, and I watch the droplets on the glass storefront racing down in wavy patterns.

Time passes; I don't know how much before Oliver's face finally appears in the window, slightly distorted by the rain-patterned glass, eyes searching until they find me.

Thank you.

I stand as he crosses the threshold.

"Flat soda?" I offer the damp cup.

He looks thrown, doesn't answer for a second. "No thanks. Now what's going on?"

"Let's walk." I throw away the paper cup and put a hand on the door to leave. He puts his hand over mine to slow me down.

"Where are we going? It's raining. And it's nearly midnight."

"I know." The performance at ManRay should begin soon, and a sick part of me wonders if maybe . . . Maybe what? Maybe more vague but ever-present humiliation awaits me? Maybe more Andy Warhols to smirk, shrug, deny? Maybe more fucking with my head, which is already fucked to the limit? No, thank you. I'm done.

I tug on the door handle. "Let's just walk. Please."

He acquiesces, and we step out into the rain, which adds a layer of noise to the evening air, a static blurred by the shush and surge of passing cars.

This rain is . . . These cars are . . . Oliver is . . . I don't even know anymore.

I lead us toward the Mass Ave Bridge, always that damn bridge, though I know we won't make it that far. Oliver gives me a single block of quiet. He's silent as we pass the hardware store, the coffee shop. At the next crosswalk, he takes my elbow and pivots in front of me.

His glasses are streaked with rain, but the eyes behind them are severely blue. Not the lazy-hazy shade of Theo's, but a crisper opaque hue.

What do you want? Oliver asks without asking. He'll give, within reason, but he needs to know what he's giving and why.

"I want to go somewhere quiet and private that's not my place and not your place." I have to raise my voice a notch over the storm, which strips the sweetness out of it, hardens my plaintive tone.

"Where then?"

"It's not far."

I reach for his hand and he lets me take it. Hand in damp hand, we go to the Hotel @MIT, and I check us in for one night.

Oliver says nothing in the elevator and is so still he could out-statue that living statue in Central Square. Would giving him a quarter get him to move? A flash of queasiness punishes the thought. He could've chosen not to be here right now. He could've left me alone with my drama and whims and confusion (is that what we're calling it now? *Confusion*?). But he didn't. He's here and he's real and if he can't do more than tolerate me on a basic level, that's still a lot.

The room could be the same one I stayed in last month, with the same view of the third floor garden. But it's a hotel, its rooms identical decorated boxes, there to evoke a generic comfort for all who enter. I don't feel it yet.

"I never noticed these curtains had mathematical formulas stitched into them." I say this pointless thing to Oliver, who is across the room, who is maybe deciding if he'll stay, maybe calibrating how much more crazy he can deal with tonight.

"Do you want a drink? I'm going to make myself one," he says.

"Sure. I can go get us some ice," I offer.

"No need."

He pulls two small bottles of whiskey out of the mini-bar, which glow like amber jewels, flips the glasses, pours from the bottles like a storybook giant, Gulliver as bartender, pops open a can of Coke, adds a splash here, a splash there. He holds out my drink.

I take it and sit on the edge of the bed. He sits in the desk chair. Our knees are inches apart, but it could be feet, miles.

"First of all, thank you." I knock back my drink and shudder.

"For what?" A wry twitch from the corner of his mouth.

I can turn this around. Rebuild. Fortify.

"I've been an idiot," I begin, but he won't let me unfurl any precious monologue.

"Let me guess why I'm here. You want to apologize. And then seduce me."

I'm like a fish pulled out of the water, dangling on a line, mouth opening and closing.

"Astrid, I'm sorry for whatever emotional breakdown you had or are having or are about to have. But you've been so absorbed in this one lost day that you've . . ."

"Gotten lost myself?"

"I would have put it in a less melodramatic way, but yes."

"You're the one who told me I was going to go on a quest. Isn't that pretty melodramatic, too? What did you expect? You indulged me in it, gave me just enough support to keep me going, to keep me intrigued, but at the same time . . ."

"At the same time what?" His eyes don't challenge or mock, not yet.

"It's like you've been waiting for me to snap out of my post-traumatic whatever-the-hell-this-is, drop the search, and choose you instead."

"*Me*? You mean a *real life person* instead of one you may or may not actually remember? Who may or may not even *exist*? Who, even if he weren't a figment, would've probably found a way to track you down by now if he was interested? Imagine that." He drains his glass, and I expect him to slam it onto the desk but it goes down softly.

Some people intimidate through strength and noise, inflict their tremors using fast fists and loud words. Oliver is the opposite. He maintains a near-violence in his stillness, conjures a silence that makes me want to fold in on myself. His wordless gaze runs an icy finger through me, leaves me in two pieces.

"I don't understand. If you think I might be so *crazy*" —I wave my hands around—"why are you even interested in me?"

"Oh no, no, no. We are not going to turn this into the Astrid Appreciation Hour where I list your fine attributes again. Though I will say this, your tenuous grip on reality is not one of them."

What can I say to that?

Nothing, so we're back in an arctic pit of silence. What I imagined could be a cozy indulgent pity party for me has instead added a new layer of shame to my evening. And it's exactly what I deserve: a nice big slice of reality cake.

"You're right," I say. "I don't know what memories of that lost day I can trust, and Theo . . . I don't know about him, either. But after tonight, it doesn't matter."

He doesn't ask, but arches an eyebrow that says, *I did tell you not to go.*

My own eyebrows twist in contrition. *I should have listened.*

He stands up. "Well, I wanted to make sure you were . . . not in any real danger . . . and you seem . . . reasonably okay."

But I'm not.

There's a movie where the guy is trying to keep the girl from leaving, and he says, let's pretend whatever it is I could tell you that would make you stay, that I just said it. I'm messing up the lines and I don't remember if she stays, but it was a beautiful copout. And even as I try to string together the right words, I know that's not what'll matter to Oliver here. No grandiose speech will sway him. There is no correct password. I only know this: if anything I say next rings false, he'll lock himself up for good, and he will leave.

"I was embarrassed," I begin. "*Am* embarrassed. And delusional. It's kind of hard to admit that you're not sure of . . . what's real. It's been easier focusing on this search . . ."Already so exposed, I don't know how to continue.

"I didn't think you'd pursue it this long."

What am I even pursuing at this point? It's not sustainable, chasing a ghost. Either he'll materialize or remain in smoke and flashbacks. And if he does appear, how could he ever match my expectations? A physical form says the wrong things, tarnishes, disappoints. Oliver and I both know this. I've been holding onto the idea of Theo like a new penny in my fist, shiny and worth little.

"Oliver," I say his name, roll it around in my mouth like the fine wines I was never able to appreciate. "There have been moments when I put all my bullshit to the side . . . moments between you and me that have been kind of great, even when they were complicated."

"They didn't have to be that complicated." He takes a step away from me.

"You're right. I want to un-complicate."

"Until the next clue, the next flashback, the next 'memory' that sets your inner Don Quixote in motion again."

"No. I'm finished with all that."

"I don't believe you."

Another step away from me. This is unbearable.

The idea of any more space between us is unthinkable, and if the price of proximity is burying one blurry gone day of my life, I'll pay it.

But is it too late?

I block his way to the door. "You have to believe me. You have your special powers, right? So if I'm full of shit, you'd know."

"It doesn't work like that, hardly ever. I'm perceptive, but I'm not a human lie detector."

The gates are closing, and I have to get inside. If he leaves now, that's it.

I put a hand up to his cheek, like a security checkpoint at a high tech fortress. I'm at the mercy of my fingerprint whorls, my map of palm lines. He doesn't move, but closes his eyes.

Let.

Me.

In.

And then a small clearance: the faint pressure of his face against my palm.

I step forward, through.

God, we're both drenched.

"Let me get you a towel," I say.

He shakes his head. I move aside some loose pieces of wet hair that have fallen into his eyes. He lets me. I take this as a good sign.

Either the temperature in here has dropped or my body has finally registered it as shiver-inducing. My teeth give a little chatter, tap dance against each other.

He looks at my mouth and says, "Your lips are blue."

"I should find the thermostat."

"Don't." He picks up the end of my braid and squeezes it until water drips between his knuckles. His jaw relaxes and his eyes take on a dreamy cast.

I grab fistfuls of his black T-shirt and wring water from it. He chuckles.

"You must be freezing," he murmurs.

I nod. He slips the jacket from my shoulders.

"That doesn't help," I say.

"Shh."

He unbuttons my shirt enough to slip it halfway down my arms and gets in close, breathes along my neck. I close my eyes and offer it to him in classic vampire victim pose, but he's already moving further down, to my shoulder, then my collarbone. He slowly licks along the edge of my clavicle, down to the hollow, where he fills it with warm air before licking across the other side, at the same deliberate pace. Holy hell, how is he finding all these nerve endings?

"I have really been wanting to do that," he whispers, then darts his tongue into my ear, a sexy punctuation.

I move to unbutton the rest of my shirt, and he guides my hands back at my sides.

"Open your eyes," he tells me.

I do.

He looks at me through rain-mottled glasses, takes them off, and those scary blue irises are full of lust and questions and an overall warning of I'll-give-you-the-benefit-of-the-doubt-this-time-but-don't-fuck-with-me.

I won't.

He removes his jacket, but before he can get to the shirt, I ask, "Can I?"

A half-smile, enough of an affirmation for me to proceed.

I want to tear it off of him, but I also want to linger on this threshold. Give him the same knee-weakening shivers he gave me. I put my hands under the wet fabric, where my thumbs find the dimples in his lower back and run small circles. I bring the hem of his shirt high enough for me to lick beneath his lower ribs, the taste of his skin salty and metallic. His stomach is damp with rain, covered in goose bumps, and I run my tongue along those, too.

This shirt has to go. He raises his arms, helps me shrug him out of it.

It's my turn to be freed of some clothing, if we're going to be fair about it, but I wait.

There's a pause where we stand there staring at each other, like opponents in a ring about to go at it, breathing hard, mentally preparing for the physical bout.

Oliver bites his lower lip and then it's goodbye to restraint as we are all over each other, racing to unbutton, unbuckle, pull or tear any fabric that obstructs bare skin. But we don't tussle like boxers, more like kittens. We scratch and nip at each other as we roll around.

"We'll do this slow and sweet later, but not right now," he says while I'm on my stomach, and he's stretched out on top of me.

He has to have me and I have to have him, so I let him in. Halfway through, he flips me over, my heels on his shoulders. Our bodies are still wet with rain and now wetter still, but I am not cold at all; I am embers brought to fiery life. I am burning from the inside out.

Afterwards, we're perpendicular on the bed, and I could sleep like this, feet dangling off the edge, bare limbs overlapping. Oliver disentangles himself and I grunt in protest.

"I'm going to turn the lights off. Get under the covers."

"I like you bossy." I comply.

"Yeah, if I tell you to do something you already want to do."

The only remaining light is coming from a digital clock, which he covers with a pillow.

"Marco," he whispers as he slips in beside me.

"Polo," I whisper back.

"Get a little bit of sleep, but not too much, because I'm going to wake you up. A lot."

He's right. I don't mind him bossy when he's telling me to do something I want to do.

Neither of us gets much sleep.

CHAPTER THIRTY-EIGHT

I'm sitting in a wooden booth, in some Irish pub. I look out the window; across the street is the Central Square Blockbuster Video. Which means this can only be one place: the Phoenix Landing.

A pint of Guinness is placed before me.

"I didn't order this," I say.

"It's what you were drinking last time."

"Last . . .?" I freeze as Theo slides into the bench across from me.

"Are you who I think you are?" I'm cautious. I don't want to play this game again.

A sly smirk. "Tom Collins. But I go by my middle name: Theo. I hear you've been looking for me. I wanted to clear up a few things."

The stout is cold and sour. I can barely swallow it over the lump in my throat. "Okay."

"Which version do you want? The one where you imagined me? The one where you're dead and this is your afterlife?" A soft laugh full of mockery. "Or maybe the one

where Oliver and I are the same person? That would make things so easy, wouldn't it?" His eyes flicker from cloudy blue to Oliver's indigo and back again, his hair darkens and returns to sandy blond.

"Tell me the truth. That's all I ever wanted."

"No, you wanted more than that. A lot more. You wanted a perfect day. One that never existed."

I shake my head and stare into my glass. "But it did. We had the kind of day I thought only happened to other people. In movies." My hands tremble. Theo puts a broad palm over them to steady the shaking.

"It didn't happen like that," he says.

It takes tremendous courage to look at him because I know I'll see things I don't want to, and I do: hesitation, sadness, and — god, it's so plain in his face, so awful — pity.

"What . . ." I struggle to quell the tremor in my voice, "What do you mean? Didn't I meet you that day?"

He licks his lips and threads his fingers through that soft, soft hair.

"We did meet, but at night. Here."

I glance at our surroundings. It could be any bar in the world; it's so ordinary.

"We met in the Harvard Bookstore . . ." I begin. I know this now.

"No, Astrid."

" . . . and then we crossed the Mass Ave Bridge and — "

"We didn't."

"Then we went to Deli Haus — "

"That's not — "

"And then the movies," I interrupt his interrupting. "Then the Copley fountain, which was filled with bubbles, then the teddy bear statue outside FAO Schwarz, where we kissed."

"Astrid, I—"

"Then we had dinner in Chinatown, then we did karaoke somewhere in Downtown Crossing. And then you came back to my place." So ugly, this desperation in my voice.

Theo holds his fingertips together and presses them against his chin like he's praying. "We did end up going to your place. But that's it. I wasn't at any of those other places. You were alone all day."

"No."

"Yes. I met you at this bar, while you were waiting for the bathroom. I bought you a drink, and we talked for a while. You said you took the afternoon off and spent the day walking all over the city. We had a few more drinks and . . . Well, you know how those things go."

The skin on my face feels like it's melting off. "No. I don't know how those things go because that's not how this thing happened. I finally remember everything. You can't change the story on me now," I choke out the words.

"I'm just presenting the facts. I'm sorry they don't fit into the little fairy tale you created." His voice pretends it's soft, but there's a hidden sharpness to it, a bed of nails under a flimsy layer of cotton.

"You're only saying that because I chose to stop looking for you. Because I'm with Oliver now."

"Is that what you think?" He grins with his mouth, but the cloudy eyes are mirthless. I didn't know a smile could be so cruel. "You think you'll ever really stop looking for me?"

"I already did."

"And yet here I am."

384 ⌒ ASLEEP FROM DAY

It's time to go. I slide out of the booth.

He grips my wrist. "Hey. We had fun. Even if you remember it a little differently."

I grit my teeth. "Let go of me."

Theo shrugs with one shoulder. "Okay, but take this." He hands me an umbrella.

"Big storm on the way. You're gonna need it." He winks.

CHAPTER THIRTY-NINE

Saturday, October 16, 1999

A faint metal clank makes me sit up with a gasp, as if waking to a gunshot.

I open my eyes and there's a sliver of sunlight cutting a yellow line across the bed. Oliver is putting on his pants, buckling his belt.

"Nightmare?" he asks.

I shrug. "I guess the sudden noise ... I don't know."

"Because I was going to tell you, you really *did* do all those things with me last night." A tentative smile, laced with a question mark.

"Oh, I remember all that. I know it really happened."

"You damn well better." He bends to kiss the top of my head. "I wish I could take you out for a big breakfast, but I have some apartments to show today. And I'm going to Waltham for an all-day training seminar tomorrow, so how about dinner Monday?"

"Sounds good."

"For the record, if it was up to me, I'd spend all day in this bed with you."

"That would be amazing. But I also have to work today. Those skulls aren't going to sell themselves."

"Well, when I get back," he brings his face in close, "we might have to pick a day where we both call in sick."

One final kiss, and he leaves.

I blink a few times, get out of bed, and put on a bathrobe.

I sit at the desk and find the hotel stationary and a pen.

Write it down before you forget again.

My scribbles are hesitant at first, but become more assertive. I almost wish I didn't remember all of it, but I do. Theo in my apartment, the rain, the sex.

I think back to my conversation with the pretentious Warhol who took my picture, about wearing masks and telling the truth. Then I recall my favorite Oscar Wilde quote: "There are only two tragedies in life: one is not getting what one wants, and the other is getting it."

Yes.

Fuck.

Yes.

I check out of the hotel and return to The Lab, where I change out of my Amelia Earhart clothes and into jeans and a light sweater. On my desk is the piece of paper with the Theo list and the map I drew on the back. I crumple it up and throw it in the empty wastebasket by my dresser. There's just enough time for a quick breakfast before work.

Sally's waiting in the kitchen like a spider in the center of her web.

"Finally! Where have you been?" She hands me a plate of cold toast.

I take a slice. "Thanks. I was at Minerva's. I left a message."

"We were worried when you disappeared."

"Naw, you probably wondered where I was for a minute or two, then flirted with some vampire-y guy and ended up sucking face with him."

She gives me a look that tells me I am exactly correct. One thing I love about Sally: I can always see through her masks.

"Did you ever find Theo?" she asks.

I spread peanut butter on my toast, take a gooey bite, and talk through it. "At last night's Andy Warhol convention? No, I've had enough. I've quit the Theo business. The search is off."

She jolts her head back as if I punched her in the nose. "What do you mean, you *quit*? You were so close to finding him."

"Yeah, but . . . If things happened the way I *think* I remember them, if it mattered to him, *he* would've found *me* by now. I've been so wrapped up in this Theo thing, it started taking over my life, taking me *away* from my life. Away from what's in front of me. I don't know, maybe it was my way of dealing with the accident." I eat the toast in five big bites. God, I am so hungry.

Sally's hands flutter the way they do when she's disconcerted, nervous jazz hands. "No, I think it's more than that. It meant something to you. *Means* something to you. You can't give up just like that."

This is where I could tell her about Oliver, where I *should* tell her. But there isn't enough time before I need to leave for work, and besides, it's still too soon. I want to savor my recent memories of him, have them belong only to me for a few hours, to turn them over like precious stones and admire every facet. I also don't want Oliver to get the brunt of her dismay; I can already hear her asking why we spent all this time looking for Theo when I had someone else waiting in the wings. No. Better to save that conversation for later.

"I'm not giving up, Sal, I'm moving on. Looking for Theo has been overwhelming and embarrassing. It's put my job at risk, my relationships—it's made me question my fucking sanity." Sally's eyebrows steeple in alarm. "I'm fine now, really. I just don't want to spend any more time on a dead end, which is what this is." Her mouth opens to protest, but I won't let her dissuade me. "Let's not argue. I can't be late for work." I scoop stray crumbs from the counter into my hand, dust them off in the sink.

"I want to hear all about your night when I get back," I add over my shoulder as I head out. "We have a lot to catch up on. Later."

Except that later doesn't happen, because when I get home from work that night, Sally is gone. There's a bouquet of sunflowers on the kitchen table with a thank you card addressed to the three of us. The note inside is brief, generic: *Thank you for letting me stay. I'm ready to move on now. You have all been wonderful.*

"Fuck," I mutter.

Why would she leave like this? I was *this close* to telling her everything, all the secrets, all the fragments of truth I'd concealed. Coming clean to Oliver last night wasn't enough—I have to confess more. This burden of withholding has grown so heavy, and who better to open up to than my oldest friend? Sally wouldn't have judged me. She's tolerated my default tendency to hide, but she's always coaxed me to fight it, to show myself. And now that I'm ready to reveal more—now that the candor is frothing inside of me, ready to erupt—she isn't here.

The phone rings. It's my father.

"You haven't returned my messages. Is everything okay?" The way he asks, he expects a dismissal of his concerns.

"Everything's fine," I begin, but stop short. Is this how I want to continue with him? To reassure, obfuscate, and maintain a polite façade? To remain near-strangers? Robin believes courage lies in stoicism and silence, but maybe he has it all wrong. Maybe he has *me* all wrong.

"Actually, things have been really fucked up," I say. "They're okay now, but they haven't been. I won't get into all of it right now—not because you don't want to hear it, but because we should talk about some things face to face. Maybe you could come visit."

His voice creaks with reluctance. "I'd like to, really. But the *Rent* rehearsal schedule is ramping up and—"

"I'd like you to make time for me. It's important."
Wow. I've never said such a thing to him before.

"Should I be worried?"

"I'm your daughter, shouldn't you always be worried about me?" The last words crack as they come out. "It's exhausting keeping so much hidden. Don't you get tired of it?" I slump into a chair, anchor my elbows to the table. "I want you to tell me about Mom. I know what really happened to her. But you've never shared your memories of her. It's painful for you, I get that, but it hurts not to know who she was. Or who you are, beyond all the theater stuff. And . . ." Fuck it. I let the tears go. "It hurts that you don't know me."

"Come on, Astrid, of course I know you."

"You really don't. And that's partially my fault. But I'd like that to change. I don't need us to be super-close, or to even call you 'Dad' but . . . I don't want to tiptoe around you anymore and make it easy for you to ignore me."

There's jagged breathing on the other line. I grab a napkin off the table and blow my nose. An ache within me predicts more tears on the horizon, but I'll cry them and then I'll move on. No matter what.

"What if . . ." He clears his throat. "I could come up to Boston next weekend."

The sunflower's petals are silky beneath my fingertips. Fragile, like most beautiful things.

"That would be nice," I say.

Sunday, October 17, 1999

It's my day off and there's a low humming in my brain that'll turn into a full blown headache if I'm not careful, so I head to 1369, a nearby coffee shop. I order something with many shots of espresso from a surly barista with a row of small silver hoops covering her ear cartilage like a mini-barbed wire fence. As I wait for my drink, I turn to a bulletin board for local services and announcements. Bands looking for drummers (always drummers, sometimes bassists; I guess everyone thinks they can sing and play guitar), tenants looking for roommates, babysitting services, poetry slams and open mic nights, clothing swaps, a pet ferret up for adoption, various items for sale (vintage suitcases, a collection of Beanie babies, Danzig concert tickets), a flier looking for—

STOP.

I take down the neon yellow paper and read:

LOOKING FOR THEO COLLINS
TALL, LIGHT HAIR, BLUE EYES,
MID-20s, AVERAGE BUILD.
NEED TO GET IN TOUCH WITH HIM ASAP.
IF YOU HAVE ANY LEADS, PLEASE EMAIL
LOOKINGFORTHEO@HOTMAIL.COM.

Oh god oh god oh god oh god.

"Astrid, Americano."

I grab my coffee and book it home.

Okay, where can I find traces of Sally's meddling? I search the living room, the den, the kitchen, but

there's nothing. I ransack every corner of my room—
desk, bed, dresser drawers. More nothing.

Check again.

Another search of the desk and . . . Oh no. Under
an issue of the *Improper Bostonian* is the piece of paper I
threw out yesterday, my Theo Rosetta Stone. It's been
flattened out and on the back of the list where I drew
the map, in the upper right-hand corner is a smiley
face.

Damn it, Sally, what did you do?

Let's take a minute here. Should I call Oliver? He's
out of town, so I'd have to leave a message. I could tell
him what I found, that it was all my best friend's
doing . . . but what if he doesn't believe me? What if
there's enough doubt to poison what happened
between us the other night? Leaving such a message
might make things tense again. Alternately, I could go
try to take down the fliers before he gets back from his
training seminar. And once things are cool between us,
I'll tell him about Sally's stunt and we'll have a good
laugh over it. That makes more sense than leaving him
some convoluted message, right?

Wrong. I can't revert back to my habit of hiding
and holding back. Oliver deserves the truth. Now.

I get the cordless from the kitchen and dial his
number. It rings. And rings. No answer, no machine.
Did he forget to switch it on? I call a few more times,
but get the same series of rings.

Well, at least I can avoid the discomfort of
explaining the fliers a little longer.

But that also means I better hurry and tear those
damn things down before he sees one of them.

I put on my sneakers. It's going to be a long day.

One thing I have to say for Sally, she doesn't do anything halfway. She didn't throw up a couple of fliers on some bulletin boards and leave it at that; she charmed her way into the store windows of 7-11 and CVS and Hubba Hubba and even the drag queen shoe store. Now I have to charm her fliers out of those establishments and others, which is easy enough ("we found Theo, thanks for your help," etc.) but time-consuming and tedious as I untangle the knots of her good deed.

My misguided friend also taped fliers to the lampposts for good measure and used packing tape to keep them secure, so I have to buy an X-ACTO knife from Pearl (where—surprise!—there's another Theo flier that needs to be removed) so I can cut them down. It takes me over an hour to clear the area between Central Square and the Mass Ave Bridge.

The thing is, I can't get angry with her for this, not after what she's been through with Corey, and my withholding so much, and then surrendering the search for Theo. When she turned twenty-one, Sally and I took a trip to the Mohegan Sun Casino to celebrate her birthday. She insisted we play blackjack, because it was one of the games with the best odds. Whenever she or I won a hand, she'd pump her fist with a triumphant "yes!" equally happy regardless of which of us beat the dealer. If one of us won, in her mind, we both won. This little stunt of hers is similar in spirit: she wanted one of us to win.

Except that this could actually make me lose, big time. God, the thought of Oliver finding one of these fliers . . . The vaguest threat of it spurs me on, makes me rush down the street with my X-ACTO like a mad slasher in a horror movie.

Over the bridge to Kenmore Square, into Deli Haus and the nearby independent record stores, down go the fliers ("Thanks again for letting us put these up. Who knows, maybe this was the one that helped us find him!"). At a pay phone, another call to Oliver yields more unanswered rings, so onward I go. Down Mass Ave and over to Boylston, where I stop at a Dunkin' Donuts for more coffee to get me through the next stretch. Past Copley Square and the fountain stands there dry, bubble- and water-free.

It's like reliving parts of the lost day in fast-forward, a blur of dialogue and action, a glitch in the video that strips out the leading man.

It's been over a month since that so-called perfect day. I don't know if I remembered it right, and I might never know. Better to keep my version undisputed, even if it's too ornate, too expansive, too much. Maybe it's more the day I wanted than the day I had. Maybe my brain got rattled in the accident and won't ever be the same. Maybe you get these days woven into your life, and then all you can do is let them go and continue forward, even if the ones that follow are less dazzling. With every flier I remove, every step I take deeper into the heart of Boston, I make a little more peace with that day and let it lie where it belongs, in it's 9/9/99 slot. Like a librarian with a stack of books, I catalog each memory and move to the next aisle, let the titles remain in their proper shelves.

There will be other great days, whether I have them alone or with Oliver or my friends or maybe even my father. I have new days to look forward to, new plans to make. I'm going to save up money so Sally and I can finally take our cross-country trip. I'm going to call Jasleen and see if she can help me find a new job in publishing. I'm going to cook my vegetable lasagna for Oliver.

Instead of piecing together an old reality, I will create a new one.

It's dark by the time I reach the bronze bear outside FAO Schwarz. I'm exhausted, but push myself toward Chinatown, where I get lost in the twist of incoherent streets. I have no idea how far Sally might've gone or if I took down every flier. I hope, I hope, I hope.

I take a taxi home and try Oliver's number again.

It rings and rings and rings.

CHAPTER FORTY

9/10/99

Astrid was on the green line heading to Park Street, her duffle bag on the seat beside her. She prayed for a speedy transfer to the red line; she was cutting it close. Her nerves jangled with happy disruption. In her head was a melody she couldn't make proper sense of, a cat walking across piano keys.

She might miss her bus. She tried not to worry.

Maybe reading would provide a good distraction. At least until she was on the Greyhound and had ample time to replay, review, relive every moment spent with Theo. She took out a book but ignored the words on the page.

"That's an unusual talent."

Before her stood a tall bespectacled man, dark hair falling into his eyes, amusement at the corners of his mouth.

"What is?" she asked.

"Being able to read upside down." He pointed to her book.

"Oh." She glanced at the cover of *Memoirs of a Geisha*, turned the paperback the right way around. "I guess my mind is somewhere else."

"Worried you might miss your bus?"

Now he had her full attention. "How did you know?"

A bony shrug. "Just a guess. I'm Oliver."

He held out a hand. Astrid hesitated, but shook it. His palm was warm, his grip confident.

"Take the next one," he urged.

"What?"

"This is going to sound strange, but hear me out. I think you should miss your bus on purpose and take the next one."

"Why?" She stared at him, baffled, dazed.

"So you can get a cup of coffee with me."

"I don't know you."

"If you get coffee with me, you'll get to know me. I think you'll like me." The words carried more levity than arrogance.

Park Street was announced over the loudspeakers. Astrid stood up.

"I . . . have to go to New York." She walked over to the train doors.

"That's too bad." His smile was accepting, but laced with regret. "Too bad."

The doors opened and she was about to step out of the car, onto the platform.

"Hang on." Oliver handed her the duffle, which she'd left under the seat.

"Wow, I can't believe myself today." She gave her head a shake, trying to rearrange her thoughts. "Thank you."

He held out a business card. "In case you change your mind about that coffee." As the train doors closed, he smiled at her again and gave her a sad little shrug.

Astrid slipped the card into her bag. She should have rushed to catch the red line, but instead she smiled back, waved at him, and watched as the train left the platform.

CHAPTER FORTY-ONE

Monday, October 18, 1999

There's no word from Oliver the rest of Sunday, which is expected, but tonight I rattle around the apartment, waiting for him to call like one of those girls I never wanted to be. I clean the kitchen and bathroom to stay busy. I read a hundred pages of a science fiction novel I find in the den that doesn't interest me but makes time pass.

There's nothing to worry about. There's nothing to worry about.

By six o'clock that mantra wears thin, especially when I call him and still get no answer and no machine. He did say dinner on Monday, right? I try again at nine o'clock, but no luck.

There's nothing to — I mean, there has to be a simple explanation here. Even if he found one of the fliers, he'd call me to hash things out, wouldn't he? Surely I'll hear his voice soon, explanations will abound, and we'll resume where we left off in the hotel room.

I do my best at self-persuasion, but there's a disturbance in the air. Something ominous has taken root in me; its black vines grow and twist under my skin.

Something is wrong.

Tuesday, October 19, 1999

I find out what it is the next day when I get home from work.

On the kitchen table is a sealed white envelope with my name on it. *This was left under the door for you*, says a Post-It written by Daphne or Zak.

This can't be good.

I hold the envelope up to the light, but can only make out a folded piece of paper.

I don't want to open it.

There's no point in putting it off, the words are already written and my stalling won't un-write them. But I was never the kind who could pull off a Band-Aid in one quick tear, even though it caused less pain in the long run. I always picked at the edges, let it tug and pinch my skin, bit by bit, until it was finally off.

I get a butter knife and cut open the envelope, slowly and neatly, as if that'll make a difference. Once that's done, I don't take out the paper inside. I let it sit there for a few minutes, the way you might let a bottle of wine aerate after opening it.

Read the damn thing already.

I finally reach into the envelope.

Damn it.

I did my best to remove all of them, but I missed at least one. The paper in my hand is one of Sally's neon yellow fliers. Oliver's note is written on the back:

> *Astrid,*
>
> *I thought the other night changed things for us, even though you were still a little distracted. I wasn't expecting a manhunt on this level. Obviously, you still haven't gotten the closure you need. This is where I step aside and let you find it. Because you're not really* here. *Maybe down the line we'll both end up in the same place.*
>
> *—Oliver*

Fists pound the inside of my head, and my stomach clenches, and I am plummeting down, down, fast and hard; I will hit cold water or jagged rocks or blunt cement any second now.

I dial Oliver's number with nervous and sloppy fingers, get it wrong twice, grit my teeth as it rings and rings and—Yes! Finally!—a click and his recorded voice tells me he's unavailable.

"It wasn't me, Oliver. I had nothing to do with those fliers. Sally put them up behind my back. It was her parting gift after I told her I wasn't going to look for Theo anymore. I wouldn't do something like that, not after Friday night. I may have gone overboard with the search, but this goes beyond anything I'd do. You have to know that. I *am* here. I wasn't before, not fully, but I am now. Please talk to me, Oliver. Call me back. Please."

I hang up the phone and read his note over and over, astonished at the ugly wreck I made.

I go into my room. On my desk, the pile of fliers from my retrieval mission. Why didn't I throw them out? I take a small stack and tear them into strips, then rip the strips into smaller pieces, until I've created small hills of sunny confetti.

Over the sound of tearing paper, I think I hear something else. Is that the phone?

I run into the kitchen and pick up the receiver.

It's him. It has to be.

"Oliver?" I answer.

"Hey. It's Theo."

ACKNOWLEDGMENTS

Terry Montimore, there aren't enough ways to say thank you. Your support, wit, wisdom, patience, creativity, and kindness are nothing short of astonishing—werewolf. You are my dream made real and your hair looks *really* good today.

Mom, thank you for getting me hooked on books early, loving me fiercely, and encouraging all my crazy ideas—like wanting to become a writer.

Erin Foster Hartley, you're the Jinkx to my Katya. We tune into the same dark and weird frequency, and I'm so grateful you receive all my transmissions.

Kelli Newby, may our inner writers forever wear eyeliner and torn fishnets. Thank you for reading quickly and thoughtfully, and always knowing when to check in.

Bridget McGraw-Bordeaux, thanks for revisiting our old haunts via this book more than once. Blood be damned, you are forever my sister.

Kez Quin, your creative writing class changed my life and helped me find my voice. Jessica Treadway, your guidance helped me hone that voice. Jessica Liese and Sharon Gerber, our little writing workshop was short-lived but kept this story alive.

Additional early readers and patient friends, I salute you. Jennifer Hawkins, the venting, commiseration, reassurance—it's meant a lot to me. Kelly Calabrese, my fellow buffalo in this blizzard, your positivity and determination is admirable. Mary Ann Marlowe, your funny quips and killer hooks have been invaluable. Kelly Siskind, you're as smart as you are foxy and I appreciate you sharing your time and wisdom.

But wait, there's more! Thank you Brianna Shrum, Alison Pantano, Amy Carothers, Nina Laurin, Missy Shelton Belote, Elly Blake, Natalka Burian, Kellye Garrett, Kristin Button Wright, Ron Walters, Shannon Monahan, MacKenzie Cadenhead, Jennifer Grunwald, Eric Leibowitz, and Will Ryan (look, I stayed the course!). Special thanks to my editor Kathleen Furin and my proofreader Carol Carlisle Agnew. Jennie Nash, Laura Franzini, Jade Eby, and the rest of the Author Accelerator team, your warmth, industry knowledge, and encouragement has been incredible. Big shout out to the Table of Trust, the Crack Den, Brenda Drake, and the Pitch Wars community.

Katie McGranaghan, this story would have no spark without you; I'll always cherish our Boston adventures.

Thank you to all the weirdoes, outcasts, lovable misanthropes, and crazy geniuses that served as my muses, companions, and even adversaries.

Finally, thank *you*. A writer is no good without readers. I'm grateful you took the time (and hey, sorry if the ending frustrated you; it had to be this way).

DISCUSSION QUESTIONS

1. The novel is set in 1999. How does the time period affect the story? How might Astrid's search be different if the story was set in the present day?

2. What importance does the Boston setting play in the story? How might it vary set in another city or town?

3. What do you think really happened during Astrid's lost day? Which version of the story do you believe?

4. Do you think Theo was real or just in Astrid's imagination? Do you think her romantic connection with him is real?

5. What about Oliver? How much do you trust his motives toward Astrid and vice versa?

6. Do you think Astrid goes too far in her quest? How does this search change her? How would you have handled things if you were in her situation?

7. How did Astrid's relationship with her father impact her attitude in life? In what ways did his remoteness help her and in what ways did it hinder her?

8. Astrid and Sally are quite different but have maintained a close friendship since childhood. What do you think each gets out of the friendship?

9. A recurring theme in the book is bravery versus foolishness. What does Astrid do that you find brave and what does she do that's foolish?

10. Some other themes include costumes/masks, feathers, angels, rain, and fire. What do you think is their significance?

11. When Astrid tells Oliver she's not going to search for Theo anymore, do you believe her? Why or why not?

12. Which character do you most and least identify with?

13. What do Astrid's dreams reveal about her? Which one(s) resonated the most with you and why? How much stock do you put into your own dreams?

14. In the final dream, Theo proposes a theory that Astrid is dead and that this is her afterlife. Is there anything in the story to support or dissuade from that theory? What about the theory that he and Oliver might be the same person?

16. For Astrid, getting hit by a car sets off a series of events that changes the course of her life. Can you think of a time in your life where you experienced such a domino effect?

17. What are your thoughts on the ending? What do you think will happen next?

About the Author

Margarita Montimore received a BFA in Creative Writing from Emerson College. She worked for over a decade in publishing and social media before deciding to focus on the writing dream full-time. She has blogged for Marvel, Google, Quirk Books, and XOJane.com. When not writing, she freelances as a book coach and editor. She grew up in Brooklyn but currently lives in a different part of the Northeast with her husband and dog.

You can find Margarita online at:
Montimore.com
Twitter.com/damiella
Facebook.com/margaritamontimore
Instagram.com/damiella

Made in the USA
Las Vegas, NV
15 June 2022

50258171R00239